WAYLAID

Waylaid

A True North Novel

by
SARINA BOWEN

Tuxbury Publishing LLC

ONE

RICKIE

Lunchtime is over on the Shipley farm, and now we're standing outside again under the hot summer sun. I've been working here for a few weeks, so I know the routine. First thing in the morning I help my friend Dylan milk the cows and the goats. Then we eat breakfast before spending the rest of the morning on hard labor.

My legs and back are already tired from digging fence post holes. I'm a city boy at heart, so the last few weeks have been a challenge.

"You've done this before, right?" Dylan hands me a wire basket with a wooden handle. "Put the eggs in here."

"Sure thing." Although I haven't collected eggs before. It sounds easier than hauling fifty-pound bags of feed around.

He also hands me a plastic milk jug, with the top cut off and a braided rope looped around the handle. "This is for picking blueberries. You hang it around your neck, so you can use both hands to pick."

"Cool, cool. Because I'm really good with my hands." I lift my gaze to Dylan's twin sister, Daphne. And sure enough, I find her watching me with curious brown eyes that sharpen immediately when I catch her staring. Again.

Flirting with Daphne is the second-best thing about working on this farm. The first best thing is the food. Honestly, I'd happily swap the order of those favorites, except the flirting hasn't gotten me where I need to go. Yet.

But it's only a matter of time. Daphne knows what she wants. It's the same thing that I want. I can't say why she's so skittish, but I've given her the time and the space to overcome her hesitation. And yet she's still keeping her distance, shooting me looks every time she thinks I'm not paying attention.

Spoiler alert: I'm always paying attention.

"Okay kids," Dylan says with a chuckle. "I'll be back in time to fence in the chickens and do the second milking. Go easy on him, Daph," he tells his sister.

"Why?" she demands. "Everyone has to do his share. Even the new guy."

"Yeah, I know. But that isn't what I meant." His eyes twinkle. "Be nice."

"Hey, it's all good," I insist. "I like your sister. A lot."

Her lips tighten.

Dylan smiles. Then he gives us a wave and lopes off toward his truck, where his girlfriend is waiting to accompany him to town to do errands.

As soon as he's gone, I turn to Daphne. "This is good. We need to talk." This is pretty much the first time we've been alone together since I arrived here. Daphne always watches me with hungry eyes. But she doesn't talk to me. When I walk into a room, she walks out.

She's afraid to let me in. I just need to figure out why.

"We're not here to talk," she says. "The berries won't pick themselves."

"Fine—should we pick berries first, then? Or collect the eggs?"

"Divide and conquer. I'll take the berries." She takes the milk jug right out of my grasp. "You get the eggs."

"But—" This arrangement doesn't work for me at all. "Why not together? We can have a nice little chat about why you're avoiding me. Besides—the chickens don't like me. Don't send me in there alone."

She halts midstride. "Wait. Are you *afraid* of the chickens?" Her brown eyes light up as if I've just handed her a precious gift.

"No way. Did I say that?" I scoff. I'm not actually afraid of the chickens. We eat chicken a couple of nights a week, so I'm pretty confident about who should be afraid of whom.

2

Their eyes are a little creepy, the way they look at you first with one side of their pointy heads before switching to the other.

But never mind. She's already looping the berry jug around her smooth neck. Daphne Shipley is all long limbs and honeyed summer skin. She has soft-looking brown hair and expressive brown eyes that can go from angry to laughing with dizzying speed.

And I have it so bad for her.

"Get the eggs. Don't miss any," she calls over her shoulder. "There should be thirteen or fourteen today." That's all she has to say before she disappears into the blueberry patch—a dozen or so shrubs arranged in three rows.

The berry bushes aren't as tall as me, but Daphne bends over and disappears, leaving me alone here on the grass, with a wire basket and too many questions and my sexual frustration.

Just another day in my messed-up life. I'm kinda used to it already.

I turn toward the coop and contemplate my strategy. The faster I get this done, the faster I can pick berries with Daphne.

Two or three of the hens are already watching me warily. At least I don't have to deal with their electric fence, which Dylan already dismantled. So the hens are milling around their coop, scratching in the grass for bugs, and waiting to slash my throat with their sharp beaks and their scaly red feet.

"Okay, ladies," I say, easing my way toward the coop. "Everybody be cool! This is a robbery."

I hear a snort from the berry patch. Maybe Daphne isn't a fan of *Pulp Fiction*. But a good line is a good line, even if the chickens are doing their best to ignore me. The coop has these little doors that open from the outside, revealing the nest boxes. It's a pretty good system, and the first one I open has an egg right there for the taking.

It's still warm. I set it carefully into the wire basket and then open the next box.

A hen glares at me from inside, her red eye angry.

"Lift up your feathered ass, girl. I don't have all day."

She doesn't budge, and I let out a sigh. Then I give her a little nudge, and spot the two eggs she's sitting on.

"This hurts me more than it hurts you," I promise her. Then, one at a time, I steal those eggs. And she lets me.

Three down, ten or eleven to go.

As I open the next box, I feel eyes on my back. I don't turn around yet, though. Daphne's watching me. She probably thinks I'm incompetent. While I was born in Vermont, I'm a military brat. I grew up all over the world. And my idea of spending a great day outside is drinking in a German biergarten or sitting at an Australian cafe drinking flat whites and reading poetry.

But it's hard to deny that the country life looks good on me. It's only been a few weeks, and I'm tanner and stronger than I've been in years. And Daphne likes that a whole lot more than she's willing to admit.

Fine. If she's going to watch me, I'll give her something to look at. I set the wire basket down in the grass and then strip off my T-shirt. Then I angle my torso a quarter turn and flex when I open the next box. I gather another egg and then cut my eyes to the right to try to catch her watching me.

Bingo. I see a flash of silver between the branches of a blueberry bush.

"Shipley?" I call out. "You need something? What are you doing with your phone?"

"Checking the time! I have a call in an hour. My new job in Burlington starts tomorrow."

Huh. I was planning to head to Burlington tomorrow too. What a coincidence.

"After you're done with the eggs, you can pull some of these weeds," she says, changing the topic. "It's a mess over here."

"Yes ma'am. We can do that together, right?"

"No way," she insists.

Damn. I go back to the eggs.

The sun beats down on me an hour later as I tug another dandelion out of the dirt. My back aches from leaning over, but my knees are saved by the green cushion I'm kneeling on. It's called The Garden

Pad, and when Ruth Shipley—Daphne and Dylan's mom—handed it to me fifteen minutes ago, her smile said, *Here, you poor, tired fucker. Don't die on my property.*

The chance of that is low, but not zero. And I'm really fucking thirsty right now. My body aches from this morning's pasture work, where I dug hole after fence post hole to keep up with Dylan and his older brother, Griffin. I'd had too much pride to take things slow. And now my poor tired body needs to lie down on this strip of grass for a nap.

I'd also like a cold beer and a smoke. But I've promised Mrs. Shipley that I'd quit smoking, so I can't light up so close to the farmhouse. And I'm a stubborn bastard. I'm going to weed this damn patch if it kills me.

Staying here for the summer was all my idea, after all. Dylan Shipley is my friend and roommate during the school year. I knew the Shipleys were always short-handed, so I'd made Dylan a deal—if they took me on for the summer, I could rent out my Burlington house and get Dylan's rent down to practically nothing for next year.

"Hell yes," he'd said. "We'd be happy to have you, so long as you know what you're getting into. The hours are long."

I've never thought of myself as a wimp. I've climbed El Cap. I've crossed jungles in Thailand. Not lately, though. A couple of years ago I was injured, and it took a big toll on my body as well as my life.

Still—I hadn't realized until now how soft I'd become. And it's taking longer than I'd hoped to adapt to all this farm work.

I plunge the dandelion fork down into the dirt and wiggle it. But when I tug on the weed, it promptly breaks off in my hand. "Fuck." The weeds know I'm not cut out for this. They can tell I'm the kind of guy who thinks *weed* is something you put in a bong. It's not a verb, damn it.

Several long minutes of digging and cursing later, I'm finally able to extract the damn root from its hole. I toss it into the ragged pile I've made. Then I throw down the hand tools and sink onto the grass like the tired man that I am.

Above me is a sky so blue that it almost hurts to look at it. The yellow sun beats down on my bare chest. Three weeks on this

Vermont hillside have already tanned my skin to a burnished glow beneath my tats. My back throbs and my limbs ache against the grass.

And now there's something crawling on my ankle. I'm too tired to see what it is. Who knew it was so exhausting to be healthy?

Slowly I sit up again and flick a spider off my foot. The view between the blueberry bushes offers me an oblique look at Daphne. She's hosing down some of the wooden barrels the Shipleys use to age their cider. After berry-picking, she hustled over there to keep her distance from me again.

She's a tough nut to crack. But I'm a patient man. I've had to be. These last couple of years have tested me in every possible way. Daphne thinks I'm cocky, and she used to be right. But these days my cocky routine is more about muscle memory than confidence. It's hard to be a shell of your former self at twenty-two.

When I flirt with Daphne, though, it's not an act. She is very interesting to me, and not just because she's ridiculously pretty. It's her attitude that really gets me going. She has a brisk efficiency that I find sexy—a no-nonsense way of moving her body. She doesn't have time for your bullshit and she doesn't suffer fools.

She's not particularly warm or friendly. That doesn't bother me, because neither am I. She's the angry Shipley. And it works for me.

I'm dying to know why she avoids me. We met a couple times before I came to stay here, and it's completely possible that I offended her and don't remember.

I sure as hell hope not. I wish she'd soften up toward me, otherwise it's going to be a long summer. We're sharing a bathroom, for starters. I'm staying on the second floor of the main farmhouse, where she and her mother also live.

Meanwhile, Dylan is living it up with his girlfriend in the bunkhouse, which is a separate building. They need their privacy, I guess, because those two have more sex than soldiers returning from war. Last week I caught them going at it in the middle of the meadow on a blanket. Had to walk an extra quarter mile just to get out of range of all the moaning.

Across the way, Daphne straightens up again. Her tank top is just a little damp from the spray of the hose, and I find myself wondering what she'd look like soaking wet.

I've had a strange time of it lately. Hookups haven't really been very high up on my list of things to do. But I'll be damned if Daphne Shipley hasn't shaken the dust off my rusty libido. There's something about those long limbs that gets me going. Her thick brown hair is always trying to escape a soft-looking knot on top of her head. I'd like to pull the clip off that hair until it tumbles down around her bare shoulders.

In the middle of this evil but entertaining thought, I hear just the slightest rustle from the other direction. The sound is far enough away that I can't tell if it's a person or a creepy-eyed chicken.

But I sit up either way. It would be embarrassing to be caught lying down on the job. So I'm back to work, tugging another weed out of the ground, when someone comes around the corner of the chicken coop. I look up, ready to call out a greeting. But the visitor is not, in fact, one of the Shipleys.

It's a black bear. A *real* one—a full-grown motherfucking bear, and it's holding a white bucket in its jaws.

And now I understand that expression *frozen with fear*. It takes me several long glugs of my heart to react, since I'm paralyzed with indecision. Should I stand up and run? Shout? Play dead? The beast is just a few paces away. I can see the whiskers on its snout.

It takes another step, and that's what gets me moving. I stand up, but my shout gets caught in my throat. I grab the dandelion fork off the grass—it's my only weapon. But when I take a step backward, I trip on the goddamn Garden Pad and go down on my ass.

The bear watches me scramble around on the ground like a wounded cockroach. I pop up again with a strangled sound. And I turn my body as far as I dare, trying to warn Daphne. "BEAR!" I yelp in a voice much too high for a grown man's.

But it's enough. Her head swings in this direction. The bear drops his bucket, and it lands with a loud smack. Even if he's about to eat me for lunch, at least Daphne can get away. I see her running toward the tractor shed. At least one of us can flee to safety.

Clutching the garden tool, I take a slow step backward. "Fuck off, bear. Go on back to the Hundred Acre Wood or where-the-fuck-ever."

He grabs the bucket's handle in his mouth again and drags it a few feet away from me. And then I edge backward, wondering if it's safe to make a run for it.

But then I hear a sound behind me. And I risk everything to take a look over my shoulder.

Daphne storms out of the tractor shed. And she's carrying…is that a shotgun? Before I can blink, she lifts that gun and blasts a shot into the sky, handling the recoil like a champ.

My head whips around again as the bear drops the bucket with a loud thump and then trots his fat ass away from me. He keeps right on going, ambling across the meadow and finally disappearing into the tree line.

"Holy shit!" I shout, turning around to see Daphne, who's watching him go. She's holding the shotgun carefully but casually, muzzle pointed toward the ground, her posture a hundred percent badass in her tiny little shorts. "Did you see that? It was a mother-fucking *bear*." I'm still in shock.

She shrugs. *Shrugs!* "They like the sunflower seeds. Those assholes. I hope he didn't break the bucket." She passes me to pick up the bucket and give it a shake. The lid is still screwed onto it, and I can hear the sunflower seeds rattle inside.

Then she walks past me again, on her way to lock the gun away. I watch her long, tanned legs march past, and I'm both turned on and a little frightened of her.

I like my women feisty. This one particularly. And I'm starting to think that this summer could be a whole lot of fun.

TWO

DAPHNE

Rickie tells the story of the bear to a rapt audience at the dinner table.

Buttering my corn bread as he weaves the tale, I roll my eyes. A bear on our property is not a big deal. It's just a Tuesday.

"And it's a *huge* bear, so I'm basically watching my life flash before my eyes." Rickie gestures wildly. The motion makes his designer T-shirt stretch tightly across the lean muscles of his chest. His tattoos peek through the V-neck.

I hate myself a little for always staring at those tattoos. Before Rickie showed up in my life, with his snarky attitude and those piercing gray eyes, I never found tats attractive.

He's not even my type. That's what I keep telling myself. But he's always catching me staring. It's so embarrassing. Today he almost caught me taking a photo of him. Thank God he didn't figure out what I was doing with my phone.

In my defense, the photo wasn't for me. It was for my friend, Violet Trevi. She keeps asking me questions about the mysterious Rickie—the guy who stood me up my freshman year. Violet had to listen to me rant about it back then too.

Also, in my defense, the staring isn't purely about sexual attraction. It's also curiosity. I'd always wondered what happened to Rickie. Almost three years ago he made a big entrance into my life. Then he exited it just as quickly.

And now—this is the truly crazy part—he seems not to *remember*

9

how we met, or the outrageous things he said to me. It's probably an act. Maybe he never expected to see me again, and doesn't want to admit that he blew me off. Or maybe I'm just that forgettable.

Ouch.

Rickie, however, is not easy to ignore. He's magnetic. My family is captivated by his stupid tale about the bear, even if they've seen bears dozens of times before.

"See, I never planned to die before I could hike the Inca Trail, so as it stalks toward me, I'm pretty bummed…"

My family laughs like they're paying guests at an exclusive comedy club.

"And I'm waving at Daphne, like, *Saaaaaave yourself!*"

More uproarious laugher.

I'm so over it. "Can someone pass the apple jelly?" I ask.

But nobody does, because they're all still listening to Rickie.

"Daphne runs into the tractor shed, so at least I have the satisfaction of knowing one of us will survive to eat that pie Ruth was baking." Again with the hilarious laughter. As if Rickie is the best thing that ever happened to them. "And then Daphne reappears— like an avenging angel in cut-off jeans—and fires that gun into the sky. That's when the bear gets religion. He drops the bucket and waddles his fat ass off toward the woods. Funniest thing I ever saw."

Everyone around the table wears a look of pure joy, from the youngest—my one-year-old nephew Gus, who's sitting on my brother's knee—all the way up to Grandpa, who's wiping his eyes with his napkin.

I'm irritated. But I get it. Rickie is both entertaining and magnetic. He's got that X factor that draws people in.

Been there. Done that. I'm never falling for his charms again.

"The apple butter?" I repeat.

Only Rickie seems to register the request. He picks up the jar and passes it down my side of the table. And, damn it, I can't help but notice the flex of his forearm muscles.

It's just unfair how ridiculously attractive some people are. He has the look of a European model between gigs. The slightly overgrown hair. The languorous body. The expensive clothes. Farm work seems to agree with him too. His color is better than when he arrived a couple weeks ago.

Not that I'm keeping track.

"So, listen," my brother Griffin says, finally changing the subject. His eyes move from Rickie to me. "Can you head out tomorrow morning at ten? I'll have the truck loaded."

I'm just about to answer, when Rickie beats me to it. "No problem."

My brother's gaze swings back to our summer guest. "It's about an hour into central Burlington. There's an alley behind the wine shop that can sometimes be a tight fit."

"Hey, wait a second," I argue. "*I'm* the one who's driving the cider into town. We had a deal." Griffin assigned me the restaurant deliveries so that I could have a few hours to do some work for a social sciences laboratory at Burlington University, where I'm transferring in the fall.

"Oh, you're both going," my brother says.

"Why?" I demand. "I can do it by myself."

"I'm taking a summer class that meets on Wednesdays," Rickie says.

"A class? Can't you just Zoom into that?"

Rickie shrugs. "It's better in person. And now I can help you make the deliveries."

"That's nice of you," my twin brother, Dylan, says without taking his eyes off his girlfriend, Chastity. They're probably holding hands under the table. Or feeling each other up, maybe. Those two are like a walking hormone. I'm surprised Dylan can even follow the conversation.

"It's no trouble," Rickie says with a shrug. "I have things to do in Burlington. And I can check on my house, do a little shopping, that kind of thing."

I take a bite of my cornbread so that I won't say anything rude. But I'm not happy about this development. Not at all.

In the first place, Wednesdays in Burlington are supposed to be my escape day. Solitude is rare when you have a big family.

And now I'm supposed to ride an hour each way with Rickie and his flirting eyes?

God, he's nice to look at, but I don't want to spend more time with him. It's hard enough sharing a bathroom for the summer. And it's already a lot of work to avoid him in my own home.

What the hell will we find to talk about in the car?

I guess I'm going to find out. At ten the next morning, when I come outside with my backpack, the truck is already loaded with liquor crates, and Rickie is seated behind the wheel of Dylan's truck.

"Here's the manifest," Griffin says, handing me a folded sheet of paper. "Easy deliveries. Enjoy your day."

"Thanks," I grunt, heading toward the passenger seat. I guess I won't be listening to the audiobook I'd planned for these Wednesday trips.

I climb onto the seat beside Rickie and shut the door. He smells good, damn it. Like some kind of spicy, exotic cologne. *Lovely. An hour alone with a man who once stood me up, and then forgot I existed.* Just what every girl craves.

"If you drive there," I say by way of a greeting. "I'll drive home."

"Nah," he says, putting the truck in gear. "I got it. Both ways."

My blood pressure spikes. "It wasn't a *request*. Women drive, Rick."

"I'm sure you're a great driver, baby girl. But I told Dylan I'd get you and the booze safe to Burlington, so that's what I'll do." He puts on the radio and guides the truck down our long driveway. "So, what are you up to in Burlington today?" he asks, unaware that I'm silently planning his murder.

"Working. A job. Once a week." My answer is as friendly as gunfire. Most people don't want to hear about public health research anyway. It's nerdy.

We roll on, and the cab is so silent that I can hear each ping of gravel the tires are kicking up. I know it's my turn to ask a friendly question, but I just don't have it in me. I have exactly one summer to untangle all the knots in my life. It's not going very well. And stress has ruined my ability to make small talk.

"Hey, can you stop so I can check the mail?" I ask as he slows at the end of the drive to turn onto the road.

"Sure, gorgeous." He brings the truck to a halt, and I try not to roll my eyes. He probably calls me that only because he's forgotten my actual name.

I climb out of the truck and open our mailbox. There's a dairy barn catalog in there for my twin brother, so I leave that alone. Dylan cares about two things—goat farming, and getting naked with his girl-friend. Not at the same time though.

Quickly, I sift through a stack of envelopes, looking for my name. I'm waiting to hear if I got a fellowship that will help me pay for my last year of undergrad. It hasn't helped that I made the sudden deci-sion to transfer from Harkness College to Moo U, and I applied for funding at the last minute.

This is what happens when you make a mess of your life.

There's one envelope in the mailbox with my name on it, but it's the wrong shape, and it's from the wrong school. So when I get back into the truck with Rickie, I'm staring at a big square envelope from the Harkness School of Public Health. Now what do *they* want? In spite of my withdrawal from the university, I must still be on the mailing list.

Rickie heads down our country road toward the highway, while I tap the envelope on my knee. My curiosity wins out eventually, and I slit the envelope open with my thumb. Inside I find an expensively printed invitation to a party in September. *Tour the Future*, it says, inviting me to a formal celebration for the new wing of the public health building where I did research last year.

At the bottom of the fancy cream-colored card is a short list of benefactors who will be thanked at the reception. In the very center is a name I've grown to hate and fear. *Senator Mitchell Halsey.* The Halseys are a big deal in Connecticut. A huge big deal.

And I'm the idiot who got stars in her eyes when the senator's son started flashing his blue eyes at me. Last year was like a slow motion disaster. It began with those blue eyes, and it ended with the realiza-tion that I had to leave Harkness if I wanted to graduate at all.

Reardon Halsey was an upperclassman with a research job in

public health, just like me. I thought we had so much in common. I believed him when he told me that we were meant to be a couple.

He lied to me. He lied to a lot of people, actually. But I'm the only one who figured it out. And when I tried to call him on it, he barely took a breath before threatening my entire academic future.

There's a note scrawled on the bottom from Dean Rebecca Reynolds, my former advisor. *Daphne, we already miss you! My door will always be open to you. ~RR*

Well that stings. Until a few weeks ago, I'd been part of an advanced program at Harkness College. I was on track to earn my Bachelor of Science and a Master's in public health, concurrently, in just five years. I could have done it, too. If I hadn't trusted the wrong man.

Even now, I'm still not really safe. Reardon Halsey could blow up my new life with a single phone call. This is why I don't sleep well anymore.

I'm tempted to throw the invitation right out the window. But Shipleys don't litter. So I open Dylan's glove compartment and shove the invitation inside before snapping it closed again.

"Not the mail you were hoping for?" Rickie asks cheerfully.

"Nope," I grumble.

"Bummer. Maybe I could find a way to cheer you up later." I groan, and he laughs. "I meant with ice cream. Can we stop for a cone on the way home?"

"Sure, pal," I mutter.

"Awesome." There's a beat of silence. "Or we could have dinner together."

"We eat dinner together every night," I point out.

"That is *not* what I meant. You look like a girl who could use a fun night out. And I'm just the guy for the job."

I'll bet you are. There's no doubt in my mind that Rickie knows how to put the *play* in playboy. But I've been down this road before. He once invited me out, before ghosting me.

I don't trust men who flirt with me. And I never will again.

"Look, I'm flattered," I lie. "But we both know you're really not my type. And I'm not yours."

"Really? What is your type? Let me guess—you like 'em clean cut and ambitious."

This is partly true. Or at least it used to be. The first man I ever fell for was clean cut. And the second one *looked* clean cut, and was certainly ambitious. But now I'm just confused. "I honestly just don't know anymore. But I'm not going to be your super convenient good time, okay? That's not happening."

He actually laughs. "You think you've got me figured out. I'm a total sleaze, huh?"

Yes. "I didn't say that."

"It's okay, Daphne. There have been times when you would have been right. I definitely went through a sleazy stage. But then I grew out of it."

"Good to know," I mumble. I never went through a sleazy stage, but I went through a naïve stage, which is surely worse.

"I'll be honest," he says, as if this conversation were ongoing. "You confuse me. Your mouth says you're not interested. But your wandering eyes say you are."

"Hey! Not true," I lie. I'm definitely attracted to Rickie, and completely unwilling to admit it.

"And what's with the photo yesterday? Did you take my picture?"

"No!" I yelp. "Why would I do that?"

"Lock screen shot?" he suggests. "I'm very decorative."

"Shut up. I was taking a selfie."

His snort says he doesn't believe me. Just kill me already. We're still at least forty-five minutes from the first delivery. This is going to be the longest ride to Burlington ever.

My phone buzzes with a series of texts, so I pull it out to check. They're all from Violet.

Helllooooo! How's it going with Mr. Hottie?

Does he have good taste in music?

Did you ask him why he stood you up for a date that time?

Can I have another photo? His face doesn't show very well in this one.

I reply with the speed of someone who feels guilty. *No more pics. Ever. I should never listen to you. He saw, and now I'll never live it down.*

Oh, don't worry! I'll tell this story at your wedding someday.

I groan. *You are a hopeless romantic. Emphasis on hopeless.*

She replies with a heart emoji. I love Violet, but I don't understand her optimism. Her luck with men isn't any better than mine.

I put my phone away and stare out the window again. But Rickie takes that as a sign that I'm available for conversation. "Look, we have to clear up a couple of things. I've got some questions."

I watch the landscape shoot by and wonder if I could survive a dive out of a moving vehicle.

"I'm wondering why you seem so jumpy around me. And I realize we met once before—"

My insides lock up, and my breath stalls.

"—but the details are sketchy to me. So here's a wild theory. Have we *already* seen each other naked? Is that the problem?"

My gasp escapes before I can help it. "No! No way." Not unless we're counting that morning last week when I glimpsed him stepping into the shower. The ass on this man is a work of art...

"Well, thank goodness." He chuckles. "Be a shame if I'd forgotten *that.*"

I make a small sound of outrage. "*Seriously?*" I squeak. "It must have been a *hell* of a sleazy phase if you think you could forget something like that."

"Oh, you'd be surprised what a guy can forget." The truck's engine rumbles as he accelerates past a log truck. "Look, I'm well aware that I sound like an asshole right now. But can you just tell me how we met before? Give me a refresher."

My head turns unbidden, and I just stare at him for a long moment. Is he even for real? I'd been assuming that he knew perfectly well how we met, but just didn't want to talk about it. But now he wants a reminder?

"Yeah, I'm serious," he says, as if listening to my thoughts. "My memory is shit."

"Lord, I'll say. Maybe you should lay off the bong."

"I get that a lot."

This is the strangest conversation I've ever had. And I still don't trust that he isn't just screwing with me. He and I spent six *hours* together. With our clothes on. But still. "My freshman year we did a weekend ride share once, from Connecticut to Vermont and then back again. You drove. I paid for gas money."

"*Oh*," he says, giving me a quick glance. "From Harkness."

"Yes. Of course."

"Right," he says, his eyes on the road. "Makes sense."

I brace myself for follow-up questions. He's probably putting it all together now. Our strangely intimate conversation. The odd way it ended.

But the questions don't come. He turns up the radio instead.

THREE

ALMOST THREE YEARS AGO

It's a drizzly autumn day in Harkness, Connecticut. It rains a lot in this oceanside town.

Daphne, a freshman, waits beneath a beautiful archway on the edge of campus. She's been dreaming of attending this school for years—since her ambitious little heart first found Harkness College in a guidebook she'd checked out from the Tuxbury town library.

And now here she is, six weeks into her first semester. Her awe hasn't worn off, even if she's not quite comfortable here. It isn't home yet.

This is deeply irritating to her. Truth be told, she thought that rolling into Harkness and moving into her dorm room would be the moment her real life finally began. The way it was meant to be.

Instead, she has a stuck-up roommate who actually brought a fur coat to college with her. Who does that?

Daphne checks the time on her phone. She's so eager to go home for the weekend that she's arrived early. She's homesick. That's just a little embarrassing. So she tells herself that the promptness is just a courtesy. She's never met the friend-of-a-friend who's agreed to drive her up to Vermont this morning.

At least he's on time. At exactly eight a.m., a boxy old Volvo slides up to the curb. With only a cursory glance at the man behind the steering wheel, Daphne darts out through the cold rain and opens the passenger door. In one hurried motion, she slides into the seat and tucks her weekend bag between her feet.

Then she turns to get a better look at her companion. And—holy smokes—he's *dreamy*. His hair is buzzed very close to his skull. Not everyone could pull off a flattop like that, but this guy can. The lack of hair makes his model-handsome bone structure stand out.

And—wow—a pair of startled gray eyes gives her the once-over. "Hi there. I sure hope you're Daphne Shipley, and not a carjacker."

"I am," she says a little breathlessly. Handsome men have always made her a little nervous. "And you're Richard Ralls?"

"That's my dad. I'm Rickie."

"Do grown-ups call themselves Rickie?" She meant it to sound flirty, but it comes out sounding a little bitchy. Story of her life. Daphne has never been able to figure out how flirting works.

"Who says I'm a grown-up?" Then he smiles, which only makes him more dazzling, and her stomach does a strange swooping thing.

"I can tell you're eager to get to Vermont," he says. "But maybe you shouldn't be so quick to just hop into a car with a stranger? You didn't even check that it was me. I had my ID all ready to prove it, see?" He holds up a photo ID from the US Tactical Services Academy.

The photo on the ID is even more handsome, if possible. Because he's wearing a dress uniform.

But Daphne isn't the type of girl who likes people to see her emotions. And she's *really* not the type of girl who lets a man tell her she's done something stupid. "Let's review," she says. "Your Vermont license plate and that haircut really cut down the odds that I've gotten into the wrong vehicle."

Another blinding smile. "I suppose you're right, Daphne. And you're Carla's friend?"

"Sort of." *Friend* was too strong a word. Carla was one of Daphne's high school classmates—one of the confident girls who'd always made Daphne feel nerdy and awkward in comparison. "Colebury High School is so small that everyone knows everyone."

Carla had mentioned once this past summer that she knew a college guy who would also be making a lot of car trips between Connecticut and their part of Vermont. So Daphne had taken down Rickie's email address, because she's a practical girl.

"Carla dated my twin brother for ten minutes or so," she says. "Everyone does."

Rickie chuckles, and the sound bounces around in Daphne's chest. "I think I'd like your twin brother."

Everyone does. She pulls out a twenty-dollar bill and puts it in the cup holder. "This is for gas. Thanks for the ride share."

"My pleasure." He puts the car in gear, and they begin their three-hour journey home. There's some kind of low music thumping through the radio, and it's warm and dry in the car as they slide down the rainy street.

The college slips away behind them, and Daphne is happy to see it go.

"So, how do you like Harkness?" Rickie asks. "And what are you studying there?"

"I'm getting a BS in biology and a master's degree in public health on the fast track program."

"Ah, ambitious. Funny that you didn't answer my first question. How do you like it?"

"It's only been six weeks."

"That well?" He chuckles.

She doesn't know him well enough to tell him the whole truth. That Harkness College is intimidating. That she's always thought of herself as an intellectual, but now she's worried if she has what it takes. And she *definitely* doesn't tell him that she feels like a country bumpkin among the slick rich kids who graduated from prep schools all over the country.

"I hear it's snobby," Rickie says, giving her an opening.

"Well, the first week somebody asked me where I was from, and when I said Vermont, they said, 'Oh, my buddy summers there.'"

"Yeah, summer as a verb. That's a look. Very *Hunger Games*."

Daphne smiles at the reference even though she hated the first book and didn't finish the series. "All right, so how about you? Do you like the Tactical Services Academy? And what are you studying?"

"Philosophy and psychology—double major."

"I notice you didn't answer the first question."

"You are a quick one. But here's the thing about USTSA. You're not supposed to like it. You're supposed to *endure* it. It's also very *Hunger Games,* but the later books."

"And you chose this willingly?"

His chuckle is dry. "Mostly. It's free, you know. So the price appealed to me. And I'm used to the military ass-kissing and jargon. My father was a colonel in the Air Force before he retired."

"Oh, at the base outside of Burlington?"

"Sometimes. I was born in Vermont but didn't grow up here."

"Where did you grow up?"

"Everywhere. Japan. Germany."

"Where'd you go to high school?"

"Choate. Where they use summer as a verb."

"Ah." This unsettles Daphne a little, because she'd assumed he was more of an ally—a Vermonter sneaking home for a weekend in rural Vermont, where everything still made sense. "So how do you know Carla?"

"I dated her for about ten minutes last summer."

Daphne should really have seen that coming. The Carlas and the Dylans and the Rickies of the world are naturally drawn to one another. They all know how to let loose and have fun. Daphne had never quite gotten the knack of it. She'd assumed that once she found her people—the nerds of the world—that it would be easier to make friends.

Maybe it takes longer than six weeks.

"Big plans for the weekend?" Rickie asks as they head up highway 91.

"Not exactly. It's peak season at our orchard. I'll probably spend the weekend driving a pony cart around the orchard so that apple-picking families don't have to walk very far to find the Honey Crisps."

"That could be fun?"

"Sure—if you like whiny kids and horse poop. The pony cart is everyone's least favorite job, but it's a crowd pleaser."

"Then what's the best job?"

"The cider tasting room. Or cashier. I'm good with numbers. I don't mind making change."

He's quiet for a second. "What's your other reason?"

"For what?"

"For going home on a random November weekend."

"Veteran's Day—we've got Monday off. That's all."

"Okay, sure. But when a girl wears makeup on a rainy Saturday morning, it usually means there's a guy."

Daphne's face heats. "Wow, six weeks of psychology classes and you're already putting everyone on the couch, huh?"

"Tell me I'm wrong." He leans back against the headrest and grins.

"Sorry, Sigmund. There's no guy."

"What? *Impossible*. Wait—a girl, then? Sorry, I should have been more inclusive."

Daphne laughs. "Nope. Maybe I really just like makeup." She doesn't. But Rickie doesn't know that.

"Nah. There has to be someone. Six weeks into freshman year..." He thinks for a moment. "You're going home to try to keep a guy, or you're going home to try to catch him. It has to be one or the other."

Daphne looks out at the wet highway as her heart flutters. The guy in the driver's seat is really not her type. He's got a bad boy glint in his eye that she'd usually avoid. But his quick wit is an awfully good time. Sparring with him is fun. "Listen, I think your analysis lacks subtlety."

"Tell me where I went wrong," he insists.

"There's this guy—"

He hoots.

"Hey! I wasn't done. There's this guy who works on our farm. And I spent all of high school thinking I was in love with him."

"An older man," Rickie says with a wink.

"Exactly. He never looked twice at me. But I didn't do a very good job of hiding my crush. A few weeks ago I found out that he's seeing someone. And I had, uh, a bad reaction."

"Ouch." He has the decency to flinch.

"Yeah. Not my finest hour. It's worse than that, because in the middle of my tantrum I was horrible to my sister, too. She's probably never speaking to me again." For good reason. Daphne is deeply ashamed of what she'd said and done. If she could rewind time and undo the damage, she would.

"So the makeup is like body armor," he says. "You have to walk back into this mess you've made, and you want to look confident."

"More or less."

"I get it. I'm stopping for gas at the next exit. I'm going to grab a drink. Want anything? Soda? Terrible gas station coffee?"

"No thanks."

He pulls into the gas station a few minutes later. Daphne is overly aware of the muscles in his forearm as he pops the parking brake. A hint of a tattoo peeks from beneath the sleeve of his uniform shirt.

I don't even like tattoos, Daphne tells herself, even if it's less true now than it was an hour ago.

Rickie sets up the pump and then heads into the store. His walk is cocky, and his uniform pants make his backside look muscular.

Daphne drags her eyes off his butt and sits back in the seat to wait. But now she's second-guessing the makeup she put on this morning. Is it really so obvious? If Rickie noticed it, maybe her family will, too.

She reaches down to unzip her duffel, and pulls out her makeup bag, setting it on her lap. Inside, there's a packet of makeup remover wipes. She uses one of these to dab at her mascara.

"*Hey,*" Rickie says a couple minutes later, setting a paper cup into the cupholder. "Don't do that. I'm sorry I mentioned it."

"It's not nice to psychoanalyze your new friends," she grumbles as the mascara comes off.

"I thought it looked hot," he says. "I should have led with that."

"It doesn't matter," she argues. "It's out of character for me, anyway."

"You say that like it's a bad thing." Rickie reaches into her makeup bag and removes her eyeliner pencil.

"What are you doing?"

He uncaps it. Then he grabs the rearview mirror and tilts it toward his face. "There's nothing wrong with keeping everyone guessing."

Daphne watches, open mouthed, while Rickie begins to do a surprisingly good job of lining his right eye.

"Don't give them that kind of power," he says, switching to his left eye. "If you're someone who wears makeup today, then that's who you are." He caps the liner, returns the mirror to its former position, and then turns to look at Daphne.

Her heart stutters as she gets a full-on view of those fiercely bright gray eyes, enlarged and accentuated by the tease of black liner. He looks twice as dangerous as he did before. "You are not what I expected," she stammers.

"Good," he whispers. Then he hands her the liner pencil and gets out of the car to put the gas cap back on.

A moment later they're on the road again. Daphne had expected him to wipe the liner off. But he doesn't bother. As they cruise up 91, he sticks an actual cassette tape into the dashboard stereo, and then sings along to Joan Jett's "I Hate Myself for Loving You."

The song seems fitting enough, so Daphne joins in.

FOUR

RICKIE

The first restaurant on our list is a steak place outside of Burlington. And when I pull up behind the building, Daphne refuses to let me carry the crate of alcohol into the restaurant. She insists on doing it herself.

She's in a *mood* today. I think she'd expected to spend the day alone. And she doesn't trust me. She can't believe I don't remember meeting her that first time.

Girl, same, I think as I watch her disappear into the back door of the restaurant. My life has been a crazy ride since those days I spent in Connecticut. I don't tell the people in my life the whole story, because I'm sick of being that guy who lost six months of his memories.

Honestly, it's easier to be a rude asshole than a freak.

Something tells me I'm not the real root of Daphne's unhappiness, either. Something else is bothering her, and it doesn't have a thing to do with me.

I have a few ideas for cheering her up, if only she was open to it.

Daphne reappears just as I'm having this thought. She's wearing a serious frown that doesn't invite discussion. And I know how to read the room, so I stick to the business at hand. The moment she returns to the truck, I point us downtown.

Our second and final delivery is to a wine bar. Vino and Veritas is on Church Street, where cars aren't allowed to go. But there's an alleyway behind it that makes the drop-off easy enough. Daphne disappears again into the back door of the place and reemerges a minute later.

"Why are we delivering this stuff by hand?" I ask as I carefully back out of the alley. "Griffin has a distributor for his cider, no?"

"The applejack is a beta product," she says. "He can't make enough of it to meet the distributor's minimum."

"Oh. Your brother is a fun guy. He's a tinkerer, right? Always experimenting with the chemistry behind various alcoholic beverages. What's cooler than that?"

"So cool," she mutters. "Can you drop me at the social sciences complex? I don't want to be late for my first day."

"Sure, gorgeous. No problem."

I do even better. A few minutes later I pull up right in front of the School of Public Health. "I'm parking in that lot," I say, pointing at the garage on the next block. "When do you want to meet me back there?"

"Um, is five o'clock too late?" She glances nervously at the building.

"No, that's fine. I have errands. And I'll kill some time in the coffee shop."

"Uh, thanks." She swallows hard, and I realize that even Daphne Shipley is capable of first-day jitters. Who knew? She shoulders her backpack and gets out of the truck.

I roll down the window. "Hey, Daphne?"

She turns back, a tiny crease of irritation on her forehead. "What?"

"You're a badass."

"What?" She blinks.

"A total rock star. Now go on. Be early. Impress the world of public health. You know you want to."

"Thanks." She gives me a smile so small that you'd practically need an electron microscope to find it. And then she strides off, long legs like honey in the sunshine, and disappears into the glass doors of the building.

And I just sit here like a bonehead, wishing I could have gotten a kiss goodbye.

The class I'm taking this summer is Ancient Philosophy, and the first lecture is a lot of fun.

After my injury, I lost two semesters of school. It took me a year to reboot my life, enroll at Moo U, and settle into Burlington. So even though I'm twenty-two, I'm not yet close to graduating.

But school has always appealed to me. And ninety minutes in a lecture hall listening to the professor explain Sophocles is entertaining.

Afterward, I spend some time in the bookstore before heading to the coffee shop like I said I would do. But only for a little while. I have another appointment in Burlington that I neglected to mention to Daphne.

It's time to visit my shrink.

Lenore is a young postdoc in clinical psychology—which is precisely what I hope to be in a few years. Sessions with her are useful in more ways than one. Not only is Lenore helping me with my issues—and there are quite a few of those—I learn things from her as well. She's smart and she speaks to me like a future colleague as well as a patient.

"My God, you're so tan!" she shrieks as I walk into her office. "And so healthy I hardly recognize you."

"So you're saying I was pale and ghostly before?" I plop myself down in my chair.

"Oh, please. You're very prompt today, Rickie. I think you missed me."

"For sure. Nobody has asked me any prying questions in a *month*."

"Well let's fix that. How've you been? Tell me everything. Are you milking cows?"

"I mostly shovel their shit. But it's still a good time." I tell her all about the Shipley farm, and my aching muscles, and yesterday's bear sighting.

"Something tells me this bear gets more ferocious every time you tell that story," she says, playing with the pendant she's wearing around her neck.

"Are you calling me a liar? Is that good patient interaction?"

"Not a liar," she says with an eye roll. "An embellisher."

"Fine. Sure. I cheated death, but you think I'm embellishing it. I see how it is."

She gives me an indulgent smile. "You seem content, Rick. And it looks good on you."

"Thanks," I say softly. And I guess she's right. These last three years have been hell. Contentment is something I thought I might never find.

"Have you seen your parents?" Lenore asks suddenly.

"Nope." I feel a stab of guilt over this. They live maybe forty minutes from where I'm staying. But things are so strained between us that I don't make visiting a priority.

"Could you have lived at home this summer?" she asks, holding me to this uncomfortable subject.

"I guess. Yeah. I would have had to find a summer job, though. At the Shipleys, the job is built in. Plus, the Shipleys aren't disappointed in me for bombing out of the Academy, and then taking a settlement."

She doesn't weigh in, yet. She waits me out, like a smart shrink would do.

"I suppose I should go visit them, just so this shit doesn't fester, right?"

"That depends," she says quietly. "There are parents who absolutely deserve to be cut out of one's life. There are toxic people in the world, and you don't owe toxic people anything. But if you think your relationship will matter to you in the future, then maybe it's time to find some common ground."

Outwardly I'm as calm as ever. But I've only been in Lenore's office for three minutes and she's already found a sore spot and pressed it. I used to have a great relationship with my parents. I'm their only kid, and we spent my childhood traveling the world together. We were tight.

Then I went off to my father's alma mater, the US Tactical Services Academy. I wasn't that excited about choosing it over Middlebury, where I'd also been accepted. I wasn't a military kind of guy, like my dad. But a few things weighed in its favor. One, the price tag. It's *free*. I could've graduated with no loans at all.

Two, my dad was proud when I got accepted. So proud. And I drank that shit in.

And, finally, I was interested in military intelligence as a career. Even if marching in formation bored me silly, I liked the idea that I could become a spy someday.

But near the end of my first semester, I went to an off-campus party and got hurt. I was in the hospital for two weeks. And I haven't been the same since.

That was the end of the USTSA for me. I dropped out. And when the college dragged its feet on giving me credit for the semester, my parents warily helped me force their hand.

"I hate lawyering up against my own college," my father had said. "But one stern letter will probably do the trick."

The lawyer had bigger plans. "Credits aren't the only thing you should be leaving with. Your doctor doesn't even know when you'll be able to go back to school. I think you're due some more party favors."

"Like what?" I'd asked.

"Like cash." So, with my permission, he asked them for a million dollars. "They'll bargain us down," he'd added.

But that's not what happened. They'd written me a seven-digit check two weeks later.

My father still isn't over it. I sued the college who gave him a free education. "I can never show my face there again," he'd raged at me. "It wasn't even the college's *fault* that you went to a damn party!"

He might have a point. Except the college has never actually told me what happened that night. When I hit my head, I lost my memory of that evening. All I know from the hospital report is that three cadets brought me into the emergency room.

We tried to find out more, but the Academy kept dishing out unsatisfying answers. "We're investigating." "There was some confusion." "It happened off campus."

After I got my settlement, they stopped pretending to take our calls. And my father lost his taste for pressing them. "I guess you don't need answers now that you're a millionaire."

Before then I'd sometimes struggled to win my father's approval. He didn't understand my intellectual interests. And he really didn't understand that I was pansexual. But he mostly dealt with that. He was a good dad.

But now I'd become a true embarrassment to him. It's not an easy thing to be. The settlement money has helped me get back on my feet. I bought a house in Burlington, and started school again, this time at Moo U. It's not like I bought a yacht or first class seats to Vegas.

It doesn't matter. He's never getting over it.

The rest of the money—after the house and the lawyer's hefty cut —is invested in bank CDs that mature right before the start of each semester. So my tuition is covered through graduation, and I don't have piles of cash free to waste on weed and booze.

I get good grades. I made new friends. My life is back on track, even if my relationship with my parents is not.

And I never miss a session with Lenore. She gets me.

"Tell me something fun about the farm," she says. "Besides the bear."

I open my mouth to tell her about the food, but then I hear myself say, "There's a girl. Daphne Shipley. I have it bad for her."

"*Really?*" Lenore sits back, and her smile is dishy. "Do tell."

"Well…" My chuckle is dry, because I sound like a middle school kid confessing his crush. "The attraction is driving me a little nuts. I'm super distracted. And I think it's mutual, but she doesn't encourage me."

Lenore cracks up.

"Wait—is that what a therapist is supposed to do? Laugh at the patient?"

"I'm laughing *with* you," she says with a broad smile. "This is great, you know? You need to celebrate the idea that you've finally got an average college guy's problem. Boy likes girl. Girl is on the fence."

I suppose she has a point. "Yeah, sure. But it's been so long since I wanted someone that maybe I lost my touch? My inner slut forgot all his best moves."

"Nah," she says, dismissing this problem with a wave of one hand. "That stuff is like riding a bike. Let's talk about Daphne. Is she Dylan's twin sister?"

"That's the one."

"Didn't you tell me Dylan's sister was moving to Burlington in the fall? And might need a spot in your house?"

"Yeah, that's the same sister. The rent is so cheap that she ought to say yes." I barely charge my friends anything. It's mostly out of guilt. Like I'm not sure I'm entitled to own a house in central Burlington, paid for by the US Tactical Services Academy. I'm trying to share the wealth with other college students who are just trying to get by.

"That's a potential complication, then," Lenore says. "Maybe Daphne doesn't want to get involved with her future landlord."

"Maybe," I concede.

"Just keep working that Rickie charm. You wouldn't be the first guy who's ever been attracted by a woman who plays hard to get."

"Yeah, but there's one more complication—we met before."

Lenore blinks. "Before *when?*"

This is where things get weird. It's where they always get weird.

"I first met her during my time at the Academy."

Lenore's face falls. "Oh, shit."

"Yeah."

We lapse into silence for a moment. This is my real issue, and the reason that I see Lenore. It's not because of my parents, or my childhood. It's because I lost six months of my memories—basically from the day I left for Academy basic training, up until the weeks after my hospital stay. And it's really freaking hard to navigate a brain where some of the crucial details are missing.

"How do you know?" Lenore asks softly.

"I recognized her face."

"And...?" She waits, hopeful.

I shake my head. "Just her face. Nothing more. Last fall she came to visit her brother in Burlington, and I took one look and just knew we'd met before." And that I'd liked her.

"Okay," Lenore says. "So that's a complication most college guys don't have to deal with."

"Yeah, I'm still trying to figure out what happened that other time. Apparently we shared a ride home for a weekend. Maybe I was an ass to her."

Lenore folds her hands. "But why would you make that assumption about yourself? Are you an ass to Daphne now?"

"No."

"Then you probably weren't then."

"You'd think." But I'm not so sure. "Daphne seems wary of me, but she won't say why. Maybe it doesn't have anything to do with me."

Except I think it does.

Lenore looks thoughtful. "Tell me why you find her attractive. What is Rickie Ralls's type?"

This is a much easier question. "She's super pretty. Tall, with dark hair and legs for days. But she's also kind of prickly. She makes me work for a smile, you know? She's angry about something, and I haven't figured out what yet."

"Huh," Lenore says, clicking her pen a couple of times. "You like your women complicated. What a shock."

"Oh, shut up."

She laughs. "I'm thrilled for you, honestly."

"Why? I just told you I'm not getting any."

"You've always told me what a player you used to be. I've heard you call yourself a slut many times. But I've been seeing you for, what, a year?"

"Yeah." My first psychologist retired, and then I lucked into Lenore when the psych department offered me a postdoc for therapy.

"Well, this has been an open question for me. Since we've been meeting, you told me right off the bat that you enjoyed sex with both men and women. And since then you haven't mentioned any new romantic or sexual relationships."

"I haven't been very interested in sex since my accident."

"Okay." She shrugs. "Does that seem a little strange? You're handling school full time. You have friends. You go to parties. You call yourself a slut. But you don't have sex."

"Long recoveries aren't very sexy. At the beginning, my ribs hurt so badly that I couldn't have imagined anyone touching me."

"Sure. Fine. But you're strong now. Why does a self-described slut stay away from the fine women and men of Burlington U?"

I shift in my chair. "Not sure."

"Let me ask it another way—have you been tempted before? Any hookups at all since your accident?"

"Not really. There was one party early on when I was trying extra hard to be a regular guy. I had some drinks and walked a girl back to her place. But I realized I wasn't feeling it, so I bailed."

"How far did it go?" she asks softly.

"Not far. Making out on the couch." I feel my face redden, because I know what she's going to ask next. Someday I'm going to be an amazing shrink. But today it's still me in the hot seat.

"When you say you weren't feeling it, was that in your mind, or in your body?"

Yup. Bingo. "It was both, actually."

"That must have been uncomfortable for you?"

"Excuses were made." I clear my throat. "But you're right, I was pretty embarrassed when my soldier wouldn't stand up and salute. Not sure she even noticed. But I just wanted to get out of there."

Lenore nods. She waits.

"After that I just didn't bother. And you know I'm still a little weird about needing to sleep by myself." That's putting it mildly. Since my accident, I can't sleep without locking the bedroom door. And I wake up several times a night, just making sure I'm still alone. It's a true phobia, and Lenore and I discuss it all the time. "Who wants to sleep with a guy who won't share his bed?"

"Oh, please." Lenore actually rolls her eyes. "If memory serves, that's like half of all college guys. Besides, a real slut could figure out how to hook up in the daylight. Boom. Problem solved."

It's my turn to crack up, because Lenore is just the best.

"So now there's one woman who's turned your head, right?"

"Oh hell yes."

"You've got your flirt on, then? Flirting seems to be your default setting, anyway."

She's not wrong. "Yeah, I'm doing my best. But she seems to have a lot on her mind."

"Unless she's just not attracted to you."

"That is *not* the issue."

Lenore smirks. "No matter what, this is a good thing. Even if you don't lure Daphne into your clutches, maybe your libido is waking up for good."

"Like, my boner might be transferrable to someone else?"

She rolls her eyes. "Make all the boner jokes you want, Rickie. But this seems important. Sex is the last part of your life that you haven't gotten back, right?"

"What?" I sputter. "You're forgetting a big one. How about my goddamn memory?"

"That will come," she says breezily. As if this two-and-a-half year nightmare will ever end.

"Will it?" Ten seconds ago we were joking about sex, but now I'm suddenly angry. Mood swings are a symptom of traumatic brain injury. They're always fun. "That's the real reason I'm not comfortable getting involved with anyone. It's the whole freak angle. 'Hey baby, let me tell you about the big hole in my memory.' Nobody wants to hear about that."

"Hang on." Lenore leans forward in her chair. "You've told *her*, right? About your memory loss?"

"Daphne?"

"No, the Queen of England. Of course I mean Daphne. If you want someone to trust you, telling the truth is step one."

Slowly, I shake my head. "I haven't told her. It's not a very sexy conversation."

"*Whoa.* Forgetting how you met someone isn't that sexy either."

With a low groan, I sink down in my chair. "I know, okay? I just wanted to move on. For two years I've just tried to get past the whole thing. But it keeps sucking me back into the vortex." I don't know if I'll ever have any peace until I understand what happened to me in Connecticut.

"Just tell her," Lenore says quietly. Her expression is both empathetic and firm. "I would never judge you for bedding whoever you want. Two consenting adults, etc. But she's your friend, right? And Dylan is your friend. Does he know about your memory issues?"

Issues. That word is entirely too sedate for the disaster I've been living. "No. I met Dylan after moving to Burlington. He knows I had a rough time, but he doesn't pry. At *all*."

Dylan has the most easygoing personality of anyone I've ever known. I would have liked him no matter when we met. When he and Keith moved into my house, I had some strange requests. "At night, we keep the doors locked up tight. And nobody enters my room for any reason."

"Sure." Dylan had shrugged. "You got it." We've been living together for almost a year now. So he knows I have a deadbolt lock on my bedroom door. And that I bought the house with money I got from a legal settlement. He's not a stupid guy. He's probably curious. But he never asks questions. I appreciate it more than he'll ever know.

"Look," Lenore says. "Is Daphne the kind of person who appreciates honesty?"

"Aren't we all that person?" I ask drily.

"Yes." Lenore smiles. "Yes we are. Honesty is sexy, Rickie. Just tell her."

"Okay," I promise.

But I sure don't want to.

FIVE

DAPHNE

My new job as a student research assistant at the School of Public Health starts like any new job—with paperwork. I fill out a bunch of forms for the HR person, who awards me a brand-new ID.

I'm not smiling in the picture, though, because starting over is hard.

All this takes a couple of hours, but finally I'm sent upstairs to find Karim, a graduate research assistant. He's a slim, friendly man with tan skin and long, dark eyelashes.

"Since I have seniority, you can bring me all your questions," he says, "I've been here for two weeks, at least."

His dark eyes twinkle when he says this, but my answer is still a very stiff "Thanks." I know he's joking, but I just can't make myself loosen up. I'll probably never trust any young, ambitious man again.

Besides, Karim is already an MD. He outranks me no matter how friendly he seems. Never again will I forget that these things matter. If I lose track of the rules, I could lose everything.

Karim leads me on a lengthy tour of the office. He explains their system of moveable workspaces. "None of the research assistants has his own desk, because we're all here on different days. You check out a laptop with your ID, unless you've brought your own. But there's no formal system for claiming a study carrel. It's first come, first served. And no fair leaving books there overnight to reserve your spot. Only an arsehole would do that."

"It was one time!" calls a voice from the other side of one of the blond wood dividers. "And I apologized!" A head pops up to match her voice, and I find that it belongs to a young Black woman with close-cropped hair and a bright smile. "Hi. I'm Jenn Washington."

"Daphne Shipley."

"Oh! You're the transfer? We're all very curious about you."

Lovely. "Yes. I'm the transfer student." *And thanks for making this awkward.* I feel my smile tighten up on my face. They probably think I couldn't hack it at Harkness, and that stings.

"Welcome," she says brightly. "Any relation to the Shipleys who make that cider?"

"That's my brother."

"Really?" she squeaks. "It's *so* yummy."

"Yeah, that's his thing," I babble. "He has a degree in organic chemistry. We're science people." Oh my God. Could I sound any more defensive right how? *Get a grip, Shipley.*

"Feel free to bring us samples," she says.

"Yeah, I get that a lot." I force another smile on my face. And when Karim continues the tour a moment later, I feel nothing but relief.

The last stop is the departmental library. "It's small, as you can see," Karim waves an arm around the room full of books. "The University has done a great job of digitizing our core research materials, and you've got Lexis/Nexis access under your new ID. But hard copies of the best reference books are kept in here. They also keep print copies of all the journal articles produced by professors and research fellows in this building. If I'm lucky, I'll have something on the shelf eventually."

"Oh, wow," I say in the same hushed, fangirl voice. One wall is *full* of peer-reviewed research publications. Karim and I have the same dream, apparently. I pull a copy of the *Journal of American Public Health* off the shelf. Sure enough, there's an article by my new boss and advisor, Vi Drummond, entitled *Modeling the Probability of Arsenic in New England Groundwater for Risk Assessment.*

"Do these books circulate? I'd love to check a few out," I ask Karim.

"Sure. Go ahead. That was Dr. Drummond's first piece about arsenic."

"I know. But it's been a while since I read it. What else should I read if I want to understand the core specialties of the people who run this place?"

He blinks. Then he eyes the massive wall of documents. "Well... Don't forget that I'm new here. But I guess I'd read the latest stuff on birthweight versus educational outcomes. And food insecurity as a factor in hospital admissions."

I spend the next fifteen minutes collecting ten more journals and checking them out under my ID number. "You can stop now," Karim says. "Before you make the rest of us look like slackers."

My hand freezes on a volume of *Environmental Health Perspectives*. "I just need to get up to speed here. It has nothing to do with you."

"Kidding," he says a little stiffly. "I was kidding."

Ten bucks says he wasn't. But that isn't my problem. If I do good work, he'll tolerate me in time. He doesn't have to like me.

"Oh, there you are."

We both turn to find Dr. Vi Drummond in the doorway. "Welcome, Daphne. I know it's almost time for you to leave. But I was hoping we could have a quick chat in my office."

"Of course." I turn to Karim. "Thank you very much for the tour. I look forward to working with you."

He has already regained his smile. "Same here. See you next week, Daphne. We'll get started properly."

Clutching my stack of journals, I follow Dr. Drummond into her office. She shuts the door and takes a seat behind her desk. "I'm really pleased that you are able to come into town once a week during the summer. It will be nice for you to settle in before you take on a full course load."

"Not as pleased as I am," I say, sitting ramrod straight in the visitor's chair, my lap full of books. "I feel lucky to have found a place here, and I can't wait to get started."

She picks up a paper clip on her desk and rotates it absently. Dr. Drummond is a white woman in her mid-fifties, with salt-and-pepper hair. She's a little more glamorous than you usually see in academia, in her elegant silk blouse and interesting silver earrings. "Your transcript is impeccable. Very few young women can manage a dual BS/MA program. And your recommendations were all glowing."

"That's nice to hear," I say neutrally. But my heart begins to pound the way it does any time I think about the mess I left behind at Harkness. If the truth got out, those recommendations would *not* glow. Not even a little.

Someday I'll make it right, I promise myself for the millionth time. I don't want to carry this burden forever.

"I have to say, Daphne..." She pauses, as my heart continues to pound. "It's unusual for us to see a student who's performing so well transfer from an advanced program like the one at Harkness to a state school. Not that we aren't proud of the work we do here. But it's not quite as glitzy or international. I did wonder why."

Right. I'd known this question was coming. And I'm prepared. "Maybe I'm not as enamored with glitzy or international as I used to be." That's certainly true. But the embellishments I offer next are not. "My whole family is here in Vermont. We have a farm, and several businesses. My brother started a family. A lot has happened since I decided at seventeen that I needed to be somewhere else."

She smiles, which is how I know I've been convincing. "There's a lot to love about Vermont. I've tried to keep our focus as local as possible. Some of the enviro-agricultural topics may be familiar to you."

"Arsenic. Nitrogen runoff. Things like that?"

"Exactly like that," she says. "And my next grant application concerns air quality. I'll fill you in more in September."

"I can't wait." I really do live for this stuff. I plan to do excellent work here. Dr. Drummond will not regret taking me on. And this job will make my grad school applications look worthy.

"All right, Daphne. We'll talk more soon. This summer you and Karim will help Jenn tidy up some data and set up some research queries, okay? And this fall we'll get on to new research."

"Great. I'm happy to help," I say. We stand, and I shake her hand with a firm grip.

This is going to work. It has to.

Okay, these research journals are *really* heavy. I lug them awkwardly back to the truck, where Rickie is leaning against the driver's side door, reading a book.

In German. That's unexpected.

As usual, I drink in the sight of him. Today he's wearing another silky T-shirt, tucked into a pair of cut-off army surplus pants. On his feet are suede ankle boots. They're not work boots. They look vintage. And there's an earring in his left ear. It's a very small hoop, which shouldn't look masculine, but it does anyway.

He closes the book as I approach, and tosses it through the open window, into the vehicle. "Ready to go? Looks like somebody hit the library pretty hard." He hurries toward me, hands outstretched, as if to help me.

"New department. I have to catch up," I explain, hoisting the books up a little further in my arms. I don't want his help. But one traitorous volume slips out of the stack and hits the pavement with a loud smack.

Rickie picks it up without comment. He doesn't try to wrestle the other journals out of my arms, either. He just goes back to the truck and climbs in, settling both our books on the seat behind him.

Somehow I make it onto the passenger seat without dropping anything else. "How was your class?" It's a feeble attempt at polite conversation.

"Great. Fine. I like school, and I'm a shitty farmer, so it was like a vacation for me. How was the new job?"

"Good," I say quickly. "I mean—new jobs are hard. I have a lot of reading to do." I smooth a hand over the journal on top of the stack, where an article about nursing mothers on food stamps is yelling my name.

"All right. I'll leave you alone to read," he says, cranking the engine. "So long as we can stop for ice cream."

I'd forgotten about that. But I like ice cream as much as the next girl. "Sure. There's a place just off exit 6B."

"Coolio. I'll poke you when we get there." He turns to give me a sexy grin.

I feel the heat of that smile. It lands in the center of my chest. This is bad bad *bad*. So I look away. I flip open the cover of the journal and try to focus on the table of contents.

Rickie probably thinks I'm a bitch. And maybe it's even true. But I cannot get lost in another man's smile. Been there. Done that. Not going back.

I read all the way to the highway exit, but I only get halfway through the first article. It's dense and full of statistical analysis that's over my head.

By the time Rickie rolls down the exit ramp, I feel the onset of a full-blown case of imposter syndrome. Dr. Drummond is expecting me to be sharp. What if they ask me to work on this type of analysis, and I can't do it?

"I see the ice cream place," Rickie says. "But there's no entrance back onto the highway. What the hell?"

"Doesn't matter," I mumble. "It's three miles down a side road to exit 6." I close the journal with a sigh. I feel so panicky right now. I've always tried to be the smartest girl in the room. But it's all an act. I'm obviously the worst kind of dunce—the kind that can't see her own mistakes until it's way too late. (See: the last twelve months of my life.)

Is it normal to have a midlife crisis right before your twenty-first birthday?

Rickie rolls into the gravel parking lot of the Dreamy Creemee and puts the truck in a shady spot. He rolls down the windows before killing the engine. It's getting toward dinner hour, so there aren't many people here. Just a couple of moms pushing toddlers on the swing set.

And I'm quietly having a panic attack in the passenger seat.

I take a slow but shaky breath. Do I even want ice cream? Is there a flavor on that signboard that could take me out of my own head? I reach for the door handle, but Rickie stops me.

"Look," he says. "About that time we shared a ride home from Connecticut..."

"*No,*" I say forcefully. If he makes me relive that embarrassing experience, I might lose my cool. "Just forget it, okay? So what if you ghosted me?"

His eyes widen. But my rant is only picking up steam.

"None of that matters. I didn't even blame you. And the only way I'm going to make it through this year is if I put Connecticut behind me, okay? Just leave it alone."

My voice cracks on that last word, and I realize that I might actually *cry*. Which is a thing I never do. But Harkness College was my dream, and I blew it. My damn eyes get hot and my throat constricts.

"S-so just forget it," I squeak. "It's already in the past. It can just stay there."

Rickie's gray eyes are soft now. And they're moving closer. To my utter surprise, he leans forward and presses a kiss to my lips.

So soft, my brain sputters.

"Shh," he says against my lips. His kiss is warm and unhurried. Like a ray of sunshine when you're shivering.

For once, my squirrel brain forgets to scurry. And I just let it happen. He kisses me again. It's still gentle. His bright eyes measure me. I don't know what he sees. But whatever it is, he decides he likes it.

Those soft lips brush and press. Again. And I'm only human. Rickie's surprisingly tender kiss has caught me at a vulnerable moment. I lean in, experimenting with the slide and pressure of his mouth against mine. A sizzle of heat flashes across my skin. It's the strangest sensation—as if he's transferred an ounce of that devil-may-care attitude across the steering column and right into my soul. I drink him in, lips parted. Ready for him to take it further.

But then it ends. Rickie sits back, his head cocked to the side, as if in deep contemplation.

I'm bereft. "Wh-what was that for?" I stammer.

I expect a smirk. But his expression remains soft. "You seemed a little freaked. So I brought you to an ice cream place on a hot summer's day. But that wasn't enough, apparently. You needed even more distraction. So I gave it to you. And I'm good at that. A real specialist."

Replying is impossible. All I can do is sit here and try to process that kiss. That *lovely* kiss.

He really has some nerve.

"Let's get ice cream now, Shipley. You promised." He unbuckles his seatbelt, as if he didn't just rock my world, which was already rocking to begin with.

I'm such a mess. But Rickie calmly waits for me to get out of the truck. He puts one hand lightly on my lower back and steers me toward the order window.

Birds chirp and the sun shines and I feel lighter. If only for a moment.

We lick our ice cream cones at a shady table. And I don't mention the kiss.

He doesn't either.

That night I hit the books again. I drag out my old statistics textbook, refresh my memory on some distribution properties, and finish reading that journal article.

It's midnight by the time I finally set aside my work to crawl into bed. The farmhouse is dead quiet. The only sounds come from my open window—the occasional deep-voiced bullfrog. Or the hoot of an owl. Sometimes we hear the howling of coyotes. But not tonight. There's mostly stillness.

A working farm always goes to bed early and gets up at dawn. I've never fit the farmer mold. I was that kid who stayed up too late reading, or daydreaming about traveling to teeming, foreign cities.

During high school, I did as much farm work as everyone else. Maybe even more than my lazy twin. But at the same time, I was plotting my escape. I was the valedictorian of my high school class. I got the highest SAT score that my school counselor had ever seen. I figured out that the very best colleges had the best financial aid. So I set my sights on Harkness. It worked, too. My Early Action application was accepted during December of my senior year. A fat financial aid award followed.

I'd done it. I'd shot the moon.

Now here I sit in my childhood bedroom, preparing to transfer to the same public university half my high school class attends. I'm bitter about it. I just can't let it show. My goal is to work so hard that everyone will be too impressed to question my motivation.

Fooling people is easy, apparently. I know firsthand. Because I'm usually the fool.

Right on cue, as I shut out the light, my mind goes immediately to Rickie. And that kiss. I still don't quite understand what happened there.

He'd kissed me when I least expected it. Who does that?

And then I'd gone along with it. The boy is seriously seductive. There's no arguing that. But seduction is dangerous.

I try to relax against the pillow. It's no use thinking about Rickie while I'm lying in bed. He's just across the hall in Dylan's childhood room, probably passed out in my brother's bed.

That's why he flirts with me, I think. I'm conveniently located a few paces away. He's horny. He's lonely. And I'm right across the hall.

I just wish I didn't find him so attractive. All that male beauty is a little intimidating. Those tattoos. That golden skin and dark blond hair...

Okay, stop it, I chide myself. Thinking sexy thoughts about him isn't going to help. I usually think of myself as a strong, independent woman. A scholar. A crusader for women's health. It's painfully obvious that I don't understand men. No—it's worse than that. When I'm attracted to someone, I seem to lose the ability to see things as they really are.

And when the right man seduces me—especially if he *praises* me— I somehow lose the capacity for rational judgment. Reardon had said I was pretty. He'd said, *I need you so much.* And I'd believed him. Every time.

Hell, even if a man smiles at me, I'm ready to believe that it means something. That's how I ended up carrying a torch all those years for Zach, our family friend. I thought his easy smile—the same one he gave everyone—meant more when it was aimed at me.

Somehow my finely calibrated bullshit meter breaks when a man gives me special attention. My inner needy girl takes over, and I lose myself too easily.

Today—in the truck with Rickie—I'd felt the familiar pull. Even afterward, watching him lick a chocolate cone while he tried to get me to laugh, I'd looked into those sparkly gray eyes and I'd wanted to *believe*.

In what, I'm not exactly sure. Attraction is the devil.

Closing my eyes, I let my thoughts drift to the afternoon. But who could blame me? Ice cream before dinner is about as wild as my life gets. That kiss was definitely a high point. And—even weirder—it worked. I felt calmer afterward, enjoying a maple creemee at a shady picnic table.

I was actually sad to leave. Rickie handed me the keys to my brother's truck and asked if I minded driving, because I knew the way back from exit 6B. It was a blessing, actually, because otherwise I probably would have spent those last few miles trying not to stare at him.

An owl hoots outside, and I'm almost ready to sleep, when I suddenly remember something strange. That time we shared a ride to Connecticut, we'd met up at exit 6B to drive back to school. I'd gotten into Rickie's car—without makeup—ready to hit the road. And I'd told him how to get back onto the southbound highway.

But today, he seemed baffled about it all over again.

I sit up in bed suddenly—as if this will all make more sense in a vertical position. But nope. It's still strange. Rickie doesn't remember our driving together. It wasn't just *me* that he's forgotten, either. It's the whole trip. It's the strange configuration of highway 89. It's like he was never there.

Like he's a different person than that Rickie I met three years ago.

I feel a chill down my spine. It doesn't make any sense.

SIX

RICKIE

The tap on my bedroom door is bashful. But I'm a psycho in the nighttime, so the sound is enough to startle me into wakefulness. I jackknife into a seated position, my book flopping off my chest and onto Dylan's quilt.

Tap. Tap. It's just a fingernail on the door. Quiet as a mouse. But my pulse is ragged nonetheless as I swing my legs out of bed and get up to face my midnight visitor.

I unlock the door and open it to find Daphne standing on the other side. She wears soft shorts that show off plenty of thigh, and a tiny little tank top.

No bra, my libido adds. There's no denying that my sex drive has roared to life, like a long-forgotten engine that still manages to catch on the first try when you turn the key.

But I step back like a gentleman and allow Daphne into the room. I close the door, just in case I'm about to get lucky.

Although the look in her eye right now is not sexual. It's pure curiosity, with a side of anger. Daphne always looks a little angry. I may have an anger kink. Who knew?

"You don't remember driving with me from Harkness," she hisses, her voice hushed.

I circle the bed and then get into it, crossing my arms behind my head and leaning back against the pillows. "I told you I had a terrible memory," I remind her.

"But you *really* don't remember," she repeats. "You don't remember the highway exit with no matching entrance. You don't remember driving there at *all*."

She's right, and I'd been willing to explain it earlier today. I was going to take Lenore's advice and spill my guts over ice cream.

But then I'd kissed her instead.

"Look," I begin. "I know it's awkward. But it's not just you. I don't remember anything from July through December of the year we met."

Her eyes pop wide, so I don't add that the following January, February, and March are a little hazy too. But I'd been on painkillers. And then I'd become dependent on painkillers, so I had to be weaned off them slowly.

It was a long nightmare.

"*What?* How do you forget six months of your life?" She plops down on the end of the bed.

This is closer to another human on a bed than I've been in... Wow. There's some depressing math. But she's not here to fuck, she's here to interrogate me. She's waiting for an answer.

See, Lenore? This is the opposite of sexy. "I got injured at the Academy. Badly. Broken bones and a head injury."

She blinks. "Like a TBI?"

"Yeah." Although I rarely use that term. *Traumatic Brain Injury.* Gross.

"And you just... forgot that semester."

"Right."

A crinkle appears between her eyebrows. "But last fall you *recognized* me. When I showed up in Burlington, I walked in and my brother asked if we knew each other. And I said no, but *you* said yes."

This, of course, I remember perfectly well. "Yeah, I know. And then I said don't worry, you'll figure it out. And then you did."

"Of course." Her cheeks pink up. "It took me a second. The context was all wrong. And you looked so different." She winces. "That was embarrassing. But your hair is so much longer now, and you weren't wearing your uniform."

"My uniform," I echo. I know I wore one. There's a photo of me from drop-off day, and I'm standing shoulder to shoulder with my dad in front of the campus gate. He's smiling like he just won the

47

lottery. I'm decked out in a green wool jacket with gold buttons, a dress shirt, pressed trousers and shiny boots. Plus a cap.

But I don't remember putting that on. I don't remember if those boots were stiff or comfortable. I don't remember if the collar of that shirt was loose or tight, or how it felt to slip the cotton onto my skin. It's a blank. And when I see that photo, it's like looking at some other guy.

"And after I heard you laugh, I realized who you were. But you recognized *me*. I know you did. So how could that be?"

I cross my arms in front of my chest. And then I actually flex, like a tool.

But it works. Daphne's eyes dart to my half-naked body. I see her drink in the view of my tattooed biceps and chest. But then her eyes snap upward again, and they narrow. "Answer the question."

Oh well. I tried. "That's happened before," I admit. "I recognize a face from that time, but I don't know why. It's..." Maddening. Terrifying. Pick an adjective. "Frustrating. But since you couldn't place me at first, I assumed we'd barely met."

She chews her pink lip. I'd like to cut these questions short and bite it for her. But I can see that she's wrestling with my story, trying to figure out if she believes me.

"Look, you wouldn't be the first person to think I was bullshitting you. Why do you think I don't explain this to people? It sounds bonkers."

"Sorry," she says, rubbing a hand across her forehead. "It's just so weird."

"Welcome to my world," I mutter. I've spent so much time these past two and a half years straining to remember those missing six months. I've visited every page of the USTSA website, squinting at photos of cadets, looking for my own face in those pictures. Looking for anything that's familiar.

I never found it.

"So what was this accident like?" Daphne whispers. She's hugging herself now. But she seems to believe me. "It must have been bad."

"Bear in mind that I don't remember." I chuckle.

"Right. Sorry."

"They told my parents that a group of cadets brought me into the

ER from an off-campus party. They said I'd climbed a wall on a dare. And then fell off."

Her perfect eyebrows shoot up. "Because you were drunk?"

"That's what I assume. But there's no evidence of that. Why else climb a wall, though?"

"Because it's past curfew?" She shrugs.

"I'd thought of that. But it was Open Weekend."

"Open Weekend," she repeats. Then she looks at her hands.

"Apparently it was one of the few times when there was no curfew. But that's all I've got. I've spent a lot of time trying to remember what happened. But it hasn't come back."

"So…" She lifts her brown eyes to mine. "You're like a character in Proust, hoping that some small thing triggers your memory?"

"Nah, this is way past Proust," I grumble. "I'd need to be Marty McFly from *Back to the Future*."

She lets out a startled laugh. "So you could go back in time and see what happened?"

"Or tell myself not to climb the damn wall. That's what McFly was trying to do, right? He wasn't there to watch. He was there to change the outcome."

"Yeah, I get it." Her big brown eyes search mine. "Can I borrow the time machine after you're done with it? I have a few messes I'd like to clean up, too."

"Sure, Shipley."

We're quiet for a minute, and I close my eyes and try to imagine myself visiting the past. I've done this before. I've tried meditation, hoping that a memory will surface. I've spent many an hour trying to picture myself climbing a wall. I concentrate, trying to imagine the texture of the bricks against my fingertips—and my feet scrambling for purchase as I struggle toward the top.

"Who dared you to climb it?" she asks suddenly, and my eyes snap open. "Don't you want to kick his ass?"

Oh, Daphne. Can't she see that we're on the same wavelength? "I would *love* to kick somebody's ass," I admit. "But the Academy wouldn't tell me who I was with." They remained silent even when my father—an alum—raged at them, begging for information.

Cadets are supposed to know better than to take a dare, they'd said. It was an attempt to shame us into silence.

It worked on my dad. But not on me.

"And you don't have friends from school who could…" She stops in the middle of the sentence. "Oh."

I snicker. "Yeah, if I had friends, I've forgotten them. And you already know that gets awkward."

"Wow, I'm sorry."

"Don't be," I say immediately. "My life was waylaid for a while there. Look at me now. I'm healthy. I'm fine." I hold my arms out wide. "Why don't you come a little closer and let me demonstrate."

This wins me a rare smile from Daphne. And, man, that smile is something else. I would like to give the word *waylaid* an entirely new meaning with her.

But then she says, "I think you only hit on me to distract me."

"No way," I argue. "I hit on you because I'd like to know how you feel underneath me."

She smirks and shakes her head.

"Fine, fine. You can ride me instead. I'm flexible on this point."

But that's when she gets up and heads for the door. "Night, Rickie. Sorry to keep you up."

"You can keep me up longer."

She gives me a wry grin and leaves the room, closing the door behind her.

I get up and lock it again, because I'm funny like that. But it's a crappy lock. So I'm also tempted to pull the wooden chair out from Dylan's desk, and lean it against the door, with the back pressed up near the doorknob, as an extra layer of security.

But I don't do it. The flimsy lock is as much leeway as I'm willing to give my phobia.

I go back to bed and shut off the light.

"Hey McFly!" Daphne shouts to me over the loud beat of live music.

"Hey, Shipley. Happy birthday!"

"Thanks!" She stands on tiptoe to speak into my ear. "I've been thinking about you."

"Yeah?" I give her a hot look. "That's good news."

She ignores this blatant come-on and says, "I can't imagine losing six months of my life. I guess it would be much more inconvenient than forgetting where you put your car, no?"

"Definitely."

It's Friday night, and we're at Dylan and Daphne's twenty-first birthday party. I'm holding the dregs of a craft beer and tapping my foot to a live band on the back patio at the Gin Mill, a bar owned by Alec, the boyfriend of May Shipley, the twins' older sister.

The good news is that Daphne is no longer avoiding me. The bad news is that she wants to ask a million questions about my head injury, while I'd rather be talking her into bed.

"How about a drink?" I ask, changing the subject.

"Sure, I'll have a Coke," she says.

"A Coke. On your twenty-first birthday?"

Daphne crosses her arms and gives me the fierce, laser-beam glare that always gets me hot. "I'm not much of a drinker. Do you have a problem with that?"

"No, no," I say quickly. "Besides, it looks like Dylan is drinking for both of you." I point at her twin, who is holding a drink in each hand and dancing to the fiddle music. He's in pig heaven right now.

"This is amazing," Dylan crows. "I can't *believe* you got Skunky Town to play at my birthday party."

"You only turn twenty-one once," May yells over the banjos.

"You're my favorite sister ever. They're not even from around here," Dylan says, his eyes following every move the fiddle player makes.

"Massachusetts," May's boyfriend, Alec, says. "I'm putting them up at the motor lodge. It wasn't outrageous."

Dylan grins, his attention still glued to the band, as it should be. He's a party boy just like me. Living in the moment is a skill we share.

"Thank you," the guitar player says when the song ends. "And now we'd like to invite Dylan Shipley to the stage to play a song with us. Where's the birthday boy?"

"Holy shit." Dylan's grin is as wide as his whole face. "I don't have my fiddle."

"It's right here!" his mother says, holding up the instrument. Clearly the fix was in.

"This is crazy," Dylan says, trading two beers for the violin. "Hope I don't humiliate myself."

That's unlikely, since he's an accomplished musician. But also, he wouldn't care that much if he did screw it up.

"What do you want to play with us?" the front man asks.

"Uh," Dylan chuckles again. "How about 'Billy in the Lowground.'"

That song title means nothing to me, but the band just nods. They let Dylan take the lead, and after he tunes up, he tears into a fast-moving fiddle tune. And then they all join in.

The Shipley clan hollers their approval.

This is a killer party by any standard. The patio is decked out with strings of tiny lights that are reflected in the river flowing past us. The place is packed with well-wishers of all ages. In the center of all this mayhem, I feel serene. I've got a cold beer and a belly full of party food.

"My babies are all grown up," Ruth Shipley says, watching her son rock out on the fiddle.

"So grown up," Daphne mutters beside me. "I found his under-wear in the hayloft yesterday."

"So grown up that he can throw his ragers in the meadow legally now," Griffin adds.

"Oh, hush," his wife says. "But who is that? Check out your grandpa."

We all turn to spot Grandpa Shipley right in front of the stage, swing-dancing with a gray-haired woman in a polka-dot dress.

"I don't recognize her," Daphne says.

"That's Mabel," Griffin says. "They met at a poker party last month. This is their third date."

"Go Grandpa," I say. "You know what they say about third dates."

"Oh, stop." Daphne knocks my arm with her own. "Is your mind always in the gutter?"

"Pretty much." I don't add that it's a recent development for me.

And that she's the one who puts it there. "All right, I'm hitting the bar." I didn't drive here, so it doesn't matter how much I drink. The Shipleys hired a school bus to ferry eight of us from the farm to the Gin Mill just for this special occasion. "One Coke coming up."

"Thanks." She nods her exquisite face, and I'm mentally kissing the rise of her cheekbone.

It'll happen. I'm a patient man.

I head indoors to the bar to pick up two drinks from a friendly Scot named Connor. And when I go back outside, Daphne waves me over to a set of wooden stairs that I hadn't noticed before. They lead down to the riverbank. But after walking down halfway, Daphne sits down on the stairs. "Have a seat."

"Yes *ma'am*." I follow her to the relative quiet and privacy of this hiding place. We can see moonlight glinting on the surface of the river. It's very romantic.

"Now I have some more questions," she says.

Of course she does.

"Did you have a roommate?"

"Your brother is my roommate."

She rolls her eyes. "I mean *before*. At macho military college."

I snort. "There are women there too, you know." And I guess I should have seen this coming. Daphne is hard on a guy's ego. People used to compete for a ride on the R-train. Now they just want to hear the morbid details of my head injury.

"But did you? Does your roommate know what happened to you? You must have *somebody's* contact information. Was he there? Isn't your phone full of messages asking you how you're doing?"

These are all good points. And I probably had plenty of friends at USTSA, because I tend to make friends easily. There's just one problem. "The rule was that you had to communicate inside the Academy's own app. It was like WhatsApp, but a private version."

"Why?" Her forehead gets that crinkle again.

"Security, I think. I still have the email that sent me the link to the app, and my login instructions. They were very clear that it had to be used at all times. And apparently I was a very well-behaved cadet, because all the messages on my phone during that time period are to people I knew outside of school."

"But it's still there, right?" she presses. "On the secure app on your phone?"

"It would be. But after I got out of the hospital, I couldn't log back in again. Once I left school, it was like they slammed the door shut on me." And that was even before I lawyered up, when my texts were shut off.

"Doesn't that seem freaky to you?"

"Sure. Although I'd prefer to get our freak on another way."

She rolls her eyes.

"To answer your question, all I've got is my roommate's name, and an email address for him." The school had sent it out during the summer, inviting us to contact one another. "His name is Paul Smith."

She brightens. "Have you called him?"

"Baby girl, I've *tried*. His voicemail says, *Mailbox full*. And he doesn't answer his emails. Some of them even bounced."

"Really?" She sets her Coke down on the stair step. "Isn't that kind of creepy? Did the zombies get him?"

I shrug, but it's creepy as fuck. My mother agreed, back when we were all more comfortable talking about it. Lenore thinks so, too. "That's really just one flower in a big bouquet of creepy. You know what's also creepy? Hearing that you and I spent six hours in a car together, and not remembering it at all."

She tilts her head and gives me a look that's uncharacteristically soft. "I'm sorry if I was bitchy about it."

"You weren't. I promise. In fact, go ahead and yell at me some more, so that I have an excuse to distract you with my mouth."

Her eyes widen. And although it's fairly dark out here, I swear she's blushing. At least I hope she is. This is the first time I've brought up that kiss.

"Or better yet—I can just kiss you again for funzies."

She tilts her head back, leaning it against the railing. And I swear she's giving this thought some serious consideration. "It's a bad idea, McFly."

I love the new nickname she's given me. "How bad?" I have to ask. "Kind of a fan of bad ideas."

She smiles and shakes her head.

And then we're interrupted. Because of course we are.

"Daphne," her sister May says, leaning down to address us in our private little hideout. "Can I see you a moment?"

Daphne actually looks put out by this request, so at least I'm making a little headway.

It's something. I'll take it.

SEVEN

DAPHNE

For a hot second, my temper flares. The sad truth is that I'm enjoying Rickie's attention. It's a good thing I'm not drinking tonight, so I don't do anything stupid. My sister's interruption is probably well timed.

And when I look up at May, I feel the usual flare of guilt. I haven't been a good sister. "It's no problem," I say, scrambling to my feet. "What do you need?"

"Well, it's almost time to cut the cake. But first I need to show you something."

"Sure. Anything." I cast a quick glance back at Rickie. He gives me a slow nod and then a wink. He looks exceedingly good tonight in a crisp, pink-and-white checked shirt which is open exactly one button further than is polite, giving me an enticing preview of those tattoos I like so much.

Until this very moment I had no idea that a man could make pink-and-white gingham sexy. But here we are. Rickie is a study in contrasts. I never know what he's going to wear or say or do. He drives me crazy. I know I ought to resist the pull. But he does *not* make it easy.

And now that I know his weird secret, he's even more irresistible. It humanizes him. Maybe I have a vulnerability kink. Although that doesn't explain how I fell for Reardon Halsey's charms last year. He's about as vulnerable as a rattlesnake.

May is shooting me sideways glances as I follow her to a corner of the deck. "Okay, I feel bad interrupting. Are you going to jump on that later?"

"May!"

"Oh please don't sound so shocked. Like the idea never occurred to you? He's smokin'."

I make a noise of irritation. "He *knows* it though." And this is the weirdest conversation. May and I aren't close. We never dish about guys.

"He's not creepy, is he?" She gives me a look of alarm as she pulls out her phone.

"No, he's not," I admit. "He's flirty, that's for sure. Really flirty. But..." It's hard to explain Rickie's unusual appeal. Every sexy word that comes out of his mouth is infused with humor. Like he's teasing himself at the same time he's teasing me. As if he doesn't mind sounding a little ridiculous if he makes his point.

I feel drawn to him, even though I don't want to admit it. He seems different than other guys.

But, ugh, he's probably not. And it's just my usual stupid crush getting in the way of seeing the world the way it really is. "He's not creepy," I repeat. "He's fine. And also *fiiiine*. Good eye candy in the upstairs hallway this summer."

"Keep me posted," she says, opening up a photo on her phone. "I wanted to show you this project I started. Now let's see..."

I wait patiently, even though I'm not very interested in all the home decorating projects she's taken on lately. My sister's life is coming together in every possible way. Her boyfriend loves her. They own several businesses between them—the bar, May's small law practice, and Alec's growing brewery operation for nonalcoholic beers, which May inspired him to start.

She used to be the fuckup that everyone worried about. Her life was a mess. But now she's super happy and accomplishing all her goals.

Meanwhile, my life is imploding. Not that I'd tell her about it because we are not close. That's *also* my fault. When she was at her lowest, I betrayed her and embarrassed her.

These days we tiptoe around each other. May tolerates me. And I should probably be more grateful.

"Here it is! See? I'm stripping and refinishing this piece of furniture. Look."

I squint at the screen. "Is that...grandma's old desk?"

"Yup! Doesn't the bare wood look great?"

"Wow." I take the phone and zoom in on the photo. My grandmother liked to sew, and she kept her machine on a beat-up old desk that had been painted an odd shade of gray-blue. But that's gone now. "Nice work. It's so pretty."

"I thought so too. Do you want it?"

"Want what?"

May looks to the heavens. "Want the *desk*. You're moving to Burlington, and you might need one. Griffin and Audrey were moving some old furniture out of the Bungalow. And I thought you could use it."

Oh geez. "I can't take that. Not after you're spending so much time on it." Like I want to owe May anything else. "Besides, I'll only be in Burlington for a single academic year. Then I'll leave again for graduate school."

"You don't have to, you know," May says.

"Go to graduate school?" I yelp. "Yes, I do." I can't change my plans. If I do that, Reardon Halsey wins.

"You don't have to *leave*," she says. "There's a graduate program in public health at Burlington U, right?"

"Sure, but..." I bite my lip. May went to graduate school right here in Vermont, and then set up shop locally. But I'm more ambitious than that. I want a degree from a top-ten university. I thought it would be Harkness. But now I'll have to look elsewhere. Like Berkeley, or maybe Johns Hopkins. "I'm probably not staying," I say. "And you should keep this." I hand the phone back to her. "It's going to look great, but I'd have to move it twice in nine months. I really can't use it."

"But..." May seems ready to argue the point. But then she closes her mouth and shoves her phone into her pocket. "Okay. Good to know." Now she looks pissed. "Happy birthday anyway. We'll cut the cake as soon as the band stops playing."

She turns and walks away.

And I'm pretty sure I failed some kind of test with her. They're the only kind of test that I usually fail. I watch her thread her way through the party, without another glance in my direction.

Shit.

My phone buzzes in my pocket, and I pull it out as a reflex. But my heart rate spikes when I see who the caller is. *Reardon Halsey.* The evil ex. Just his name makes me experience a fight-or-flight reaction.

Swiftly, I hit the button to decline the call. And then I take a deep, shaky breath. There's no reason for him to call me. And I really don't want to know why he did.

A little later, Audrey reveals our birthday cake. It's really two cakes joined together in the middle. Audrey made it the way people divide toppings on a pizza—chocolate on one side and lemon on the other. A rich buttercream frosting covers the whole thing.

There are blueberries lining the edge, and Audrey has drizzled a message across the top in chocolate sauce: LOOK OUT WORLD. DYLAN AND DAPHNE ARE 21!

I choose a piece from the lemon side, and my brother chooses chocolate. We have never liked the same things, or read each other's minds, or had a secret twin language.

Often, when I tell people that I have a twin brother, they say, "That's so cool!" And Dylan *is* pretty cool. That's why he has so many friends, most of whom are here tonight. His aim in life is to collect friends wherever he goes.

My aim has been collecting achievements. Not that I lack friends. But I poured all my energy into my life in Connecticut, and then walked away from it all. And I let my old high school friendships fall by the wayside. Now I'm lonely with nobody to blame but myself.

Nevertheless, I paste a smile on my face and thank Audrey for the cake.

And the wish I made when I blew out a candle beside Dylan was a simple one. *Please let my twenty-second year be a little less terrifying than the last one.*

When the band starts up again, two different men ask me to dance. But one of them is Roddy, my cousin's boyfriend. And the other is my grandfather.

I say yes to both. But honestly, do I look *that* lonely?

After they reel me around for a song apiece, I treat myself to a single glass of champagne. I have never enjoyed getting drunk, because I don't like to feel out of control. Especially in a room full of my extended family.

Eventually the band stops playing, and our friends begin to say goodnight one by one.

By the time we all climb onto the bus to head back to the farm, it's one in the morning. I sit beside my grandpa.

"These dancing feet are tired. Happy birthday, Daphne. If you're twenty-one, I'm probably legally dead."

"You look fine to me. Did you have fun tonight?"

"Yes, until my date went home early."

"Bummer," I sympathize.

"Pick a wild one, Daphne."

"What's that?"

"Whomever you choose, make sure he knows how to party. Life is short, but the nights are long when you're bored."

A head swivels around to look back at us. It belongs to Rickie. He winks at me.

When we get home, I get ready for bed, but I'm strangely wired. That's why I end up standing in front of the bathroom mirror, checking my phone. There's a text from my ex. It says: *Happy birthday, Daphne. Hope it's a good one*.

I eye this little missive the way you might look at a venomous spider. It makes no sense, for starters. The last time we spoke, he threatened me.

The result was that I didn't tell Reardon I wasn't returning to Harkness. After our ugly argument, if you can even call it that, I just quietly made my escape plans. I quit my job and finished my semester, head down, behaving as if nothing had changed.

Only then—after the last final exam—I went to the dean of my program and announced my departure. I never told Reardon. I don't even know if he's heard the news.

He's probably on a golf course somewhere, *summering*. How does he even know it's my birthday? Did I tell him that sometime? Some night after sex, when I still believed all the lies that came out of his mouth?

Just thinking about kissing him makes me squirm now. How could I have *ever* been so dumb?

And yet I'm afraid to ignore his weird little message. I'd like to leave him with the impression that our breakup had no lasting consequences. He should think that as long as he can.

So maybe a quick reply makes sense. I want to appear completely nonthreatening, at least until I figure out how to deliver him the justice he so richly deserves.

Thanks! I add a really banal smiley emoji and I hit send.

Five seconds later the phone rings in my hand.

"Shit!" I almost drop it on the tile floor.

My phone seems to ring for a year before finally going to voice-mail, and I pause in the hallway to see if he leaves a message.

Nope.

"Shit. *Shit shit shit.*" I do not want to talk to him. And now he knows I'm awake and evading his call.

My heart beats wildly, and all for a ringing phone. But I feel as though I've summoned a monster. On my birthday, no less.

Before I make it into my room, the door to Rickie's room swings open, and there's Rickie in nothing but a pair of boxers and—bizarrely—a silk bathrobe, his tats on full display between its open halves. "Hey. Is everything okay?" he asks.

"Yes." *No.* But I've been cursing it up out here. "I was just, um…"

In my hand, the phone rings again. And I give a full-body jerk that probably makes me look like a nervous freak.

"You sure?" he asks.

"No," I finally admit. "Can I ask you a weird favor?"

"Of course. The weirder the better." He gives me an easy grin. Then he beckons me into his room.

Hastily, I close the door behind myself. "I do not want to talk to this man. Would you answer my phone? Maybe, um, pretend like we're hanging out together and he's interrupting?" It's a good thing the light is so dim in here, because my face is probably crimson right now.

Rickie's smile widens. "Oh, that's no hardship." He grabs the phone out of my hand and swipes to answer the call. "Hello? Awful late for a phone call, pal."

I lean in, my head close to Rickie's. And he tilts the phone a little to make it easy to hear the reply.

"She won't pick up, huh?" The sound of Reardon's voice actually makes me shiver. "Can you give her a message for me?"

"Sure, man," Rickie says. "This better be important. Just saying."

"Oh, it is. You tell Daphne that if she so much as breathes my name to anyone in our program I will bury her. Vermont isn't that far away, you know?"

My heart might actually detonate, it's pounding so hard. And I feel my legs start to shake.

"Interesting," Rickie says in a strangely light tone. "Got some anger issues there, pal. I'll let her know you called, so she can get that restraining order prepared."

"Who is this?" Reardon demands. "Have we met?"

"Nah," Rickie says. "But if you want to keep your face in one piece you'll keep it that way." Then he ends the call and drops the phone onto his bed like it's made of hot coals and it's burning his hand.

EIGHT

RICKIE

That *voice*. Like Lucifer himself. The moment I heard it, I felt cold inside.

But forget me. Daphne is actually swaying on her feet. That's the only reason she lets me ease her toward my bed, like you'd do for a frightened child. I deposit her against the pillows, where she hugs her knees to her chest and grips them, white knuckled.

"Hey, you're trembling," I whisper, climbing onto the bed beside her. She doesn't even protest when I wrap an arm around her. She actually leans in. That's how I know things are bad.

"Okay, who's your violent friend?" I manage to ask the question casually. But I'm not fooling anyone. That kind of brazen threat can only come from some kind of psycho.

The world is full of terrible people. I know this. It's just that I can usually make it through a Friday night without talking to any of them.

"He's my..." She shudders, and I pull her a little closer. "I guess you'd call him my ex. Reardon Halsey. And if the name sounds familiar, he's the son of Senator Mitchell Halsey."

Does that name sound familiar? Each time I hear a name these days I hold it up to the white mist of my memory and ask myself why it's not *more* familiar. Did I once know it and then lose it? Or did I never know it at all?

Fun times with my brain.

"He was part of my graduate program," she says dully. "A transfer from your school, actually."

Goose bumps rise up all over my flesh. "From the Academy?"

"Yeah."

"Isn't that weird?" I ask. Because I think it is. Any mention of my former school puts me on high alert.

"Not really?" She shrugs. "There are several joint science programs between Harkness and other schools. There's one in bioengineering, and one in biochem. But the Harkness joint BS/MS program is fairly novel, so we get a lot of transfer students."

Nonetheless, my pulse has notched up to a higher setting. "And you dated this guy?"

"Yes. I guess. Dating makes it sound so civilized. It was more like a secret fling. Nobody knew. It was a *huge* mistake."

"Why is that?"

She props her head in her hands and takes a deep, shaky breath. "We were working on a project together. I was really flattered that he wanted to hang out with me. He was a year older than I was. Rich, powerful family."

"And he was super attractive," I add drily.

She lifts her face out of her hands. "You know who he is?"

"Nope. But girl, that guy sounds like the worst sort of human, and you are as smart as they come. So he must have a face like Adonis and a nine-inch cock for you to see past his attitude."

Daphne pushes a fist against her mouth and laughs, even as her eyes get damp. "He was really pretty, I guess."

"His face? Or his cock?"

"We are not talking about his—" She laughs and cries at the same time. I didn't know that was humanly possible.

"About his dipstick? Fine. I'm a fan of cocks, though."

"Really?"

"Yup. Pansexual but heteroromantic. It's not a secret."

"Oh." She hiccups. "We're still not talking about it. I'd like to forget I ever saw it."

"So it ended badly, huh?" Of course it did. Because exes don't usually call you on your birthday to threaten physical harm. He sounded like evil in a human form, and I'm not likely to forget the ice-cold tone of his voice anytime soon.

"It never should have started," she says, leaning back against the headboard and closing her eyes. "He flattered me. Just little things at first. *You have the prettiest eyes.*" She groans. "I ate it up. I'm not used to men showering me with compliments. And then one night he invited me up to his apartment for a drink..." She shakes her head. "I went for it. We started, um, seeing each other even though it was against the rules."

"Wait, why? Two students hooking up isn't very newsworthy."

"Technically, I was his boss," she whispers. "He was assigned to my unit of the research project. And even though he's a year older than I am, and we're both students, it was still against the rules."

"Okay," I say slowly.

"My writeup on his work would become part of his file." Her voice is so soft that I can barely hear her. "So after a month or so of..."

"Hanky spanky?" I offer.

"He broke it off. I was almost relieved, because I'm not the kind of girl who's comfortable breaking rules."

"You? A good girl complex? You don't say."

She gives me a weary glance. "If only my good girl instinct had been stronger, I wouldn't be in this position."

"Why? What happened? Didn't he like what you wrote up in the file?"

"Oh, it was *glowing*." She rolls her eyes. "He's highly intelligent, so the writeup was easy, even with my guilty conscience. I used very specific examples of good work that he'd contributed. I thought I'd learned a lesson, and paid the price only in excessive guilt and crushing shame."

I'm not convinced that *crushing shame* makes sense in this scenario, but I'm smart enough to keep that opinion to myself. "I take it that something went wrong? Otherwise he wouldn't feel the need to lash out like a cornered pit bull."

"He cheated. At work," she adds quickly.

"Like, on a test?"

Daphne shakes her head, and silky strands of her hair brush the bare skin of my shoulder. "We were working on a big study that follows healthcare workers' health all over the country. Our office processed surveys from all over Connecticut. Thousands of them. So every day we got these responses either online or in the mail. And I eventually realized that Reardon was throwing responses away."

"What? Why? To lighten the workload?"

"No." Her head thunks against the headboard. "He was throwing out responses from Hartford County. It's sort of a miracle that I ever noticed. But I had been given a research assistant position that was pretty far above my pay grade, so I was kind of psycho about counting and double counting everything that we got."

"And then the piles shrank?" I guess.

"Yes, but only certain piles. Reardon was digitizing the data that came in on paper. We all were. It's boring work. But quite a few responses went missing in four zip codes."

"What's special about Hartford County?" I have to ask.

"Cancer," she whispers. "There's some preliminary evidence of a cancer cluster. It would make his father look bad. That's my theory, anyway. But I can't prove he was throwing away surveys from cancer patients. I didn't even form that theory until recently. But the numbers kept coming up wrong, so I confronted him. That was my second mistake. I should have told someone else first. Or I should have tried catching him in the act. But I just thought there must be some explanation or misunderstanding. And then when I brought it up he was *terrifying*. Just psycho."

Oh shit. "What did he threaten you with?"

"He said I was crazy. That I had no proof. And that I'd invented this whole thing because I was so upset that he dumped me. He said he'd file a sexual harassment claim." Her voice shakes. "He said he could make me look like a crazy stalker. He had the text messages to prove that he's the one who broke it off."

"Oh my fucking God."

"He said if I tried to take him down, he and his father would make sure I never got a diploma from any university anywhere. And I believe him."

My heart hurts now. I wrap an arm around Daphne and pull her close to me. "And you never told anyone this story, did you?"

"Not a single person," she says. "I never wanted anyone to know. And I don't even know why I just told you."

I do, though. Because this Reardon guy is a terrifying motherfucker. And sometimes fear just spills over whatever container you're trying to keep it in.

"Okay, okay," I whisper. "I won't tell a soul."

"I'm a coward," she murmurs. "I pretend to care about science and public health. But all that data is fucked because I'm too afraid to report him. God, my head." She rubs her temples.

I reach over to the bedside table and flip off the lamp. "This won't fix itself tonight."

"It won't fix itself period," she says. "Now that he knows I've left Harkness, he's nervous."

"Yeah, but…" I think it over for a moment. "He's nervous, but he can't do anything. It makes no sense for him to make accusations against you now, because that invites countermeasures from you. You'd be forced to defend yourself by telling your side of the story. That's why threats are his only option. He needs you to be terrified and stay silent."

"It's working," she says. "I'm terrified every day."

"Jesus," I whisper.

We sit quietly for a while. I feel Daphne relaxing by degrees. Her breathing slows down, while I think through everything she's told me. What a mess.

Daphne makes more sense to me than she did an hour ago. No wonder she's so angry. No wonder she hasn't been very receptive to all my fun suggestions. I've been trying to get her naked, while she's been trying to keep her life from running off the rails. "The best thing you can do for yourself is to try to relax," I whisper.

"Mmm," she sighs against me.

"Put him out of your head." I'm quiet for a moment. "You know what's really relaxing? Orgasms."

I expect her to complain that my joke is ill-timed. But she doesn't. And when I glance at her to find out why, I realize she's fallen asleep on my chest. Figures.

But she's so cute when she's sleepy. Her face has softened, her long eyelashes practically touching her cheeks.

I don't mind being Daphne's pillow. Don't get me wrong—I would rather tire her out with sex than trauma. But I can't deny that this is nice, too.

Doesn't that just figure? I've been trying to get her into bed for a couple of weeks now. But not like this. And what's more, I won't be able to sleep with her here. Ever since my accident, I need solitude and a locked door to fall asleep.

Still, I don't have any urge to wake her, or to get up. I relax against the bed and watch the moon rise out the window. Daphne breathes slow, even breaths that I can feel against my bare skin.

It's peaceful. And maybe I'm still frustrated by all the difficult things that have happened to me these past few years. But at least I'm on an upswing.

And there are worse places to be than on a bed in Vermont, under the moon, beside a sleeping beauty who needed me tonight.

NINE

ALMOST THREE YEARS AGO

"Now you make a right at this stop sign. And a mile from here you'll see a sign for the highway again."

"Got it," Rickie says. It's kind of weird that this highway exit has no matching entrance. But whatever. He's happy to take directions from Daphne.

He's back in his uniform shirt, pointing the car southbound this time. Seventy-two hours passed very quickly, and now it's time to drive back to Connecticut, and go back to the Academy.

Rickie fights off the dread in his gut. He knows that the upperclassmen are making his life hell on purpose. Plebes are mistreated so that they can learn to bear up under pressure. In a year or two it will be his turn to make the plebes' lives hell.

It's not that appealing, honestly. And the worst of the bullying is getting on his last nerve.

The bullying is not directed at Rickie. He's too smart to attract their attention. But still, it's hard to watch. The way they target his roommate is just evil.

Christmas break will be here soon, though. There are only a few weeks to survive before exams. Then he will have completed Gauntlet Term, as it's called. Six long months of both military training and classes, July through December. All plebes endure it together. It's supposed to build character, as well as muscle.

"How was your weekend?" Daphne asks.

"Pretty great." He gives her a quick glance. She's not wearing makeup today. Not that it matters. She's the prettiest girl he's ever met, and he's met plenty.

She's a first year, too. That's lucky. There will be more of these car trips, so long as the ancient Volvo doesn't die before they both graduate.

He makes a mental note to have the oil changed.

"*Pretty great?*" she repeats with a throaty chuckle. "Where's the detail? We've got three hours, here. Or wait—maybe you can't tell me. Too scandalous?"

Daphne Shipley is *teasing* him. And he likes it. A lot.

"Well, I can't talk about the sex and the drugs. But I also went to the shooting range with my dad, like real men do."

"Real men who call themselves Rickie."

He grins. "This again? I told you—my father is Richard. So I'm Richard junior. And Richard is a boring-ass name."

"It's the name of kings," she points out. "Richard the Lionhearted is a badass name. *Rickie* is a little punk with a slingshot."

"Sure, babe. Walking around referring to yourself as Richard the Lionhearted wouldn't be weird at all."

Now they both laugh.

"First I became Rick, so we didn't get confused about who Mom was calling. And since I'm not a very serious person most of the time, my friends started calling me Rickie. And I just went with it. At the Academy I'm *Richard* all the time, which I don't particularly like. So if friends want to call me Rickie for twenty more years, I don't really have a problem with that."

"Makes sense," she admits somewhat grudgingly.

"Your turn," he says. "Daphne is…a flower? It's a pretty word. But are all the people in your family named after plants?"

"No. My oldest brother is August, named after my grandfather, who was born in August. But he goes by his middle name, Griffin. My older sister is May, because she was born in May…"

"So why don't you have a month for a name?" he asks.

"Well, I'm a twin. And you can't name *two* kids July, so…"

"All righty." He grins. "That's why you became a flower."

"A Daphne is a boring little flower, true, but it's also two other things, so I'm open to interpretation."

"Do tell. What are the two other things? Wait—isn't there a Greek myth about Daphne?"

"You are correct—a super depressing myth. Eros shoots Apollo to make him fall for Daphne. But he shoots Daphne with something that means she can't *ever* fall for a man."

"So they're star-crossed lovers," he says.

"Oh, it gets worse. He pursues her mercilessly, including disguising himself so he can spy while she bathes in the river. He's basically going to rape her, so she asks her father—a river god—for help. And he turns her into a laurel tree. Forever."

"Ouch," he says. "Okay, what's the third thing? Because at this point, a boring flower is looking like your better option."

"It's a water flea," she says, trying not to smile.

"Say what?"

"You heard me. Daphnia is a genus of tiny crustaceans. Filter-feeding plankton."

"Omigod." He laughs. "And here I thought Richard was a bad draw."

"Stop."

"I don't know if I can look at you now without seeing a water flea. Sorry."

"Just know that I did some shooting this weekend, too."

He laughs. "Seriously?"

"Don't look so surprised, Mr. Tactical Services. I grew up on a farm. When it's time to slaughter a pig, the shot has to be right between the eyes. Otherwise you make the animal suffer."

"You took out a pig this weekend? All I shot was a paper target. What did you use?"

"A rifle."

A laugh escapes from his chest. "You are *surprisingly* sexy, Daphne Shipley." He gives her another very appreciative glance. "Don't lose my email address."

She rolls her eyes, as if he's teasing her.

He's not. Daphne is *totally* his type. She just doesn't seem to know it. "Do you hunt?"

"I have," she says. "But that ended when my father died when I was fourteen. I don't miss it. Hunting is boring. I don't mind killing an animal for food, but I do mind sitting around all day in the snow waiting for it to wander by. I don't need to make a sport out of my dinner."

"But you could argue that venison is more ethical than those pigs you said you raised. Bambi is free and happy in nature until the moment your bullet finds his heart. The pig is enslaved from birth to become your sausage links."

"I never said my way was more ethical," she points out. "But we only have organic livestock now. That pig has a lot more space and privacy than I ever had in a house with three older siblings, including a twin brother."

"That pig never has to ask for the remote control, huh?"

"You're an only child, right?" She sniffs.

"Maybe. Why?"

"One does not ask for the remote. One fights for it with sweat, blood, and sharp elbows."

"That sounds like an average night in my barracks. Have you considered a career in the military?"

She smiles and shakes her head.

Rickie makes himself turn his eyes to the road. But he really just wants to look at Daphne. Seeing people is his superpower. And what he sees of Daphne he likes.

She's a little lost right now, which he recognizes from personal experience. Starting in a new place is hard. As a military brat, he's done it so many times. This is her first time living away from home, though, so it will take her a little longer to find her stride.

But when she finds it, the rest of the world better watch out. There's a fierceness to her that can't be hidden. He's especially drawn to this.

The drive is long, and they make a lot of small talk. He promises himself that he won't ask her any personal questions about her weekend. His curiosity about people and their relationships sometimes makes his friends twitchy.

But he loves that shit. That's why he's going to become a spy. And when he's had enough of espionage, he'll go back to graduate school to become a clinical psychologist. He has it all planned out.

Somewhere in Massachusetts, he can't stand it anymore. "You haven't told me about your weekend."

"Is that a requirement?" she asks, pulling her hair back off her shoulder.

The motion shifts the air between them, and he catches a whiff of her shampoo. Lemons, maybe. He wishes he could get even closer and do a thorough analysis.

"I suppose not," he admits. "But you kinda left me with a cliffhanger. Did the guy say anything? Is your sister still mad? Did the ponies shit everywhere?"

She laughs. "No, of course not. Yes she is, and yes they did."

"Pfft. No details?"

She faces away from him, her gaze out the window. "I made everything weird at home. My sister won't even look me in the eye. And the guy is extra *polite* to me now. Like a stranger. I was happier when he treated me like an amusing sidekick."

Well, ouch. "The weirdness will pass eventually, right?"

"I guess," she mutters.

"And there will be other guys. You probably have a few picked out already. Maybe go back to your practice guy and give him another turn at bat."

"My practice guy?"

"Yeah. Some high school hookup. He'll swallow his own tongue if you tell him you want a rebound. There's got to be someone like that in your past." Rickie tries to toss off this suggestion in a casual way. Like he's not privately waving a hand in the air, volunteering as tribute.

Except there's a very telling silence from the passenger seat. And his heart sinks. He's put his foot in it *again* with this girl.

But really? She *waited* for her crush? Who does that?

He clears his throat. "You know, I'm happy to pull a Katniss, here. Any day of the week."

She snorts.

"Dead serious. Maybe you're having a moment in your life when you need to get out more."

"That's my whole life, apparently," she mumbles.

"Ah. Well, I'm kind of a specialist at having fun. Maybe we could have fun together."

She finally glances in Rickie's direction, trying to see if he's serious.

He is. "I've got an idea, okay? Hear me out. At the end of the semester we'll have our first Open Weekend."

"Open Weekend?"

"Yeah, the Academy is a closed campus most of the time. No visitors. But there are these weekends when the rules are suspended. All the cadets party off campus like savages. Here." He picks up his phone from the cup holder and unlocks it. "Text yourself from this, so I'll have your number. When our plans are set, I'll invite you to a party. It's some annual thing that happens at a boathouse. It's supposed to be epic, although people exaggerate. I'm game to find out."

She holds the phone without entering her number.

"Come to the party," he says. "If only for a drink before I take you home. It doesn't have to be, uh, a big deal."

"A party," she repeats. "With or without the pity sex?"

He snickers, and falls a little more in lust with her than he already was. Most women wouldn't call out his bullshit quite so plainly. "There would be no pity involved, I can assure you."

"Uh, thanks."

"Leave me your number. I hate email. And you can decide whether or not you're coming after I send you the details."

"Fine," she says, possibly just to shut him up.

But she taps in her number nonetheless.

Satisfied, he turns on the radio. "Creep" starts playing through the speakers. It's a fun singalong, but Daphne doesn't join in. "You know this one?" he asks.

When he glances over at her, she's mouthing the words. It's such a dark song about not belonging. Everyone can relate, at some point or another.

And then—on the second verse—she starts singing. Holy shit, her voice has some power. But forget the skill—it's the raw emotion she puts into it that floors him. Just wow.

Daphne Shipley could bring a guy to his knees.

If he's lucky, he might just be that guy.

TEN

DAPHNE

I wake up the next morning to the sound of my mother's voice in the hallway. "Daphne? I have to run to the feed store. Would you get breakfast on?"

Lifting my head off Rickie's pillow, my first thought is: *oh shit.*

My second thought is: how do I end up in so many awkward situations? If I call out an answer, she'll know I'm in the wrong room. And where *is* Rickie? I'm alone in this bed.

"Daphne?" she calls again. "Are you in there?"

It's not the crime that gets you. It's the coverup, right? When will I learn? I slide off the bed, march over to the door and yank it open. "I'll make the breakfast."

My mother turns her head. Her eyes widen.

But that's when my bedroom door pops open, too. Rickie is standing there, blinking sleep out of his eyes.

My mother's confusion doubles. "Will *someone* start breakfast? I guess it doesn't matter who."

"Sure," Rickie grunts.

"I'm sorry I fell asleep on your bed," I stammer.

He shrugs. "No problem. Yours was available."

"The bacon is defrosted," my mother says. "I'll be back in an hour." She turns around and marches back down the hallway toward the staircase.

Rickie and I spend a long moment just watching each other. I have

75

a hangover, but not from alcohol. It's the vulnerability. I hate looking weak, and last night I just spewed all my poor life choices at Mr. Hot and Broody.

"Sorry," I mutter again.

He just shrugs.

"Now she's going to imagine that we're..." I clear my throat.

"S'okay." He yawns. "I imagine it every day, too. So we'll have that in common."

Then he slips past me and nabs the bathroom before I can get in there.

Figures.

Lucky for me, Reardon doesn't try to call me again. He doesn't text, either. But now I'm always on edge. Every time my phone lights up with an incoming message, I have a moment of panic.

But as the days pass, I start to relax. Rickie and I don't speak of it again. He knows I don't want to. Although I have to admit that spilling my guts has made me feel a little calmer. It makes me feel less crazy to hear someone else's thoughts about it. *Threats are his only move*, Rickie had said. And I appreciate this logic.

It doesn't stop me from worrying, though. And it doesn't stop me from feeling deeply embarrassed. I told Rickie about the academic land mine I'd created. But that's not the only thing that Reardon destroyed.

He took my self-esteem, too. It's just gone. When I started dating him, I thought I was smart and maybe even sexy. Now I'm just a dumb girl who screwed a liar. Oldest story in the book.

When Wednesday arrives again, Audrey sends us off to Burlington with another shipment of applejack for two new restaurants.

This time, there's a holdup at the first one—nobody is there to receive it. And we burn fifteen minutes trying to call the phone number on the manifest, until finally someone shows up at the restaurant and takes the delivery.

"I'm going to be late for work," I complain, eyeing the clock on the dash.

"Nah, it's fine," Rickie says. "I'll drop you off, go to my class, and then make the delivery afterward."

"Really? Could you?" The desperation in my voice is evident.

"Uh huh. Because I can tell the idea of being late to your second day at a new job is making all your good girl sensors ping like crazy."

He's not wrong. "Someday you're going to be an excellent shrink."

"Aw, careful, Daphne. I think you just paid me a compliment. I might get cocky."

"Too late," I snap. But there's no bite in it. I watch the red bricks of the Moo U campus approach, and I wonder how it came to this. I'm actually starting to *like* Rickie. And that's dangerous.

He pulls up in front of the School of Public Health a couple minutes later. I reach into the back seat for a box of pastries that Audrey sent with me this morning. *For your new friends at work,* she'd said. *I was testing blueberry recipes.*

"Whoa, what are those?" he asks.

"Just bribing my coworkers so they'll like me. It's what you do at a new job." Thank God for Audrey's social impulses. I'm well aware that I was frosty last week. It's almost like Reardon Halsey has made me forget how to feel optimistic about people.

Rickie rolls down the window so he can talk to me after I shut the door. "Don't forget we're stopping for ice cream on the way home."

"Again?" I turn around on the sidewalk to wave goodbye to him.

"It's what we do, babe. It's our thing. Don't mess with tradition."

"Fine. Later."

"Later!"

I turn around, only to find Karim holding the door for me. "Good morning," he says.

"Morning."

"Rickie Ralls is your boyfriend?"

I laugh. "Not exactly. We live together." That came out wrong, but it's accurate. "Like roommates."

"Oh. Cool." He shrugs as I follow him through the lobby and into our office space. "Sorry. It just made sense to me. Like all the attractive, super intelligent people should really end up together."

I think Karim just called me super intelligent. And attractive. Weird.

"Last year I was a TA. For a cognitive psych class. And the professor interviewed Rickie in class about his amnesia. That was interesting. But Rickie knew more of the neuroscience we were learning than most of the graduate students in the class. And then there's the whole speaking three languages thing. It does things for my competence fetish."

"Karim, do you have a man crush on my friend Rickie?" And just listen to me! I'm teasing my new coworker like a normal, well-adjusted person.

"Oh, it's a full-on crush," he says. "Those eyes. Those tattoos."

My surprised laugh comes out as an undignified snort. "Don't *ever* let him hear you saying these things. His ego is king-size. He does enjoy flattery, though. Just a tip."

"Really?" Karim's eyes sparkle. "So you're saying there's a chance?"

He leads me into a conference room, where Jenn is already waiting. "Morning!" she says, hoisting a postal service tray out of a box and onto the table. And with one glance I know what we're going to be doing today. The envelopes stacked into that tray are identical to the ones causing all the trauma in my life.

I actually shiver.

"This is the—"

"Northeast Healthcare Workers survey. Vermont edition," I say, sounding like the worst kind of know-it-all. "Sorry. These envelopes haunt my dreams."

And I mean that literally.

"No problem! It's great that you've done this before. Once you get comfortable I'll just go over our procedure, because there could be differences?"

"Absolutely." I shed my heavy backpack and slide Audrey's pastry box onto a corner of the table.

Then I listen like a champ as she explains the procedure. The surveys are separated from the envelopes, but the envelopes are retained by zip code.

We did the same thing, of course. But Reardon had disposed of the extra envelopes too. It was the first thing I'd checked.

It turns out they do things exactly the same way in Vermont. So we get to work. I'm already a pro at zipping the letter opener across the top of the envelope without slicing the papers inside, and the work goes quickly.

"I brought treats," I say after an hour. "Blueberry scones."

"Does that mean it's time for a coffee break?" Karim asks.

"Yes!" Jenn shouts. "Our coffee break ritual is an episode of Cold In Death."

"The true crime podcast?" I ask.

"That's the one. Are you a fan?"

"Not yet. But first I need to duck into the library anyway and swap some journals."

They both stare at me. "You didn't," Karim clears his throat, "finish reading those already?"

"Well, sure. But I had a whole week. And I don't have a life, so..." I chuckle nervously.

They exchange a glance. "Wait until she finds out our other favorite pastimes," Jenn says.

"They're very intellectual," Karim explains. "Darts at the bar. And karaoke."

"I can play darts," I insist. "My grandpa taught me. He's a shark. Karaoke and I don't mix. Like, at all." I don't like to be stared at.

"Eh, one out of two ain't bad," Karim says with a shrug. "Can I have a scone now?"

"You can have two." I slide the box toward him on the table. I already like these people. I can't help but feel a little whiff of hope.

Reardon seemed nice, too, my battered ego points out. *You can never really tell.*

New friends are too risky. I learned that the hard way.

ELEVEN

RICKIE

"Hey," Lenore says as I bounce into the chair across from her. "Thanks for pushing back a half hour. I know you were waiting around."

"No problem." She'd texted to say that she had a patient in crisis, asking me to meet her a little later than usual. "I did an errand and went to the coffee shop."

"Is that why you look so jittery right now? How was your week?"

"I don't even know where to start."

"Another bear?"

"Nope. Everything I faced down was human. I did what you said. I told Daphne about my issues."

"Oh!" She clutches her heart. "That's so healthy of you, Rickie. You deserve a cookie." She wiggles her eyebrows. "Did you get a cookie?"

"Your use of the word cookie confuses me. It's almost like you're making it sound *sexual*."

She snickers.

"Nothing happened. Yet. But it turns out that Daphne is dealing with some things, too. She has a crazy ex who's threatening her. It's a long, weird story. And get this—he transferred from USTSA. A senator's son."

"Okay?" Lenore plays with her earring. "Does that feel meaningful to you?"

"Of course it does. I can't remember my own life, so every mention of that place feels like a sign. Like I'm living through the second act of a horror movie, waiting for the big reveal."

"And I take it you didn't recognize his name."

I shake my head.

"Or his face?"

"Nah, I didn't Google him. Not yet, anyway. I was distracted when Daphne fell asleep on my half-naked body. On my bed."

"Oooh!" Lenore claps her hands together several times and looks far more entertained than a shrink is probably supposed to. "There you go burying the lede. Then what happened?"

"Nothing. I lay there a while wondering why I can't fall asleep with someone else in the room. It makes no sense. Daphne isn't going to throw me off a wall. But it doesn't matter. I couldn't do it. I had to sneak out of there after a while and sleep in her room."

"Okay, let's dig into that," Lenore says. "What were you feeling right before you decided to get up and leave? Was it fear?"

"Discomfort, I guess. I was tired, but I feel like I can't let anyone else catch me asleep."

"*Catch* you," she repeats. "That's an interesting word choice."

"I know it's weird," I admit. "I didn't use to be like this. I'd fall asleep on trains, or wherever. Like a normal person."

"Falling asleep is the most vulnerable you can be," she says.

"Defenseless," I agree.

"Falling asleep *naked* would be the only way to make yourself even more vulnerable."

"Yeah, maybe," I tell her. "But nudity doesn't bother me. And yet I can't stand the idea of napping in front of anyone. It gives me the willies."

"This is really bothering you all of a sudden, isn't it?"

"Yeah," I grunt. "Because I thought I was doing so good lately, you know? But Daphne has got me all stirred up in every possible way. And I swear to God I could write off six missing months of my life if I could just get back to a life of bad decisions, seduction, and sleeping wherever I happen to land."

Lenore bites back a smile. "Let's try to figure out why you can't.

Why don't you tell me about the weeks just *after* your accident," Lenore says. "You were in a hospital, right?"

"Right, but I don't remember much. I was on a lot of meds. Broken bones are really painful." And I had a bunch of them.

"You must have fallen asleep in a hospital room in front of lots of people."

"Sure. Fine. I can see what you're getting at. But actually the sleeping in a locked room thing didn't start until after I'd been home for a while. A couple months, maybe."

She perks up. "Really?"

"Yeah. I was trying to wean myself off the pain meds—which was no fun. And opiates fuck up your dopamine receptors. So I'd wake up at all hours."

It's been a while since I've thought about those awful weeks. I was still in a brain fog half the time, too. But it's hard to pinpoint when I started locking my bedroom door.

Now here I sit, straining to remember something that other people would have no trouble with. Story of my life. The seconds tick by, and I just get frustrated. "I don't know, Lenore. I can't remember what I was thinking when it started. Maybe I thought it would help me sleep, because nothing else was working? I just don't know."

"Okay," she says gently. "Don't force it. I can tell that this aggravates you."

"It *does*." My own vehemence surprises me. "Because I can't understand my own compulsion. The truth is I don't really *mind* if the whole Shipley clan were to see me sleeping. Even if I'm drooling on the pillow or whatever. I don't really care what people think of me."

"You are gifted in that way," she says. "You could give seminars."

"But that means it's a *fear*. Some kind of phobia. Even if I don't know where I got it."

"Okay, good reasoning." Lenore crosses her arms. "So what are you going to do about it?"

"Isn't that your job?"

She just smiles.

"I guess…exposure therapy," I grumble. "That's all I got, right?"

"It's certainly the most direct route to resolving this. You could sleep outside under the stars. Naked. Hey—where did you say you saw that bear?" Then she slaps her knee.

"I hate you."

She smiles.

Two hours later I'm sitting at a picnic table, eating an ice cream cone with Daphne. My lengthy dry spell means that it's practically a sexual experience watching her lick the cone slowly. Her damn tongue on that scoop of toasted coconut is the most sensual thing I've seen in years.

And the torture isn't even intentional. I can tell her mind is miles away, while I sit here quietly dying. "I'm sorry I was late getting back to the truck," I say in a blatant plea for attention. "My appointment ran late."

Her gaze returns to the present moment. "Appointment? I thought you had class."

Well, shit. There's nothing like outing yourself as a mental patient to the woman you're crushing on. "I do have class. But after class, I see my therapist."

"Oh." She shrugs. "Actually, being late may have helped me. I was just sitting there with a dead phone, and it made me realize something."

"Did it make you realize you want to see me naked?"

She frowns. "It made me realize something about the US Postal Service."

"Okay. I'm down for licking your stamps."

Her tongue meets the creamy cone again. "You might need to workshop that joke. It isn't quite there yet."

"Noted. Now tell me about this postal thing."

"Today at work we opened a whole bunch of surveys—just like my old job. And they explained the whole procedure to me, even though I already knew what to do. Just as a formality, right? Hearing it all again gave me an idea."

"For what?"

"Revenge," she says slowly.

Oh, Daphne. Can't she see that we're soulmates? I drop my voice. "Tell me this revenge fantasy. I'm listening."

"It's *not* sexy." Her brown eyes dance.

"I'll be the judge of that."

"Okay. So if you want people to return surveys, you pay for their postage."

"Sure."

"But you *don't* buy a stamp for all 70,000 envelopes, because only half of them are going to be returned."

"And your poor little research budget can't handle it?"

"Exactly. So return mail is a thing where the USPS charges you only for the ones that come back."

"I see where this is going. It's a way to prove the discrepancy. You paid for a number of stamps that should be greater than the data you entered into the system."

"Right. It *should* prove my theory. Nobody looks at those bills too closely, because nobody would bother to embezzle postage. But there's one post office login for the whole study."

"Do you have the login?" I ask hopefully.

"No, but I know where it is. I can picture the sticky note that's taped inside the procedure folder, in the filing cabinet at Harkness."

"Okay." I chuckle. "How are you going to get it?"

In answer, she gets up and crosses to her brother's truck, while I try not to stare at her ass in that slim little skirt she wore to work today. When she returns, she hands me a party invitation. The event is seven or eight weeks away, in September.

"Oh baby," I whisper. "You're going to do this James Bond style? Drink a martini and then sneak into the office for espionage?"

"It's academia, Rickie."

"Ah. Cheap white wine and cheese cubes. Got it."

She leans forward across the narrow table, giving me a giant smile. "You do understand."

"So much," I whisper. And I lean forward, too, drawn in by the magnetic pull of her brown eyes. She looks so *happy* for once.

And now we're close enough that if I lean a little further over the table, I could take her mouth in a kiss. She knows it, too. And that bright spark in her eyes tells me she likes this idea.

Or maybe not. Because before I can seal the deal, she suddenly swings her legs over the bench and gets up. "We should get home," she says.

Right.

Maybe next time.

———————

That evening after dinner—and after I wash dishes like a good house-guest—we go outside to horse around. Dylan is trying to teach Jacquie, one of his goats, to jump through a hoop.

I'm holding the hoop, while Dylan does all the coaxing. "Come on, cutie," he says, clicking his tongue. But she keeps trying to go around the hoop to reach the treats in his hand. "No, baby. This way." He makes a kissy sound with his lips.

"You have such a way with the ladies," I tease.

"She just needs a minute to get used to the hoop. Then she'll bend to my will."

"Why are we doing this again?" I ask. "I bought some beer for us. And I was hoping to drink one in a rocking chair on your front porch."

"Ooh, beer," Dylan says, instead of teasing me about being as tired as his grandpa. My shoulders still ache from tossing bales of hay up into the loft all day yesterday.

"The good stuff, too. Sip O' Sunshine," I say, hoping to move things along.

"Five more minutes," he presses. Dylan has to feed his goat a metric ton of the treats in his pocket, but Jacquie finally walks through the damn hoop.

"Yes! Done. Beer time."

"Awesome," Dylan agrees. "Porch, or movie?"

"Oh, so Chastity is busy tonight?"

Dylan freezes, the hoop in his hand. "Am I really that bad?"

"What?"

"I am terrible, right? Ditching you every night. I'm sorry."

"Hey, it's fine. I just like teasing you."

Dylan gives me a sideways glance. "All right. If you say so."

SARINA BOWEN

"Besides, your grandpa is really improving my chess game. Although he prefers poker. Last week he got Daphne and Ruth to play, and he cleaned us out in half an hour."

"Yeah, you got to watch your wallet with Grandpa." Dylan closes the gate of the goat enclosure behind us and we head for the house.

"We were playing for cookies. Your sister almost got him in the last hand, though. So close." I snicker at the memory of Daphne's frustration when her grandfather revealed a straight, beating her three tens.

"How's she doing, anyway?"

"Your sister? Fine. Why are you asking me?" I actually feel a rare flush of guilt at this question. And it's not because of all the dirty thoughts I have when I'm with Daphne. It's the fact that an asshole is threatening her, and her family doesn't know.

"Because she might talk to you? She doesn't talk to me. I thought deciding to switch schools was supposed to be a good thing for her. But she just seems so tense this summer."

"Did you ask her about it?" I hedge. It's not my place to tell him Daphne's secrets.

"Nah, she'd never tell me. I'm the fuckup and she's the over-achiever. I'm the last person she'd tell if something was wrong."

"Oh." I don't have siblings, so I don't really know how that works. "I'll try to pay attention," I lie.

"Thanks," Dylan says. "Now let's get our beer on."

Later, after watching a shoot-em-up with Dylan, I turn in for bed. The night is still, and the only thing I hear through the open windows is a chorus of frog song, punctuated by the quick flash of firefly light outside my bedroom window.

This is the safest, most serene place in the world. So I purposely leave the bedroom door unlocked as I climb into bed.

I'm challenging myself. Aversion therapy is a time-tested way of getting over a phobia. Studies have demonstrated that the majority of phobia sufferers can experience relief from aversion therapy, sometimes quickly.

It's not like I have to plunge my hand into a box of spiders, here. All I have to do is sleep with the damn door open.

But ninety minutes later, I'm still staring at the ceiling, wondering what the hell is wrong with me.

At one thirty in the morning, I get up to lock the fucking door.

After that, I fall immediately asleep.

TWELVE

DAPHNE

That weekend I do some babysitting for my little nephew. And I feel crazy tonight. Sitting alone in the stillness of my older brother's home isn't good for me. I'm full of buzzy energy.

It's probably because I've never plotted revenge before.

Okay, that's not strictly true. Anyone with a twin brother has plotted revenge. But this is on a whole new level. It requires a party, a theft, and delivery of an anonymous email that I will try to spoof so that it appears to originate from inside the Harkness system.

It's a lot to plan. I'm either a genius or a psycho. Possibly both.

As soon as I see Griffin's headlights turn into the driveway, I slam my laptop shut with a guilty click.

Audrey enters her kitchen a minute later, where I'm still sitting at her table. "How was he?" she asks, meaning her son.

"Fine," I insist, even though it took me an hour to get my nephew to go to sleep.

"Fine, like *easy*? Or fine like your eardrums will eventually heal?"

I laugh. "The second thing. But I'm a softie. When he whimpers, I run back into his room."

Little Gus just doesn't like to go to sleep without his mom and his dad at home. But he's only one, and his mom is pretty great, so it's hard to blame him.

"How was the dinner party?" I ask as my sister-in-law sits down opposite me.

"It was chill," she says. "Just an excuse for May and Alec to see some friends, I think. This is for you." Audrey puts two twenty-dollar bills on the table.

I make a sound of petty outrage and push them back toward her. "I don't need your money. I like to spend time with Gus. Besides, I was mostly reading in your kitchen, which is much quieter than my kitchen."

"I told you she wouldn't take it," my brother Griffin says, coming through the door.

"It's not really fair for you to skip your own sister's party for me," Audrey says.

"It was a couples dinner, you goof," I argue. Besides, May would rather see Audrey anyway. Everyone knows it. I lift my laptop from the table and stow it in my backpack.

"How about a drink before you go?" Griffin asks. "Or three drinks. I have some new applejacks to sample."

"Ooh, twist my arm." While I've been out trying, and failing, to save the world, Griffin has been busy learning to make all kinds of yummy and profitable things. He's a respected family man and a community leader.

I am a failure. But I am here to celebrate his success, especially if it means a taste test.

Audrey gleefully sets out nine tiny tasting glasses, while my brother gets bottles out of the cabinet. "The two year is finally ready," he says. "Let's compare it to the 90-day aged, and the unaged."

"Let's," I agree.

I taste the clear, unaged liquor first. I roll a drop of it around on my tongue. "Crisp," I say. "Notes of citrus and paint thinner."

Audrey laughs, and Griffin kicks me under the table.

"What? I'm not a boozer. Maybe you asked the wrong girl."

"Try this one," he says, pushing the two year toward me.

I take another little taste. "Ooh. This one is more my speed. It's deep and bold. Notes of plum, and pretentious leather upholstery."

"You're just fucking with him now." Audrey giggles.

"It's good, I mean it."

Griffin gives me a smile. He's great at his job, and we both know that my opinion doesn't really count here. He sets the third shot between the other two and then takes a drink for himself. "You know Mom is on a dating app?"

"*What?*" I nearly choke on my third taste. "She is not."

"She is," Audrey confirms. "I helped her with her profile picture."

"Why?" I demand. "Those sites are full of con artists and assholes."

Griffin's eyes lift. "You have a lot of experience with this?"

"No," I say firmly. "But I read. And the news isn't good."

"Mom is too smart to be conned," Griffin says. "But I wish she could just meet a man at the church coffee hour."

"Why does she have to meet a man at all?" I whine.

"She's only in her fifties, Daphne," my brother chides. "In a couple of years you'll be gone to God knows where, and your brother will be shacked up with Chastity somewhere. Do you want Mom and Grandpa to be all alone?"

"What's wrong with being alone?" I ask the happiest couple in America.

They look back at me with identical pitying smiles.

I pick up one of my shot glasses and drink it down.

An hour later I'm walking carefully down the wide, grassy aisle that cuts through row upon row of our apple trees. I rarely allow myself to get tipsy. I like to stay in control. But the applejack had begun to loosen the big ball of stress in my chest almost from the first sip.

So I'd drunk plenty. And why not? The journey home is only a quiet walk across our own property. It's a quiet summer night, and yet I'm not completely alone. Up ahead, at the halfway point, I see an unfamiliar creature. Someone is lying on a blanket and staring up at the stars.

As I get closer, that person suddenly sits up, his body tense, and stares in my direction.

It's Rickie. And I feel myself smile in spite of myself. I don't know how a guy can seem sexy and strong and still a little hapless and silly all at the same time. It's something to think about later, after I metabolize all the apple brandy I just drank.

"Hey McFly," I call out. "You're awfully jumpy."

"Bears," he says, clutching his chest. "I have to look out for bears."

"Not in the dark," I argue, dropping to my knees on the edge of the blanket. "Deer wander around in the dark, though. So do coyotes."

"Good to know," he says, dropping back down, his hands behind his head. "What are you doing out here?"

"I was babysitting my nephew. What are *you* doing out here?"

He points upward. "Absolutely nothing. Just watching the night sky. Your brother and Chastity went to bed early."

"Of course they did."

He grins.

"And people wonder why I didn't jump at the chance to move into your house in Burlington. Who wants to overhear sibling sex?"

Rickie reaches out and covers my hand with his. "Well, it depends on how we organized the rooms. You might need to stay off the second floor. That third floor room is a little small. But it's very private."

I look down at his hand on mine. It's a good-looking hand. Strong. Broad.

There's a reason I don't drink.

"Are you thinking about moving in?" he asks.

"Not sure," I say, holding my cards close. "Why should I?"

"Well, it's cheap, just like me." He gives me a sleazy wink. "And noise-canceling headphones cost less than Burlington rents. Just saying."

"Cheap is good," I admit. "In this case."

"Don't forget the location, on one of central Burlington's most convenient streets. And then there's the view."

"The view?" I don't think you can see the lake from that part of the city.

"The *view*." He pulls up his T-shirt to show me his abs.

Apple brandy makes me look. And look. And lick my lips.

Rickie makes a low chuckle. Then the jerk does an ab crunch so that he can *remove his shirt entirely* and cast it aside. "Any questions?"

He leans back, supporting his weight on his hands. Suddenly, I can't even remember what we were discussing. I'm locked into a staring match with Rickie's abs, and those wings that are tattooed onto his delicious pecs.

"Come here," he says softly.

"Why?"

"Because our last kiss was bitchin', and I want a rematch. We're all alone out here, right? What's the harm?"

What's the harm? echoes the alcohol in my bloodstream. "But why me?" I blurt out. That's what's really holding me back. I don't understand his interest. And I've been burned before.

Rickie tilts his head to the side, as if confused. "What the fuck kind of question is that? Why *you*? Because you make me crazy with your short skirts and sass and your big opinions. And if you don't come over here right now and kiss me, I'm going to think you're afraid of kissing. You're chicken."

"*Chicken?*" God, this man knows how to push all my buttons. The youngest of four children can never resist a dare.

Still, the youngest of four children also likes to argue. "I'm not afraid of *kissing*. But I really dislike *bullshit*. The last man I kissed was only in it for career advancement, okay? He talked me into his bed, and now I'm moving to a different state and hoping nobody ever finds out that my actions have compromised ten years' worth of research. So pardon me if I ask a few questions first."

In the silence after my outburst, I regret everything. A very sexy man asked me to kiss him. And I gave him a lecture instead.

Is it really that surprising that I rarely go out on dates?

Rickie doesn't react the way I expect. He doesn't get up and walk away, or even tell me to forget it. He tilts his head, considering me. And then he whispers, "He really did a number on you, didn't he?"

I swallow hard. "Why yes, I suppose he did."

"I see." He beckons to me. "Come here and I'll answer your question."

"My question," I repeat.

"Yeah, I'm ready to explain why I want kisses from you." He crooks his finger. "But you have to sit on my lap if you want to hear the answer."

I move forward without really thinking it through. Because I *do* want to hear the answer, damn it. Why does he have to be so stunning in the starlight, with that bare chest practically reeling me in like a trout on a hook?

As I approach, Rickie puts his hands around my waist and hauls me onto his thighs, so I'm straddling him. My short little skirt rides up, and I smooth it down, as if I had any dignity left to maintain.

His lips twitch. "That's better." He reaches up and brushes the hair away from my face. "You know what the great philosophers had to say about sexual desire?"

I shake my head for two reasons. First, I have no idea. And second, I'm trying not to give any more lectures tonight. Because now that I'm this close to him, I would like another one of those kisses, please.

"The answer is *nothing*," he whispers. "Barely a word about man's most natural instincts. Maybe they considered it too base to discuss. Or—and I like this theory better—maybe Plato didn't think I needed a reason to kiss a pretty girl in the moonlight."

My face is still tingling where he touched it a moment ago.

Rickie leans in, and I hold my breath. But he doesn't kiss me yet. Instead, he traces my cheekbone with his lips. "There are so many reasons why I want you," he whispers. "It's a lot of things at once. It's these long legs..." He trails a hand down my bare shin.

And, wow, it's been a really long time since someone touched me like that. I shiver under his fingers.

"It's your perfect face." He places one slow kiss on my cheekbone. "But it's also the snarky things you say with this smart mouth." He runs his thumb over my top lip. "And it's your attitude—like the world would just run a little better if they'd let you be in charge, you know?"

"Well it *would*," I whisper.

He smiles.

"You have a thing for pushy women?" That's the word Reardon used when he was irritated with me. *Stop being so pushy, Jesus.*

"Apparently I like 'em feisty," Rickie says, his fingertips skimming lightly down my back.

I can't believe I'm sitting in Rickie's lap, letting him touch me. And I can't believe how much I *like* it. My skin is dotted with goose bumps. And my lips are tingling, as if begging to be kissed.

"Your anger turns me on," he says, tracing the shell of my ear with the tip of his nose.

"What? Why?" I shiver again. "That makes no sense."

"Doesn't it?" he asks. "Maybe because I'm angry, too."

I'm just trying to decide if that sounds like bullshit when those serious eyes come closer. And I might die if he doesn't kiss me already.

Once more I'm startled by Rickie's gentleness. He moves in, barely touching our mouths together. As if he knows that inside me beats the heart of a frightened little forest creature who might run off if he makes any sudden moves. Soft lips skim over mine. My goose bumps redouble.

But then it finally happens. My insides go *whoosh* as our mouths meld together for real. There's some serious heat behind all that gentleness. Rickie's arms come around me, until all the muscle cages me in.

God, it's delicious. This is still a bad idea. But I'm doing it anyway. I lift my hands to his bare shoulders and sigh. Hard heat and muscle. Soft kisses and whiskers.

I feel him smile into the next kiss. He tilts his head and deepens our connection. It's more aggressive this time. Searching. When I lean in and kiss him back, he escalates by penetrating my mouth and tasting me.

Oh yes. It's on.

What's the harm, he'd said. I'm sure I'll find out later. But right now, everything is wow.

My hands need to move and explore, so I put my palms on his bare chest. And now it's his turn to shiver under my touch. Honestly, it's a revelation. Can I make him do it again?

I brush his chest with light fingertips, experimenting. My thumb finds his nipple ring. And he makes a sexy grunt into our kiss. I wonder what he'd do if I put my tongue on it...

But I'll have to find out later, because Rickie owns my mouth. It's his now. Each kiss is followed by another. And another. I can't pull back or I'll miss one.

Meanwhile, his hands roam my body in a way that would be awfully presumptuous if it wasn't making me so hot. His knuckles drag down the valley between my breasts. Then he bends his legs, prompting gravity to slide me further into his lap, until we're chest to chest.

His thumbs sneak under the fabric of the little summer top I'm wearing, and my belly quivers at the contact of his skin against mine. Maybe I *don't* need a reason to kiss a bad boy in the starlight. It's such a damn relief to sink into his touch. And to stop thinking so hard.

I hear nothing but a static fuzz in my brain as we make out. It's blissful. And his hands are magic. His touch knows things. It knows the sensitive spot at the base of my spine, where his fingertips make me shiver. It knows the undersides of my breasts, where dragging a thumb across the soft swell is enough to make my nipples peak and tingle.

My heart beats to a steady rhythm now. It says *more, more, more.* Unbidden, my own hands roam Rickie's bare chest, tracing the shadowy outlines of those tattoos.

And I can't help but notice that I'm not the only one who's loving this. There's a hard ridge between my legs now. And when my fingers venture lower on those rock-hard abs, he hums his appreciation.

Funny. I always thought bad boys weren't my type. But now that seems like a miscalculation. It's not like I've needed anyone's help at screwing up my life single-handedly.

And bad boys are really *really* good with their hands.

THIRTEEN

RICKIE

Plato said: "You can discover more about a person in an hour of play than in a year of conversation." And maybe he *was* talking about sex. Because I'm learning a lot about Daphne right now. How she tastes, and how eagerly she moves against me as we touch and tease each other.

But she has trust issues. So I'm not going to strip her down and bang her under the stars. Even if I want to.

Badly.

I pull her a little closer against my chest nonetheless. I drop kisses down the smooth skin of her neck, and her answering gasp of appreciation is all I need in this world. Her hand wanders reverently across my bare back, venturing down to my ass. And I smile into our next kiss.

I used to be the kind of guy who could hook up and think nothing of it. Parties were for cruising. Names were optional. But I'm not that guy anymore. This is big for me. The desire coursing through my veins is a wondrous thing. I'll never take it for granted again.

Daphne's kisses mean more to me than she will ever guess. I'd forgotten how this feels—the heat of skin against skin, and the electric sizzle of my nerves every time she finds a new place to caress.

I kiss her deeply, and she moans, needing this just as much as I do. My tense, angry girl has finally let herself loose in my arms. It's beautiful the way she shivers under my tongue. There are a couple of layers of clothing between us. But the heat of her core is unmistakable against my cock.

Reaching under her skirt, I palm the back of her thigh and then drag my fingertips upward. She's so responsive. Each new inch of skin that I claim makes her quiver. Her ass feels exquisite in my hand. So I can't resist tugging her a little more firmly onto my body.

God, I've missed sex. Our tongues tangle and tease. And Daphne begins to ride me slowly. It's sweet agony. My dick strains against these shorts, desperate to get closer to the action.

Daphne's clever fingers squeeze between our bodies, and she toys with the button of my shorts.

Nope. I'm not going there yet. So I gently steer her hand away, placing it on my chest instead.

She groans in frustration. I've clearly created a monster—a long-legged, sweet-smelling sex-monster. Her smooth fingers move on to teasing my nipples. And I really want to lay her out on this blanket and fuck her like a beast.

Our kisses grow desperate. I haven't felt so wild, so free with myself in a long time. This is the stuff that dreams are made of. Hot kisses in the cool night air, and the whisper of the breeze in the grass.

Daphne moves against me hungrily. I slip my hand beneath her skirt, squeezing her ass, and she moans against my tongue. So I slide my fingers past the elastic of her panties, all the way down between her legs, cupping the heat of her core with my palm.

"Rickie," she pants, and my name on her lips is like a drug.

"Let go, sweetheart." I let my fingers slide and tease. She's so wet for me. I feel like a sex god. "I've got you."

She drops her face into my neck and issues a whispered curse.

"Shhh, beautiful girl," I say as she rides my hand.

Her mouth traces my neck, and we both shiver. Then she lets out a beautiful whimper and clenches around my naughty fingers.

"Fuck, you are so lovely." My voice is raw with unfulfilled desire. "So hot." I force oxygen into my lungs as she sags against me.

"Oh j-jeez," she stammers. And then she lets out a gasp, and a long, sweet moan, before collapsing against my body.

"Nice," I whisper, holding her snugly. It isn't easy for Daphne to set aside her control. I know this. We breathe into the stillness, our hearts thumping together. My dick is as hard as one of the fence posts I worked with today in the back meadow. But I don't even mind. It makes me feel alive.

I lean in and kiss her swollen lips again. Slowly.

And then my phone lights up on the blanket, pinging with a text. Twice.

Daphne pulls away suddenly.

"Ignore it," I say.

But she doesn't. She removes herself from my embrace. The damn phone pings again. And then I hear a screen door slam in the distance. "Rickieeeee!" Chastity calls. "Are you out here?"

Daphne slides off my lap and stands up, looking flustered. She plucks her backpack off the grass.

"Hey now." I rise on unsteady legs. "No need to bolt."

"But we...Actually, just *me*. I—" She gulps.

I bite back a smile. "Are you okay?"

"Yes. Fine." The words are like machine gunfire.

"Are you going to play poker with us? Sounds like Dylan and Chastity are still up after all."

"No, I don't think so." She hitches her pack onto one shoulder. Then she looks down at herself and straightens her skirt with frantic motions. "I've...got to go."

"You look fine. Perfect, actually." I lift my hands to her hair and smooth it out of her face. Then I place a soft kiss onto her cheekbone.

She lets out a breathy sigh and hurries away toward the house.

I watch her go, feeling both wistful and victorious at the same time.

For days after our epic makeout session, I barely get within ten paces of Daphne. This is her choice, not mine. She chooses chores at the opposite end of the farm from wherever I'm working. She sits at the other end of the dining table.

A less confident man might worry that he'd lost his touch. But she's still sneaking looks at me, and I see how it is—the poor girl just can't handle the indescribable hotness that arises when we're near each other.

So I'm patient. Again. And after three days, I finally run into her in the upstairs bathroom one night when we both pick the same moment to brush our teeth.

"Hey there, stranger," I say, leaning against the door frame.

"Hey, McFly, she says, bending over the sink to spit.

"I could swear you've been avoiding me."

She dries her mouth. "Yup. Absolutely."

Her honesty catches me by surprise, and I laugh out loud. "Okay, usually people lie about that."

"Why, to save your ego? That thing is made of titanium."

She kills me. "Fair enough. But I still don't know why you'd avoid me. Seems like you should come back for more."

"Sure, no problem." She folds the hand towel and sets it primly back onto the bar. "But I only get drunk about twice a year. Does December work for you?"

"Huh. And here I thought you were a woman of science."

"What does that have to do with anything?" She picks up her hair-brush and frowns at me in the mirror.

"There's a flaw in your logic, baby girl. If I was only attractive to you when you're drunk, then you wouldn't have to avoid me when you're sober."

She rolls her eyes in the mirror as she begins to brush. Now that I know how soft her hair feels between my fingers, I definitely need more.

"I think you just can't handle the hotness," I say.

"Of you?" she sniffs.

"No baby. Of *us*. There's something there, and you like to pretend there isn't."

Daphne is finished with her hair, which is a shame, because I was really enjoying living vicariously through that brush. "I'm just being smart. You and I are a terrible idea."

"Why? Give me three reasons."

She holds up a finger. "One, I gave up men. Second, we're room-mates, and that's awkward."

That's true, but it doesn't bother me as much as it should.

"And three, I gave up men."

I snort. "Are you into women?"

"Nope."

"Bummer. There goes that threesome I was planning for us."

"Too bad." She stalks past me and leaves the bathroom.

Although I see her checking out my bare chest in the mirror as she goes. Her mouth might be telling me that it's not going to happen. But her eyes tell a different story.

FOURTEEN

DAPHNE

And then it's Wednesday again. Another chance to impress my new colleagues. And another hour-long ride in the truck with the man who makes me crazy.

I grab my computer bag out of my bedroom and put on my game face as I descend the stairs.

"Ready for another delivery?" Audrey asks, bouncing Gus on her hip in our kitchen. "It's a big one this time."

"Am I ever going to taste this perfect brew?" Rickie asks. He's parked against the counter, wearing another one of those V-neck T-shirts that shows me a peek at his tats. The same ones I rubbed my body against this past weekend, like a cat in heat.

God, just kill me. I can't believe I did that. The man says a few sweet words to me and tells me he wants a kiss. And what do I do? Climb on top of him, slobber all over him and then ride his hand until...

Yikes. I'm never drinking again. And as Audrey describes today's deliveries, I feel the prickly heat of embarrassment creeping up my neck. And we're not even on the road yet.

"Sorry about the timing," Audrey is saying. "But it's a bar, not a restaurant, so they're not open for deliveries early in the day."

"We can do that one on our way back," Rickie says. "Daphne likes to work until five anyway. We'd get there at maybe 5:45?"

"That's perfect," Audrey agrees.

"Take," Gus says, lifting his chubby little arms. I expect him to reach for me. But he's reaching for... Rickie of all people.

I feel you, little man.

"Oh, I think he likes you," Audrey says. "Sorry, Gus. They're on their way out."

"Take," Gus demands. He gives Rickie a devastating, chubby smile.

To my surprise, Rickie plucks the chubby toddler out of Audrey's arms and pops him onto a hip. "You're a little devil, aren't you?"

Gus laughs and pokes a finger against the tattoo that's visible on Rickie's chest.

"He's smitten," Audrey says.

Aren't we all, kid. Aren't we all.

"Strap in, Gus," Rickie says. "The rush hour traffic is headed outside. Ready?"

Gus waits with wide-eyed fascination.

"And we're off!" Rickie shouts, then he sprints for the door, a giggling Gus holding on tightly. A moment later they appear out the window, where Rickie is galloping around the driveway with Gus in his arms.

"What's that on your lip?" Audrey asks.

"What?" I touch my lips. There's nothing there.

"Oh, it must have been a little drool." She cackles. "You have a thing for him, don't you?"

"Shhh," I hiss. "You're not funny. I do not have a thing for him."

"*Sure* you don't," she whispers back. "How could you not? He's so hot." She waves a hand in front of her chest, as if cooling herself.

"He's not my type," I grumble.

"Oh my God, he is *exactly* your type. Smart enough to keep up with you. Great taste, but not a snob. And that body." She lets out a low whistle. "You need to get on that."

I follow her outside, knowing she's a hundred percent wrong. I need to stay *off* that. And every other man, too.

The three delivery crates are already stacked neatly into the back of Dylan's truck. Audrey hands me the manifest. "Have fun today," she says with twinkling eyes.

"Thanks," I grunt.

"I made you these for the office," she says, opening the back door to reveal another pastry box. "Spinach and feta croissants. There are five of them in there, plus a separate one for Rickie."

"Hey! Thanks!" Rickie says, carrying a flushed Gus over to where we stand. They're both panting. "You're the best, Audrey."

He isn't wrong. "Thank you, Audrey. That is really nice."

She takes Gus from Rickie, and he goes to start the truck. When he's out of earshot, she turns back to me. "I know that starting over is hard," she whispers. "We've all done it."

I look down at my shoes. This isn't my favorite topic. And now I know I haven't been doing such a great job of hiding my stress. Yay.

"Maybe someday you'll tell us why you have to start over," she continues. "But either way, I'm here for you."

"Thank you," I choke out.

"No problem. Have a good day at your new school. Play nice with the other kiddos."

"I will."

―――――――――――――――

Rickie stops at the post box for me again today.

And, wow, I finally get the piece of mail I've been waiting for. But I'm too chicken to open it. So I shove it into my backpack and stress over it instead.

Rickie isn't stressed. He hums along with the radio as we cruise up highway 89. "I have a big idea," he says.

"Oh do tell. I love your big ideas. They never end up embarrassing me."

"Huh." He shoots me a sideways glance. "I'm feeling the cool breeze of irony in that statement."

"You're a sharp one."

"Embarrassing you isn't a goal of mine, Shipley. And I don't think you should be embarrassed about wanting my hot body."

I snort, because who talks like that? Even though I do want his hot body, and I hate myself a little for it.

"My big idea, since you asked—"

"I didn't."

"Well you should have. My big idea is that we go out to dinner in Montpelier after we make the delivery."

"Why? Dinner is free at home."

He shoots me another look. "Because it would be *fun*. And different. Besides—your brother and Chastity are going out tonight, to a drive-in movie."

"Which really just means they're going to have sex in a new location," I grumble.

"Right. But my point is that it's going to be another nice summer night. We could sit outside somewhere, have a beer and some food. There's a noodle shop in Montpelier that's barking my name. It's been a while since I had cold sesame noodles and crispy duck."

That does sound delicious. But I have so many questions. "Do you mean... like a date?"

"Absolutely," he says.

"But we're not dating," I point out. "I'm not dating *anyone* right now."

He shrugs. "I'll let you sort out your own semantic arguments. But I'd like to take you out for dinner. What have you got to lose, anyway?"

"Besides more of my dignity?"

He laughs. "You know, it kills me that I can't remember meeting you the first time. Were we super polite to each other? Or was it just as snarky?"

"Snarky from minute one," I admit. "You were nice to me, but I couldn't figure out how sincere it really was."

He looks over to me again, and his expression is filled with so much warmth that I'm taken aback. "I was sincere," he says, before turning back to watch the road. "Not that I remember it. But I just have a feeling."

My heart thumps like a bunny rabbit's. *But then you stood me up.* I keep that detail to myself. My dignity is in enough jeopardy already. And it's not like he can explain himself. He doesn't even remember meeting me.

I don't have room in my life for warm glances and dinner invitations. Rickie is very distracting. And I cannot let myself get distracted.

"So?" he asks. "Dinner? It will be like an hour-long vacation. Have some noodles with me, Shipley. It won't hurt. I swear."

"Maybe," I say. "I'll text my mom and see what she's planning. If she has big plans for dinner, I wouldn't want to bail on her."

"Fair enough," he says. "Ask her, then."

Fine. Whatever. I pull out my phone and send a message to Mom.

But she hasn't answered by the time we finish our first two deliveries in Burlington. That's not unusual. She's a busy lady.

"Oh well," I say, feeling relieved. "Maybe we should have given her more notice."

"Maybe," he says as he pulls into a parking spot near the School of Public Health. "Why don't you give me your number and I'll text you to check in later." He pulls out his phone and looks at me expectantly.

"It's..." I pause, because it's just occurring to me that we've texted before. Shit.

"It's what?" He's waiting.

"I think I have your number already. I'll check. And I've got to run." I grab Audrey's pastry box, leaving Rickie's pastry behind in its own bag. Then I open the truck's door and hop out.

"Wait, really?"

"Really."

And now he'll realize he can look for those old texts. And he'll know that he stood me up, and that I failed to mention it, because I was embarrassed about that too.

Lovely. That's the problem with secrets. They never stay buried.

"See you at five," I say. And then I run for it.

FIFTEEN

RICKIE

Daphne hustles away from the truck, and I gather my things and cross the campus in the other direction. Outside the lecture hall, I take out the savory croissant that Audrey made for me and eat it slowly.

I guess it makes sense that Daphne and I corresponded before. If you're doing a ride share with someone, you'd do that.

I'm just so tired of the big gap in my memory. I don't even know what I don't know. It's exhausting.

After finishing my excellent pastry, I sit in the last row of the lecture hall and pull out my phone. While the professor talks, I search my phone for 802 numbers. There are a bunch of them. There aren't any Daphnes. And the only Shipley is Dylan.

But eventually I find one for a "SHark," which must stand for some blend of Shipley and Harkness. Who knows what nineteen-year-old me was thinking?

When I open it up, I find a conversation from fall of three years ago. It begins with a boring conversation about where to pick her up —at a gate on Elm Street. Then we negotiate a meetup spot for the ride home. It's at the same exit as the ice cream place. Just like she'd said.

A chill snakes down my spine, even though I'm reading the dullest exchange of text messages ever written. It's just that I know I'm the guy who wrote this. But I don't remember, so it feels like someone else did it. My double. My evil twin.

Then I keep reading. We chat again ten days after our car ride.

RR: Have you given any more thought to my invitation?

SHark: What invitation was that again? I forget.

RR: Well played. Or maybe you get countless offers from men willing to stamp your V-card.

Wait, what? I read it again. And then I let out a groan.

The guy seated closest to me looks up from his notebook with a shaming glance. Oops.

But seriously. Two strangers shared a ride to college, and then I offered to take her virginity? The evil twin theory is looking pretty good right now. I read on, even though I'm a little afraid to.

SHark: There's this thing called subtlety.

RR: Never heard of it.

SHark: [eyeroll]

RR: Look, I know I'm a bastard. And half the things I say are meant to get a rise out of people. But come to the house party anyway. I don't actually expect a private party for two. In fact, bring a friend if it makes you feel more comfortable. We'll all have a good time.

SHark: Does that mean you're planning a ménage à trois?

RR: How many times did you have to type that before auto correct stopped turning it into something even dirtier?

SHark: OMG, three. But the only way you'd know that is by typing it a lot.

RR: Nah. I text in a couple different languages, though, and the results are often heinous.

*SHark: *cough* Humblebrag *cough**

RR: Busted. But to answer your Q, I'm not expecting anything at all. I just think we could have fun. Whatever kind of fun you decide is your speed.

SHark: Maybe you'd rather find another date to this party. One who is more of a sure thing.

RR: Nah. Come with me to see this place. We'll use summer as a verb. We might need to Uber you home, if that's okay. But happy to pick you up before I get my drink on.

SHark: Okay, fine. I could use a little adventure. Text me the details?

RR: *Will do tomorrow. Later, Good Girl.*

SHark: *Later Bad Boy.*

Well, parts of that are embarrassing to read. But not all of it, I guess. I was only fifty percent asshole. And you can tell that I really liked Daphne.

Of course I did.

I keep scrolling, and it doesn't end well. I text her a time and date for the party, and I tell her to look for my Volvo at the gate at eight o'clock. She agrees. But then, at eight fifteen on the established date, I see this:

SHark: *Okay, you're fashionably late. But I'm outside in a thin little jacket. Just saying.*

SHark: *35 minutes, really? I'm starting to take this personally.*

SHark: *Okay... No call. I guess you found a more fun date after all.*

Jesus Christ. What did I do? I reread the entire thing a couple more times, and it gets worse with every reread.

All this time I've been trying to seduce Daphne. I keep telling her we'd be good for each other. Stress relief, or some bullshit. Like I was doing her a favor.

But, nope. I'm the guy who offered to do that before and then left her standing around in the cold, waiting for my no-show ass.

Hell, when was this? It could have been really cold.

I hold my finger down on the last message to see when it was written. And the timestamp makes my heart seize.

That afternoon, I practically gallop into Lenore's office. As I'm waiting for her door to open, I receive a notification on WhatsApp. It's a new message from Daphne.

Clever girl. She switched apps, probably hoping I wouldn't find our old texts.

Too late.

Daphne: *Guess what? Mom says you and I are going to be on our own for dinner anyway. Seems everyone else has plans.*

Let the healing begin.

Rickie: So we can have noodles, right?

It ought to make for an interesting dinner. Me stammering out an apology that's two and a half years overdue.

Daphne: We might as well. It's either that or we're foraging for leftovers.

Rickie: Cool, cool. I know I'm only your dinner date of convenience but I'll take whatever scraps you throw me.

Then I send her a GIF of a cute, begging dog. It's just the opening foray into the round of groveling I owe her.

It's not a date, she replies. Then she sends me a GIF of a door closing in a guy's face.

Now that I know I deserve her wariness, everything makes so much more sense. No wonder Daphne doesn't trust me.

I send back a picture of a dozen roses anyway. Because it's hard to give up being the irritating bastard that I am.

When I sit down in the chair a minute later, Lenore asks me if I've made any progress on my homework.

"Oh…a little." I've forgotten all about aversion therapy. It's the furthest thing from my mind. "Yeah, I started thinking about it. I went outside at night, and lay on a blanket to put myself in the mindset of being exposed. But then I got distracted."

"Another bear?" she asks.

"Nah. Daphne. But look—something weird just happened."

I unlock my phone and show her the godawful texts I exchanged with Daphne all those years ago. And she winces at all the same places I did.

"But that's not even the strangest thing," I point out. "This Saturday night when Daphne was waiting for me? I'm pretty sure it's the same one that I ended up in the hospital."

Lenore's eyes widen. "You think it is? Or you *know* it is?"

"Well, this was for the Saturday night of Open Weekend. I woke up in the hospital two days later. And they said I was injured at an off-campus party."

"You were supposed to take Daphne to an off-campus party," Lenore says slowly.

"Right."

"*Wow*, Rickie. Maybe you didn't stand her up at all. Maybe you got hurt and never read these texts!"

"Maybe," I say slowly. The timing doesn't quite work, though. Unless… "Hey, can I ask you a favor?"

"Sure?"

"Can you pull my file and look at the oldest stuff in it? The date of my injury wasn't really interesting to me before. But now—"

"Yeah, okay," she agrees. "But I do remember that the medical stuff in there was super thin. The Academy didn't send us much to go on. But I'll try. No matter what, you're not the kind of guy who stands a girl up without a good reason."

"Aren't I?" I lean back in the chair, and close my eyes. The usual blank wall greets me. And it's just as frustrating as ever. No—it's worse. A man is supposed to take responsibility for his actions. And I don't even know what mine were.

I open my eyes again. "That's really seductive thinking, Lenore. Like—if I don't remember what happened, I get to choose. I can either decide that I was this dick who screws around with virgins. Or I can be this romantic ideal—the sleeping prince who broke seven bones and couldn't reach out to the princess. That just sounds too convenient. Did you ever read *Choose Your Own Adventure* novels?"

"Sure." She grins. "I liked that one with the unicorn. Sue me."

"Well, I used to cheat. I'd keep my thumb in the page where I made the last choice. And if I didn't like the outcome, I'd flip back and try again. That's me right now deciding whether I'm unlucky or just a dick."

"Now hang on." She leans forward in her chair. "First of all, every kid cheated with those books. I had an elaborate system of numbered bookmarks so I could reverse any decision."

I bark out a laugh. "I knew you were an overachiever."

"Shut up. And second—you're *still* no different from the rest of us. Reframing your past is what everyone who sits in that chair is doing. Every guy who's telling me about his own failed marriage is trying to decide if he's unlucky or just a dick. You're not that special. Nobody needs to *forget* his past to realize that it has several different interpretations."

"Oh, please. Like it wouldn't be helpful to know what my intentions were?"

She smiles really sweetly at me, and it's irritating as hell. "Rickie, look. You don't have to remember the events of that night in December to know who you are."

"God, if you're about to tell me to click my heels together and say, 'There's no place like home,' I'm asking for my money back."

Lenore belly laughs. But after she's done, she gives me a wise smile. "Look. We are *all* trying to survive our pasts, so we can live with ourselves in the present. Even if you woke up tomorrow remembering every minute of your lost year, it wouldn't matter. You can *choose* which Rickie you are. Just decide. And whatever choice you make will be the absolute truth."

"Okay," I agree, because that excellent speech deserves acknowledgment.

I only wish I believed her.

SIXTEEN

DAPHNE

I'd thought that Rickie would be smug about my decision to have dinner with him. But he's quiet as we make the final delivery of applejack to the bar. I watch through the windshield as he carries the crate inside, muscles bulging, eyes feral. He looks angry, honestly.

Not at me, though. When I approached the truck after work, he'd given me a soft look. And then he'd let out a sigh.

Something is bothering him. I can feel it.

Once again I'm struck by the realization that men just confuse me. Rickie always gives off a dangerous vibe. It's more sexual swagger than violence. But now he's in a mood that should probably frighten me. But it doesn't.

Reardon, on the other hand, looked like a Vineyard Vines advertisement in crisp preppy shirts and white-toothed, harmless smiles. Yet he stabbed me in the back at his first opportunity. And when I called him on it, he screamed at me and called me a stupid whore.

And he *slapped* me. I was terrified. That's the part I never mentioned to Rickie, or anyone else. It's just too embarrassing.

I truly believe that most women are born with an instinct that helps them figure out who's scary and who's safe. But mine just never kicked in. This is why I avoid men. It's a pretty good reason, too. I should have said no to dinner.

But I didn't.

At the noodle shop, we're given a plum table by the window. I put my napkin in my lap and pick up the menu. Honestly, this is a treat. Rickie is right that I never go out anymore. I haven't had the emotional energy to reconnect with friends, or go out on dates. Anxiety has eaten my life.

I glance around at the restaurant, which only has a few patrons so far, because it's early. But everyone here looks so relaxed and happy. This is just what I need—a short break from reality. For the next hour, I can be just a lucky girl who's out for dinner with a ridiculously attractive boy.

The waitress arrives, and we order. Rickie thanks the waitress. Then he turns those gray eyes on me, and asks me a polite question. "How was work today?"

"Fine. Good, actually." He listens respectfully while I prattle on about data collection.

"So why public health?" he asks suddenly. "How'd you choose it?"

"Well, at first I thought I wanted to be a doctor and literally save lives. My father died young of a heart attack."

"Right. That really sticks with your brother, too."

"I know. So I started college as a premed bio major. But then I took some classes on healthcare policy."

"And you loved it?"

"No, I got angry."

Rickie grins. "Go on."

"The way we deliver healthcare in this country is so screwed up that the doctors can't even do their jobs. I mean—there are politicians who can't stand the idea of food stamps for hungry children, because one able-bodied guy might accidentally get a free sandwich he didn't earn. Those same guys will defund women's healthcare—all of it—no matter that the data shows that free healthcare for poor women reduces *all* government expenditure. They will *burn it to the ground* just so one undocumented immigrant doesn't get a handout, or just in case somebody gets an abortion."

And now I'm getting worked up. Again. It's a real mystery why I don't have a lot of dinner invitations.

But Rickie just reaches across the table and smooths his thumb across the back of my hand. "Go on."

"I just need science to win. That's all. Public health is about making good policies. I need the grown-ups in the room to make the decisions. Or we're all lost."

"That's admirable," says the new, subdued Rickie.

"Okay, what's wrong?" I finally ask. "You're quiet and it's creeping me out. At least when you're flirty and crass, I know how to handle you."

"Sorry." The smile he gives me is sheepish. "Rough day."

That's when the waitress brings us two steaming bowls of food. I've ordered the salmon fried rice, and it looks like heaven. I unwrap my chopsticks eagerly. God, I need to get out more often. And I will eventually. After I unfuck my life. Somehow.

Rickie ignores his own bowl to watch me dive in. Then he puts his beautiful face in his hand, and asks me the question I was hoping he wouldn't ask. "So tell me—why did I once crassly offer to stamp your V-card?"

Crud. I never wanted to have this conversation. "What if we just pretend that never happened?"

He waits.

I take another life-giving bite of rice and then sigh. "Oh, this is going to sound ridiculous. Because it was. I told you this truly pathetic tale of imagining myself in love with someone. And I confessed that I'd..." Yup, this was going to sound stupid. "I'd *waited* for him, if you catch my drift. And he'd just found the love of his life when I met you. I was a little depressed about it."

I smile like it's all hilarious, but he doesn't smile back. "So I was going to swoop in and show you a good time?"

"Well, you offered. I didn't know whether I was going to accept."

I probably was, though. I'd felt reckless, and I wanted my life to have a little more danger in it. Besides—Rickie is hot and smart *and* funny—which really *does* make him my type.

He finally picks up his chopsticks and pokes at his ramen soup. "I suppose that sounds like something I'd do. But that guy in those texts sounds a little creepy."

"Eh. I thought you were awfully forward. But never creepy. You asked me in a way that was half joking. But I liked how different your outlook was from mine. As if the world was just here for your amusement. Like—let's just go where the night takes us."

"Interesting." He takes a slow sip of his beer, and seems to think about it.

"Honestly, I liked the way you didn't care so damn much about every little thing. I was jealous of your attitude, and I wanted to borrow it for a night."

He's quiet for a couple of minutes. And I hope we can move on. "Listen," he says eventually. "I want to tell you something, although it's probably just wishful thinking. I'm pretty sure that Saturday night of the party is the same one I ended up in the hospital."

My iced tea stops halfway to my mouth. "Really?"

He nods.

"I guess you're *really* sorry that you stood me up, then."

He smiles sheepishly. "Hindsight. Am I right?"

"Or—" The realization dawns. "Maybe you got hurt, and didn't even mean to leave me standing by the gate in the rain for forty-five minutes."

He tips his head from side to side, considering. "See, I love that idea. But it's a stretch. How I could accidentally get wasted if I was planning to come and get you? And fall off a high fence, all before eight o'clock?"

He makes a few good points. And I love this idea a little too much as well. If he'd already been hurt, then I'm not the nerdy virgin he'd abandoned when someone better came along.

"But either way, Daphne, I'm sorry. I apologize. You must think I'm such an asshole."

"Well, I know you a little better now and I find you to be a very entertaining asshole."

Finally he smiles. "I'm still sorry."

"I know you are. And I accept your apology."

He glances down at his overturned phone. "Those messages though, so smug."

Uh oh. A contrite Rickie is even more dangerous to my libido than a crass Rickie. It makes him more real. I can't let myself like him this much. "Can we just drop it now? Besides, you're still smug."

115

"About some things," he says. "But I've been taken down a few pegs lately."

"You too, huh? Welcome to my quarter-life crisis."

He picks up his beer and takes a swig. "The offer to take your virginity still stands, but I assume that ship has sailed."

I reach across the table and poke him with my chopsticks.

"Yeah, I thought so."

For the hundredth time, I wish he weren't so ridiculously attractive. The simmering heat I feel when he smiles at me is very distracting.

He settles in to eat, and I relax. After a minute, he stretches one hand a few inches across the table, just far enough for his fingertips to brush mine. It's the lightest brush, and then it's over. "Look, I'm *very* drawn to you," he says quietly. "My gut tells me that I must have been drawn to you then, too. Right from the beginning."

"Well, there's proof of that." I try to sound nonchalant. "You offered me sex."

He flinches. "I just wish I had that time machine, you know? I'd like to think I handled you with care."

Suddenly, my insides are all gooey. And my heart is sparking dangerously, like the flux capacitor on Marty McFly's DeLorean.

The moment is broken when my phone pings with a couple of texts. But I don't want to look away. No man has ever watched me the way Rickie does. Like he's waiting for a sign.

"I'm sorry," I whisper. "I don't know how to explain how we were with each other. And I can't say for sure what you were thinking." I *still* don't know what this man is thinking and he's sitting right in front of me.

"Don't apologize," he insists. "I'm the one who's sorry. I can't even offer to make up for lost time, because my offer was pretty sleazy in the first place."

"Unless it wasn't meant to be," I hear myself point out. See? I'll always be that hopeful girl—the one who thinks that this time the boy wants me for more than just sex.

"I'm not willing to give myself the benefit of the doubt." He picks up his chopsticks again.

"Fine, but believe it or not, I'm over it. I went on to meet *far* sleazier men than you, who proceeded to do far worse damage than standing me up."

My phone keeps pinging. "Better see who that is," Rickie says. "Also, there's two guys over there watching us, and they look familiar."

I reach for my phone while also glancing over to see who he means. And I spot my cousin Kieran and his boyfriend across the room, menus in hand. When I turn my head, they give me twin smirks.

I frown as a reflex. And of course the texts are from them.

Kieran: Who's your hot date?

Roddy: Nice muscles. And those tats! @Kieran, did you know Daphne had a bad boy kink?

I groan.

"Everything okay?" Rickie asks, frowning.

"Sure. It's just my cousin giving me a hard time." I pick up my drink and take a sip while subtly showing the guys my middle finger.

There's a burst of laughter from their table, and I can hear it all the way over here. Rickie glances in their direction and smirks. "Oh yeah. I remember them from your birthday party. Hey, guys." He gives them a wave and a smile.

Is it weird that I'm relieved to see that cocky smile come back—the same one that I sometimes want to wipe right off his face?

"So," I ask, hoping to change the subject. "What are you writing that paper about?"

"Subjectivity in Aristotle," he says. "A hylomorphic analysis."

"Huh. Well that sounds…"

"Boring?" he guesses.

"I was going for complicated."

Richie gives me a secretive smile. "Sure you were."

"No, really. From one nerd to another—you shine on. One of my goals in life is to always put at least one million-dollar word in the titles of all my papers."

His smile grows hotter. "I knew you were special."

My phone beeps again. I send a suspicious glance toward Kieran. But he and Roddy are deep in conversation.

"Did you know your grandpa likes this restaurant?" Rickie asks.

"What?"

He nods to a table behind me. And when I swivel my neck around, there sits Grandpa. He's eating the salmon fried rice with a fork, not chopsticks, and he's seated across from that woman he was dancing with at my birthday party.

Grandpa waves with his fork and gives me a wink. Then he taps his phone on the table with one of his bony fingers.

"What the hell?" I gasp. I pick up my phone and look at the text.

Grandpa: *You and the new roommate are dating? I see how it is.*

I let out a little shriek of dismay. "Why can't I just eat some fried rice without a peanut gallery?"

Rickie's smile gets a little wider. "Your family is hilarious, Daphne. Just roll with it."

I tap out a quick response. ***Gramps, I'm not on a date. Also it's rude to text at the table.***

Grandpa: *Then why are you replying?*

"The man makes a good point," Rickie says.

"Don't read my texts. And I hate you." I power the phone all the way down.

"No, you don't," he says, and the cocky expression that I know so well is back. "Not that I deserve it, but you don't hate me."

Fine. Fine. So I ate out with Rickie and I liked it. And I hate that I know how good a kisser he is. There will be no more kissing.

And this *wasn't* a date. Even though Rickie doesn't let me pay my half of the check. "My idea, my bill," he says.

"Thank you," I say a little stiffly. "We're still not dating."

"I heard you the first time," he says with an easy smile.

Only it turns out that I'm the only one in Vermont who's not on a date tonight. As we're leaving the restaurant, Rickie holds the door open for...

My mother. My *mother* is walking into the noodle shop in a dress, with a man I've never seen before.

"Oh!" She stops short in front of me. "Daphne, honey. Hello."

"Mom," I say curtly. "Who's your friend?"

"This is Gil," she says, nodding a little too vigorously. "Gil, my daughter."

The man smiles and shakes my hand nervously. He has a salt-and-pepper mustache that needs a trim. "What a wild coincidence, running into family tonight."

"It's not such a wild coincidence, apparently." My voice is tight, and my mother gives me a disapproving glance. But she's about to see for herself. "Maybe you'll get our table by the window. Have a nice meal."

Mom and I just blink at each other awkwardly for one more moment, and I realize that I'm really not emotionally prepared to see my mother on a *date*.

"See you at home," she says. And then she walks into the noodle shop.

SEVENTEEN

RICKIE

Back in the truck, I punch the button to turn on Dylan's radio. Music fills the cab, and Daphne turns her face away from me to look out the window.

"Are you okay?" I ask. "Do you not like that guy? Gil?"

"I'm fine," she bites out. "Gil is probably a terrific human being. It's just new, okay? My dad died seven *years* ago, but my mother never said a word about dating before this summer. It's just a strange idea for me."

"Must be something in the water. Every member of your family is out there dating. Including Grandpa."

She groans.

"You're the *only* Shipley who insists she isn't dating," I say, driving the point home. "Mom is out there having a great time. And you say you're giving up men?"

She turns her chin to give me a critical glare, and I give her a sleazy wink. She tries to hold on to her expression. But I see her lips twitch with humor. "Maybe I didn't *actually* give up men. Maybe that's just an excuse I thought up to let you down easy."

"Nah," I insist. "Impossible."

"Oh, really?" I can see the eye roll even without looking. "That sure of yourself?"

"Daphne, seriously. Who could resist a guy with *this* face, *this* body, and a tendency to proposition hot young women and then leave 'em by the side of the road?"

"And still I've met worse," she mumbles. "Where is all this traffic coming from?"

It's true—Montpelier is jumping tonight. "The whole world is dating, see?"

She growls.

After five minutes of stop-and-go traffic, I finally get the truck back on the highway. Then we're cruising south, as the radio plays on. "I hate to keep bringing up my gross inadequacies," I say into the companionable silence. "But could I ask you a couple questions about our early car rides together?"

"Sure."

"When I originally invited you to that party, how did I describe it?"

"Jeez. It was a long time ago."

"I know. Just do your best."

She blows out a breath. "It was going to be hosted at a boathouse of some kind."

Huh. "Like a yacht club?"

"Well..." She hesitates. "I got the impression that it was private property. But that could have just been my take on it. I don't have any friends with boats. I don't know the lingo."

"Okay. Did I happen to mention how far a drive it was from Harkness?"

"Nope. Sorry. I got the feeling you didn't have too many details yet. But it was some kind of annual tradition. You'd heard stories. You wanted to see what the hype was all about."

"That sounds like me." This is a dead end, though. How could Daphne know anything about a party that I failed to bring her to? And I don't want to pester her all night. "Just one more question," I insist as I put on the signal to get off the highway.

"Wait, where are you going?" she asks.

I take the highway exit and brake slowly toward the street. "I want ice cream. Duh. I didn't think our nondate should end until we got some ice cream. Is that okay?"

"Sure."

"Your enthusiasm overwhelms me."

She smiles. And I'm such a sucker for that smile.

There are a surprising number of people here at the Dreamy Creemee, too, so I ease the truck into the lot, where a gaggle of children are poking each other in and around the line. I cut the engine at the far corner of the gravel parking area. Then I turn to Daphne again. "My final question is an easy one."

"Okay?" She unclips her seatbelt and then waits for me to ask it.

"Did I kiss you?"

"What? When?" Her eyes dip.

"In Connecticut. After our car ride."

"No, you didn't." She shakes her head.

"Oh good."

Her brown eyes leap to mine. "Why is that *good?*" Then she seems to realize what she's just admitted—that she craves my kisses. "Never mind." She reaches for the door.

"No, this is crucial." I catch her hand before she leaves the truck. "You know how I recognized you, even though I didn't know why?"

She nods, her face impassive. But I can see her pulse fluttering at her throat.

"I recognized you. But it wasn't just like remembering a word I'd forgotten. When I saw your face, I knew I'd met you. And I also knew I'd liked you. I wasn't ambivalent. I thought—*there she is.* And..." I thread our fingers together. "It might kill me if I'd forgotten even one of the kisses that I'd ever shared with you."

"*Rickie,*" she breathes.

"Yeah?" I move a little closer.

She looks away. "I'm trying to give up men."

"Yeah? How's that working out?" I ask. Then I reach up and brush my thumb lightly across her cheek.

And when her eyes turn to me again, they're blazing. So I lean in to kiss her, and not gently this time. I've been craving the press of her mouth against mine. Pulling her close to me, I feel all lit up inside.

Daphne shivers into our kiss, and her smooth hands land in my hair. Her mouth softens beneath mine. And then her body softens, too. All at once. Like an offering.

Holy fuck. I kiss her deeply, my tongue stroking her top lip until she opens for me. And I swear to Christ I hear an angel choir as we slide into each other's arms. I don't deserve a second chance with her. But this is it. She and I are happening. I just want to lose myself right here on the front seat of Dylan's truck.

But I can't. I make a desperate, unhappy groan as I wrench myself away from the hottest kiss of my life.

Daphne blinks up at me, cheeks flushed, pupils blown. I stunned us both. And it takes all my willpower not to dive right back in.

My phone is ringing. And more importantly, we're sitting in a busy parking lot at the ice cream place. Whatever we've started will have to wait.

Daphne gets out of the truck and slams the door. Either she really wants ice cream, or she wants a moment to compose herself. My money is on the latter. Daphne isn't comfortable losing her cool. She prefers to have her emotions well under control.

I get it. I'm not the same, but I do understand.

Needing a few deep breaths myself, I grab my phone and my wallet and slowly extract myself from the vehicle. She's staring up at the signboard with unseeing eyes.

My phone chirps again.

"Who's calling you?" she asks.

I slip a hand into hers, and her fingers thread between mine, as if we've held hands a million times before. "I'm not sure. It's..." I pull out the phone with my free hand. "Your brother." I swipe to answer. "Hello?"

"Rickie! Come to the Goat!" he says. I can hear a crowd of people in the background.

"Where?" I ask.

"The Mountain Goat! It's a bar. Is Daphne with you? She knows where it is."

"We're in line for ice cream. I thought you guys went to the movies?" The line moves forward, and I follow the gentle tug of Daphne's hand.

"That was the plan," Dylan says. "But then you didn't bring the truck home in time, so I got Griffin to drop us here for dinner. I told him you'd pick us up later."

Daphne snorts, so I know she's hearing the whole conversation.

"You could have taken my car," I point out.

"Nah, I need my truck at the movies," he says. "It's more comfortable, if you know what I mean. So get over here. We've got a table."

"Okay, man. After we get ice cream, we'll come to the Mountain Goat and pick you up." So I guess my nondate is going to be cut short, even though I'm still buzzing from Daphne's kiss.

"Come in when you get here," Dylan says. "It's two-for-one beers and we'll play some darts."

I glance at Daphne, who shrugs. She's got her armor back on, even if she's still holding my hand.

"Sure, man," I say. "We'll see you soon."

Daphne removes her hand from mine, and the line advances again.

EIGHTEEN

DAPHNE

The cold lemon sorbet was just what I needed to cool off the hormone surge caused by Rickie's kisses. I lick the sharp, sweet cone all the way to the Mountain Goat, calling out the directions as they arise.

Rickie's ice cream is slowly melting in a cup. And when the truck comes to rest in the gravel parking lot of the Goat, I hand it to him.

He spoons up a scoop of chocolate and smiles at me. "You feel like playing darts?"

"Do I have a choice?"

"I can rein in your brother. I'll just tell him about the bottle of good whiskey I've got stashed, and he'll be down for a quick exit."

"Eh, let's go in," I say. Maybe if I'm surrounded by people I'll stop thinking about his mouth. And those clever hands. And the heat that pours off his body whenever we touch each other. "Do you like to bet on darts?"

His smile is immediate. "Maybe. Are you a shark, baby girl?"

"You'll find out, won't you?" I say, fighting my own smile. I'm pretty good at darts. Grandpa taught me all kinds of games. My dad did, too. Everyone in my family is a life-of-the-party kind of person.

Everyone except me, of course.

I follow Rickie into the Goat. The sound of laughter and conversation rushes at us as we step into the crowded room. But Dylan and Chastity have got a booth, and an empty pitcher of beer.

"You two work fast," Rickie says, lifting the empty pitcher and giving it a shake.

"Because you're driving," my brother says with a chuckle. "You steal my truck, you get to be my chauffeur."

"I'll drive home," I pipe up from behind Rickie. We've already established that I can't handle the potent combination of alcohol and Rickie.

"Yes!" my brother hoots. "Come on, Rick. Let's get our drink on."

"You're welcome," I grumble as Dylan pulls Rickie toward the bar. Rickie has the decency to look back at me with apology in his eyes.

"What was that?" Chastity asks, watching them go.

"What was what?" I drag my gaze off Rickie's ass in those faded jeans and onto Chastity, my brother's live-in girlfriend.

She looks like a pixie with her blond hair and her apple-cheeked smile. "That *look* Rickie gave you. Are you two...?" She wiggles a finger between us.

"*No*," I say without waiting to hear how that sentence ends. Because whatever she was going to ask, it's not happening. I've got to stay away from that boy, with his dangerous mouth and those eyes that see way too much.

"Okay. That would have been weird, anyway."

"It *would*? Why?" I squeak. Maybe I've given up men, but I'd rather not be written off as hopeless.

"Because Rickie doesn't date," she says. "He doesn't fool around, either. He doesn't even let anyone into his bedroom. For any reason."

Oh. So this isn't about me at all. "Are you sure? He carries himself like a total player."

Chastity props her heart-shaped face in her hand and drops her voice to a conspiratorial register. "Well, we talked about it one night when we were sitting up late watching a movie together. It was a Hallmark movie, and the couple just had their big kiss under the mistletoe. And I asked him when he was going to liplock somebody, you know? He always refers to himself as a party boy and a man whore."

I shrug, as if this topic isn't fascinating. But it totally is. "And what did he say?"

"He just hasn't wanted anyone since his accident. He isn't as comfortable with having people in his bed, or as interested in having people in his pants. That's a direct quote." She smiles. "Trust Rickie to try to make a sad thing funny, you know?"

"Yeah," I agree. Although I'm deeply confused. He seems both comfortable with and interested in me. That kiss in the truck? I'm surprised we didn't set the front seat on fire.

A whistle pierces the loud social chatter around us, and I look toward the bar. It's Rickie, his T-shirt straining against his biceps as he gives me a wave. *What do you want to drink?* he mouths.

"A Coke!" I shout.

He makes his fingers into a gun, shoots me and says, "You got it."

"That was thoughtful," Chastity says, her eyes dancing. "Are you sure you two aren't gonna become a thing?"

"I'm super sure," I say, as my brother arrives back at the table with a full pitcher of beer and a couple of extra glasses. He sits down next to Chastity, and they smile at each other. They're in that early stage of love that's hard to tolerate, with the tender glances and the hand-holding and staring into each other's eyes 24/7.

Not that I have firsthand experience. But I've watched Griffin fall, and then May, and now Dylan. Like a stack of dominoes. If Grandpa and my mother are also out there dating, I really *am* the last Shipley standing.

Wait—no. I'm relieved to remember my cousin Kyle. He's permanently single. And he's older than I am by eight or nine years.

"Beer, Daphne?" my brother asks.

"No thank you. I'm your chauffeur, remember? Too bad you're a shitty tipper."

"Don't bitch," he says. "If we're all drunk, you'll clean up at darts."

"I clean up at darts no matter what. Just admit it."

And half an hour later, I do.

NINETEEN

RICKIE

A couple hours later, after I've lost twenty bucks at darts—to Daphne —she drives us home, as promised.

I'm in the back seat, pleasantly drunk, trying not to stare at the back of her kissable neck.

Beside me, Dylan reaches forward to put his hand at the juncture of Chastity's shoulder and neck. He strokes her skin with his finger.

I spent the past few months giving him a lot of shit for how handsy they are all the time. But it's sweet, and I'd happily eat my words if I could have what they have.

In Dylan's shoes, I'd be the same way. I'd claim my girl, and let the whole world know that Daphne was mine. If she wouldn't give me a death glare and accuse me of acting like a macho asshole, that is.

She would, though. And that would make me smile just the same.

I've got it bad.

When we get back to the farm, Daphne notes the presence of her mother's car. "I hope her date went well."

"You don't *sound* like you hope so," her brother snickers.

"Shut up. I'm trying."

Dylan laughs. And the minute he and Chastity are out of the truck, they go skipping toward the bunkhouse, probably to have loud sex all night. In fact, Dylan actually sweeps Chastity up and carries her toward the bunkhouse, while she shrieks in protest. They bounce off into the darkness together.

I catch Daphne watching them. So I brace my arms and bend my knees like I'm about to scoop her up, too.

"No," she says, holding out her palm to stop me.

I straighten up, laughing. "Kidding. I wouldn't dare."

"Good."

"Apparently I like my women prickly."

"Apparently you do," she says, opening the kitchen door and marching inside.

Daphne goes to greet her mother, and I slink upstairs alone. I take a turn in the shower, and by the time I'm done, she's in her room with the door shut.

She would have left it open if she wanted my company. So I go into my room and lock the door. As one does.

I lay down in bed and listen as Daphne's door opens. She takes her turn in the bathroom and then returns to her room.

No knock on my door, either. I hug my pillow and wonder what she's doing. She's probably propped up in bed, reading something brainy.

If I were lying next to her, I'd pick up a book, too. I'd put a hand on her smooth knee, and stroke her skin with one hand while I turned pages with the other.

Daphne is smart, and very invested in her work. So it's possible she wouldn't toss the book aside and jump me. I'd have to work for it. I'd let my hand roam her long legs. Then I'd close my book and roll over to drop kisses on her smooth stomach...

And, yup. One of us is horny already.

Ah well.

As a distraction, I haul my laptop onto the bed and run a few internet searches. After all, I have some new material to work with. *USTSA yacht club party.*

Nothing.

Boathouse party. USTSA Christmas party. Bash. Open Weekend.

Nope. Nothing.

I've tried some of these terms before, of course. But until now I never had the clue of "boathouse" before.

Still, I try a couple dozen permutations and come up empty every time. If this party was a secret, or unsanctioned, people probably knew better than to label their selfies. What I need are names.

I try my roommate's name. I've put him into a dozen internet searches before. *Paul White boathouse party.* As usual, I get some hits for a country music singer with a similar name. This time I also turn up a French impressionist painting called *The Boating Party.*

Not helpful.

So I plug in the one other Academy name I can think of— Daphne's horrible ex. *Reardon Halsey Christmas party.*

I sit up straight as the screen *fills* with images. I choose a thumbnail at random, and get a photo of four guys in tuxes holding champagne flutes.

I scan the faces, and *bam.* My gut clenches in recognition of the guy on the end. I know that face. I *hate* that face.

Holy shit.

Honestly, I need to look away from the screen for a moment and take a slow breath. My pulse is elevated, and I actually feel nauseated.

My eyes flit back to the screen, though, because I've waited so long for this. A clue. *Any* clue to those lost months at the Academy.

In spite of my pounding heart, I force myself to catalogue his features. He has shiny dark hair and brown eyes. He has an aquiline nose, and a strong but well-proportioned jaw. He's an objectively handsome prepster.

And the internet is full of photos of him. His dad is a senator, and they're frequently photographed together. Daddy Halsey went to USTSA too, I note. There's a short piece in the *Hartford Courant* from four years ago, announcing the senator's son's acceptance into the venerable yet secretive program. "Training the next generation of officers, innovators and spies," it reads.

Or not, apparently. Because this guy turned up at Harkness with Daphne.

Sure enough, when I search for Halsey at Harkness, his name comes up on that research study Daphne told me about. He's still listed as a senior research assistant, whatever that is.

I search him six ways to Sunday, and it's midnight by the time I realize how exhausted I am. And I'll be up at six o'clock to help Dylan in the dairy barn. I need to sleep.

But first, I make myself look at his photo one more time. It's another party pic, although I never did find evidence of a boathouse party anywhere. Halsey attends a lot of his daddy's political soirees.

I look him right in the digitized eyes. He's smiling widely, his teeth white, his tie straight. He looks about as dangerous as a well-bred Golden Retriever.

But I know better. And when I stare into his smiling eyes, I feel nothing but cold disgust.

I get up and set the computer on Dylan's desk, and then shut out the light. Back in bed, sleep doesn't come easily. I don't know what to do with this new information, because it really *isn't* information. It's just recognition. And dread.

And *that's* Daphne's ex? What does that even mean?

I bury my face in the pillow and try to sleep.

It works. Mostly. But sometime before dawn I become aware of a presence in the room. My eyes flip open, and the guy is *right* there, lying next to me in bed, staring at me. And then he smiles, like it's all a joke.

I try to lift my arms to push him off the bed, but I can't. I can't move.

He grins.

I open my mouth and howl out a tortured, strangled sound.

It's probably my scream that wakes me up for real. I sit up fast, alone in Dylan's bed, sweat pouring off me, my heart trying to pound its way out of my chest.

"What the fuck was that?" I gasp into the dark.

"Rickie?" comes a sweet voice. Then there's a gentle tap on the door. "You okay?"

Yup. Daphne's knock arrives at exactly the wrong moment. Story of my life. "I'm fine," I call. "Bad dream."

I do not get up and let her in.

She doesn't knock again.

I start the day in the barn with Dylan, shoveling cow shit while he does the milking. I'll never be a farmer. I'm not half as interested as Dylan, who's at the other end of the barn chatting up the cows as he hooks them one by one to the milking thing.

But as summer jobs go, this one is very low stress. We've got tunes on the radio, and after the milking I'll be fed a huge breakfast. So it's all good.

Even after that horrible night, I almost feel normal. But I must not look it.

"You look tired today," Ruth Shipley says at breakfast.

"Oh, I'm good," I insist. "Just stayed up too late watching TikTok videos."

Daphne shoots me a curious glance. She's probably wondering why I did some yelling in my sleep. On and off I have nightmares, usually about claustrophobia. Sometimes I dream about getting locked into a closet or a coffin. Lenore is always fascinated.

But last night is the first time I saw a face in one of my bad dreams.

And it was so vivid. I suppose I could pump Daphne for more information about Reardon Halsey. He left the Academy. I left the Academy. Maybe we did so at the same time. It could be important.

But it probably isn't. And I hate flying the freak flag in front of Daphne. What would I even say? *I Googled your ex, and his photo made me almost puke. Please pass the maple syrup.* Yeah?

No.

"What's the plan for today?" I ask instead.

Dylan drains his coffee cup. "You and Chastity are meeting Zach in the orchard for pest prevention. You're hanging bait traps."

"Cool, cool. So long as you don't use me as the bait, it's all good. I'm kind of irresistible, so…"

Everyone smiles except Daphne, who's giving me another searching look. And if I'm not mistaken, it's underscored with heat.

I have no idea when she and I are finally going to get together. I just know that when it happens, it's going to be spectacular.

TWENTY

DAPHNE

I don't know how many times Rickie caught me staring at him this morning. Quite a few, I'm afraid. It was bad enough when I was only struggling with his raw sensuality.

But it's even worse now that I have Chastity's whispered gossip playing on repeat in my head. *Rickie never hooks up.*

First of all, that is incredibly hard to believe. I've never met someone more comfortable with his sex appeal. And secondly...*never*? Does that include kisses in the truck, and heavy make-out sessions on a blanket in the orchard?

Because that happened.

On my best days I don't do all that well with uncertainties. But now they're driving me crazy. After breakfast, my poor wandering eyes get a break when Rickie and Chastity head outside to hang pest traps in the orchard.

The rest of us have a family meeting. That means Griffin, Mom, and Audrey run the payroll, and then we all talk about plans and expenses for the coming month. Even May drives out to the farm for a family meeting.

"Where'd Dylan go?" I ask as we all sit down.

"Here!" he says, sliding into his seat at the last minute. He hates family meetings, they make him fidgety. I'm not a huge fan, either, but I show up out of obligation, and also to help my mother plan Thursday dinner, which is a family tradition.

"First order of business," my mother says. "Tonight's dinner will be served outdoors. It's just too hot to have twenty people in the dining room."

She's right, it's going to be a scorcher. But the number sounds high. "Wait, how many chairs do we need?" I ask.

My mother picks up her pen and starts jotting names down the margin of her legal pad. "Griff, Audrey, Gus, May, Alec..." She keeps going, adding herself and me and Dylan and Chastity and Rickie. "No Zach tonight, but Kyle, Kieran, and Roderick are coming."

"That's thirteen," I say. "Plus Grandpa is fourteen."

"Is he bringing a guest?" Audrey asks with a smile. "I'll just ask him." She pops out of her chair and disappears into the TV room.

When she returns a moment later, she's shaking her head. "No guest?" my mother asks, pen poised above the paper.

"Actually, he's just not sure."

"I got a bit of a situation," Grandpa says from the doorway. "It could be a plus one, a plus two, or a big fat zero."

"How's that?" Griffin asks, looking amused.

"Well, I'm trying to date Mabel. But she said she's too old to start over. And I think that sounds like horse-pucky."

My mother is still clutching the pen. "Should I write down Mabel as a maybe?"

"Then I danced with Patrice at the twins' birthday, just to give Mabel something to think on. And it backfired."

"*Really,*" Audrey says slowly. "Who knew that a blatant exploitation of a woman's emotions could backfire?"

He gives her a sour look. "Now she says I'm too much of a bad boy for her taste. Do I look like a bad boy to you?"

"*Yes,*" says everyone at the table, in unison. It might be the only time we've ever agreed on anything as a family.

Grandpa scowls. "I invited Patrice to dinner. But now Mabel is asking me what I'm up to tonight. She's fishing for an invitation. It's a very fluid situation. Anything could happen."

"Keep us posted," my mother says. "We'll assume Grandpa has one date tonight. That makes our grand tally about seventeen people."

"Fifteen," I correct, because accurate data is kind of a sticking point with me. Oh, the irony.

"We'll be seventeen," she says firmly, writing down that number and circling it.

"Do you have two dates tonight, too?" Griffin asks.

"I guess you'll find out," she says crisply.

There's an awkward silence at the table. Dylan and I exchange a glance. It asks: *what is up with everyone today?*

"So," Audrey says, her sunny voice puncturing some of the tension. "What's on the menu?"

"I was thinking we should have a taco bar," Mom says. "Grilled chicken and slow-cooked beef, and a lot of toppings."

"Excellent." Audrey claps her hands. "I can make a couple of sides. Mexican rice? Spicy black beans? Ooooh—guacamole!"

"Roderick is bringing that," my mother says.

"Even better," Audrey chirps. "His guacamole is great."

"I can make sangria, and lemonade," I offer. "But what about dessert?"

"Pies," my mother says. "We'll make them after lunch. Will you help?"

"Sure," I say quickly. "No problem."

"Okay, on to finance," Griffin says, opening a file folder. "I'm trying to decide the best timing for investing in solar. There's a nice tax incentive that would cut down the cost. But the up-front expenditure is still kind of steep."

"How steep?" Mom asks.

"The proposal is right here. But I haven't seen this year's tuition bills yet. Who's got numbers for me?"

Oh boy. This is the moment I've been dreading. I pull my financial aid award out of my back pocket and hand it to Griffin. "This came a week ago. They took their time."

Griffin unfolds the document, which he quickly scans. "Whoa. Why's the cost so much more than last year?" He looks up. "Shouldn't we be saving money with you at a state school?" His eyes dart from me to my mother.

Mom just shakes her head.

"No, unfortunately," I explain. "They, um, just don't have the same endowment as Harkness. Dylan's full-time bills look just like mine."

"I thought that was because Dylan is a B and C student," Griffin says.

"You're kidding right now, right?" my twin asks. "That's not how financial aid works."

"I didn't know that," Griffin grumbles, scanning the page again, as if the numbers would change. "Is it because Daphne applied late?"

"No! But thanks for asking," I snap.

"Hey!" He holds up two hands in surrender. "I just thought maybe there was a chance we'll do a little better for the second semester."

"No," I say, drowning in my shame. "The aid is just not as good. And I couldn't determine that before I switched. Also, last year I got a fellowship. And, uh, this year they didn't fund me."

Everyone stares at me with pity in their eyes. And I actually feel worse than I did last night when I finally dared to open the envelope.

"Okay," Mom says gently. "It is what it is."

"I could take out an additional loan," I offer. "Just for this year. To replace those funds."

"But what about grad school?" Griffin asks. "That's still your plan, right?"

"I'll, uh, worry about that later. I'll be applying for other fellowships."

There's an awkward silence. Griffin scans the numbers again and jots something down on his notepad. "I still am not a hundred percent clear on why you're transferring. Actually, I'm zero percent clear."

"Griff," my twin warns. Dylan hates conflict. "She doesn't have to explain every decision."

"This was a big one, though," Griffin says quietly. "Can I not ask?"

Another silence follows, and everyone is staring at me. They're all wondering why I spent my teen years saying I couldn't wait to go somewhere more cosmopolitan, only to come running home a year before I received my degree from one of the nation's most elite colleges.

"It wasn't the right place for me," I say eventually.

He sighs. "Okay. If that's what you're going with."

"Does it matter?" May asks. "What if I loaned the farm a couple thousand dollars, so you don't have to choose between the tuition and solar panels?"

Oh *hell* no. "I'm not taking your money," I say, and it comes out sounding *way* too sharp.

May sits back in her chair, like I've just slapped her. And Dylan just shakes his head at me.

So I'm the bitch again. Lovely. But I really don't want her paying for my mistakes. I have enough sister guilt, thanks.

"Never mind," Griffin says. Now that he's stirred everything up, he wants to move on. "I'll pause the solar until spring. Moving on to payroll... we have all the help we need right now, which is nice. Why is the bank account out of balance with QuickBooks?"

"Rickie hasn't cashed his paychecks," my mother says.

"Ah," he jots down a note.

"Daphne, can you remind him?" Dylan asks.

"Why me?" I squeak. Is it really that obvious that I spend way too much time thinking about Rickie, and his wicked mouth?

Dylan gives me a look like I'm an idiot. "Because you two go to Burlington every week, where he banks?"

"Oh, sure." I *really* need to just keep my mouth shut this morning. Where's the duct tape when I need it?

"All right," Griffin says. "So everything is on track for the remainder of July and August, personnel wise. But I'm worried about September and October. Daphne, Dylan, Chastity, and Rickie are all back to school. We'll need bodies."

"Especially on the weekend," Audrey adds.

"Do we know anyone from church who's taking a gap year before college?" my mother asks. "Recruiting was easier when Daphne and Dylan still had high school friends."

"This does get harder every year," Griffin admits. "Kieran and Kyle used to give us hours. They're both too busy now. Isaac moved away. I need a new plan."

"Chass and I will still come home on the weekends," my brother says. "We're both available for U-pick season. If the bunkhouse is full, we can stay in my room."

"I'm more worried that the bunkhouse will be empty," Griffin says. "I'm going to call the guys at the agricultural extension and ask about hiring some Jamaican apple harvesters. I've never wanted to take on all that immigration paperwork, but we really need a new play."

"I'll come home on the weekends," I hear myself offer.

Everyone blinks. "You *never* do that," Dylan says.

"No kidding, I used to be three or four hours away. Besides, I'll need a part-time job. Why should I work in a Burlington bookstore when I could be working at the farm stand instead?"

"Okay. That's helpful," Griffin says slowly. "Thank you."

I can see that he doesn't actually believe me. And that's what I get for spending most of my teenage years telling everyone who'd listen that I couldn't wait to get out of Vermont.

We had family meetings when I was a little girl, too. My father liked to gather everyone around the table, and explain whatever changes he was making for the new season. He'd tell us about his choices—whether or not to regraft a set of trees, or whether or not to buy a new cow. Then he'd ask our opinions.

"You choose, Daddy," I'd always say. "I'm not a farmer."

My views haven't really changed, but my circumstances have. And since I'm not twelve years old anymore, I understand that sometimes you just have to pitch in and help your family.

They don't believe me. They don't trust that I'm sincere. That's my fault too, I guess.

So many things are.

TWENTY-ONE

DAPHNE

After the family meeting, I help Mom set up the tables and chairs outside for Thursday dinner. Then I take a basket of sandwiches and cold drinks out to where Dylan, Chastity, Zach, and Rickie are working.

Today is a scorcher, so the men are all shirtless, of course. *I will not ogle Rickie's tattoos. I will not ogle Rickie's tattoos...*

"Aren't you going to eat lunch with us?" Chastity asks as I plunk the basket down and turn to go.

"Sorry, I'm in the middle of...a thing," I say as Rickie climbs off a ladder, his hot body glistening in the sun. He's wearing a pair of steel-gray shorts, and that's basically it. Just sun-kissed skin and lean muscle as far as the eye can see. "Later guys!"

He gives me a smirk as I walk away.

But avoidance only gets me so far. After lunch, Zach and Griffin load up three juvenile bulls to deliver them to the slaughterhouse, while Dylan and Chastity head out to measure and map out the farmland we bought from the Abrahams, and plan their future together.

Rickie is sent back to the farmhouse to help prep for Thursday dinner with me and Mom.

"Put me to work," he says, pulling his close-fitting T-shirt down over his head. As if that even helps dull my attraction.

"Fine." I grab an apron off the pantry door and toss it to him. "Suit up. We're making pies."

He drops the apron over his head. It's blue-and-white calico with a ruffle across the hem. I may have grabbed the girliest one we have, accidentally on purpose. But it doesn't even put a dent in my hormone spike. He crosses those strong arms in front of his chest and smiles. "Teach me your ways."

Wow. Just wow.

Dragging my eyes off him, I tug the kitchen scale into position and set a big mixing bowl on top. "First you sift the flour. Here." I fetch the sifter out of a cupboard and set it on the work table. Then I heft the flour canister onto the table and open up the top. We buy flour by the fifty-pound bag because we use so much of it.

"What does this do?" Rickie picks up the sifter and squeezes the handle, which turns the mechanism.

"It makes the flour lighter and easier to work with," my mother says. She's arranging fresh cherries, blueberries, and frozen strawberries on the countertop.

"Awesome." Rickie scoops the sifter into the flour and aims it at the big metal mixing bowl.

"Wait!" I yelp just as he starts to squeeze the handle. "You *have* to tare out the scale first."

Rickie holds up his free hand like a busted perp. "I don't know what you just said, but okay."

"Sorry." I reach over to set the kitchen scale properly, and my knuckles brush against the ridges of his abdominal muscles. Not even a frilly apron can disguise how cut he is. Wowzers.

Like I need to be any more distracted than I already am. "We use three hundred grams per double crust, and we can do two double crusts at once," I ramble. "Six hundred grams. Go."

"Yes sir, thank you, sir!" he barks.

My mother chuckles. "Daphne can be a bit of a drill sergeant. She can't help it. She was born into chaos, and she hates chaos."

Et tu, Mom? "I'm right here, you realize?"

"Yes, you are." She picks up the cherry pitter and gives me a knowing smile.

Rickie squeezes the sifter repeatedly, and I kind of hate myself for noticing the flex of his forearm muscles on every stroke. "I know," he says. "We can sift Daphne to make her lighter and easier to work with."

"Excellent plan," my mother agrees, and I want to smack them both.

The kitchen is just too small. Coming home already felt claustrophobic. I have secrets to keep, and a family to appease. My inconvenient curiosity—that's the word I'm using—about Rickie shrinks it even further.

And did I mention it's legitimately hot in here? The thermometer stuck to the outside of the kitchen window says 86 degrees.

My mother pulls the stems off the season's first cherries, while I measure out salt and a bit of sugar for the crust.

"What else do you use?" Rickie asks. "Oil? Shortening?"

"*Butter*," my mother and I say at the same time.

"And then ice water," I add. "The butter and the water have to be absolutely frigid. Like my cold little heart."

The two of them laugh. And when my eyes meet Rickie's, I feel an unwelcome tremor. His smile sees right through my bullshit and confusion. There's heat in those gray depths.

Just what we need around here. More heat.

"Brace yourselves," my mother says, which is funny because I've spent the whole summer doing just that. "I'm going to preheat the oven."

"Gawd," my grandpa says, shuffling into the room. "It's going to be hotter than the devil's armpit before these pies are baked. Totally worth it, though." He glances at Rickie. "Nice apron, boy. A real man can always rock the ruffles."

He holds up a fist, and Rickie bumps it. "Damn right."

I busy myself checking the total weight of Rickie's flour and then whisking in the other ingredients. But my mind is back three years, to the day when Rickie put on that eyeliner and told me, *Don't give anyone that power.*

But how do you stop? I've spent a lot of energy trying to be a certain kind of person. The smart twin. The ambitious kid. The overachiever.

It's so exhausting. But I can't find the off ramp. It's not like I could just suddenly unload my troubles on my family, either. I'd get six or eight conflicting opinions about how best to unfuck my life. No thanks.

"Okay, now what?" Rickie asks.

"Now we quickly add butter chunks. You'll use this." I hand him the pastry blending tool, which is made of wires attached to a wooden handle. "You're going to break up the butter into gravel-sized globules, surrounded by flour. Then we add just enough ice water to bring it together."

"Let's do this. Butter me." He picks up the blending tool, giving me a lazy wink.

He means it as a joke, and yet I still feel it in some inappropriate places. And the kitchen seems to shrink yet again.

"Ruth, we're going to make it to that library talk, right?" Grandpa says. "I heard there's mini cheesecakes after."

My mother glances at the clock and frowns. "I hope so," she says. "An hour isn't much time to finish four pies, and we're just starting."

"With all this labor?" Grandpa asks. "I'll help, too. Rickie got the fun apron, but mine is still here somewhere, right?"

"I'm sure it is," Mom says as Grandpa disappears into the pantry.

He returns a moment later, wearing an apron that reads: *I turn all the grills on*. "Now pass me that cherry pitter, Ruth. This old man wants to go to the library talk."

"What's the book?" I ask.

He shrugs. "I'm in it for the air conditioning and the snacks. Is that so wrong?"

"Not wrong at all," my mother says.

I drop chunks of butter into the bowl of flour, while Rickie uses vigorous strokes to cut it in. I try not to sneak peeks at his cupid's bow mouth as he whistles happily.

And the temperature in the kitchen rises yet again.

"Okay, good work, team." My mother closes the oven door and sets the timer. Then she lifts the edge of her apron to dab her flushed face.

"We're off, are we?" Grandpa lifts the apron over his head. "I just need five minutes to get beautiful."

Rickie is washing dishes in the sink, a job that he volunteered for in a hurry, probably because it involves splashing cool water around beside the open window. I'm stuck scraping pastry dough off the table and wiping everything down.

"Daphne, you'll take these pies out when they're done?" my mother asks. "There's fifty-five minutes on the timer."

"Of course," I say as a trickle of sweat runs down my back. "I might have to escape to the air conditioning upstairs while I wait."

"That's probably wise." She removes her apron. "See you in a bit."

The kitchen is shipshape a few minutes later, and my mother drives Grandpa off to town. I toss my apron onto the counter and eye the oven timer.

Rickie turns around, parks his muscular ass against the sink and spreads his delicious arms wide. "Gosh, how shall we spend fifty minutes? Got any fun ideas?"

"Nope," I grunt.

Except I do. And the arrogant man in the frilly apron knows it. He pulls that ridiculous thing over his head and tosses it on top of mine. I'm overheated in every possible way.

Rickie's eyes never leave mine as he takes a glass out of the cupboard, fills it with water and gulps it down. And a few things become crystal clear to me:

1. There is nobody else home.
2. It's very hot in here.
3. Rickie and I are alone together, and I don't trust myself.
4. I can't leave, either, because of those pies.
4(a). I don't even want to.

He sets the glass down on the counter. "You're thinking so hard there's steam coming out of your ears."

"That's just the weather."

He smiles dangerously. And why does sweat look so good on him? It probably looks pretty awful on me. In fact, I'm sure it does. And now I know exactly what to do with the forty-odd minutes before the oven timer dings. I need a cool shower. Stat.

I break off our little staring contest. "You know, I think I'll head upstairs and…"

Rickie slides his body sideways before I finish, his movement stealthy. Where is he going?

My competitive instincts kick in, and I make a move toward the stairs. But Rickie has a head start. He turns and darts ahead of me, grasping the railing, and leaping up the first stair treads two at a time.

Now I'm in hot pursuit. What the hell? I didn't even say the word *shower* out loud.

But it doesn't matter. At the top of the stairs, Rickie breaks to the left and disappears. By the time I reach the second-floor hallway, I find him in the bathroom, where he's cranking on the water.

I barge in, livid. "You said you were an only child!"

"Yeah, I am," he says, testing the water temperature with one hand.

"I call bullshit. That was a classic sibling move."

He laughs. "Some people need training, Shipley, and some people are natural-born assholes." Proving his point, he flips his hand, and a spray of water arcs onto my face and sweaty tank top.

"Y-You...!" I sputter, while he laughs. Then he reaches back with one hand and strips off his T-shirt.

And there it is at close range—his shapely, infuriating, tattooed chest, glistening with sweat. How can a girl *think* with that in her face?

"You *knew* I wanted the shower!" I complain.

"Don't be a sore loser, Shipley. There's room for two." He pops the button on his shorts.

Then? He leans in and kisses my shocked, angry mouth.

For once, I'm not even surprised. But that doesn't mean I'm ready. I'll never be ready for one of Rickie's kisses. I feel a jolt when those firm lips land on mine. It's like waking up to find yourself in the middle of a terrific party. Your whole body is invited, but your brain forgot the date and time.

He doesn't ease me into it, either. He's all slick heat and salt and pressure. It's a kiss that demands an answer.

And I fold like a bad hand of poker. I step closer instead of backing away. His confidence is like a drug, and the sound of the shower muffles the loud arguments in my head.

Rickie licks into my mouth with the finesse of a man who already knows that he's won. The slide of his naughty tongue against mine delivers another jolt to my overtaxed hormones.

He makes a soft sound of pleasure, and his wet hands lift my top over my head. "Come on," he whispers between kisses. "Cool off with me."

My last rational decision is to kick the bathroom door shut.

TWENTY-TWO

RICKIE

Until I met Daphne, I didn't know it was possible someone could look so vexed and so turned on at the same time. She *hates* the fact that she's so attracted to me. And when she actually starts to like me, she'll hate that even more.

I can't fucking wait.

In the meantime, I quickly undress her. And when I lean her against my body so she can step out of her panties, she lets out a hungry whimper.

"That's a good girl," I say between kisses. "Now come here."

She lets me guide her into the shower. I tug the curtain closed, and then I pull her into my arms. She makes a noise of pleasure as the tepid water rains down on our overheated skin.

"You see?" I whisper. "Isn't this nice?"

"So nice," she breathes, her fingers sliding across my pecs.

"Now she gets it." I kiss her on the jaw. On the ear. And on the neck. She runs her tongue along my shoulder and my groan echoes off the tile walls. My hands are full of her sweet ass. And my cock is poking her rudely in the stomach.

Daphne doesn't mind. She presses her wet, sleek body against mine and shivers. I need her mouth on mine again, so I take her in another deep kiss. She gives in, letting me run the show, and I take sip after sip of her hungry mouth.

We are nothing but slick skin and questing hands, deep sighs and deeper kisses. I let myself touch her everywhere—cupping her breasts, trailing a thumb down her ribcage until she shivers. Sliding my fingers in a teasing rhythm between her legs as she moans into my mouth.

It's been a long fucking time since I felt like this—heated and invincible. Halfway to debauched.

But—as usual—Daphne walks her own path. She moves her pussy out of my greedy reach, and kisses her way down my chest, as the water beats down on her back. She wraps a hand around my hard length, and I let out a gasp of shocked pleasure. Before I can even get a breath, she takes my cockhead into her mouth and sucks.

"*Fuuuck.*" The noise causes Daphne to lift her face, which only gives me a better view of her lips wrapped around my cock. I have to brace my hand against the tile wall and remember how to pull air into my lungs.

She's pleased with herself, too. Maybe it's the stunned look on my face, or the shaky breath I take to try to calm myself down. But those brown eyes burn with victory. She doubles down, sucking and licking and running her hands up my thighs.

Holy hell. I need to calm down, or this is going to end well before I'm ready. I close my eyes and restate the Münchhausen trilemma. But then Daphne teases a finger across my taint and I forget my own name.

"Okay!" I bark. "If you're trying to prove something, you win. Whatever it is." I wrap my hand around her wet hair and tug.

She glances up, and I am saved from humiliation by the water turning cold. The sudden spray of icy water calms my body right down. But it takes an extra beat for Daphne to notice the chill. Her dark eyes take on a look of distracted confusion, until she finally pops off my dick.

Hastily I turn the water off. Then I push the curtain aside and grab a towel, which I wrap around her body as she rises. "Oh my God," she breathes. "What are we doing?"

There goes her squirrel brain, barging in on my fantasy. "Look." I pull her close, whispering right into her ear. "I've put some considerable effort into convincing you to let me have my evil way with you."

She gives me a startled smile.

"And I know how much you appreciate honesty. So I'm going to be *very* clear about what I want from you. Are you ready?"

She gives me a slow nod.

"First, I want you to lie down on my bed. On your back. And don't dry off first, because I'm in too big a hurry. Besides, it would be a waste of time. Because I'm going to run my tongue all over your body, until you come on my face."

She makes a soft, delicious sound of longing, and I press my aching erection against her hip, because I need the contact so damn bad.

"And *then* I'm going to suit up and pound you right into the mattress. That will probably take about two minutes, tops. Because I've been wanting to do that for at least six weeks, and probably three years. But we're running out of time. So if that works for you, I'm going to need you to show me some hustle right now."

She blinks, her pupils dark and wide.

Just to get things moving, I step out of the tub. I'm dripping on the bath mat and I don't give a damn. I give Daphne one more long glance—the kind that could accidentally set a forest on fire with its heat. And then I leave the room. She'll either follow me or she won't.

Naked, I walk down the hall, turning left into my room, listening for her footsteps behind me.

I hear her. She's right there. But I'm not going to ask again. I'm not going to beg. It has to be her decision.

Just as I start to lose hope, she steps through the doorway. Then she drops her towel.

"Thank fuck," I breathe. "Now get over here." I dive for the bed.

She's more graceful in her approach. But she's here nonetheless, stretching her long-limbed, willowy body out beside me. Each breast is a perfect handful. I can't wait to touch her everywhere.

I pounce, kissing her neck with a vampire's eagerness. I need her so bad it hurts. My cock swings, engorged and heavy, against her hip as I lean over her. "Should I close the door?" I manage between kisses. Then I lick a droplet of water off her nipple.

She shivers before she can answer. "N-no? I have to listen for the oven timer."

"Fuck the pies," I mutter into her breasts. Then I suck one nipple into my mouth, and she moans. But the truth is that I work well with deadlines. I bet I can make her yell my name in the next five minutes. Her hands are already roaming my skin.

Daphne might be skittish, but she knows her own mind. And right now her mind is focused solely on me, and my mouth, and the wicked play of my fingertips low on her belly. I'm relentless with my tongue and my teasing hands.

A hot breeze blows through the open window as she shifts her hips restlessly on the quilt. She's too stubborn to ask me for what she wants. Whereas I'm too stubborn to ever shut up about what I want.

I nudge her legs apart. "Lie still," I say, just to be a jerk. Then I run a fingertip lightly across her mons.

She whimpers. I chuckle.

"Rickie." Her tone is accusing.

"I know, baby girl. I know." Then I stroke a thumb across her clit and she arches off the bed in pleasure. "Goddamn." She's so responsive. I lean in and take a slow lick of heaven, and her moan is the sexiest sound I've ever heard.

Now there's no way to hold myself back. I'm relentless with kisses and licks, and the more I give, the wetter she gets. It's good to know that I haven't lost my magic touch. Her fingers tangle in my overgrown hair as she lifts her hips to meet my tongue.

And even though my cock is leaking against the quilt, and my balls ache, I still draw out the process, slowing down my deep kisses to her pussy, clutching her hips in my two hands. This is goddamn beautiful and I know not to rush a good thing.

"Rickie," she pants. That's as close to begging as my girl is willing to go. She writhes in my grasp, her knees shaking. "Why are you so *good* at this?"

"Because I enjoy it." I tease her with my fingertips again, and she throws her head back and moans. "Look at me."

Daphne lifts her face. Holding her eyes, I kiss her inner thigh, and deepen my touch. One more kiss on her throbbing core, and she shatters in my arms. It's the sexiest thing I've ever seen. She arches back into the pillow and lets out a whispered curse, her chest heaving.

Angling my body off the bed, I grab a condom out of my shaving kit, and I put it on with clumsy, eager hands. Daphne watches me with a flushed face and bright eyes. And when I return to the bed, she pulls me down and lifts her face for a kiss.

"You make me crazy," I murmur against her lips.

"Bullshit," she whispers, tracing one of my tattoos with a fingernail. "You were already crazy."

I laugh into the next kiss, and I take both her hands in mine, stretching them over her head.

And then a deafening crash slams through the room, and I jolt off of Daphne's body like a man who's been electrocuted.

TWENTY-THREE

DAPHNE

Yikes.

It was just the wind—a sudden gust blew through the house, slamming the bedroom door.

It was loud. I definitely startled.

But Rickie is even more rattled. "Whoa," he gasps, kneeling on the bed beside me. "S-sorry. I just…need a minute."

"Sure," I practically slur, because the man just gave me a *spectacular* orgasm. I can barely feel my face, let alone speak. It's fair to say that I haven't felt this relaxed in *years*.

And if Rickie says, "I told you so," after this, I don't think I'll even be irritated. He's been telling me all summer to just give in and let go. And then I finally did. He made it easy for me. The happy look on his face as he kissed me in the shower? I'm never going to forget it. For thirty minutes, I forgot all my troubles.

It's a revelation.

The breeze moves the curtains again, and somewhere in the house another door slams. The sound is muted by the closed bedroom door.

Rickie leans down and rests his head against the mattress. His back rises and falls with rapid breaths.

I'm just about to ask him if he's all right when I hear another unwelcome sound—tires on the gravel driveway outside.

Oh boy. This is really going to kill our buzz, isn't it?

Rickie groans. The poor man. He's about to be left hanging *again*. I rise to my knees and peek out the window at the driveway below.

The car is unfamiliar to me, with New York plates. The driver pulls to the side and kills the engine. And when the door opens, I'm startled to see my friend Violet Trevi get out.

"Omigod!" I shriek. Then I lunge for the wet towel on the floor. "Violet!" I call out the window.

She turns around to find me. "Surprise! Get down here and give me the tour, quick! I want to see apple trees, but I think it's going to rain!"

"Give me two minutes! I'm—" *Naked, with horror movie hair.* "Just out of the shower!"

I expect a snarky comment, or a complaint, from Rickie. But he's facedown and oddly silent.

Parking my hip on the bed, I put a hand on his damp hair. "I'm so sorry about this. I had no idea she was coming."

In answer, he reaches a hand up and slides it on top of mine. Tonight I'll probably be seeing those long, talented fingers in my dreams.

But he doesn't say a word.

"How long do you expect to lord this interruption over me, exactly? I'm just trying to plan my week."

Finally he lets out a snort. But he still doesn't speak. He just massages my hand with his own.

I lean down and kiss his messy head. "Come and meet Violet when you can. She's a lot of fun. Much more fun than I am."

"Not possible," he croaks. "Go on." He removes my hand from his hair and gives me a playful shove toward the door.

Reluctantly, I go. And the moment I open the bedroom door, the oven timer dings. Because of course it does.

I close Rickie's door on the way out.

After pulling myself together in exactly three minutes, I race downstairs.

Violet has shut off the oven timer, and she's leaning against the work table, sipping a glass of water. "The pies are just starting to brown," she says. "I thought you should make the call about whether or not they're done."

"Thank you!" I grab her for a big hug. "I can't believe you surprised me like this. Wait—does my mother know?"

Violet beams. "Yup! I called on the house phone and asked her which would be a good day to show up. She invited me to Thursday dinner. I've always wanted to come to a Shipley Thursday dinner!"

"I hope I didn't oversell it," I say with a laugh. "I mean, the food is always terrific, but you also have to put up with all my crazy family members."

"Sign me up." She claps her hands. "When do I get to meet the tattooed hottie?"

"Shhh!" I hiss, and my eyes flick toward the staircase. "Don't you dare let him hear you say that. I'll *never* live it down."

"Is he here?" she whispers.

"Let's go for a walk," I say. It would be rude of me to kiss and tell. But Violet's highest talent in life is information extraction.

"Can I pet a goat?" Violet asks.

"Sure."

"A cow?"

"Absofuckinglutely. Let me take these pies out of the oven and we'll go."

Outside, I introduce Violet to Jacquie and Jill, my brother's dairy goats. And then I walk her past the cows in the meadow, and past the mobile chicken coop.

"Oh, they *love* you!" Violet coos when the hens come running.

"No, they love treats," I clarify. "Usually I have sunflower seeds in my pockets if I need them to move from one spot to another."

"Well, it's good to see you haven't changed." Violet rolls her eyes.

"What?"

"So quick to brush off any praise. Is it so hard to believe that chickens love you?"

"Please," I snort. "Let's find you some sunflower seeds so you can become their favorite human, too."

The minute I pull out the bucket, the clucking grows louder. We each take a handful and I instruct Violet to be stingy with her love for a couple of minutes while I move the flexi-fence, post by post, to a fresh bit of the meadow. "Just watch where you step," I say. "You don't want chicken poo on those sandals."

She has a fine time tossing seeds while I shift their habitat. And then we toss the rest, all at once, creating a feeding frenzy.

"Okay, fine," she admits as we cross the grass toward the orchard. "So they'd like Genghis Khan if he had treats. Doesn't make you any less lovable."

"Thanks, babe." I walk her past the cider house, toward the orchard.

"Look at all the little green apples! There must be millions of them. Is this a good year?"

"So far." I mentally knock wood. "It's been a little dry, but nice and sunny. It's only July, though. A lot can go wrong before October. One bad hailstorm can ruin a whole crop. There are diseases. Pests. Any number of problems. At one point or another, we've had them all."

Violet flips me a sideways glance. "And you wonder why I think you're a pessimist."

"Farming is *literally* the riskiest job in the world. There's a reason I'm not going into the family business."

"I just like to bust your balls. Besides—the sky is starting to look like the beginning of *The Wizard of Oz*."

She isn't wrong. Suddenly it's as dark as a solar eclipse. "My mom said it was going to rain this afternoon."

But Violet has already forgotten the weather. "Ooh! Look at the nice little moos!" She takes off at a trot toward the fenced area where the calves are kept. "So cute!"

I don't explain that these are the last of the boys, and that they don't have long to live. We give them a great few months on grass and milk. But then they're off to the butcher, where they'll become ethical veal on a restaurant menu.

There's a rumble of thunder, followed by a strong breeze that makes the grass whispery.

"Uh-oh," Violet says, looking at the sky. And a calf bleats in agreement.

"I think we're about to get wet," I say, just as the first fat drops begin to hit the earth around us. "Come on!"

Violet and I make a dash for the tractor shed. Raindrops pepper my still-damp hair. We just make it inside when a drenching shower begins to beat down onto the grass.

"Wow," Violet says, twirling around in front of the open doors. "That's impressive. Can I climb on the tractor?"

"Knock yourself out."

She steps up, seating herself on the Kubota. "This is my color." She pats the orange body. "Choosing a tractor to suit your skin tone is a totally rational thing, right?"

"Totally. Although you'd also look nice in John Deere green," I tease her.

She tosses her hair. "That's my evening tractor."

"Cool, cool. So where is this cabin your brother rented?" I have a vague memory of Violet mentioning a possible trip to Vermont. But I never expected her to surprise me.

"It's not far. It's really more of a house, at this place called Green Rocks."

"Oh, I know where that is." It's an enclave of summer rentals.

"Tomorrow he and his wife are going hiking with Dave and Zara. Can I hang out with you instead?"

"Sure you can. I'll take a day off. You could stay here tonight, actually."

"Oh goody. Because I brought an overnight bag. Now I just have to call Leo and tell him I'm keeping his car. Dave will have to pick him up to go hiking. Oops!"

"Oops!" I laugh, feeling so grateful to her for showing up. "I've missed you terribly." Violet graduated from Harkness in May, and got a job in New York. It won't be easy to keep in touch from here on out.

"I miss you, too, babe!" Violet's eyes practically glow with happiness. "And how unlike you to say so out loud. So it must be true."

"Well, get used to it. I miss you so much that I'm not going back to Harkness because you're not there anymore."

The smile falls off Violet's face. "You're not allowed to make that joke until you tell me the real reason you're transferring."

"I can't," I whisper. "It's complicated."

"It's Reardon's fault, right?" she growls. "I know it is."

"But also mine," I say firmly. "And I don't want anyone to know how stupid I was."

"Come *on*. Like we haven't all been there. I've got my share of stupid. My family would crap their collective pants if I told them all the scrapes I got into before graduation."

That might even be true. But Violet never managed to upend her entire life like I have. And I won't burden her with my ugly story. It would put her in a strange ethical position.

"I'll tell you what," she says. "I'll stop asking you about Reardon if you tell me something dishy about this tattooed hottie living in your house."

"Fine," I say quickly. "He's a really good kisser."

"Omigod!" Violet's shriek echoes off the sides of the tractor shed. "When did this happen? Tell me *everything*."

I hesitate. That would honestly take weeks. Somehow the story of Rickie and me has become a twisty epic journey punctuated by strange encounters and intimate conversations.

"Oh *wow*," she says, drawing her own conclusions about my silence. "You did the nasty with the bad boy hottie. Where? In a hay loft? Actually that sounds sneezy. On the bed of a pickup truck?"

There must be something wrong with me because both of those options sound dreamy. "Not quite," I say slowly. "But we were getting there."

"What stopped you?"

I think back to the slammed door and Rickie's reaction. Bad timing is a theme with us. "Actually, you're the culprit," I tell Violet. "He and I were fooling around when you drove up the driveway."

Her jaw drops comically. "You're. Joking."

"I'm not." I try to hold a serious expression, but my lips twitch, because Violet is so funny when she's freaking out.

"Oh my God! Oh. My. God." She covers her face with her hands. "I'm sorry. I thought it would be fun to surprise you."

"It is fun." I give her toe a gentle kick. "Stop with the dramatics. It's fine. I'm sure we'll pick things up again another time."

"You *have* to," she says. "I can't be responsible for getting in between you and a great guy's generously sized dick."

"How do you know he's a great guy?"

She hoots. "So he *is* generously sized? You didn't argue that part. And I already know he's a great guy."

"He's definitely not Reardon," I point out.

"That's a good start. But honey, we learn from our mistakes. You wouldn't be so caught up in Rickie if he was anything like Rear-end Halsey."

"Wouldn't I?" This is my biggest problem of all. "I don't know anything anymore. I don't trust myself at all."

"You should," she says, swinging a leg over and hopping off the tractor. It's still pouring outside, and the rain smells like fresh ideas and the color green. "Honestly, you made one mistake. Just one. And there's something broken about that asshole, Daph. He's not normal. I'll bet he doesn't even know anymore where the lines are, or when he's crossed them."

She isn't wrong. But I fell for it anyway. I'd like to think it wouldn't happen again.

But I'm still scared.

TWENTY-FOUR

RICKIE

I raise my head off the quilt. I hardly know what day it is, let alone the time. But I hear voices outdoors. They're drifting in through the window, which is only opened a crack.

Waking up isn't easy, especially when the afternoon's disasters come back into sharp relief. After Daphne left my bedroom in a hurry, I'd locked the door and then sat down on the bed, burning up with humiliation. I discarded the condom I hadn't needed. And when it began to rain, I closed the window most of the way and then fell into a dead sleep.

Now Thursday dinner is underway, and I'm still only halfway conscious.

Shit.

I rise and take a little care getting dressed. I put on a nice linen shirt and my best pair of shorts. In Vermont, that's practically black tie. I brush my teeth and tame my slept-on hair.

And when I look in the mirror, I'm startled by how sharp the guy looking back at me appears. I mean, I'm a good-looking man. That's a given. But the guy in the mirror looks solid. When in truth, I feel like a hot mess.

This afternoon, a door slammed, and I'd practically lost my mind. Who does that?

I grab my flip-flops and descend the stairs toward the laughter and the voices. When I exit the kitchen door, I see that I haven't even missed dinner. A very long dining table has been arranged in the grass. It's set with real dishes and silverware. Running down the center are a parade of mason jars. In every other one are flowers from the garden that I've helped weed. And there are candles in the alternating jars, burning where the wind can't knock them out.

A dozen or so people stand around on the grass, drinks in hand. The rain showers have knocked a lot of the humidity out of the air, so it's a beautiful night for an outdoor dinner party.

And I feel nothing. Like I fell asleep and never fully woke up. Like I forgot how to feel alive.

"Hey, there he is." Dylan taps a frisbee against his thigh. "What happened to you this afternoon?"

"I took a nap, and it almost killed me." I cross to where he's standing. Nearby, Chastity is chatting with Daphne's cousin and the cousin's boyfriend—the guys we saw at the noodle shop.

"Want a beer?"

"Of course." Dylan fetches one from a metal tub full of ice, and opens the top with a church key in his pocket. "Thanks." When I close my hand around the bottle, the sensation of the icy glass against my palm is the first sign that I might eventually be alive.

I take a refreshing sip as my gaze wanders around the lawn of its own volition. But I don't see Daphne anywhere. What the hell must she be thinking right now? I came at her like a beast today. I talked a good game. And then I got spooked, and couldn't close the deal.

My face heats at the memory of jumping away from her on the bed, like I'd just been tasered. Then I collapsed on the bed, panic crushing my chest. I was instantly clammy, as if someone had drained all the life out of my body. My heart had raced so fast that it honestly felt dangerous. All I could do was lie on the bed and try to remember how to breathe.

"So what did you guys do today?" Dylan asks. "You and Daphne."

"Why?" I bark.

Dylan shrugs. "Chastity and I came in after the rain, and there was nobody at home. Those pies were just sitting there on the table, you know? I feel like I deserve some recognition for not sampling."

I make a shocked face. "Hands off my pies. Who knew those took so much work? And I'm no good at rolling them out, so your sister literally pried the rolling pin out of my hands and forbid me to touch the crust."

"Daphne? Nah." Dylan snickers.

"Then your mom took your grandfather to some event in town. And the wind was kicking up, so it didn't look like a good gardening day. So we were going to have sex but then we said nah."

Dylan snorts then shakes his head, just like I knew he would. "I know you say these things to freak me out, but it doesn't really work on me. You'll have to try Griffin."

"Good to know." I swig my beer. "Actually, it started raining, and then I turned into Rip Van Winkle. What did you do all day?"

"Drew a bunch of diagrams of the Abrahams' fields. Googled crops and acreage. But then the rain chased us back into the bunkhouse for some recreational activities." He wiggles his eyebrows.

"Planning out your future farm makes you horny?"

Dylan shrugs, smiling. He was always a happy guy. But he and Chastity are #squadgoals. Seventy years from now they'll be that ancient couple who's still holding hands in the grocery store.

I'll be lucky to be alive in seventy years. And forget having a partner of my own. I'm such a wreck.

"Dinner is served!" Ruth Shipley clinks a spoon against the mason jar several times. "Line forms to the right of the buffet!" She's such a goddess. I hope she finds a man who makes her happy. Nobody with that much love to give should be alone.

"Does your mom have a date tonight?" I ask, spotting the mustached man at her elbow.

"Yup. That's going to take some getting used to."

"I bet."

Dylan chuckles as I follow him to the back of the food line. "Daphne wants to run a background check on him. She says she doesn't trust men with mustaches."

"I'd better stay clean shaven, then."

Dylan ignores this comment. And a moment later I finally spot Daphne coming out of the cider house with a brown jug in her hands. She carries it over to the table. Her eyes flick just once in my direction.

But her friend—I think Violet is her name—gives me a long stare and then a big smile that could truly mean anything. They've obviously been discussing me.

Uh-oh. The old Rickie didn't mind being the subject of female speculation. But the new one is a wreck, apparently.

"Oooh, guacamole," Dylan says, handing me a plate. "These tacos don't stand a chance."

The dinner looks glorious, of course. I make myself a full plate and follow Dylan and Chastity to the table.

"Check out Grandpa," Chastity whispers. "He has two dates!"

Sure enough, I spot Grandpa Shipley at the head of the table, a woman on either side of him. He looks to be telling a story, and they're both laughing.

"Go Gramps," Dylan says. "If he stays out all night, I'll give him a standing ovation at breakfast."

Yup. An octogenarian has more confidence than I do tonight. What the hell is my problem?

I take my first bite of the spicy black bean and corn salad that Audrey prepared. And, wow, it's amazing. I feel the first hint of optimism that I've felt tonight. Then I eat a pulled pork taco with lime and guacamole, and it does more good things to my attitude.

Feeling eyes on me, I glance up to catch Daphne sneaking a look from down the table. I wink at her, like the old Rickie would have done.

I miss that guy. I really do.

After dinner, Dylan plays a few fiddle tunes for the crowd. Then his grandpa asks for a turn on Dylan's instrument, and he happily hands it off.

"Smoke?" Dylan whispers to me. "It's the last of our stash."

"Sure."

I follow Dylan around to the far side of the cider house, out of view of everyone else. "Oh, look," he whispers. "The old picnic table we're heading for is already occupied by Daphne and Violet. "Maybe you should sit next to my sister's tasty friend."

"Why? Daphne is the hot one."

He laughs like I'm joking. "Evening, ladies. Can we smoke here in peace? Or will Daphne rat me out again?"

Daphne flips up her middle finger without even glancing in his direction. "It was *one* time," she says. "And you totally had it coming."

"Did you?" I ask Dylan.

"Probably," he mumbles, throwing a leg over the bench and plunking down beside his sister.

I sit down across from Daphne, and she gives me a smile that's a little bit shy.

"What did he do?" I ask her.

"Well, I was trying to plan a surprise party, and he *told* the birthday boy! There are kindergarteners who are more capable of keeping secrets."

"I didn't *realize*," Dylan argues.

"Because you don't listen," Daphne fires back. "Ever."

He pulls a baggie out of his pocket, and begins rolling our last joint. "Eh. I like parties, but I hate planning things. I probably tuned you out so you wouldn't ask me to make a contribution."

I snicker, because that sounds like Dylan. "Whose surprise got ruined?"

"Zach's," Dylan says, pulling a lighter out of his pocket too.

"The farm hand?"

"Yeah, he used to live here. Daphne was hot for him for, like, forever." He lazily flicks the lighter. I glance up at Daphne as her face pinks up.

Huh. No wonder Dylan is the frequent target of Daphne's revenge plots. He does not give a fuck what others think of him, and he is probably incapable of understanding why his sister would. But Daphne guards her heart more closely.

"So how'd you get even with this motormouth?" I ask her, hooking my thumb toward her evil twin.

Her smile is very satisfied. "I handed his stash of weed over to Mom, with a lengthy document on the perils of pot on the teenage brain."

"Good one. Shows concern, but also infuriates the target. I'll give you an eight out of ten."

"Wait," her friend Violet says, her eyes appraising me. "What would make it *ten* out of ten? How evil are you?"

"It's a fair question. Eight is a solid score, of course, but I took points off for not going the extra distance. I would like to see Daphne mixing in a few grams of oregano, to ruin the stash and make the crime look worse than it is. And adding some cases of White Claw, to question not only his values, but his taste in manly beverages."

Dylan laughs. Then he offers the joint to the table. "I know Daphne won't partake, but maybe Violet is more fun?"

The look on Daphne's face is murderous now, but Dylan doesn't notice.

Violet takes the joint between her fingers, but then hesitates. "Do you trust the dealer?" she asks. "Our friend had a bad experience once."

"Yeah, I do, because we grow our own," Dylan says.

"It's not even illegal," I pipe up. "Six plants each, under the new Vermont law."

Dylan holds up a hand and I high five him.

Daphne looks heavenward. "You can take the boy off the farm, but he'll just grow pot in his garage."

"I think I like Vermont," Violet says, taking the first puff. "But give your sister a break, maybe? I don't think future public health officials are into pot as a rule."

"Not for anyone in their twenties, and only medicinally," Daphne says sweetly. "Science is so damn inconvenient sometimes."

She has a point, but that shit feels medicinal tonight. I'm on edge, but I don't let it show.

Instead, I stretch my legs out under the table and capture one of Daphne's feet with mine. Her eyes widen, but she doesn't pull away.

"Tell me more about Vermont," Violet says. "What's it like growing up here?"

"Let's see," Dylan says, drumming his fingers on the table. "Everyone knows how to drive in the snow. And you never really have to dress up for anything."

"This is accurate," Daphne agrees. "Don't bother wearing nice shoes, they'll just get trashed. And don't bother washing your car. That's what rain is for."

"Everyone has sex in a pickup truck," Dylan adds.

"Huh," I say slowly. "I can confirm this is true."

"But you drive a Volvo," Daphne points out.

"It was her pickup truck." I shrug, and everyone else laughs. "It's universal."

"It's not," Daphne mutters.

"No?" her brother asks, looking amused. "Eh, never mind. I don't really want to know." He moves on, telling us a story about chasing his goats away from a patch of poison ivy. But I'm still thinking about truck sex with Daphne.

We shoot the shit and share the joint until it grows tiny, and until Chastity pokes her head around the corner of the cider house. "Dylan! Come and help me serve dessert."

"Sure, baby cakes." He hands me the remains of our joint. "Don't miss me too much."

"Why would I? It's easier to hit on your sister when you're not around."

"You're hilarious." He hauls his long frame off the bench, chuckling. Then he lopes off after Chastity.

"Nobody believes me," I mutter. Then I press my hands down on the table and lean over, bridging the distance between Daphne and myself, and kiss her.

For a split second she is frozen with surprise. But her mouth softens after a moment, and I kiss her slowly. It's not indecent. But it isn't quick, either.

And when I sit back down, Violet stares comically between us. "Well, that happened."

Daphne is blushing all over the place, but I don't embarrass. Not over a kiss, anyway. I stub the last scrap of the joint out on the metal table frame and toss the evidence into the wet, tall grass.

"Are you sure you want me to stay over tonight?" Violet asks teasingly.

"Of course," Daphne says quickly. "You can stay in my room with me. Or maybe May's old room, if we can find the air mattress."

"I'll stay in your room," she says. "We can bunk together. Unless you plan to sneak out in the night. I saw at least two pickup trucks in the driveway. Or, wait—isn't Rickie's room right across the hall?"

She grins, and I do too, for a second. But I can't actually sleep with anyone in the room, and Daphne probably knows that.

So I feel glum again anyway.

TWENTY-FIVE

RICKIE

Later, after the party is over, I pause in the upstairs hallway, listening. And I hear wild laughter from behind Daphne's door.

I'm rocking a pair of low-slung athletic shorts and nothing else. But it would be rude not to say good night, right? I knock on the door.

"Yes?" Daphne calls. "Come in."

I open the door and lean against the frame.

"Well *hello*," Violet says from the bed, where she and Daphne are seated together, a laptop propped up between them.

"Evening, ladies. Maybe you could keep the giggling to a low roar? I need a lot of sleep to look this good all the time."

Daphne tries to roll her eyes at me, but it doesn't quite work. She's too busy admiring me. So I cross to the bed and lean down, dropping a kiss to the top of her silky head. "Good night. Have pleasant dreams."

"Oh, she will," Violet says.

"You shut up," Daphne mutters. "Night, McFly."

"Night, gorgeous."

I stride out of there without a backward glance. But as I'm closing the door behind me, I hear Violet's next comments. "Christ on a cruller, that boy is hot. I'd be jealous if I weren't so happy for you."

"Shhh," Daphne hisses.

I step away, grinning. But there's no fist pump. No victory dance.

I'm still a wreck, who locks his door on the way into the room. The chair mocks me from its place against the wall. But I don't move it against the door. I stay strong.

Then I pick up my phone to text Lenore. *Do you have any time for me tomorrow? I had a weird day.*

Her response comes almost immediately, and I feel a little guilty texting her so late. Someday that might be me—the guy getting panicky messages from patients at all hours. *Could you make it to my office at 10? I could give you thirty minutes.*

Sure. I'll be there.

Are you okay right now? Need to call me?

I'm okay. I promise. See you tomorrow.

Early in the morning I meet Dylan in the dairy barn. I shovel cow shit at top speed while he does the milking. "Hey, D? I need to go to Burlington at breakfast time. Sorry for the late notice, but I need a couple hours off."

He pops up from behind a cow. "Yeah, okay. No problem. Is there anything wrong?"

"Nope. Just an appointment I forgot about. You need anything from town? You can text me if you think of something."

"I'm good," Dylan says. "You'll be back for the afternoon? Griff wants to finish the pest traps and do some cleanup from that storm."

"Yeah—I'll be back around noon."

"Hey Rick—cash your checks while you're in BTV."

"What?"

"Your paychecks. Stop by the bank when you're done, and cash them."

"I don't really need the money," I point out.

"Nobody cares," Dylan says, patting a cow on the rump so that she steps a little closer to the milking machine. "Everybody who works here gets paid. Even if they flake off to Burlington on the hottest day of the summer."

"I'll be back for the hottest part of it," I point out.

"Likely story." Dylan gives me a careless smile. "You can make it up to me in beer."

"Now there's a plan. I'll pick something up on my way back."

"I got one more big idea if you want to hear it," Dylan says.

"Hit me."

"Let's fuck off this weekend and go hiking."

"Where?"

"I was thinking of the Presidentials," he says. "Ever climb Mount Washington?"

"Yeah, once during high school." The White Mountains peaks of New Hampshire are some of the best hiking in New England.

"Well, I haven't," he says. "If we hike up and take the railway down, it could be a day trip."

I consider this. "We should probably stay in an AMC hut, right?" That's what I did in the past. The huts are a really unique experience. They can each house a couple dozen hikers at a time in barracks-style rooms. For a reasonable fee, you get a bed, a blanket, a pillow and a hot dinner and breakfast. You bring your own sheets, and there aren't any showers. But you can refill your water bottle and wash up in the bathrooms.

"I thought of that," Dylan admits. "But there wouldn't be locks on the, uh, bedroom doors. So we don't have to stay up there. We could get cheap hotel rooms and do two different day hikes."

Dylan doesn't really have the money for a hotel room. And it's just stupid that my strange sleeping habits are preventing me from going on the kind of adventure that I'd enjoyed as a teenager.

"Look, why don't you see if any of the huts have space?" I ask slowly. "I can deal with a couple of nights of crappy sleep."

Dylan tilts his head to the side, as if trying to read me. "Are you sure?"

"Yeah, I'm sure," I insist. It's just dawning on me that this is exactly the aversion therapy setup that I'd been trying to envision. A room full of well-intentioned strangers sleeping on top of a mountain for adventure.

Maybe I'll conquer this shit. I'm tired of being a mess. I'm so sick of me.

A couple hours later I'm sitting in Lenore's office, feeling a little fool-ish. She's waiting for me to explain my emergency.

Let's face it—I just drove more than sixty miles because I got pissed off when my penis took a time-out when I was about to have sex.

"So just how weird was your weird day?" she asks into the silence.

"Well…" I clear my throat. "Maybe your hunch was right about me. That there's something weird going on with me and sex."

"How do you figure?" she asks.

"You know the dual control model of arousal? Accelerators and brakes?" It's a dumb question, because of course she does. It's like asking a shrink if they've heard of Freud.

"Of course," she says. "Excitation versus inhibition."

"My inhibitions are really easily triggered," I say in a casual voice. But I don't feel all that casual about it. "Yesterday we were, uh, fooling around…"

Lenore grins. "You and Daphne, huh?"

"Don't get too excited. I mean—I did. But then all of a sudden I didn't."

"What triggered you?" Her expression is calm and open.

I trust Lenore completely, and therapy is an excellent tool. But this is surprisingly hard to talk about. "It was just a door slamming in the breeze. It was loud, but completely understandable. But my dick didn't care. I had, like, a full-on panic attack."

"Tell me exactly how you felt in that moment," she says.

"Uh, cold. Clammy." I remember the way my sweat cooled into goose bumps. "And my heart felt jumpy. I was on, like, high alert. And I didn't want anyone to touch me."

"Okay." She folds her hands on the desk. "And how did that play out? Was it embarrassing? What did your partner do or say when this happened?"

"I was embarrassed. I still am. But it could have been worse. Daphne's friend drove up a few seconds later, interrupting us anyway. So I'm not even sure Daphne noticed my…" I cringe.

"Dick deflation?" Lenore provides.

"Is that good clinical practice?" I yelp. "Putting words in the patient's mouth?"

She merely shrugs. "I hate to break this to you, but losing an erection due to a moment of stress is perfectly normal for any man, at any time. Even a twenty-two year old Casanova. You know this already."

"But it didn't feel normal at the time," I argue. "I felt like a basket case. I still do."

"All right. So tell me why it feels like an important realization in your life, and not an instance of really unlucky timing."

"Because I'm so—" I try to put it into words that don't make me sound trivial. "My sleeping alone thing is already weird, and disruptive. You pushed me to think about why I don't have sex anymore. And I can't really explain it. Where's the connection between head injuries and skittish sex?"

Lenore's smile fades. "What if there isn't one?"

"A connection?"

She nods. "Let's just suppose for a second that your problems are larger than the brush-off I just gave you. Let's suppose you're experiencing a true sexual dysfunction. Why would you assume it's connected to a head trauma?"

"Because that's the thing that *changed*." Isn't it obvious? "Did you happen to read my file, by the way? I know it's only been a couple days since I asked."

"Yes," she says quietly. "I pulled it Wednesday night and read the whole thing."

"So... did you find any dates in there?"

"Yes," she says. She reaches for a sticky note and shows it to me. *Saturday, December 10th.* No surprises there. "That's the night you were admitted to the hospital." Then she swallows uncomfortably.

"Anything else, Lenore? You kind of look like you saw the devil."

That's when she chews on her lip. It's her tell, and I rarely see it. But she's nervous about something. "I read the whole file twice. Every word. The last time I read it was during the month we began working together. But now I know you better, so it read differently to me."

"And?"

She sighs. "And there are some things in there that seem strange."

"Are you going to tell me what they are?"

"Yes, but first I need to tell you that this is all speculation on my part."

"Just please tell me what you saw."

"First of all, the information they sent over about your medical treatment is woefully incomplete. It's not actually a medical file, like you would get from the hospital. It's more like a one-page summary that somebody typed out to send to us. And it is barely sufficient."

"One page? I was in that hospital for weeks."

"I know that. It's just a summary of injuries. I know which of your ribs were broken, but I don't know what drugs you were given for the pain."

"Do you need to know that?"

She shakes her head. "Not necessarily, because you're not being treated for addiction. But it's not right. A request for medical records should never have been answered with this half-assed information. As for your head, it only says that the patient was confused, due to a probable head injury."

I snort. "Wow. So forthcoming."

"Right." She chews her lip again, and I can tell we're not done yet. "By comparison, the file included much more information about your academic history, including a transcript of your first semester grades. Nice work, by the way, all A's."

"Thank you. I didn't take any of those exams, but I did everything else. That's why I lawyered up in the first place, to get the credits."

She looks down at a note on her pad. "You took chemistry, an intro to psych, a math class, a course on Chaucer, and Spanish. You got credit for courses you don't remember taking."

"They couldn't have predicted my memory loss at the time," I point out.

"Right. That's why it didn't seem strange to me the first time I read it."

"And now it does?"

She frowns, and I feel a tingle of awareness at the back of my neck. "A month or so ago, you and I got off on a tangent about liminality in *The Canterbury Tales*."

I chuckle. "Sure, yeah. It's more fun to talk about Chaucer than about myself."

"Right." She smiles. "When's the first time you read Chaucer?"

"Like, any of it?" I ask. "I have no idea."

"Did you read *The Canterbury Tales* in high school?"

I'm sweating now and I don't even know why. "Those stories are everywhere. They're referenced in a million other works of literature."

"Uh huh. But you can quote from "The Knight's Tale" in Middle English."

It's starting to hit me what Lenore is saying. "You think I remember some of that class."

"You remember Chaucer," she says carefully. "But not sitting in the class."

"Right," I agree. "Or the professor's name. Yeah. Okay, that's weird. Head injuries are weird."

"Yours is especially weird," she says.

"In what way?" I demand.

She puts her elbows on the desk and then puts her head in her hands. "Rickie, I don't have any medical experience with TBI. So I did a bunch of reading this weekend, and I couldn't find a single TBI case with memory issues that are similar to yours, where so much material is retained so perfectly."

"There are other cases. Like that CEO who slipped in the bathroom and lost his entire life's memories."

"I read about him," she says quietly. "His brain scan revealed a loss of blood flow to the right temporal lobe."

That's true. And yet my brain scan showed no abnormalities like his. "That man also had learning issues after his accident. Difficulty forming new memories. I didn't."

Lenore nods calmly.

Nothing inside me is calm. Because I know what Lenore is trying to imply. "You think I don't have a TBI anymore."

"That's one explanation," she says with deliberate care.

And I realize it's even creepier than that. "You think I *never* had one. You think my memory loss is only traumatic?" My voice gets high and weird. "Like...a dissociative fugue. Wh-what is the new term for that?" Then I answer my own question. "Dissociative psychogenic amnesia." My heart pounds, and I hear a rushing sound in my ears.

"That's an extreme interpretation," she says. "That brain fog you suffered after the accident sounds very much like a concussion."

"But that went away in *weeks*."

She watches me, and waits.

Bile climbs up my throat. I might actually vomit. When did this office get so small? I stand up and quickly unlatch Lenore's window, and roll it open to the summer air. I stick my head outside and breathe. The sight of the green lawn below us makes me feel a little calmer.

Just breathe, I remind myself. I haven't had a panic attack in a long time. Months. And now I'm on panic attack number two in two days.

Panic attacks, by the way, are a very rare symptom of TBI.

What if I never had a TBI?

When I turn back to look at Lenore, her eyes are worried. I'm scaring her right now. And, honestly, that's the most frightening thing yet. Her fear. "Shit, I'm not going to *jump*."

"I know," she says quickly. "I'm no doctor, okay? I struggled with whether to bring this up. But after rereading that file, I had certain suspicions. And I shared them with my advisor, who thought that you and I should have a discussion."

A *discussion* sounds so benign. "You think my entire memory loss is psychological."

"I think it *could* be. This honestly isn't the first time I've wondered," she whispers.

"And you never *said* anything?" Anger surges inside me, and I know she doesn't deserve it. But when will the hits stop coming?

"Rickie, you are the smartest client that I have, perhaps the smartest person I know…"

"You wanted me to figure it out for myself," I say heavily.

"It was just a suspicion," she says. "My job is to lessen your trauma, not increase it. And there wasn't any proof. And let's not forget my lack of medical experience, and the lack of a decent medical file here. Although I was open to exploring that idea if you ever went there yourself."

But I never went there myself. Some shrink I'm going to be. "I could get another scan," I suggest. "Mine came up clear."

"You could," she agrees. "There might be a hospital somewhere with a more sensitive machine. We could investigate. But if a new set of scans is clear, then you still don't know anything. It could still be a medical condition that we can't find on an MRI."

"I'm so tired of not knowing," I say uselessly. "And I hate this theory of yours."

"Why?" she asks.

"What do you mean *why?* I've been so angry about my memory loss and now you're telling me that it's my own fault."

"Whoa now," she says, pointing a finger at me. "That is a very bad take on this discussion."

"I know," I grunt. "But last year I was a guest speaker at that cognitive psychology course. Remember? Everyone was so impressed that I knew the ins and outs of memory loss diagnoses. It's just that I had mine all wrong."

"Rickie, I hate to break this news—but if you're going to become a clinical psychologist, that means a *lifetime* of interpreting other people's psychological issues without ever being sure that you've got a good grasp on your own. We are all our own worst patients."

"I realize that," I grunt.

"One problem at a time," she says gently. "This changes nothing."

"How can you *say* that? My treatment should change. I should be considering hypnosis or some shit."

"That option has always been open to you. But you told me hypnotism is for suckers. Those were your actual words."

My laugh is bitter. "It's true." I get up out of my chair. "Our time is up, right?"

"Almost," she admits. "But sit down a sec. I don't want you to walk out of here feeling angry and confused."

"I've been angry and confused for a couple of years now," I point out. "Today is no different."

"It is, though," she says quietly.

I know she's right. I just don't know what to do about it. "What if you call the Academy? It's been at least a year since anyone bothered them about me. What if you reached the infirmary and asked for another copy of my file?"

She taps her fingers on the desk. "I'm game. But if they weren't helpful before, they probably won't be now."

"Probably," I admit. "But what if you get someone new on the phone? Somewhere, someone knows what happened to me that night. I mean—lie to them if you have to. Say I'm in crisis. Tell them I'm psychotic. Ask them if I was shot at or blown up. I don't care how outlandish you make it. If they issue a denial, they might throw you some more details. Do whatever it takes."

She takes a deep breath. I can tell she's thinking about it.

"Please," I whisper. "I know it probably won't work. But just try."

"Okay," she says. "Okay."

"That's all I ask." On that note, I make my exit, leaving Lenore's worried face behind.

TWENTY-SIX

DAPHNE

I'm very frustrated. I suppose that's nothing new. I've spent the whole summer feeling frustrated by my situation.

Except now I'm also *sexually* frustrated. That's new. And it's all Rickie's fault.

After Violet's departure—and the promises she extracted from me to tell her absolutely everything about the future developments between Rickie and me—I'd expected to have some free time with him.

But that's not what happens. Instead, my idiot brother takes Rickie on a guys' hiking trip to the White Mountains, where they summit three of the Presidentials in the span of four days.

Guess who has to milk the cows while they're gone? This girl. It's Chastity and me in the barn at the crack of dawn for four days straight. She's ridiculously cheerful at seven in the morning. A year ago she was worried about starting college and worried about finding her place in the world.

But now Chastity behaves like she's found a secret trove of happy pills, and won't share. She's living her dream, planning her future with my brother and so in love that she might as well be skipping through a field of daisies at sunset.

Meanwhile, the second-floor hallway is way too quiet for my taste. The weather has finally cooled off, but I haven't. I lie in bed every night listening to the crickets chirp, and feeling lonely.

Is it crazy to miss somebody that I thought I wanted gone? I spend a lot of time remembering the view of those gray eyes as he kissed me in bed. Like I was a precious gift to hold and explore. Sometimes I catch myself smiling so hard that I roll my face into the pillow and sigh.

The pull I feel toward him is uncomfortable for me. Whenever I feel this way, it usually ends in disaster.

"Come on, Daphne," Violet had said before she left. "Rickie seems great. And they can't *all* be like Reardon." That didn't sway me very much, because my data set is still small.

But then she'd said something else that got to me. "If you don't take a chance, then Reardon wins."

And that's true. I can't let Reardon Halsey have a lasting effect on every part of my life. He may ultimately ruin every professional ambition I have, and that's on me. I will pay for my mistakes.

But I won't pay for his. And if Reardon is the last man I ever make myself vulnerable for, that would be horrible, right? The man outmaneuvered me for now. He can take my job, but he can't take my happiness.

I won't let him.

In theory, anyway. My bold decision has me flopping around in bed, and not even the cool Vermont air blowing in through the window can cool my heated, yearning skin.

Rickie and my brother drive back on Tuesday night. They roll up at sundown in Dylan's truck, while I'm in the kitchen with Mom, prepping tomorrow's meals.

My heart leaps as soon as I hear their voices outside. And it takes tremendous effort to keep on peeling carrots when I'd rather run for the door, the way Chastity is doing right now.

"Hey! We're in the middle of a game, here," Grandpa complains from the dining room.

"You're winning anyway," she says, laughing. Then she plants a kiss on Dylan the minute he appears in the kitchen doorway.

"Greetings!" he calls out after kissing her hello. "We are filthy dirty and Rickie got himself a sunburn. But we smashed all three peaks."

"Congratulations," my mother says, wiping her hands on her apron. "Did you have dinner?"

"You bet we did. We'd better take turns in the outdoor shower. It's that bad. But then I'll come back in and take care of this laundry." He drops a bag in the mudroom. "But you come with me, lady." He takes Chastity's hand, and they disappear outside.

Rickie doesn't enter the house at all. I have half a mind to run after him for my own kiss hello. Or—let's be honest—a glimpse of his naked body in the outdoor shower by the bunkhouse.

But I play it cool, and I wait.

Guess what? Playing it cool is the pits. Rickie doesn't knock on my door at all on Tuesday night. I don't even get a glimpse of him until Wednesday morning at breakfast, where I'm hovering in the kitchen making pancakes and watching the stairs like a stalker for his appearance.

When he finally shows his face, the first thing I notice is that his sunburn is already fading to a golden tan. But the second thing I notice is the way he avoids my gaze.

"Morning," he says, his voice subdued. "How've you been?" His eyes are elsewhere.

"Fine," I reply, but my heart drops. I pour him a mug of coffee, but then I *force* him to look at me when I hand it over. And I brace myself to see regret or disinterest on his face. Why else would he be avoiding me if there were no second thoughts about our hot and heavy shower last week?

He lifts his gaze to mine, finally, and I'm shocked to see dark circles under his eyes. He looks like he hasn't slept in a week. And I must be pretty bad at disguising my surprise, because he winces. "You okay?" I whisper.

"Of course," he says. His index finger slips artfully across the back of my hand as he takes the mug of coffee from me, leaving tingles on my skin.

I look up at him, encouraged by this small display of warmth. But the back door opens, and Rickie turns away from me as Dylan enters the kitchen, with Chastity bringing up the rear.

"Oooh, pancakes," my brother says, grabbing a plate.

"You're on cleanup duty," I point out. "It's Wednesday, so we're heading to Burlington at ten."

"Yeah, I know," my brother says, stealing one right off the griddle and handing the plate to Chastity. "Rickie is staying here today."

"What?" I say, and it comes out as a squeak. "Why?"

The man in question uses the ladle to pour another pancake onto my griddle. "I'm gonna help Dylan catch up on some maintenance, and just Zoom into my class."

"Oh," I say, thrown. That's exactly the suggestion I'd made to him a few weeks ago, back when I was trying to stay out of Rickie's orbit.

And now he's taking that suggestion, and I'm so disappointed.

"But don't worry!" Dylan says, oblivious to my despair. "Chastity is going with you instead. You'll have to drive, but she'll hop out and make the deliveries, so you don't need to park."

"Okay, sure," I say breezily. "But what's she going to do for five hours while I'm at work?"

"Buy a computer!" Chastity crows, bouncing back into the kitchen. "I've been waiting for this day for a long time. And I finally have the cash." Her smile is like sunshine.

Even I'm not a big enough bitch to rain on that level of glee. "Okay, that's really great."

"After the store sets it up for me, I'll entertain myself at the library. It's all good."

I guess that's settled, then. I make a couple of pancakes for myself, and for my mom. And then I get ready to hit the road.

An hour later I'm burning up the highway miles toward Burlington, with the applejack delivery—and Chastity—in tow.

Conversation doesn't flow easily. Chastity will probably become my sister-in-law someday, so I should really make an effort.

She and I have never had much in common, but that's not the real problem. I'm so distracted by the questions swirling around in my heart. Why did Rickie look so beat? And why is he blowing off our Wednesday?

Our Wednesday. Just listen to me. I don't even know myself anymore. A new wave of frustration washes over me. Who's going to make me stop for ice cream and give me the fuck-me eyes?

This is why I avoid tattooed hotties with pretty gray eyes. They're addicting.

"Hey, Daph?" Chastity says suddenly.

"Sorry, what?" I ask guiltily. "I'm a little distracted."

"That's okay. I was just thinking about the school year. And I know money is tight this year. I mean, money is always tight. But I also know that it, uh, bothers you."

"True enough." Have they been discussing me? Is it worse than I even realized?

"I just wonder why you never considered living with us at Rickie's place in Burlington. There's one more bedroom. And it's *so* cheap."

"How cheap, exactly?" I hear myself ask. When Dylan had brought up this possibility last Christmas, I'd said that I wasn't interested. I didn't want my brother all up in my business.

I still don't. But my first housing payment is due very soon. And now I have a fuller picture of the financial strain, plus grad school to consider.

"Rickie owns that house. I'm not exactly sure how. He doesn't talk about it. But next year Dylan and I are only kicking in, like, a hundred dollars each every month. Rickie is covering the taxes by renting it out this summer."

"*One* hundred dollars?" That can't be right.

"That's what he said. It covers heat and utilities. But Rickie says he doesn't need to charge actual rent. So Dylan and I decided we're going to cover all of the grocery bills, too. Even if we're always treating Rickie, it's still a whole lot cheaper than a dining hall plan."

"Wow. That's crazy. Rickie is crazy. He could get so much more than that."

"You're not wrong. But the money doesn't seem to matter to him. So think about it, okay? That fifth bedroom is pretty small, and there's no bed in there yet. But if you were joining us, I would take that tiny room and use it as an office. Because, let's face it, I'm mostly going to be sleeping in Dylan's room."

I snicker.

"Yeah, I know," she says. "But we could tone it down if that helps."

"Tone what down?"

"The PDA, and the sneaking off early every night." She sighs. "I know we're a little much. But I don't want to be the reason you pay for a dorm room. I don't want to scare you off from a situation that could really help the whole family."

Yikes. "Chastity, you're not scaring anybody off. I promise. When Dylan mentioned the house to me, I told him no as a reflex. I didn't want to crash anybody's party."

"Oh," she says quietly. "But why would you assume you were? Dylan wouldn't have suggested it to Rickie if he didn't want you there."

"I suppose you're right," I say, although I'm unconvinced. Dylan thinks I'm an uptight drag. He was probably asking out of obligation, and hoping I'd say no.

"Just think about it," Chastity says. "I think it would be nice."

"Too much testosterone in that house?" I ask with a chuckle. As it stands, she'll be the only woman with three men.

"No, that's not it. I just like your company. The world is full of cliquey women that I don't understand. But you shoot straight every time."

"Oh," I say, taken aback by this compliment. It's a really nice take on my overly direct personality. "Thank you."

"You're welcome." Silence falls again, but only for a moment. "Hey, Rickie said that sometimes you get ice cream on the way home. Do I get ice cream, too?"

"Sure," I say quickly. "Why not?"

TWENTY-SEVEN

RICKIE

The sun beats down on my bare back as I kneel down to remove a white paper sleeve from the base of an apple tree. Dylan and I are making a sweep through the orchard, removing spent pest traps, and picking up any early drops and tossing them into a compost bin hitched to the back of a tractor.

"If we let 'em lie there and rot, we get pests and disease," Griffin had explained.

It wasn't hard work, but the day was shaping up to be another scorcher. And I keep getting interrupted by texts from Lenore, who's unhappy with me for canceling our appointment this morning. My phone chimes three times again in rapid succession.

"Problem?" Dylan asks from the opposite side of the same orchard row.

"Sorry," I mumble. "Let me just tell her I'm busy."

"Sure, man. We need a water break anyway."

I pull out my phone.

Lenore: Please check in. You were upset when I last saw you, and this seems like the wrong time to miss an appointment.

Rick: I'm fine. I'm just tired from a long weekend of aversion therapy. That didn't go so well but I'll tell you all about it next week.

Lenore: I thought we were going to *discuss* that plan before you put it into action.

Rick: I had an opportunity. 3 nights in AMC huts. No locks anywhere. It's all about trust, right? And sleeping near sweaty strangers.

Lenore: That sounds like my version of hell. Did you make it all 3 nights?

Rick: Barely. I actually slept some the 3rd night. Not sure if that was progress or just exhaustion.

Lenore: Please check in with me tomorrow. I could make time on Friday again.

Rick: Next week. Regular time. I swear. Sorry for the cancelation.

I look up to see Dylan watching me. When I put my phone away, he tosses me a bottle of water. "Is everything okay?" he asks.

"Yeah. Fine. There's someone I usually see on Wednesdays in Burlington. She's just pissed that I canceled on her."

Dylan's eyebrows lift a millimeter, which is basically as shocked as Dylan gets. "You got a girlfriend in BTV? No way."

"Nah. It's not a girlfriend. We both know I'm hung up on your sister."

Dylan grins and shakes his head.

"My standing date on Wednesdays is with a therapist."

"Oh," he says. And there isn't even a twitch of surprise at this little revelation. Dylan just rolls with it, as usual. "If you've got your phone on you, can you look at the weather? I didn't think it was gonna be this hot again. It's only noon."

"Sure, man." I pull out my phone and check. "The high will be eighty-eight today, ninety tomorrow."

"Christ." He drains his water bottle. "At least we got the cooler weather for hiking."

We put the water bottles onto the tractor and Dylan drives the compost bin further down the row. Then we get back to work. My legs are sore from climbing three four-thousand footers in as many days. And I'm weary to the bone from lack of sleep.

Last night I got eight hours in the farmhouse behind a locked door. But it barely made a dent in my exhaustion. The AMC huts were—as I'd remembered—the perfect aversion therapy setup for someone who's unable to fall asleep near others. Aversion therapy forces you to confront the things that freak you out. It's supposed to prove to your psyche that there's no reason to be afraid.

It's controversial, because patients hate it. And many therapists hate it too. Who wants to make their patients cry or have a crisis?

On the other hand, it works. For example, teens who experience social anxiety often respond very quickly to aversion therapies that force them to engage with strangers in an otherwise safe environment.

That's the idea, anyway. And it's true that my nights in the various mountaintop huts forced me to confront my phobias. I felt twitchy even walking into that room to put my pack down on the bed before supper. There were eight beds—four sets of bunk beds built into the walls of the place.

Just looking at those bunks gave me a creepy feeling. "Can I take the top?" I'd asked as Dylan removed his pack.

"Sure," he'd said easily.

I'd put my pack onto the top bunk and walked right out of there again. But a few hours later I'd found myself climbing onto that damn bed, dread pooling in my stomach. Even the creak of the wooden ladder made me edgy.

It didn't make a lick of sense, either. The other hikers were chipper twenty-somethings like us, full of smiles and good manners. The bed was comfortable enough. And there was a cool mountain breeze blowing through the open windows.

But it didn't matter. I lay awake for hours, listening to other people snore peacefully. They got their much needed rest, while all I got was angry.

Up until last week, I'd believed that all my troubles were the result of a physical injury. I'd felt stupid knowing that my own recklessness had upended my life. But it still felt like something that could happen to anybody. Just a dose of stupidity compounded by some bad luck.

Now I didn't know what to think. What kind of trauma was so awful that I could have forgotten it just to protect myself? That's ridiculous, especially when all I really want is to remember.

It was just a bump on the head, I'd insisted to myself at three or four in the morning.

But why then couldn't I sleep? And what's with the panic attacks?

There aren't any answers for me in the orchard today. I take another dropped apple in hand and hurl it at the compost bin with such force that it bounces right back out again and hits Dylan in the ass.

He whips around. "What the hell was that?"

"Sorry," I clip. "Bad bounce."

He squints at me. And I must look half deranged, because he looks concerned instead of angry. "Are you okay today? You seem off."

"I'm just tired," I growl. "The whole sleeping near strangers thing didn't really work for me."

His face falls. "I'm sorry. It was a bad idea."

"It was my idea to try it," I insist. "And I'll live."

After a beat, Dylan decides not to worry about it. He turns around and picks up another apple.

God bless the Shipleys. Dylan is as solid as they come. Like his whole family.

I never should have gotten myself involved with Daphne. What a dumb idea that was. Who'd want a piece of this?

Bending over for the four hundredth time, I find myself thinking about her at work in Burlington. What's she doing right now? Plotting to take over the world, probably.

I smile like a fool. But then I remember the look on her face this morning when Dylan told her I wasn't going to Burlington today. Disappointment.

That bothered me. I'm basically famous for disappointing her by now. Let's review—first I stood her up. Then I came on strong and freaked out in bed. It's going to be a while before I can think about that afternoon without wanting to slink off somewhere and hide.

"Hey, Rick?" Dylan interrupts my self-recriminations.

"Yeah?" I stand up and face him.

"I gotta ask—are we still looking at a pretty low monthly rent in Burlington for this coming year?"

"Yeah, of course. Nothing's changed. I'm just asking you guys to help me cover the heat and the utilities. This summer's renters paid the taxes."

He tosses a stick into the bin. "Daphne hasn't said she's in. So you'll have to do the math again, right?"

"Maybe?" I shrug. "I probably don't need to, though. We're talking small sums, here."

"Okay." Dylan rubs the back of his neck. "But you still haven't cashed those checks? I'll take the low rent deal so long as you take a paycheck this summer. We're still coming out ahead."

"Yeah, okay. Fine." I turn around and crouch down to remove the sleeve from an apple tree.

"One more question," Dylan continues. "I want to know if you think this is crazy. But what would you say if I told you I was thinking of proposing?"

My hand stops halfway to grabbing an apple out of the grass. My first thought is: *that's ridiculous. You're too young to get married.* But after a few seconds tick by, I realize that Dylan's situation isn't the same as mine. And he doesn't need to hear that kind of negativity from his friends.

I close my fingers around the apple and stand up. "Honey, I didn't know you felt this way about me. I'm flattered but I don't think I'm ready to take this big step with you."

Dylan looks heavenward.

"Sorry," I chuckle. "I'm a little surprised, but also not. Anyone could see that you guys will end up together. Why now?"

"Because I just don't see the point of waiting. And Chastity doesn't really have any family of her own, you know? I want to give her that. She deserves to feel like a full member of the team."

Well that's just humbling. And now I'm glad I kept my trap shut. "Guess you'd better start saving up for a ring."

"That's actually the biggest kink in this plan," he says with a shake of his head. "There's this jewelry store in Montpelier that uses all Vermont designers. I figure the rock doesn't have to be huge if it's nicely done, right?" He winces.

"Dylan, this may come as a shock to you. But Chastity's not into you for your vast fortune."

He barks out a laugh. "Okay, yeah. That's a good point."

"It's the same reason I don't rent out those bedrooms for a profit. I'm not willing to share a house with just anybody. I need people around me I can trust."

Dylan gives me a sideways glance, before plucking another insect trap off a trunk. "Someday you'll make a great shrink."

"Let's hope so," I grunt.

"Don't you have to log in for your class now?"

"Crap." I yank out my phone and check the time. "Yeah, sorry. I'd better run."

"Go on. I'll see you at lunch." Dylan waves me off.

I grab my shirt and my water bottle and jog through the orchard toward the farmhouse. I make it up to my room on time, and log in before the professor starts the lecture.

While I'm waiting, I sign all three of the checks from Shipley Farms, then use my banking app to deposit them. It's about 2400 dollars all told.

That done, I settle in to listen. But the lecture bores me almost from the first minute. Maybe it's my piss-poor attitude, or maybe it's the on-screen disconnect. But my mind wanders, and I find myself searching the interwebs for a jewelry store in Montpelier that specializes in local artisans.

It's not difficult to find. So I call them up and purchase a gift certificate for a Mr. Dylan Shipley in the amount of two thousand dollars. And the moment the confirmation email comes through, I forward it to Dylan.

"This is for you, bro. And by the way—I finally cashed those checks."

TWENTY-EIGHT

DAPHNE

This week, Thursday dinner is at our friends' house in Montpelier. Sophie and Jude like to host every few months, and the Shipley clan always caravans over there to make it happen.

But Rickie begs off and stays home.

There's something up with him. I can tell. But I can't seem to get him alone for a minute to ask. Whenever I walk into a room, he walks out of it.

He's basically playing the same game I was a month ago. I avoided him like the black plague for the month of June, even when he smiled at me. Especially then.

I'm trying hard not to take it personally. My gut says that he isn't suddenly tired of me—that there's something else going on. Those dark smudges under his eyes are new, along with the weary look on his face.

But it's so easy for all my old insecurities to sneak up on me. My heart is like our old Kubota tractor that's always in need of repair. You replace one part on it, and something else immediately breaks.

And the fact remains that no man I've ever had feelings for has returned them with the same fervor. Never. And I'm starting to wonder if one ever will.

It doesn't keep me from hoping. I follow Rickie with my eyes wherever he goes. On Friday afternoon I walk past the cider house where he and Dylan are supposed to be scrubbing out barrels in preparation for the first press next month.

And they're arguing. So—like anyone with three siblings has learned to do—I stand beside the open door like a creeper and eavesdrop.

"You shouldn't have done that," Dylan is saying.

Oh no. Could this be about me?

"I wanted to," Rickie says in a low voice. "I can do as I please."

My face heats. *Please don't let this be about me.*

"It's too much," Dylan says. "I don't like owing anybody."

Rickie makes an irritated sound. "That wasn't why I did it. You don't owe me anything. We've been over this."

"I could have waited, you know. I'm patient."

"Yeah, but now you can be choosy about your timing. I didn't need the money. Money is, like, the only thing I don't have to worry about right now."

My heart gives a little sympathetic squeeze. What is Rickie so worried about?

"Dylan—" my other brother's voice cuts in. "Just say thank you already. This is not that complicated."

"Yeah, yeah," Dylan mutters. "Okay, thank you. It's gonna make me look like a bigger stud than I already am."

Rickie laughs, and the sound of it gives me a fluttery feeling in my chest. "There, was that so hard? You're welcome, punk."

I'm just about to walk away when I hear Dylan say my name. "Hey—Chass asked Daphne about her housing situation this fall. And she sounds like she might actually consider moving in with us."

"Oh," Rickie says slowly. "That's cool. That will make it so much more convenient when we're dating."

My eyes bug out.

"Come again?" Griffin grumbles. But Dylan laughs.

I trot away from that door as fast as I can. Everything about Rickie confuses me.

Everything.

———

On Friday night, it's hot again, and really sticky, too. We're all a little beaten down by the unrelenting heat and the humidity. Mom puts a window fan in the dining room so we can get through dinner without melting. She serves Caesar salads with fresh bread and grilled chicken that Grandpa tends on the Webber outside.

Rickie sits at the opposite end of the table. Again. But even so, I keep catching him staring at me when he thinks I'm not looking. And the expression on his face is soft, too. There's a fondness there that's hard to hide.

But he's staying away from me, and I don't understand why.

"Let's go to the swimming hole after dinner," Dylan says. "Griff and Audrey have been hanging out there with Gus. Griff told me he even mowed the grass."

"Where is this place?" Rickie asks.

"Down the road, just a mile and a half. We can bike it or drive."

"Sounds fun," Rickie says. Then his eyes flicker toward me again before he looks away.

And I ask myself an important question. *What would Violet do?*

It only takes me a minute to think of the answer. Wear a tiny bikini.

Duh.

Two hours later I'm sitting on my towel, which is spread on the grass at the edge of the swimming hole. This place is about the size of a modest backyard pool, filled by moving water and surrounded by rocks. It's fed by a creek that drops the water down a two-foot waterfall.

My brothers are geniuses, I guess, because I feel so much better now that I've dunked myself into the water. And now we're eating ice cream cones that Audrey and Griffin brought us.

"Why haven't we come here every night?" Rickie asks, licking his cone. He looks cheerier than he's looked in days.

"We never used to come here," Dylan admits from the pool itself, where he's standing with Chastity. "Why is that?"

"Because Chasternak was a jerk about it way back when he owned the land," Griffin says. He's holding onto my nephew, while Audrey shares a cone with the little guy. "There were *No Trespassing* signs posted on every tree. The one time I brought friends here, he called Dad and made a stink about it."

"But it's ours now," Dylan says. "Another perk of buying the Abrahams' land."

"You and Daphne had a baby pool," Griffin continues. "I don't know if you remember, but May and I used to have to watch you in it so you two didn't try to drown each other. It was like a full-time sibling rivalry cage match with you two."

"Dude," Dylan says. "It's funny, but now that you mention it, I still feel an urge to push her underwater."

"Try it and die," I say as a reflex.

Rickie laughs. He's sitting on a blanket on the grass beside me. And I've been doing my best not to stare at his shirtless, dripping wet body. Now he says, "I've got twenty bucks on Daphne in this fight."

"Maybe we'll stop at one child," Audrey says.

Griffin only grins. "Thank you for the ice cream, baby. Shall we go home?"

"We should. This one is up past his bedtime."

Gus gives her a wary look and pouts.

They say their good nights and make their way through the trees toward the dirt road, while Rickie helps Audrey carry her cooler back to the car, and Griffin carries his cranky son.

Meanwhile, my brother pulls Chastity back into the water and starts kissing her while she laughs. Then she stops laughing and wraps her body around him.

"Check, please," Dylan says. "We should head back. It's getting late."

I roll my eyes. It's not even nine o'clock. The sky is still bright in the west.

"Go on," Rickie says. "You know you want to."

Dylan climbs out of the water. "Should I leave you the bikes or the pickup?"

"The truck," I say quickly. I felt like a doofus riding my bike here in a bikini. But it was worth it. Rickie has been as broody as ever tonight. But his eyes keep finding their way over here nonetheless.

And now we're going to be here all alone.

"Keys are in the ignition," Dylan says, climbing out and wrapping a towel around his waist.

"Sleep tight," Rickie snickers.

Chastity's face is pink as she says goodbye. And then the two of them are gone. I hear bike tires on the gravel a minute later.

And that's it. Rickie and I are the only people left. He is stoically licking his ice cream cone. And the silence thickens around us. This is just the sort of moment when Rickie usually hits on me.

But, nope. Silence.

"What are you thinking about?" I finally ask.

"I'd rather hear your thoughts," he says.

"But I asked you first."

He smiles slightly. "Fine. But it isn't all that exciting. I was thinking about how three years ago, almost exactly, I went with some people to the chutes in Thetford. You've been?"

"Of course."

"Well, I hadn't before. It was a hot summer day, and we spent it jumping into the river and basically getting into trouble. And I remember it with perfect clarity."

"Were you there with Carla?" I blurt out. I've never forgotten that they dated. Carla is my polar opposite—easy and fun.

Rickie blinks. "Yeah. How do you know?"

"You mentioned her the first time we met. That's the person we knew in common. She gave me your email address."

"Oh, right." He glowers.

"So what happened at the chutes?"

"Nothing."

"Then why do you look so angry right now?"

"Because I remember the deli sandwich I ate for lunch. And I remember we were teasing one guy about his tight bathing suit. It's so goddamn strange that I remember *everything* that happened up until the minute I left for college."

"Oh." I swallow. "But not after."

"But not after," he repeats. "It drives me straight up a tree."

Okay. So Rickie's in a dark mood. I've been there.

After a beat, he moves over, bridging the distance between us. He puts a palm on my knee, and it's cool from swimming. "Your turn," he says. "What are you thinking about?" He takes a bite of his ice cream cone.

If I told the truth, he'd probably drop the ice cream in surprise. *Well, I was actually thinking about your dick and how I hope to see more of it.* "Just wondering where you went inside that head of yours." That's as much truth as I feel able to deliver.

His expression softens. "I've been neglecting you, haven't I?"

"What? No. That's silly."

"Is it?" His smile turns sly. Then he tosses the last bit of his ice cream cone over his shoulder, without even looking to see where it lands. "Come here, Shipley." His voice is gravel.

I shiver. "Why?"

"Because I need a closer look at this bathing suit you're rocking."

"You really don't," I argue, even if I've been hoping for this moment for the last hour.

"Oh I disagree." He moves closer, sitting next to me on my towel, his strong legs hanging off the rock, feet in the water. His fuzzy knee brushes against my smoother one, and I can't help but want more.

I won't ask for it. A smarter girl wouldn't be at war with herself like this. And I don't mean to be coy. But I can't help feeling like Rickie is more than I can handle. I'm no Carla. Any minute now he's going to realize that I'm not half as sexy and desirable as he thought.

If I said that to Violet, she'd yell at me and make me take it back. And maybe she's even right. But you can't always help the way you feel.

My thoughts must not be loud enough for Rickie to hear because he lifts my damp hair and tucks it away over my shoulder. He's casual about it, as if we always do this. Then he leans in and kisses my neck, smooth as you please.

Tingles shoot across my body. And then they redouble as he slips a finger under the shoulder strap of my bathing suit and runs the length of it, down to my breast. "Did you wear this for me?" he whispers, as his breath tickles the shell of my ear.

"No," I say. But what I mean is, *yes, but I shouldn't have.* I just spent several days wishing he'd pay more attention. And now that I have his attention, I've forgotten what to do with it.

But Rickie hasn't. "I like it anyway. And I like *you*." The compliment just rolls off his tongue. And I turn my chin to look into his warm gray eyes. They crinkle at the corners when he smiles back at me. "You look hot in this. But I still want to take it off you."

Instead of replying, I just stare at him in wonder. He makes it sound so easy. *I want this. I like it. I like you.* I wonder if that will always be hard for me, or if the fear will seep out of me some day, so that I can look at a man and say, *I want you, too.*

"You're mad at me," he whispers.

"No," I say quickly. "I'm really not."

"Yeah, you are. A little bit. Because I've been stuck inside my own head. I've been neglecting you."

"You've been distant," I say carefully. "But that's me on a good day."

He laughs, and I feel it rumble inside my chest. "You're not distant. You're cautious. And you have reasons. He hasn't contacted you again, has he?" After asking the question, Rickie wraps an arm around me and scoops me onto his lap. Suddenly we're nose to nose. "Has he?"

"N-no," I say.

"Good. Do you have anything else to tell me?"

"No? Why?" His gaze at point-blank range is so distracting.

"Because I'm going to kiss you in a minute, and you'll forget whatever you had to say."

"That's arrogant."

"No it isn't." His smile teases me. "Because I'll forget too. I've got it bad for you. And I'm sorry to send you mixed signals this week. We're more alike than you think."

"We are?" I ask as his hand cups my face. I lean into the pressure of his palm. I can't help myself.

"Yeah," he whispers. "Messy lives and greedy hearts. That's us, Shipley."

"Oh." It's hard to argue with that. Especially when Rickie starts dropping soft kisses at the corner of my mouth. I'm impatient, though. I know what's coming, and I know I won't actually resist. So I turn my face and find his mouth with my own.

With a chuckle, he brushes his lips across mine, still teasing me as my body lights up in anticipation of more. "You kill me, Shipley." His long fingers brush down my body until he grips my hips in two firm hands.

My head jerks upward, because I'm in a perilous position right now—on his lap, at the edge of the pool. It would be so easy for him to toss me right in the water. With both hands, I reach for his biceps and hold on.

"Hey—there's a zero percent chance I'm about to throw you into the water."

"But you could," I say quickly. And I still don't relax my grip. I've been tricked before.

"When are you going to learn? Pushing you away is not in my plans," he says. And then he tightens his grip on my hips and pulls me in close, until we're nose to nose. "Pushing you down on that blanket? Now there's a plan I can get behind."

Whoosh goes the breath out of my lungs. And I get goose bumps as he tugs us both away from the edge of the water, then falls back onto the blanket.

I follow him on all fours, looking down at him, halfway shocked by this turn of events, and also at my own audacity, because I'm practically straddling him now. "Rickie?"

"Yes, baby girl?" He reaches up and runs his hand right over my ass, and I feel my body respond immediately. I'm hungry for his kisses. But now he's waiting to hear my question.

"Um," I hear myself say. "Chastity told me you never hook up."

His eyes widen a fraction. "Well I guess she'd be surprised if she came back for her pocketbook right now, wouldn't she?" With playfully slow fingers, he eases the strap of my bikini top down my shoulder, until it threatens to fall off.

"But is it true?" I ask. I'm teetering on this emotional precipice, trying to decide if I can do this—if I can put myself out there one more time, even though my love life is a perpetual disaster.

I want this. I really do. And he knows it.

"It's true," he says, running his fingertips down my jaw, then teasing my lip with his thumb. "I haven't hooked up with anyone since before my injury."

I stop breathing. "Really? That long ago?"

"Really," he says, almost absently. His talented fingers trace the top edge of my bikini top, over the swells of my breasts, teasing my sensitive skin. "I used to think something was wrong with me. But now I think I know better." Those gray eyes look up, boring into mine. "I was missing you. I was waiting all this time for you to come back into my life. And now you're here."

A shiver runs up my spine. But it's the good kind. "You are very persuasive," I whisper.

"It's easy to be when you're telling the truth. Now come closer and let me show you." He beckons to me with a crooked finger. "That's a girl. A little further. And feel free to crawl toward me at any time. *Yesss.*" His hands reach for me, skimming my bare ribcage, pulling me in. I land on him, and it isn't very graceful.

But no matter. He rolls, pulling me to the blanket, his generous mouth finding mine. His kiss is a searing press of lips and heat. He licks into my mouth a moment later, and I open for him, as obedient as a baby bird.

"*Yesss,*" he murmurs again, rolling us until he's on top, braced on strong forearms above me. "That's more like it." He kisses me again, while I give in and explore his sculpted chest with my fingertips.

He was right about one thing—it's easy to lose your train of thought while kissing Rickie. My hesitation evaporates faster than the water that's still clinging to our steamy skin. He leans in, chasing kiss after kiss, his strong body a needy weight against mine.

I've never done this before. I've never kissed a man on a blanket under the trees. And I've certainly never let one tug the straps of my bathing suit off my shoulders, and then expose my breasts one by one to the dusky sky.

"Take the top off," he murmurs, leaning down to tongue my nipple. "I need it out of my way."

My hands do his bidding, even if getting naked outside feels brazen. As the cool air peaks my nipples, it occurs to me that I'm not a good girl anymore. I tried to be, but I failed spectacularly.

And the casual slide of Rickie's roughened thumbs across my bare breasts has me too distracted to care how far I've fallen. I just want more of this reckless feeling. I thread my fingers through his hair and pull his head down to my chest. A moment later, his wicked tongue runs amok over my nipples.

This is exactly what I need. My hands find their way to the waist-band of his bathing suit. I slip my fingers past the fabric and wrap my palm around his hard length.

The kiss he's delivering to the valley between my breasts halts its path. And he makes a low groan of surprise and delight as I stroke him. "I love that," he says huskily.

"Of course you do." I swipe a thumb across his tip, and he makes a masculine grunt of pleasure.

"Baby, you can touch me all day long." He rolls lazily out of my grasp. "But that's not what I meant. I love it when you let go. When you finally say *fuck it* and take what you want. Now *that's* sexy."

Then he lifts his hips and turns away, shedding his bathing suit, tossing it aside. When he turns back to me, he's wearing nothing but a fearless smile. Confidence is my drug of choice, apparently.

We lean in at the same time, and my smile rejoins his. He moans into our kiss, and the sound is so raw and hungry that I feel it between my legs. Then his hand is there, pulling off the last scrap of my bathing suit. My body quivers happily.

And then I'm naked on a blanket with Rickie, ready to give him anything and everything he wants from me.

TWENTY-NINE

RICKIE

During high school my parents were briefly stationed in the United Kingdom, where their rental flat had a gas fireplace. You turned on the gas and tossed in a match, and it instantly lit with flames.

That's how I feel whenever I touch Daphne. Yet I've tried to hold back the wave of need that rolls through my body whenever we're together. She deserves a better man. One who's less of a wreck.

Yet I'm the one she wants. And she's so beautiful when she decides to let loose. The arch of her back as I kiss her. The hot look in her brown eyes asks for more.

And I've got more. I've got deep kisses and skin that sizzles as soon as it brushes against hers. I've got clever hands, and a whole lot of hunger. Daphne never believes me when I tell her how much I care for her. She doesn't trust it. But I'd give every last piece of myself to her, if she'd let me. Every damn drop.

Promises aren't on her mind right now. Just sex. And I aim to deliver. Dropping my hips onto hers, I rest my cock in the cradle of her body, where she can't miss my arousal or my crude intentions.

Even though it's a hot night, she shivers beneath me, lifting her hips on a whimper. Upping the ante, I spread her legs with mine. Our next kiss is wild and deep. Her long legs tangle with mine, and her hands skim all over my skin in a way that's more desperate than tender.

I love it. But God, I need to slow down. My body is tightly coiled with need. I run a hand down and up the smooth skin of her inner thigh, and I swear my fingertips are shaking as I delve between the petals of her body.

"Oh *yes*," she whimpers as my cock gives a helpless throb.

I take a deep, slow breath, and lower my mouth to her breast. I kiss her slowly there, even as her heart thuds against my cheek. "Sweetheart," I rasp. "What are the odds there are condoms in your brother's truck?"

"Who cares?" Her hands land in my hair and stroke. "We don't need one."

"You sure?"

"Promise," she breathes. "Women's reproductive health is my jam."

Holy hell. I let out a choked laugh and give a silent prayer of thanks for my good fortune. My celibate streak no longer seems weird at all to me. Clearly I was waiting for Daphne Shipley.

The wait is over. So I rise up onto my elbows and reverently kiss both her breasts again. Then her neck, and the tender place beneath her ear.

Then I brace her in my arms. And, looking down into her serious brown eyes, I nudge her entrance with the head of my cock. We lock gazes as I slowly feed it to her, inch by slow inch, taking my time not because I have to, but because I don't want to forget even a moment of this.

Her kiss-bitten lips fall open as she moans my name. And I realize I'm holding my breath, for good reason. I'm in a wet, tight heaven, with nothing between us. I can feel everything, and it's almost too much to handle.

I draw a slow breath, feeling very much like a bomb that might suddenly go off.

"Rickie," she whispers.

"Yes, gorgeous?"

Her eyes seem to find their focus. "I like *you*, too."

"That is really good to hear." My next kiss is soft and sweet. But that's the only part of me that is. I have to move. And when I slowly roll my hips, we both groan. Daphne arches up to meet me, her cheeks flushed with pleasure.

If I can make this last more than a few minutes, it'll be a damn miracle. Especially since she starts making heady little gasps every time I thrust. *More. Yes. Harder.*

I move slowly, drawing out each shift of my hips. I'm sure I've never concentrated so hard on anything else before in my life. I don't want to miss a moment of this bliss. Soft lips caress my own, and long fingers grip my shoulders as I move.

Daphne strains upward against me, needing more. But the ground is hard beneath us, and I don't want to bruise her. So I hook my arms around her and roll onto my back.

She looks down at me a moment later, a little dazed. But she wastes no time bracing her hands on the earth and beginning to ride me.

Sweat is dripping off me now. Everything is sweet, sweet heaven. Her steamy gaze holds mine as she moves.

And even if I fall off *three* more walls—head first—there's still no way I could ever forget this perfect moment.

"Rickkkk," Daphne breathes. Her forehead creases with effort, and she bites her lip. And a new wave of lust rolls through me as I watch the storm gather behind her eyes.

"Have at it, baby," I whisper, trailing my fingertips down her body. "Love watching you ride me." Then I drop my hand to the place where we're joined.

On a high-pitched gasp, she turns her face away from me, catching her bottom lip in her teeth.

"Christ, you're beautiful. Eyes over here," I rasp, as my balls tighten dangerously. I lift a hand to her chin and turn her head, begging her to look at me.

When she does, I get a glimpse of everything she hides from the world. Her expression is pure fire, and pure need.

And I'm done for. "Look out," I say, clamping my jaw together to stave off my climax. But it doesn't work. I break like a seawall in a hurricane. My hips slam upward and I groan as it slams through me.

"Oh yes. Oh—" Daphne gasps.

I roll my hips again, and she slides down onto my chest with a moan and a blissed-out shiver. I clamp my arms around her and hold on tight, unwilling to let go of her yet. And she flops her head onto my shoulder with a tired sigh. "Holy macaroni," she mutters.

I look up at the darkening sky and smile like the crazy man that I am.

THIRTY

DAPHNE

Wow.

Just wow.

I'm slumped onto Rickie's body, feeling like I might never move again. But as my brain comes back online, a few important realizations are making themselves known to me.

1. That was mind-blowing. Seriously. I had no idea.

2. We're still joined together, and his arms are braced around me.

2a. I like it. A lot.

3. I'm probably going to do it again. If I get the chance.

3a. I hope I get the chance.

Rickie lets out a low chuckle suddenly, and I wonder if I did or said something ridiculous in the throes of passion. So—with great difficulty—I pick up my head and look at him.

He's grinning broadly.

"What?" I demand. I'm feeling the first twinges of a vulnerability hangover already.

He pushes the hair off of my sweaty face. "I'm just happy, that's all. I'll probably be smiling for a week."

"Oh." My face flushes with self-consciousness, and I lift my hips off his body, finally separating us. And he lets out a happy groan.

I scramble to my feet and walk back over to the swimming hole, where I jump right in. Even this feels ridiculously sensual. I haven't ever been skinny-dipping before. I was always the kid who was too self-conscious to throw off my clothes and jump in with the others.

But I just had naked outdoor sex with my brother's roommate. Now there's something I never planned to do on my summer vacation. I guess I'm not the shy kid anymore. Go figure.

There's a loud Rickie-sized splash beside me, and I try to wipe off the look of wonder I must be wearing on my face and play it cool.

But Rickie doesn't give me the chance. He hauls me closer and kisses me, his wet skin seal-like against my own. "Damn, Shipley," he says against my tongue. "We are totally coming back here. Probably tomorrow."

"It's supposed to rain tomorrow," I say, because I never was cool. "Eighty percent chance."

He doesn't roll his eyes, or smile. He just looks at me with a serious expression, his gray eyes darkening in the fading light. "The hayloft then," he whispers. And then he kisses me again.

I manage to play it cool when we drive up to the house in our bathing suits and towels a little while later. Cool enough, anyway. My mother is on the phone, which helps. I don't have to look anyone in the eye and try to explain why I look dazzled and frazzled.

I head straight upstairs. And a half hour later I hear Rickie whistling in the shower. I hide in my room, lying curled up on the quilt, my body more relaxed than it's been in ages.

Desire is a wonderful drug. I'm happy for the dose I just had. But old habits die hard, so I'm already bracing myself in case he distances himself after this.

Honestly, even if he forgets my name again tomorrow, it might have been worth it. Nobody has made me feel sexy in a long time. And even if Rickie is out of my league, I know in my heart that he's no Reardon Halsey. He's not going to lie to me or betray me.

My hair is still damp, and my muscles are loose. The sultry summer air blowing into the window smells sweet.

And when my phone chimes, I almost don't bother checking it. I don't want anyone to kill the high I'm riding. But maybe it's Violet. And curiosity wins, so I peek.

It's not Violet. It's Rickie. *Gorgeous, can I come in for a second?*

Maybe, I say, playing coy. *What do you need?*

A good night kiss, he says.

All right, I agree.

The door opens a few seconds later. Rickie appears, chest bare, hair damp. And my heart leaps at the sight of his smooth body slipping into the room as he pulls the door shut behind him.

He wastes no time climbing onto the bed beside me and leaning in for a kiss that's surprisingly sweet. "Promise me something," he whispers.

"What?" I ask, my brain temporarily scrambled by the way his strong arms gather me up and hold me close. My cheek comes to rest against his chest, and I can feel his stubble graze across my other ear.

"Promise me you won't climb inside your head and think up fifty reasons why that was a terrible idea."

"Okay," I agree immediately. Even though it's a distinct possibility.

"Uh huh," he says knowingly. "You may not realize it yet, but this is happening."

"Pretty sure it already did," I mumble against his warmth.

"I don't mean the sex. Although there's plenty more where that came from. I mean this." He lifts my chin and stares deeply into my eyes. Then he gives me a slow kiss. "And this." I receive another kiss. "But also more dates. Dinners out. I want it all."

I blink up at him, feeling a little dazed by another Rickie-inspired hormone rush. "All of what?"

"All of you," he says with a low rumble. "I realize you're still getting used to the idea."

My stomach does the swoop thing. "I tried not to like you. But it didn't work."

"I know, baby girl." He gives me his cockiest grin. "Sorry about that. What can I do to help take away the pain of this failure you've suffered?"

He's joking, but I'm not. "Just don't ever lie to me. That's what I need from a man."

"Ah." His expression goes serious. "All right. I promise."

"Thank you," I whisper. I wish he'd stop being so dreamy. A girl can't think with a man like Rickie holding her in her bed.

"Don't mention it," he says. I get one more kiss. "Good night and sweet dreams."

"Good night."

He gets up and walks away. And just the view of his backside starts those good dreams flowing even before I shut out the light.

THIRTY-ONE

DAPHNE

It's August, and the first apples are ripening, which means the farm is suddenly busy again. And my first semester's tuition has come due in full, so I'm a little stressed out about money, even though I know Mom already wrote the check.

When you blow up your life, there's a lot of damage control afterwards. I knew my summer would be complicated.

But then there's Rickie, with his hot glances and surreptitious kisses. As much as it kills me to admit I was wrong about someone, I'm a convert now. Maybe it's the sex we've been sneaking around to have in odd places. Maybe it's the way he sneaks into my room to kiss me good night every single evening.

I like him a little more every day. That doesn't mean I find it easy to say so again. I'm still wary, and still wondering whether he'll get sick of me. I hope it's not soon, because Rickie makes everything more fun.

This morning he's entertaining the whole breakfast table with a story about having a stare-down with a porcupine. And instead of scowling, I'm laughing along with everyone else.

"See, I didn't know what they might be able do with those quills," he says, his glass of iced tea sweating in the grip of his strong hand. "I thought—can he shoot them like guns? Can this porcupine turn me into swiss cheese?"

"No!" Dylan says, laughing. "That's ridiculous."

"But I didn't *know* that," Rickie explains. "And I wasn't about to sign myself up for some accidental acupuncture. So I just stood there on the path, holding my ground, you know? I flexed my biceps, just to make myself as fearsome as possible. Just in case this porcupine was easily impressed."

He flexes in his chair, and everyone howls.

"He wasn't, by the way. He just stood there, and I was afraid to turn my back on him. Finally I sort of made a run for it around him. And that is why I was five minutes late for breakfast. At least you're not planning my funeral, you know?"

"No one has ever been killed by a porcupine," my mother says, dabbing her eyes.

"As far as you *know*," Rickie corrects, while Grandpa slaps his knee.

I get up and fetch the coffeepot, because I want another drop before we get on the road to Burlington. It's Wednesday now—my favorite day of the week. When Rickie drives me to work and kisses me goodbye in the parking lot.

In the kitchen I grab both the coffeepot and the iced tea pitcher, because I've figured out that Rickie isn't really a coffee drinker if there's tea available. So I keep the pitcher full when I can.

Back in the dining room I pour coffee for Grandpa and myself, and then pass the pot to my brother. Then I refill Rickie's glass, and I feel his fingertips graze the back of my knee. It's just a discreet touch of gratitude.

But I love it. My pulse quickens whenever we're in the same room, too. It's been a long time since I let myself feel this kind of joy. It's heady. It's risky. But I can't help myself.

"You're done with your class now, right?" my brother is saying. "What will you do after you turn in the paper?"

"I'm picking up the keys to the house from the rental agent," Rickie says. "My renter left town yesterday, and the house is all mine again. While Daphne's at work, I'll go to the storage unit and load up our boxes into your truck, and drive them back to the house."

"Oh, man," Dylan says. "You should have said something. You want help?"

"Nah, it's fine," Rickie says quickly. "I don't mind moving your stuff around. It's just a few boxes of books and clothes. You can carry it upstairs yourself, okay?"

"Of course," my brother says. Then he glances up at me. "Any more thoughts about your housing situation, Daphne? Have you been looking for a place?"

"I looked at a couple listings," I say casually. The truth is that I haven't done much, and there's only three weeks left. "There's always the dorms."

"Maybe you should stop by the Spruce Street house after work," Dylan says. "Take a look at Rickie's extra bedroom and see what you think."

"What a great idea," Rickie says brightly.

I don't dare glance at him because I'd probably blush furiously. He's mentioned the house a couple of times, but I keep deferring the conversation. If everything goes south with him, I don't want us to be roommates.

On the other hand, I need somewhere to live, and I need a plan. Fast. "Sure, I'll take a look." Then I carry the coffeepot back to the kitchen to end the conversation.

On the way into town, I become absorbed with reading something.

So absorbed that I don't notice we've arrived at the first delivery site until Rickie kills the truck's engine.

I look up, startled. A whole hour has gone by while I ignored him? "Sorry," I say quickly.

He snickers. "You used to fight me on who could drive the truck, babe. I'm not complaining that you're busy reading..." He leans in to see my laptop screen. "A grad school application? UC Berkeley?"

"They just went live," I explain, clicking my laptop shut. "It's application season again. And since my transcript is going to look incredibly strange, I need to do an A+ job on the essays and supplements."

"I see," he says quietly. "California, huh?"

"Maybe. Or Baltimore. Cambridge. New York City. I need to apply to every top program and pray that one of them can see past my senior year transfer."

He nods slowly. "Got a safety school picked out?"

"Sure. I could probably stay here in Vermont. My summer job—which will soon become my all-year job—means I can probably win over the Moo U crowd."

Those gray eyes measure me. "But you don't want to stay here."

"I can't stay here," I say quickly. "I mean I could, but I just can't."

He cocks his head. "Come again?"

"Well, it's just that I—" How to put this in a way that won't make me sound like a snob or a bitch? Seconds tick by while I come to the realization that there *isn't* a way. Maybe I am a snob and a bitch.

He waits.

"I've invested everything into this career path," I say slowly. "Other girls had lots of fun. And other girls had boyfriends. I studied. I put all my chips on one thing, and that thing was an Ivy League education. My family invested in me, too. Dylan went part-time to school when I went full-time."

"That was his choice," Rickie points out.

"Yeah, mostly," I concede. "But it kept costs down at home. And now he's behind and trying to catch up so he can graduate and get back to taking care of business. I have to finish what I started. That means getting into a top program and getting great funding."

"So this is about money?" He gives me the eyebrow quirk. "Burlington would cost more?"

"It's unclear," I admit. "But it's not a top program."

"What makes a top program a top program?" he asks.

"Um..." This is not a question I want to answer. "Bigger programs do more research. They have more connections. For later. Berkley is a huge program."

"I see," he says calmly. But I hear something else in there. Like I've let him down somehow. "You like California?"

"I've never been," I admit. "But it's really far away from Harkness, Connecticut. And that's the other reason I need to get into a top program. If I don't, if I settle for second best, then *he* wins the battle."

"Uh huh," Rickie says flatly. "Course, if his actions send you five thousand miles away from people who love you, arguments could be made that he's still driving this bus."

My jaw drops. But before I can formulate a response, he opens the truck's door, gets out, and delivers the first crate of liquor of the day.

I put my laptop away. And I'm simmering with irritation when he comes back to the truck. But I don't say anything, because Rickie isn't wrong. Everything I do is informed by *My Biggest Mistake*.

Not that it's any of Rickie's business.

And it's not like I have a choice. My own mistakes got me here. All I can do is make the best of it. Berkley, California would be the best of it.

Not that I really want to move five thousand miles away and start over making new friends. *Again*.

My thoughts fester as we make two more deliveries. And I've worked myself up into a Major Snit™ by the time Rickie pulls into a parking spot right in front of the School of Public Health.

I grab my backpack off the floor and reach for the door handle.

"Hey, Shipley, hold up." He pulls the keys out of the ignition and turns to face me. "I'm gonna need a kiss before I go."

Even though I'm a little annoyed at him, my stomach does the same swoopy thing it always does when he trains those perceptive eyes on me.

But a glance out the window shows me that Karim is standing right in front of the building, his phone to his ear. And I don't want to make a spectacle of myself at work. "Make it quick, McFly," I say. "My coworkers can see us."

He reaches up and cups my face in his hand. "See, I don't have a problem getting you all hot and flustered in public places. But that's just me."

I roll my eyes, even though his touch feels so nice. "Trying to be a professional here. Stop making it difficult."

He chuckles. Then he leans in and kisses me softly. It's quick, and leaves me hungry for more.

"Damn, Shipley. When you look at me like that, it's tough to let you walk away."

I swallow hard. But then I open the door and climb out.

"Daphne!" Karim calls out. He's watching me now with a smile on his face. *Oh boy.* "How's it going?"

"Great," I say as Rickie climbs out of the other side of the truck.

"We're doing karaoke tonight at the Biscuit," he says. "You guys should come."

"What time?" Rickie asks, as if this were up to him. "I'm Rickie, by the way."

"I know," Karim says, walking closer and offering his hand for a shake. "I was in the psych seminar last year when you were a guest speaker."

"Ah, yeah. It was fun to be the class freak for a day, I guess." Rickie crosses his tattooed arms, and Karim blatantly checks him out.

"Hey, I thought your story was so cool," says my coworker, Rickie's new fanboy. "We head over to the Biscuit in the Basket from five-thirty onward," he says. "First we eat two-for-one wings, and then karaoke starts up around six."

I open my mouth to shoot down this idea. But not before Rickie says, "Awesome, we'll be there."

What the...?

"Cool!" Karim says, with a smile a mile wide.

And I can't believe I've just been snookered into karaoke. Although Karim and Jenn have been hinting that I should join them, and it feels wrong to say no all the time. But *karaoke*? That's not something you do with new coworkers. *Yikes.*

I shoot Rickie an evil glare.

He smiles.

"I have to text my family," I say stiffly. "In case I'm needed at home."

"Get on that then." Karim points at the building. "I'd better go in."

"Right," I say quickly. "Me too." I shoulder my pack. "I'll just be a second."

I wait for Karim to walk out of earshot. Then I turn on Rickie. "What did you do *that* for?"

"Because karaoke is fun?" he shrugs, like this is so obvious. "I won't drink more than one beer, so I can still drive home."

"You can go ahead and drink," I hiss, "Because there's no *way* I would get drunk with a microphone in my hand in front of colleagues. Jesus."

He laughs. "Okay. It's a date. Before that—meet me at the house at five? To see the place. You remember where it is?"

"Yes," I grunt.

"Great. See you then." He tugs on my hand and gives me a quick kiss. "Later, gorgeous."

My cheeks flame. "Later."

He walks away, smiling.

Naturally, Karim is waiting for me by the door. "You sneaky Pete!" he crows as soon as I enter the building. "You told me you two were just roommates."

"It's complicated," I grumble. "He's hot, but annoying."

"My heart is breaking," he says, sneaking one more look through the glass doors at Rickie's departing figure. "That boy looks *tasty* with a suntan."

Damn it all, he isn't wrong.

"Does he have a good voice? If he sings some kind of sexy ballad at karaoke, I may not recover."

"I haven't heard him sing," I say. But then I realize I have.

Twice.

THIRTY-TWO

RICKIE

Even with my class finished, my Wednesday is a busy day. I turn in my last philosophy paper, then pick up my keys from the rental agent. Then I head over to the house and check the place out, just to make sure the tenants left everything in order.

They did. The place is spotless. But as I walk around my empty house, listening to my own footsteps, I remember why I always fill the place with roommates. I do better with people near me. Not in my bedroom, but near it.

Christ, I'm weird.

Even so, I practically bounce into Lenore's office for my session.

"Someone's in a good mood," she observes.

"Yeah, it's been a good week." I actually drag the chair closer to her desk and prop my feet on it.

"Comfortable?"

"Yup. I got my house back today. I'm moving back in soon."

She cocks her head. "With or without a new roommate?"

"Daphne hasn't said. But I'll win her over." I give her a dazzling smile. "Short commute to my bed and all."

"So I take it things are going well in the Daphne department."

"I've got no complaints, and neither does she."

Lenore laughs. "Noted. How are you sleeping?"

"Apart, if that's what you mean."

"I meant generally. Any more nightmares?"

213

"Well, sometimes." I kick my feet back down onto the floor. "And now I see his face in them."

"Daphne's ex?"

"Yeah." I rake a hand through my hair. "It's creepy as fuck."

"What does he do in these dreams?" Lenore asks me. "Anything new?"

"No—not one thing. I see his face by my bed. And then I always wake up."

"Okay." She chews her lip. It's her tell, so now I'm wary. "Did you pick your classes yet?"

"For the fall? We can't turn in a schedule until the twenty-seventh."

"But have you thought it through?" she asks.

Good grief. "Lenore, why are you suddenly so interested in my course load? Avoidance is not a good look on you. Whatever you have to say, just say it."

She blows out a breath. "I called the Academy. I made another attempt to find out more."

"Oh." My blood stops circulating. "I forgot about that."

"It wasn't helpful," she says quickly. "It was merely infuriating."

Something inside me relaxes, and I'm not even sure why. "Okay. Were they dicks?"

"You could say that." She picks at a fingernail. "I went off script, Rick. And it didn't even help."

"What did you ask?"

She lifts her eyes to mine, and they are so sad. "I said you had PTSD, and we couldn't discover the source of it."

"That's not, uh, inaccurate," I point out.

"Right. But then I said that it might be sexual in nature." She presses her hands together, as if trying not to fidget. "This guy was a stone wall. So then I implied that I was treating you for symptoms that a rape survivor might exhibit."

I feel a nauseating rush inside my chest, and the question screaming through my brain is, *Why would you say that?*

Then again I'd asked Lenore to shake things up. "And what was their response?"

"He said..." She puts her head in her hands. "He said—*that's ridiculous. A man can't be raped.*"

"Oh," I say slowly. It takes me a second to realize that this doesn't have a thing to do with me. But Lenore is upset. Her eyes are red, and her lips are tight. "That's a shit thing to say, right?"

"It's a *horrible* thing to say. It negates a very real problem and perpetuates a societal stigma. I've treated men who have been assaulted, and they don't need that kind of *bullshit* in their lives."

"You're right," I say quickly. "It's awful."

"So bad." She rubs her temples. "I'm sorry I couldn't wheedle anything out of them. They said to call the hospital, which I will do. But the hospital won't actually have any kind of incident report. Just treatment details."

"Okay. It's all right, Lenore. You tried. I'm sorry it was upsetting."

She looks up at me, her expression sad. "I sit here all day asking my patients to deal with difficult truths, you know? It's hard work to tell the truth. And some asshole at a military academy tells me that sexual assault doesn't happen to men."

"It's outrageous," I agree. "What a shittastic place. Good thing I don't remember a single thing about it." I give her a sly smile.

"Stop," she says. "You're not supposed to have to cheer your therapist up. I'm sorry. I'm just angry."

"Me too, lady. But not today."

She smiles. "No? Why?"

"Got nothing to be angry about. My girl is slowly coming around. I'm not free and clear yet, but I'm getting close."

"I see." Her smile reappears. "And what's your big plan there?"

"Karaoke. It's the secret to life."

"I'm sorry, *what?*" Lenore giggles.

"Daphne thinks she has to always have her shit locked down. Like it would kill her to show any weakness. But her coworker invited us for karaoke tonight. She didn't want to say yes, but I forced her hand."

"Women love that," Lenore deadpans.

"Yeah, yeah. She needs to be social with these people, though. She already admitted that. And karaoke has this way of making you realize you don't have to be amazing all the time to have fun and be loved."

"You went all guru there, didn't you?" She waves a hand toward me. "It's a good look on you. This poor girl doesn't stand a chance. What are you going to sing?"

"I haven't decided yet. Something devastating."

"Looking forward to the video of this," Lenore says. "Feel free to share."

I spend the afternoon unpacking my first-floor bedroom. It's satisfying to stack my winter clothes back inside my empty dresser drawers. I make my bed, too, with the mattress pad I'd stored away, and my clean sheets.

This house is a rift between my father and me, but I sure like having a place that's all mine. I'd actually wondered if letting strangers rent this house for the summer would bother me.

But, nope. This room still feels like my sanctuary. The shelf over my bed is just waiting for me to stack the reference books there in a tidy row. I have framed maps on the walls of all the places I've been— the city in Germany where I lived for a few years. And the one in Japan.

And there's a box of knickknacks that I save for last. It's full of souvenirs from various trips I took over the years. There's a carved set of dragons eating each others' tails that I found at a flea market in Hong Kong. And a weird little mermaid figurine from Copenhagen.

The doorbell rings, and I realize I've lost track of time. It's five o'clock already. And I am more than ready to see if Daphne is still pissed at me. I hope not. I'm ready to drag her off to eat two-for-one wings and sing in front of her coworkers.

I trot through the house and pull open the front door. "Hi, gorgeous. Miss me?"

"Looking for compliments, McFly?" She crosses her arms over her chest.

"Still pissed about the karaoke, huh?"

"Only because you didn't ask me first." She cocks her head to the side. "I should go out with those guys. They're good people."

"I'm glad," I say, waving her into the foyer. "You deserve good people around you. Like me."

She sniffs. "Give me the tour, McFly. Then we can eat some chicken wings and I can listen to you sing."

I take her hand. "I was thinking we could do a duet."

"Nope. You're the only one who's going to sing."

"Huh." I guess I can press this issue later. "This is my living room." I wave a hand into that room. "It needs new furniture, but I like to throw parties, so I'm afraid to upgrade. We really only sit in there on the weekends, when we're trying to get over our hangovers."

"My weekends don't usually include a hangover," Daphne shares.

"Well, that's your loss, then, because I make an excellent hangover tea, and I'm pretty good at soups, too. Come and see my kitchen."

I lead her toward my favorite room in the house, with its sturdy wood floors and its old-fashioned windows. The appliances are old, but in a fun way. There's a curvy green refrigerator and a matching range. There are orange Formica countertops in a spacious L shape, and a roomy nook for the mid-century diner-style table and the chairs I'd picked out.

"Oh. This is so *cute*," Daphne says.

"Isn't it?" I agree. "It's my favorite room for studying or cooking or just wasting time with your brother." I park my hip against the counter and study Daphne, who is trying so hard not to like my kitchen, or picture herself in it. I can see the fight raging behind her brown eyes.

My girl is so afraid to settle in to anything. She thinks that if she trusts me, I might betray her. And if she makes herself at home in this kitchen, she's afraid she might not want to leave again. "Take a breath, baby girl. You don't have to plan your whole life today."

Her eyes narrow with irritation. "I wasn't trying to plan my whole life. Just the next year."

"Yeah, my bad. Come on. I'll show you the best stop on the tour."

"The empty room?"

"Nope. Even better. My room."

"I should have known." She gives me a quick smile, and when I hold out my hand, she takes it.

As I thread our fingers together and lead her toward the back of the house. I congratulate myself for having made the bed. *Well done, subconscious.* This is the most privacy she and I have had together in a while. Possibly ever.

"Nice," she whispers when I lead her into my sunny bedroom overlooking the backyard.

"I got a lot done today." That's why it's so tranquil in here already. The books are back on the shelves. The empty boxes are already gone. The only thing left is the remaining knickknacks I've half unpacked.

That box is on the bed, so I pick it up and empty the last few things onto the top of my dresser, to sort later.

"What's this?" Daphne picks up a large coin and turns it over on her palm.

"That's from Thailand."

"God, I want to travel," she says with a sigh. "So badly. But there hasn't been time. Or money."

"I took a gap year. Worked a bunch of jobs. Took some trips." It was amazing, and I wish Daphne could do the same.

"What's this? And this?"

She touches each of my trinkets with gentle hands, while I explain every coin and object. "That's just an ordinary espresso spoon from the flea market on Portobello Road in London. I try to find something small to bring back from a market in every county. Bonus points if it's something useful. If I don't find the right object, I keep a coin instead."

"And this?" She taps a little wooden box. "Where's this from?"

"Ah, that's from Vermont. But it's a mystery."

"What do you mean?"

"That got shipped home from the Academy with the rest of my stuff. I had some Christmas presents in there—a book for my dad, and something for my mom. But this thing didn't have a tag on it. I don't know who it was supposed to be for. And it's weird as fuck. Open it."

She lifts the lid of the little wooden box to reveal the world's strangest piece of jewelry. It's basically an ugly insect-like critter cast in silver, on a silver chain. "Apparently I mailed a photo of this thing to my mom and asked her to get one of her friends from the League of Craftsmen to make it. But I don't know why."

Daphne makes a strange sound. Like a choked gasp. When she looks up at me, her brown eyes actually fill with tears.

"Whoa now," I say, wrapping an arm around her. "What did I miss?"

"It's a water flea."

"Um..." That means nothing to me. A tear escapes from her eye, and I catch it with my thumb.

"The other name for it is a daphnia."

"Wait, what?" I lift the strange pendant out of her hands and stare at it. I see a strange creature with awkward appendages near his head. "Are you joking?"

She slowly shakes her head. "We had a discussion about my name. I told you that it was three things—a boring flower, a really depressing myth, and..."

"A water flea," I finish.

"You remember?"

"*No*," I choke out, dropping the pendant onto the dresser. "But I know *me*. And if I really liked you, it wouldn't stop me from propositioning you. But I would also go to the trouble to get a damn water flea cast in silver, and bring it to you on our date. So where *the fuck* did I go instead?" My hands are suddenly balled into fists. I'm sick to death of not knowing.

"Hey now," she says gently. "It's... I think it's really neat. This was waiting here all this time. And I found it."

"Yeah, so neat," I bite out, still angry. But I throw an arm around her and haul her against my chest anyway. "My little water flea."

One of her arms wraps around my back, and her hand lands on my abs. "No, it was sweet. It *is* sweet. I want to keep it."

"It's yours." I drop a kiss to her temple, but I'm so angry with myself that I'm practically bursting out of my skin.

"Nobody ever gave me such a thoughtful gift," she says, and her voice is almost as soft as her hands that are stroking me now. Calming me.

"Babe, maybe you didn't notice, but I failed to give it to you. You told me you have shit taste in men, right? And I had the balls to argue."

"Don't," she whispers. "Don't *do* that. Don't take back all the things you've said about us. Some bad things happened. But you're not allowed to pretend like none of the nice ones happened, either."

I let out one more angry curse, but I'm fighting a losing battle. Because Daphne is kissing the underside of my jaw. It doesn't seem to matter that I'm not in the mood to be soothed, because her mouth is soft and generous. My next harsh breath loses steam, becoming a shudder as she kisses her way down my throat, and into the V-neck of my T-shirt.

My anger is no match for her loveliness, apparently. Because suddenly I'm kissing her. And then—when her hand finds its way onto my thickening cock—I lose this little contest of wills.

Maybe it makes me a selfish bastard. But her hunger is all it takes to burn away my hesitation. I dive into the next kiss. I'm greedy for it, and I let her know, yanking her close as our kiss deepens. Bullying my tongue into her mouth.

If she wants this wreck of a man, she's going to get him. And I'm not in the mood to be subtle.

She isn't either. She tugs my T-shirt up, slipping smooth hands across my back. And I up the ante by grabbing the fabric and hauling it up and off my body. "Is this what you're after?" I growl.

She doesn't speak. But her serious eyes assure me that it is. Then she dips her head to taste the tattoo at my collarbone.

Once again I pull her in. Her hair is so soft between my fingers. And her tongue curls across my skin with a lovely stroke. She's making it hard to stay angry. She's making me just plain hard.

Especially because Daphne never does this—she doesn't come for me. I'm the one who has to ask for it.

But not today. She's kissing my neck. Her hands are in my back pockets.

I back her up toward the bed, since that's where this is headed. I lift off her blouse and toss it onto my desk chair. She's wearing a plain black bra, and the sight of it gives me a possessive rush. Daphne doesn't like to show her cards. But she shows them to me.

Only to me.

"You want to cheer me up?" I growl. "Then get on that bed."

Eyes wide, she sits down on the end of it and scuttles backward.

"Good girl."

I'm preparing to join her when I realize I've forgotten something important. Spinning around, I grab the pendant off the dresser and bring it with me to the bed. "This is yours," I say roughly. "I want you to wear it." Then I unhook the chain and drape it around her neck.

"Thank you," she whispers as I attach it.

She touches a finger to the pendant, where it's perched above her breasts. Her eyes get soft and lazy, like she sees right through me. Like she knows the storm will pass.

My anger ebbs a little further. And when I lean down for another kiss, it's the tender one that she deserves.

THIRTY-THREE

DAPHNE

We're on a bed. An actual bed. It's a damn miracle.

Late afternoon sunlight slants through Rickie's window as he nudges me further onto the mattress and removes my skirt.

Then he removes my panties.

Then he removes my bra.

And when he kicks off the last scraps of his own clothing, all that's left between us is a piece of jewelry depicting a daphnia in all its weird glory.

Rickie fingers the pendant, and his expression burns with promise. "Better late than never, I guess."

"Yes, I—"

Words desert me as he lowers his mouth to my breast and swirls his tongue around my nipple. I gasp as a sizzle of sensation rips through me.

I moan shamelessly, because I'm not shy anymore. And I'm no longer afraid to love him. So I shamelessly reach for his cock and stroke him.

He groans, and I smile up at the ceiling. It's not that my heart is suddenly bulletproof. It's just that I no longer have a choice about how I feel. He's gotten to me. And if I hold myself back, I might miss something.

That seems like a bad idea, since every touch of his hand sets me

222

on fire. Now he's dotting me with kisses, dropping them everywhere. My neck. My shoulders. My stomach. My—

I let out a shivery moan as he kisses his way up my inner thigh. "You don't have to go slow," I prompt. "I'm done resisting you."

His chuckle is low and throaty. "What if I want to?" He strokes a thumb so slowly over my core that I moan and clench my thighs.

Then he lowers his head and gives me his mouth. His kisses get hotter and wetter until I'm gripping his plain white comforter in two hands. "Please?" I hiss. "Now. I don't want to wait."

He looks up at me with molten eyes. "You ask so nice when you want me, Shipley." He pushes up, prowling up my body. Then— finally—he fits the blunt head of his cock against my entrance.

When he slowly, torturously, begins sliding home, I realize that I recognize the look on his face. It's a messy mix of hope and awe—and it's the same one I wore when I wondered how badly it would hurt if he loved me and left me.

I try to pull him down to kiss me. But he won't come. He hovers, watching me, drawing out this moment. I need him to move. So badly. But he's staring into my eyes instead. "Better late than never," he repeats, his voice raw.

"Yes," I gasp, too turned on to be articulate.

Then he leans down, right where I want him. "Christ, I need you," he says, pressing his mouth against mine. The kiss is slow and intentional.

Only then does he begin to move. And it's perfect.

Needless to say, we are late to karaoke.

After the slow, mind-melting sex, we stay curled up on the bed for a while. He mindlessly strokes my hair, while I indulge in sleepy daydreams about coming home at the end of the day to this man in this bed.

I know I'm getting ahead of myself. But when you're curled up naked next to Rickie, it's hard not to dream.

Eventually we get up. We shower together, which leads to shower sex.

Only after that do we pull ourselves together and walk over to the sports bar. When Rickie and I stroll in holding hands, someone is just finishing up a Cindy Lauper song on the little stage, and everyone starts clapping.

Since it's an August Wednesday, and this is a college bar, the place is only half full. It makes it easy to spot the public health crew at a large table along the wall. Jenn and Karim wave us over. They're accompanied by two graduate students I've met at work.

"You made it!" Jenn says, clearly surprised.

"Sorry we're late, we had a few things to take care of." Rickie says this with a straight face, and I hope I'm not blushing. My fingers find the daphnia pendant at my neck and worry it.

Maybe all the clichés are true, but I feel like a new person after spending an hour or so in Rickie's bed. It's not just that I am more relaxed than I've been in a long time. Maybe ever.

But I also feel like we're a team. And I've never had that before—this sense that I'm building a strong bond with someone. Rickie and I know each other's secrets. We've seen each other's pain.

Until now, I didn't understand why that was sexy. I would have thought the opposite was true. Who wants to share pain and misfortune?

Me, apparently. When Rickie got angry today, I just wanted to soothe him. Because I've been angry, too. And he deserves better. So I told him—with my body. And he listened.

Now he pulls out a chair for me, and his hand on my lower back is more than just a caress. It's an acknowledgment. Of us.

"Here guys," Karim says, pushing slips of paper toward us. "Write down what you're singing."

Rickie grabs a menu. "This requires some thought. And probably some french fries."

"Yeah, okay. But if you need a partner for a duet, I'm your man," Karim says to Rickie.

"I'll keep that in mind," Rickie says, grinning. His hand slides onto my knee. "What are you singing?"

"Nothing."

"Hey," Karim complains. "Everybody sings."

He's winding up to say more when the DJ interrupts with an announcement. "The next singer is Karim. And Jenn is on deck."

Karim slides out of his chair. "Pick a song," he insists as he goes.

"I'll help you pick," Jenn says. She slides a stack of laminated lists toward us. It's held together by a metal ring. "I'm working my way through Whitney Houston's repertoire."

"You probably have a great voice."

"Nope!" she says gleefully. "Whitney is probably turning over in her grave. But it's fun." She turns her attention to Karim, and the first bars of his song play as he grips the mic.

"I don't sing," I whisper to Rickie. "At least not in front of coworkers."

"Daphne," he says, his rich voice right in my ear. "You're not supposed to sound amazing. It's a bonding experience. The point is to show your soft, off-key underbelly to your colleagues, so they know you're human."

I know he's right, but I still don't want to.

"What if we did a duet?" Rickie offers. "You can pick the song."

"Really?"

"Sure." He pulls one of the paper slips toward himself. "I'll do one by myself, too. What the hell."

On the stage, Karim starts to sing. The song is "Father Figure" by George Michael. It starts off kind of low and whispery. And he sounds competent enough.

But then it rises in pitch and tension, and he nails every note. Rickie leans forward in his chair. "Wow, right?"

"Wow," I agree.

"He's our ringer," Jenn says. "And he has a thing for George Michael. If you don't know what to pick, just put him down for a duet on 'Freedom' and be done with it. Everything sounds good with Karim."

Rickie nudges me under the table. "I want to sing with you."

"You do?"

"Totally. Although I suppose we could have a threesome."

I actually giggle. "Just the two of us is plenty. I'll pick something."

"Anything," he says, kissing my cheek as Karim croons into the mic.

"What if you don't know the song?"

"I'll fake it." He shrugs. "Want a four-cheese bacon burger and fries? That's what I'm getting."

"Yes, please."

He flags down the waitress while I scan the karaoke list like there will be a test later. What would Rickie sing with me?

My eye stops on a particular song. It's one that I *know* he knows. Hmm.

Karim finishes the song with a flourish, and we all cheer loudly.

"Come on, Shipley," Karim says when he returns to the table, flushed with victory. "Pick a song."

"Fine, fine." I scribble down my song just as the waitress arrives to take our order.

"Huh. Interesting choice," Karim says, shamelessly looking over my shoulder. "That's a little dark, Shipley."

"What did you pick?" Rickie asks.

"You'll find out in time to sing it with me."

"Mine is a duet, too," Rickie says. "Karim, can you help me with this?" He passes my coworker a slip of paper.

Karim hoots with laughter. "Oh, man. Totally. You are a good time." Karim hands both slips of paper to the waitress.

"What did you pick?" I ask.

"You'll find out," Rickie says, repeating my own irritating words to me.

The waitress peeks at the slip of paper in her hand. "Ooh, I'm going to make sure I'm not on break when you sing this." She gives Rickie a big smile. "Now what would you like from the bar?"

"Tequila," I grunt. "But it's a bad idea. I'll have water instead."

Rickie laughs.

As I wait for my song, my discomfort turns to dread. The waitress brings our food, and the burger is delicious, with a garlicky local goat cheese on it. But I only eat half. Rickie also ordered me, of all things, a Shipley cider.

"Thought you could use the comforts of home," he says when I recognize it on the first sip.

"That's so cool that your family makes cider," Jenn says.

"My brother has plans for world domination," I tell her. "He's making applejack now, too. They have it at Vino and Veritas on Church Street."

"Oh, I like that place," Karim says, bobbing his head. "Hey Rickie! Our song is up!" He cackles. "Brace yourself, Shipley. Your man is about to sing you a poppy love song. I can't even handle it."

"Which poppy love song?"

Rickie gives me a smack on the cheek. "You'll see."

He and Karim confer as they walk toward the little stage. They each get a mic, and the introduction kicks in. Both of them sway back and forth, and Karim snaps rhythmically to the easy beat.

"This song is for Daphne," Rickie says, just before he begins to sing.

My face heats, and I still don't recognize the song. But Jenn lets out a hoot. "Omigod, he's doing Meghan Trainor! That is adorable."

It takes me another minute. I paste a smile on my face as Rickie sings an easy sequence about a dream. Then the fictional dream ends, and he wakes up bereft.

But then the chorus kicks in, and I remember the song all at once. It's called "Like I'm Gonna Lose You." He looks right at me and sings his heart out, while every woman in the room starts feeling light-headed from how attractive he is.

Or maybe that's just me.

"Oh!" Jenn elbows me. "Karim is taking the John Legend parts! This is epic."

It is super, super cute. And I'm not worthy—of this song, or the hot man singing it.

He seems to think I am. So I can only try to live up to the hype.

Karim and Rickie ham it up at the end, and everyone in the bar claps and whistles. I feel flushed and self-conscious as he walks back to the table and then leans down to kiss me.

Somebody does a cat-call whistle. I might die now. But it will all be worth it. "Nice job, McFly. I loved it."

Grinning, Rickie plunks down in the chair and steals one of my french fries. "Thank you, Shipley. What's the duet we're singing?"

"You'll see." I pick up my cider and take a gulp. Singing in front of strangers? How did I agree to this?

I worry about it while someone from another table sings a passable rendition of "These Boots are Made for Walking." But then the DJ calls my name, and I'm almost glad.

"Let's get this over with," I grumble, and everybody laughs.

Rickie springs out of his chair. "It won't hurt a bit."

"Liar," I gasp. And then I straighten my spine and head for the stage.

THIRTY-FOUR

RICKIE

Aw. Daphne is really nervous. I feel bad about pressing her to do this.

I'll just have to make it up to her later. That could be fun.

"Okay, let's hear Radiohead's 'Creep,'" the DJ says with a smile. "Awesome song." He hits a button.

"Interesting pick," I say. "A little dark, but it's a killer track. I like it."

She gives me a funny little smile. Then she switches on her mic, and I do the same. The intro kicks in, and she taps her toe easily to the rhythm. I put a hand on her shoulder and give it a squeeze.

And we start to sing.

The first part of the song is pitched a little low for her. She stands very still and sings the lyrics carefully, and I help, without drowning her out.

We sound awesome, if I do say so myself.

When we hit the chorus, she sings it full-out. And I instantly get the chills. Her voice is silky over the crunchy guitar, and I feel her voice roll over me.

It's exhilarating.

The next verse goes the same way, and I'm really enjoying myself as we hit the chorus again. And I risk a glance to the right as we build up to the crescendo on *weirdo*.

She picks the same moment to glance my way. And she smiles.

And then... I don't know what happens to me. I get a prickly

229

sensation all over my scalp. My face gets hot and it's suddenly hard to get oxygen into my lungs. I glance at Daphne again, and it's like hardcore déjà vu. As if I've been here before, but maybe on an acid trip.

I keep singing on autopilot. Or maybe I'm just mouthing the words.

It's a short song. Daphne sings the last quiet line alone, and then the bar erupts in cheers, especially from our table against the wall.

Daphne smiles, but it's forced. She's shooting me strange glances.

What the hell just happened? I'm having a panic attack for no reason at all.

We walk back toward the table, but the tightness in my chest isn't loosening up. "I'm gonna smoke," I grit out. Then I make a beeline for the door.

Outside, it's a pretty summer night. The light is fading already. That's August in Vermont. I kick a foot against the bricks, lean against the building and tilt my head up. And I just breathe.

I stay out here alone for a few minutes, just trying to figure out what triggered me. That song, maybe. But why?

The door opens and Daphne comes out, her bag over her shoulder. "I paid the bill. We can leave if you want."

"We don't have to," I grunt.

She shakes her head slowly. "I think we do. What happened in there?"

"No idea." It comes out as a sigh, because I'm so tired of making excuses to this girl. "Why, uh, did you pick that song? It made me feel…" Crazy? Possessed? I don't even know how to explain it.

She looks uncomfortable. "Because we sang it together before."

"What?" The prickles on my scalp are back. "Where?"

"In your car," she whispers. "On our road trip."

"Fuck. Really?"

She nods.

"Holy shit." I put my head back against the wall. It's tempting to bang it right into the bricks.

"God, I'm sorry. I wasn't trying to screw with you. I just saw it on the list."

I reach out and grab her hand. "It's okay. I *want* to remember." As

I say these words, I am nearly consumed by self-loathing. "But aside from having an episode of the creeps, I don't *actually* remember. *Christ.*" I'm a delicate fucking flower, apparently. "What else did we sing in the car?"

"Whatever was on the radio. And also, um, things you had on cassette tape. Joan Jett and the Black Hearts."

My laugh is bitter. "Prince?"

"Yeah, 'Purple Rain.'"

"Journey? Or maybe not. I wouldn't have wanted you to think I like Journey if I was trying to impress you."

"Maybe you *did* like me, because there was no 'Wheel In the Sky.'" She squeezes my hand.

"Of *course* I liked you," I snap, sounding like an asshole.

"Joking," she whispers.

"Sorry. Can we go home?"

"Yeah. Come on."

Daphne offers to drive, but I turn her down, as usual. She doesn't argue, but she shoots me worried glances for the first few miles.

I'm a broody asshole all the way home, too. And when we pull into the driveway, I realize I haven't said a word for thirty miles.

Shit.

I kill the engine, and the silence practically throbs.

"Sorry," I grunt. "I'm a little tired."

"Oh please," she says, not letting me off the hook. "You're freaked out. Can't you just admit it?"

"I'll be fine."

"Uh huh. I know you will. But you just spent the whole summer trying to get me to trust you. And when I finally decide to do that, you clam up. So why do I have to show you my whole bag of crazy when you never show me yours?"

"It's not the same."

She snorts.

"I'm serious. Everything that's gone wrong in your life right now is someone else's fault."

231

"That's crap, Rickie," Daphne fires back, with her trademark lack of bullshit. "What you don't understand is that the only reason I *do* trust you with the darker things is because I've gotten a glimpse of yours, too. You make me feel like I don't have to be perfect all the time. That song? 'Creep?' It's like our little secret."

I hang my head. I don't feel like anyone's safe place tonight. But I am definitely a weirdo, like the song says.

"Look—my ex was really good at pretending he had everything figured out. And he turned out to be the scariest person I've ever met."

"Jesus. Don't compare me to that violent fucker."

"I'm not, and you know it. But if you want me to really trust you, you have to be willing to share."

"Hell," I curse. "You're too smart for your own good." I reach across the seat and take her hand in mine, smoothing my thumb across her palm. She's right, of course.

And now I realize I have another problem. I recognized her ex, too. But I haven't told her that. I recognized him enough to tell Lenore about it, and to dream about him, too. Yet I haven't shared, because that's just freaky. Why stir up the specter of that jerk for nothing?

She opens her mouth again, and I expect another plea for me to talk. But she changes the subject instead. "Rick, we forgot to go upstairs for a look at the empty room in your house."

I lean back against the headrest and smile. "We did, didn't we? Never made it past my bedroom."

"Chastity says nobody is allowed to go in your bedroom. Ever. But I did."

"I thought I explained this already. You're not just anybody. You've already had a first row seat to my bag of crazy. And now you've got a backstage pass."

She laughs. "All right. Then I'll take that empty room in your house. Sight unseen."

"Yeah?"

"Yeah," she says. "Because I trust you. And even if things don't work out for us, I'll still know that you're a good guy."

I let out a shaky breath. "I don't really deserve you, Daphne Shipley."

"Just try to, McFly. That's all I ask. The whole Meghan Trainor thing was a nice touch, by the way."

"Was it?" I really had enjoyed watching her blush while I sang it. So now I hum the chorus again, and I can feel her smiling in the dark.

"Encore?" she asks, hopefully.

"Depends what kind you're asking for, really." Then I hitch myself closer to her on the truck's seat, and pull her in. "There's all kinds of ways I could interpret that. Just saying."

The kiss I give her is sweet, and deep, and it's everything I need.

THIRTY-FIVE

DAPHNE

I'm making out in a pickup truck with Rickie. Maybe I'm a real Vermonter after all.

Lately my libido is cranked up to eleven. I feel shameless. In fact, I'd like to become a card-carrying member of the sex-in-a-truck club, please.

Except we're parked in my family's driveway. So it's probably a very bad idea.

Rickie pulls back, studies me, and then kisses me on the nose. "We'd better go inside."

"I guess so," I sigh.

He laughs and climbs out of the truck.

I grab my pack and do the same. And it isn't until I get closer to the house that I realize my entire family is on the front porch. The *whole* family, including Grandpa, my mother, Griffin, Audrey and Baby Gus. Also Dylan, Chastity, and even May and Alec are sitting there.

And everybody's holding a champagne flute. "Oh, boy," I stammer. "What did we miss?"

"I was just wondering that same thing," May says slowly.

"Didn't you guys pull in, like, ten minutes ago?" Dylan asks. "What were you doing out there?"

Uh-oh. I don't risk a glance toward Rickie. But instead, I try a page out of his book. "Making out, of course." I wave a hand, like it's a joke.

Dylan laughs.

But May squeals.

"Ohhhh finally," Chastity says.

"What?" Griffin asks.

Doesn't it just figure that I can't pull off the same slick tricks that Rickie gets away with? So now I'm standing here, my face heating, wondering what to say next.

"She's just kidding," Dylan says, reaching over to pull his girl-friend's ponytail.

"No. Nope. She's not," Chastity says. "You don't pay enough attention to Daphne. Nobody does."

"Hey!" I yelp. "That's not true. Moving on."

"No, it *is* true," my mother says from her rocking chair. "We always expect Daphne to be okay, and to do her own thing. We don't pay enough attention."

"I get that," Griffin agrees. "Daphne doesn't even feel like she can tell us what's wrong in her life. Transferring colleges during your senior year? We should be asking more questions."

"I'll ask 'em!" Grandpa volunteers.

"*Hey*," I argue. "There's no need. Everything is great with me."

Rickie clears his throat. "Oh the hypocrisy."

"Okay, fine," I mutter. "Everything is a little screwy with me right now. But it's fixable. I'm not going to crash your party with my drama. Now what are we celebrating?"

"What *aren't* we celebrating?" Griffin booms. "It's Big Announcement Day here at Shipley Farms. Don't feel bad if you missed the memo, because I did, too."

My sister laughs. "We're, um, engaged." She lifts up a hand to show me the ring on her finger.

"Oh my GOD!" I squeal. My joy is real, although a portion of it is due to shifting the conversation away from myself. "Congratulations! That's beautiful." I scoot over to look at the ring on her hand. It's a diamond solitaire in a very classic shape. "So pretty!"

"But wait, there's more," Grandpa says. "Everyone is gettin' hitched, apparently."

I look up quickly. "Not you, too, Grandpa?"

"No, no. Still having woman troubles. Your twin, though. He's got it all figured out."

My gaze flies to Dylan, who gives me a sheepish smile. "Check it out." He lifts Chastity's hand, and there's a ring on her finger, too. It's an artsy swirl of silver—almost like a river—with three stones in it.

"Holy cow, you guys!" Lord, I'm not a crier. But my eyes get misty. "That's gorgeous. Congratulations."

"We didn't mean to upstage May," Dylan says. "It was a coincidence."

"Must be something in the water," Grandpa says.

"Nobody is upstaging anyone," May chirps. "Want some fake bubbly?" She lifts a bottle out of an ice bucket—it's a fizzy ginger beer that we keep around for celebrations, because May doesn't drink alcohol. "Daphne? Rickie?"

"I would love some," I say. "Let's have a toast."

After they pour me a glass, and we toast, I perch my ass on the porch rail near my mom and May. Everyone else drifts away from the porch, talking on the lawn or inside the house.

"Okay, tell me everything," I demand of my sister. "Did this all happen today? Where did Alec pop the question?"

"Alec made me a nice dinner at home, and surprised me to bits by pulling a ring out of his pocket. I said yes immediately." May shrugs. "That's the whole story. But let's hear about your thing."

"Is there a photo?" I press. "We're not talking about my thing. I'm not spoiling your night with my drama. You of all people."

May narrows her eyes. "Why *me of all people*?"

Seriously? "I already have the Worst Sister Ever trophy," I explain calmly. "I'm not looking to add extra bonus points by raining on your parade."

"Daphne," my sister gasps. "It was three years ago. Can't we just move on? I forgave you for that a long time ago. I'm over it."

"Maybe Daphne isn't," my mother says quietly.

I stare down at the ginger bubbles in my glass and say nothing. But she's right. Three years ago I outed my sister to the woman she was in love with. "I was just *evil* to you. I have regretted it every day since."

"Well, I haven't," May says gently. "It's a thing that happened, and then it passed. You were a teenager, for God's sake. And I'd been pretty hard to live with that year. You just kind of exploded."

This is all true. "But I still feel icky about it."

"That's because you're a good person," my mother says. "So maybe you should give yourself a little credit for recognizing when you've hurt someone. And then get past it."

My eyes are hot again. "Okay. I'll try."

"I'd appreciate it," May says firmly. "Or else you're just going to be polite and distant to me until the end of time."

"I'm very good at distant," I grumble.

"That's why we're all fascinated by your thing with Rickie," May says, clasping her hands with obvious glee. "What's that all about?"

"He's, uh, a pretty interesting guy," I say lamely. But how much detail could I be reasonably expected to supply with my mother sitting right here? "He's fun. He got me to do karaoke in a bar tonight."

Mom and May burst into surprised laughter.

"What?" I complain. "Lots of people do karaoke."

"Lots of people who aren't *you*." May cackles. "Is there a video?"

"God, I hope not," I say, and they both laugh again. "Why are we talking about this when you're the one getting married?"

"Come on," May says. "The fact of my marriage is not that big of a surprise. Dylan and Chastity, on the other hand..."

We all glance toward the lawn, where Chastity is standing with Audrey, who's admiring her ring.

"They're young," my mother says softly. "But that's okay. They need each other."

"Who's getting married first?" I ask.

"Me," May says. "We'll get married this spring, I think. Probably at the church, with a reception right down the hill at *Speakeasy*. I want something simple."

"There's plenty of time to plan a wedding," I point out.

"There is," May agrees. "But I watched Lark spend a lot of time and energy trying to throw a wedding that met her mother's expectations, and I just don't want a lot of fuss. I don't want a big puffy dress. I don't want to throw a sit-down dinner for three hundred people. I want a catered barbecue and contra dancing. I don't need to reinvent the wheel or throw the wedding of the century."

"That sounds fun," I admit. "I'll help you, if you want. I'll be here in Vermont."

"About that..." my sister says.

I groan. "We'll get into that another time. I made some mistakes last year. I complicated my own life. But it will be fine. I promise."

"We're here if you need us," my mother says.

"I know. Thanks." It's nice to hear.

I just wish that they didn't have to say it.

I make the rounds, congratulating all the soon-to-be-married people. Alec is calm and joyful, while Chastity seems happy enough to burst. When I ask her what kind of wedding she wants, she says "It doesn't matter. As long as Dylan is there."

"Can I make a speech?" I ask. "I've been saving up embarrassing anecdotes about him for a *long* time."

"Have at it," she says. And then she looks down at her hand to admire her ring again, as if she can't believe it's really there.

The last person on my list to congratulate is my twin brother. But I have some trouble finding him until I go into the farmhouse and climb the stairs.

He and Rickie are in the bedroom, and as I walk down the hallway, their conversation ceases.

"Okay," I say, propping myself in the doorway. "You can stop talking about me now. Or I'll tell Chastity that I once convinced you that aliens had taken your real sisters away on their ship and left behind a set of imposters."

"I didn't *actually* believe you," Dylan grumbles. "I was just acting scared."

Locking my eyes into an unseeing expression, I drift toward the bed with a strange gait.

"Oh, cut that out," he says, rolling to get out of my path. "That's creepy."

Rickie bends in half, laughing.

My brother gets up, looking disgruntled. "You've always been good at changing the subject."

"It's my super power," I admit. "That and finding things you would rather keep hidden. But I came up here to congratulate you on your big proposal. That's a power move."

"Thank you," he says, his smile quick.

"The ring is super cool."

"There's a store she likes." He shrugs. "Some idiot gave me a ridiculously big gift certificate there, so I could afford the ring."

I glance at Rickie, who smirks. "I don't see any idiots here. Do you?"

"Not touching that, McFly," I smirk back at him.

Dylan looks from me to Rickie and back again, his expression puzzled. "Okay, I still don't quite get it with you two. It might take me a few days."

"Whatever." I walk over to where Rickie is seated on the bed, and he takes my hand and kisses my palm. It's just my hand, of course. But Rickie is just about the most sensual man on the planet, so there's a lot of intention in that slow, sliding kiss.

"Okay. Well." Dylan looks flustered. "I'll leave you two, um, to it."

"To what?" Rickie asks playfully.

"Blergh," my twin says. "Never mind. Bye, kids."

"Bye," Rickie says teasingly.

But Dylan doesn't walk right out the door. Instead, he steps toward me and then grabs me into a quick, tight hug. "Love you," he says gruffly. "Don't be a stranger."

"Love you, too!" I say to his departing back. Then he's gone.

It takes me a beat to turn around again. Rickie's sitting there, smiling at me like he's pleased with himself.

"Was that weird?" I ask. "He seemed weird. Did you talk about me?"

"Only a little. Come here already. We might as well make out, because that's what everyone imagines we're doing right now."

I suppose that's true. So I plop down on the bed.

Rickie pounces, pushing me down against the pillows and rolling until he's on top of me. He smooths the hair away from my face and gives me a lip touch. "You okay?"

"I'm great," I admit.

"Dylan didn't really give you a hard time over this, did he?"

"This what?" he asks, eyes twinkling. He drops his hips onto mine in a meaningful way.

"This...whatever this is," I say, trying not to rub my body against his like an affectionate cat.

"Whatever this is," he repeats. "Do you want to put a label on it?"

"Not really."

He laughs, and I love the sound of it. "You're hard on my ego. What if I want to put a label on it?"

"Which label?" I reach up and run a hand down the V-neck of his T-shirt. I'm not even a little bit hard on this man's ego. I can't stop touching him.

"You are my girl, Shipley. My woman. My person. You belong to me."

"Huh. Did you put it that way to see if I would throw a feminist fit about your possessive words?"

His eyes twinkle. "No, I put it that way because I feel very possessive of you, in a completely enlightened, nonstifling way."

I snort.

"We're dating, Shipley. You aren't onboard?"

"I'm onboard," I admit.

He grins. "And, since you asked, your brother did not give me a hard time. Except that he told me to be careful with you, because something was obviously not going right in your life. And did I mind telling him what that was?"

I stop breathing. "Did you tell him?"

"No way, Shipley. I told him to ask *you*. Not that he liked that answer. So he asked me if there was some guy he needed to beat up. And I said, again, he needed to speak to you directly. But also maybe he should work on his uppercut and his left cross."

"Wow, okay," I say quietly. "Thank you."

"Don't mention it. Your brother said he'd get in a few hours of practice with the heavy bag at the gym. From where I sit, your family is a bunch of cool, slightly crazy people. They're just looking out for you."

"I know."

"Maybe we'll work on my family next," he whispers.

"Okay." I know things are strained with his dad. "Good plan."

"Meanwhile, you're going to move into my house. We'll have to think hard about who's in which room. For privacy purposes."

"That should be a consideration." I smile up at him, hoping he'll kiss me for real now.

But he's still talking. "The third floor is kind of far away from me. But then you wouldn't have to share a bathroom with your brother. Chastity has dibs on the empty first-floor bedroom. But maybe you two should discuss a swap."

"Really—I don't care which room it is. It's only for a year."

"So you say." He smooths my hair. "Either way, you'll save money. And even though you'll be busy rebooting your life and applying to grad school, I'll still get to see you at home."

"That's true." And, yup. It does sound pretty nice.

"We're going to have a great year, Shipley. Hard work and good times," he says.

And revenge, I mentally add. Because I haven't forgot my big plan. In a few weeks, I'm going to make Reardon pay.

But Rickie isn't thinking about that at all. He finally leans down and kisses me slowly. His lips tease and press.

And I forget all about Reardon Halsey.

For now.

THIRTY-SIX

RICKIE

"Oh my God, my arms are so tired," I complain. "It hurts to hold the steering wheel."

"You want me to drive?" Daphne asks.

"Nope." I accelerate past a Hyundai and gun it toward Burlington. "Just like to complain."

She laughs. "Such a whiner. Can I put on *Purple Rain?*"

"Sure."

She pushes the cassette into the player. Prince starts singing "Let's Go Crazy."

We're in my Volvo, with a load of Daphne's clothes and books in the back seat, and I'm counting down the exits. This is it. School is starting again. I had a great summer with my girl, and—apart from my muscle pain—I feel pretty great about life.

Daphne had been slow to pack up her room, so Dylan and Chastity drove the truck back ahead of us. Tomorrow we're all registering for fall courses. Then there are two days of classes before we go back to Colebury to pick apples again.

The last three weeks have been crazy busy. I have mad respect for the Shipley clan, especially Dylan. I always knew my friend was a hard worker. But I never quite understood what the busy season meant for him. It means picking the earliest apples from sunup to sundown, while also preparing the farm for an invasion of tourists. Meanwhile, the cows and goats still need to be milked.

And August is just the start. There are miles upon miles of ripening apples in that orchard. As the season progresses, they'll turn red faster than the Shipleys can pick them.

Dylan puts the "full-time" in "full-time student." That's for damn sure. And Daphne has agreed to go back with him and Chastity on the weekends to help out.

Which means I'll probably do the same sometimes, because I fall a little more stupid in love with Daphne every day. That's me—falling for a girl who thinks she's moving across the country a year from now.

I guess I'll deal with that when it happens. For now, I'm going to enjoy her.

Although, since the night her family learned we're a couple, we've barely spent any time alone together. Daphne doesn't want to fool around in the house where her mother and grandfather might hear, and I don't blame her.

So we haven't found many moments of accidental solitude. Except for one fun night when we parked Dylan's pickup truck on a deserted country road and had a quickie on the back seat. That was a good time. And now I get to tease Daphne about being a real Vermonter.

My foot is heavy on the gas pedal as the first Burlington exits finally appear. I'm eager to get back to the house—and sleep past six a.m. tomorrow morning for the first time in weeks.

"Almost there!" Daphne says from the passenger seat. She reaches over and gives my arm a happy squeeze. She seems lighter and happier than she's been in a long time.

I like to imagine that I'm at least partially responsible. "What if we didn't haul this stuff up to your room yet?" I ask. "We could collapse in my room and watch a movie instead."

"Sure," she says easily. "What do you want to watch?"

"Who cares? I'll probably tune it out and strip you naked after the first ten minutes anyway."

She laughs. "Okay, I'll rephrase. What do you want to watch ten minutes of? Pick something exciting so I don't pass out early."

"Did I say ten minutes? I meant five."

When we reach my house, the truck is in the driveway, but there's nobody downstairs. Even Keith's door is shut when I troop upstairs to drop a box of clothes on Daphne's new floor.

"I don't know if I can live in such a noisy house," Daphne whispers when I return to the first floor.

"I know, right?"

She puts a box of books down in the living room. "Can I park this here for now?"

"Of course. You want a beer? I stocked up on Wednesday."

"I'll just have a sip of yours," she says, yawning.

I steer her toward my room. "Pick a show to watch. I'll be right there."

A few minutes later, we're both nestled comfortably in my bed. We're watching one of those singing competition shows, because when Daphne had flipped past the channel, someone was covering "Like I'm Gonna Lose You" by Meghan Trainor.

"Yours was better," she'd said. And now we're watching a four-teen-year-old girl sing an opera aria.

Or—wait—I am. Daphne is asleep. She's snuggled onto my chest, eyelashes curled down to her cheeks, breathing peacefully.

I sip my beer and watch the silly show. Having Daphne here in my room is exactly what my heart wants. But I'm still that guy who can't fall asleep with company. Last time this happened, I'd solved the problem by going to sleep in her room.

And maybe I'll have to do that again. But I'm not going down without a fight.

So I slide out from beneath her and get ready for bed. I shut all the lights off, and check all the locks on the doors. Then I go into my room and close that door too. I lock it, of course.

When I'm lifting the covers, Daphne rolls over. But she doesn't wake up. She only sighs deeply.

I strip down and lie beside her, closing my eyes. I'm so tired. My muscles ache. And I just want to do this simple thing that other people can do—fall asleep in a bed where someone else is. *This is so peaceful*, I tell myself. *There are so many people I care about under this roof.*

Logic doesn't always matter, though. Ask anyone with a phobia.

Tonight, the message seems to be penetrating my tired brain. *I'm safe*, I remind myself. My trauma is in the past. I can't pretend it isn't there, lurking in the shadows. That doesn't work.

But right here, right now, everything is fine. I listen to Daphne breathing steadily beside me. And I slow down my breathing, matching my rhythm to hers. It's like a meditation, except instead of focusing on my own breathing, I'm focusing on hers.

Until I'm not anymore.

The bed moves suddenly. That's the kind of thing that ought to startle me. Except Daphne's voice says, "Omigod. I'm sorry."

My limbs are heavy. I only slit my eyes open to see sunlight pouring into my room. Then I close them again.

"Rickie. I slept here. And you slept, too!"

"Still doing it," I slur.

She laughs. "Isn't this great? I don't mean that it's great that I overstayed my welcome. But you don't look like you minded. Were you awake all night?"

"Nuh uh," I breathe.

"So that's progress?"

"Mmm." She's not wrong. But now that I've figured out how to sleep, I'm down for the count.

Daphne runs a hand though my hair, and slides off the bed. I hear her unlock the door and leave, closing it softly behind her.

My consciousness is a half-formed, floaty thing. The bed is warm, and I'm hard, because I'm so comfortable and the pillow smells like Daphne. Everything in my life is wonderful, because I slept in a bed with my girlfriend like every other horny guy on the planet. Go me.

A little later, it gets even more wonderful, when a freshly show-ered Daphne comes back into the room a half hour later with a mug of tea.

"Is that for me?" I mumble. But of course it is, because Daphne is a coffee drinker.

"Yes, sleepyhead." She sets it down on the bedside table.

"I'm unworthy." I push myself up into a sitting position.

Her eyes widen at the view, because I sleep naked. "Good morning to *you*."

"Isn't it?" I reach for the hot tea and take a sip. I let the comforter stay where it is—low on my thighs. Then I give her a sexy smirk.

Daphne gulps. "I'm liking Burlington a little more than I ever expected to."

"Are you now?" I run a shameless hand over my tattooed pecs. "Why don't you close the door?"

She does it.

"I like your first day of school outfit." She's wearing another of her short skirts, with a pretty blue shirt. "But please take it off."

"We only have an hour until we're supposed to leave," she whispers.

"Darling, that's plenty of time." I put the tea back down on the table. Then I toss the covers off my body. "You need some help?"

"Sure," she says, biting back a smile. "Why don't you show me what you have in mind?"

I lean over and catch the back of her smooth leg in my hand. And I run my fingers very lightly up the back of her thigh, under her skirt, until she shivers. My cock thickens against the sheet, and I let out a happy sigh.

As I unzip her skirt, Daphne lifts her shirt over her head and tosses it onto my rug. "Take off your bra," I whisper. "Come closer. Let me love you."

She begins to obey, but I'm impatient. So I wrap both my arms around her legs and pull her onto the bed, where she topples onto my body.

And she's laughing—until I shut her up with my mouth.

The lady said we didn't have much time. So I ply her with kisses. And it isn't long until I have her spread out on her back, her hands gripping my shoulders as I move inside her. Our morning together is made up of white sheets, sunshine, and bare skin.

Then she catches me off guard, suddenly tensing her body with a sweet, climactic gasp. She pulses around me, and then moans.

So I'm done for, too. I plunge my tongue into her mouth and groan as I come fast and hard.

And then I bury my face in her neck and laugh.

246

"What's so funny?" she pants, her arms flopping out to her sides.

"Nothing. Everything. I don't know." I grin against her smooth skin. "I spent so much time trying to get back my old memories. But all I had to do was make some new ones."

"Yeah, okay. True. This will probably be a top-twenty memory for me."

"Twenty?" I yelp. "Sweetheart, please. I'm climbing your leaderboard a hell of a lot faster than that."

"I'm just leaving some space, McFly," she whispers. "It's only the first day of school."

"I like how you think."

She squeezes my hand. And I squeeze hers right back.

THIRTY-SEVEN

DAPHNE

Maybe I'm just a snob who was ripe for a lesson in humility. But I hadn't expected to like Moo U very much. I thought it would be big and impersonal. I thought the classes would be easier than the ones at Harkness.

But nope. My professors are every bit as sharp and engaging as the ones I had at Harkness. So the homework starts piling up almost immediately. It's a good thing I only have four academic classes: a senior seminar on reproductive biology, a history course on voting rights in the twentieth century, an English course, and an upper-level statistics class.

Because I also needed a phys ed course to meet Burlington University's requirements. This came as an unwelcome surprise. "At least there won't be any homework," I'd grumbled to Rickie.

"I've been putting that off, too," Rickie had said. "Any ideas on what you'll choose?"

"Um, I was considering badminton," I'd admitted. "It sounds easier than weight training, or swimming, or any of the others."

Rickie had laughed. And then he'd signed up for badminton, too. So now on Tuesday and Thursday afternoons, we're swinging at birdies together. And Rickie wears a vintage tennis outfit—a tight polo-collar shirt with sleeves short enough to show off his tats, and a pair of short white tennis shorts—just to troll me.

So that burden has become a blast. I don't know what's more

surprising—enjoying my phys ed requirement, or the fact that Rickie is the one who makes me love it so much.

It's hard to deny how important he's become to my whole life. I'm not the only one who appreciates him, either. It's been eye-opening to see him in his natural habitat. People just turn up at the house on Spruce Street every Thursday and Friday night. They bring booze and pot and music. He's magnetic, and I'm not the only one who notices.

Yet I'm the one he kisses every time he comes home. It's a little mind-blowing.

Meanwhile, I'm still working Wednesday afternoons at the School of Public Health.

"We're going to need you at karaoke again," Karim points out during the third week of school.

"Weeknights are for homework. Besides, you're not interested in my singing," I point out. "You just want Rickie there."

Jenn giggles. "You may be right about him. But *I* want you there, Shipley. Boyfriend or not."

And I'm pretty sure she means it. I've made friends whether I meant to or not. Go figure.

Life in Burlington—and on Spruce Street—is a whole lot nicer than I expected. Just to keep up the appearance of my independence, I sometimes sleep in my own room. But just as often I end up in Rickie's bed. All night long, too. Waking up to his naked body curled around mine is heaven. Sometimes, when he smiles at me, I just want to pinch myself.

Honestly, it's a problem. Rickie is on his way to becoming the first man I ever really loved. He's already the first one I've ever trusted with my heart. And if I ever get these grad school applications done, it's not going to be easy to walk away from him.

But I know I'll have to.

As promised, I drive back home to the farm with Dylan and Chastity every Friday night or Saturday morning. The orchard hours are not helping with my workload. I should be writing my grad school essays instead of picking apples. But Griffin is so grateful for the help. And my mother is happy to see me.

Besides—I've been away for so long that I'd forgotten how good the cider house smells when my brother is pressing apples. The last time I experienced that was the weekend I rode home with Rickie from Harkness. That was almost three years ago.

"Bet you don't miss the pony cart," my brother says one afternoon as we sort apples for the farmers' market.

"You'd be right," I agree. When the Abrahams moved away, they'd sold the horses. So now the apple pickers actually have to *walk* to where the Honeycrisps grow.

"Me neither," he agrees. "They're pooping their way across someone else's farm now."

I snicker. "And we don't have to argue about that job anymore."

"Right. Really appreciate having you here, though," he says, tossing a wormy apple into the compost can. "Means a lot, Daph."

"No problem," I say quickly. "Wish we could get even more of this done before tonight."

He gives his head a little shake. "We're doing fine. It's nice having you around again. Here and in Burlington. That's all."

"Really?" I blurt out.

My brother laughs. "Really. We weren't *always* trying to drown each other in the baby pool, right? We had fun sometimes."

"Yeah. We did," I admit.

"You could stay in Vermont longer than a year, you know. Just saying."

I lift my head to argue with him. But I'm not fast enough. He's already grabbed his empty bushel basket and walked off, whistling to himself.

Dylan likes having me around. But he also likes having the last word. That's how it is having a twin brother.

And I can't say I mind.

Not much, anyway.

It's a Thursday night in September, and we're finishing up the Chinese food we all ordered together. I dump the last bit of fried rice onto my brother's plate. "You know you want this." Dylan is a bottomless pit, and always has been.

"Thanks. I totally do."

I carry my plate over to the sink and rinse it. Rickie joins me there. He places a hand lightly on my back. "I ran into Karim in the library. He wants a karaoke rematch. Can you swing it next Wednesday night?"

"Um, no," I say. "There's something I need to do. Actually..." I drop my voice to a whisper. "I have a favor to ask. Can I talk to you privately?"

"Any time, baby girl." He takes the plate out of my hand and puts it into the dishwasher. "Why don't you step into my office? We can do some *filing*." He wiggles his eyebrows at me.

Dylan, with a mouthful of fried rice, makes a disgusted sound. "Stop it with the creepy euphemisms."

Rickie snickers and leads me into his room, where I close the door. "Do you really need a favor?" he asks.

"Yes." I sit on the bed.

"A sexual favor?" He climbs behind me and starts rubbing my shoulders.

"No, but you can keep doing that anyway."

Soft lips kiss my neck. "What can I do for you?"

"Can I drive the Volvo to Connecticut next week? I'd borrow Dylan's truck, but I don't want to explain where I'm headed."

Rickie's hands go still on my shoulders. "Where *are* you headed?"

"Harkness. Remember that invitation I showed you? The reception is on Wednesday. I plan to drive down, stay for less than an hour, and drive back."

He doesn't say anything for a moment. He goes back to massaging my shoulders. "Are you just going to schmooze?"

"No." I shake my head. "I'm going to slip into the office and get the postal account password out of that file folder."

"Daphne, baby. What if you didn't?"

"What if I didn't *what?*" I demand.

"Didn't get it. Don't take that chance," he says, dropping his hands. "Is it worth it?"

"Yes," I say immediately. Then I spin around so I can see his solemn face. And there's a dark look in his eye that makes no sense to me. "I need to fix what he did."

Rickie sits back, propping himself up on muscular arms, frowning. "You didn't make that mess, Daphne. It isn't yours to clean up."

"But it's *science*," I insist. "It matters."

"So write a letter telling the dean where to find this information."

"No way. If I strike out at him, it has to be ironclad. I need to see the evidence first. Otherwise he'll bury me."

He pinches the bridge of his nose. "You're not going to let this go, are you?"

"No. I can't," I insist.

Besides—he's wrong. I *did* make this mess. I was in charge of this data. And if I hadn't slept with Reardon, I would have been able to ring the alarm the moment I saw something was wrong. I wouldn't have let him blackmail me.

I'm such an idiot. But if I can fix this problem, I won't have to feel like one anymore.

"Okay," Rickie says.

My heart lifts. "I can use the car?"

"I'll drive you down there," he says. "You let me go with you."

"Oh my God. You don't trust me with your car?"

His gray eyes widen. "Baby, I trust you with my car, and I trust you with my *life*. But I *don't* trust the violent fuckface you had the misfortune to date before me. So if you want my wheels, you take me as your plus one."

"Oh." My heart practically explodes. "Well okay, then. This thing is Wednesday night. It's a four-hour drive."

"I'll make time, Shipley," he says, laying a hand on my knee. "I don't want you to go alone. We're a team, okay?"

"Okay," I say softly, because I really like the sound of that. "Okay."

THIRTY-EIGHT

RICKIE

That night I lie awake for the first time in a long while. I can't sleep.

Daphne is curled up in my bed, breathing deeply. Her presence is not the reason for my troubles. It's just the opposite.

The truth is that I'd forgotten about Daphne's big plan. I'd been too busy enjoying my new life with her to think about it. I'd been too busy cooking meals with her in the kitchen and snuggling in front of the TV. Too busy making love to her every chance I got.

It's not like me to be dismissive. And I know Daphne pretty well. The moment she'd shown me that invitation, I should have known she'd go through with it.

But I'd let my guard down. I'd stopped beating my head against every available surface.

She hasn't, though. This isn't over for her. I'm busy falling in love. But she wants revenge. She wants her career, and grad school at a top-five program somewhere far away from here.

It stings a little. But I already knew that. My new problem is how to keep her safe. I wanted her to be done with Reardon Halsey.

But she isn't done. So I guess I'm not, either.

I spend the next couple of days feeling broody about our upcoming jaunt to Connecticut. And Daphne is pretty quiet, too. On Friday morning, I catch her looking at the floorplan of a building on her laptop—just like James Bond.

But she closes the computer quickly as my footsteps approach.

"It's just me," I whisper. "Was that the place? Want to share?"

She shakes her head. "I really don't want to involve you if I don't have to. Technically I'm planning to commit a crime. Even though I'm not stealing anything."

"I'm going to be standing next to you." I lean over and kiss the top of her head. "I'm an accessory, right? That's what the TV cop shows would call it."

"That's just it." She swivels to look up at me. "I don't think you should go. I'm well aware that this plan is crazy. It might fail. And I will take full responsibility." She swallows hard.

"Hey now." I sit down beside her on the couch and pull her close to me. She's wearing the daphnia necklace. She never takes it off. "Look—I can't sit at home here next Wednesday night and wonder if you're okay. I just can't. So I'm going with you."

"But Rickie..." She buries her face in my flannel shirt. "I don't know what I'm doing. This will either work great, or it will make things worse. But I have to try."

Do you really? I want to ask. But I don't say it. Daphne has to figure this out for herself. I don't want to be the kind of guy who tells her what to think and do.

But I worry.

Daphne goes home with her brother for the weekend, and I keep worrying. The house is too quiet with just me and Keith at home. I read Aristotle and brood.

Then, on Saturday night, I have another damn dream. It's just like the ones I had this summer—where I open my eyes and Reardon Halsey is lying on my bed, smirking at me.

Then I open my eyes for real and wake up sweaty. And not in a fun way. *Shit.* It's three in the morning. And I can see his face so clearly in my mind's eye.

Why is that?

I turn on the lamp, which chases the shadows out of the room. I pull my laptop onto the bed and open it up. I google Reardon Halsey again, and find all the same photos as last time. It's not a great use of the wee hours. But I recognize his face, and it's driving me insane.

So I open up my email and try something I've tried a million times before. I write another email to paulywhite123.

Paul,

Hi, it's me again. I've written before, but I don't know if you got my earlier messages. I'm still out here looking for answers. I still don't remember how I ended up in the hospital.

There is a lot that I need to know. Can you help?

Hell, I don't know if you've ever read one of these messages. I don't even know if we're friends. But if you know what happened to me on the Saturday night of Open Weekend, I need to know.

Or even if you don't know, please reply so I know you actually still exist.

Yeah, that's dark. But my mind has been to some very dark places recently.

Sincerely,

Rick Ralls

I spend Sunday writing a paper about Freud. Plus I check my email about a thousand times.

Later that afternoon, on the 1001st try, there's a bolded, unread message at the top of the stack. From paulywhite123.

I actually close my eyes for a moment in surprise. But when I open them again, it's still there. The time stamp is only a few minutes ago.

When I open the message, it's only one line long. He writes: *Are you getting help for those dark places? You should.*

Holy heck. Now we're having a conversation. So I reply.

Yes, I did get help. My therapist's name is Lenore. She's terrific. She even laughs at my jokes. 10/10 would recommend.

It's nonthreatening, and it asks nothing. So I hit send. And then I pray, and watch my inbox like a hunter in a deer blind.

But night falls, and I still have no response. Daphne comes home with her brother and Chastity, and I smile and try not to look like the jumpy fucker that I am.

255

"Can we order pizza?" she asks. "And I brought home lettuce for a salad."

"Sure, baby. I'll make the salad. I need something to do with my hands."

"Another innuendo?" Dylan mutters.

"Believe it or not, no," I say, taking a bag of groceries out of his hands. "I'm just a little stir crazy."

"Is Freud kicking your ass?" Daphne asks. She gives me a kiss on the jaw.

"Yeah," I say immediately. "I had, uh, a long day of paper-writing." God, it feels trashy to lie. Daphne is the last person I want to deceive. But I know nothing more than I did when she left on Friday afternoon.

I need to know more. So I spend the evening pretending to write a paper while watching my inbox. Nothing happens, until Daphne crawls into bed with me at midnight, and I force myself to shut off the light and pull her into my arms.

"Did you miss me?" I ask, kissing her neck.

"You know I did," she murmurs.

"Why don't you show me how much?" I ask, trying to find my normal self.

"I think I will," she says.

Monday night I'm alone in my room, checking my phone one more time before I go to sleep. And Daphne is upstairs, pulling a late night for homework.

Checking for a new message is just a habit by now. But suddenly there it is.

Rick,

"10/10 would recommend." I heard that in your voice. And the joke means that you're going to be okay. Not sure what to say about your memory. You probably won't believe me, but not remembering could be a blessing.

P.

• • •

Now I have goose bumps all over my body. He still isn't giving me what I need. So I write back.

You're right. I am going to be okay. It took me a while, but my life is back on track. I spent the summer on a farm. Now I'm working on my degree full time, at Burlington U in Vermont.

Contacting you was a selfish act. I want to know what happened. I want to know if I was to blame for blowing up my life.

I don't need to know. But I want to.

Please tell me you're going to be okay, too. You have me imagining the worst.

—Rick

I try to wait up for his reply. But it never comes, and I fall asleep clutching my phone like a talisman.

On Tuesday his message arrives while I'm in class.

Rick,

I know you want a full accounting. I can hear how hard you're trying not to demand some answers. But I can't help you.

At first I couldn't answer you because I couldn't stand to think about you, or anyone else at the Academy. Pretending it didn't happen was the only way I could go on.

Then I broke down, and couldn't read your messages because I was institutionalized for more than six months.

And now I can't give you what you want because I signed an NDA.

I know that's a shitty thing for me to say. That my tidy little settlement is more important than your sanity. But my tidy little settlement is paying for my continued sanity. And I bet your thick philosophy books say something about how going forward is more important than examining the past.

If they don't, they should.

—P

. . .

After reading this, I gather up my stuff and walk right out of the seminar. It's rude, but I have to keep him talking to me. I'm taking Daphne to Connecticut tomorrow. And Paul knows what happened.

Paul—I know it sounds crazy, but I don't remember anything from that Saturday night. And I can live with that. I don't want you to put yourself in harm's way.

But my girlfriend is up against a creep who left the Academy the same year I did. My gut says it's not a coincidence. I'm trying to decide how worried I should be about him.

Anything you can tell me without hanging your ass in the air would be sincerely appreciated.

—Rick

P.S. I signed an NDA too, by the way. It just means a little less when you can't actually remember.

Daphne calls me while I'm sitting at the Green Bean, the campus coffee shop, eating a croissant and staring at my phone.

"Hey, baby girl," I answer, sounding more chipper than I feel.

"Hi, McFly. I called to ask you what time you'll be ready to hop into the DeLorean and leave tomorrow. I was hoping we could go at 2:30. I took the day off from work."

"Okay," I agree immediately. "What do I wear on this adventure?"

"Khaki pants, button-down shirt," she says.

"Noted. What do you want for dinner tonight? Your mom sent home some chicken. I thought I'd make tortilla soup."

Ding. My phone alerts me to a new email. And now I can't even concentrate on the conversation.

"That sounds great," Daphne is saying. "What can I make on the side?"

I fail to answer her, because I'm already holding the phone away from my ear, already reading Paul's words.

"Rickie?" she prompts.

"Uh, sorry gorgeous. I'd better go."

"Is everything okay?" she asks, her voice worried.

And that's when I make a terrible error. I don't tell her about this crazy conversation I've been having. And I don't tell her why.

"Yeah. See you at home," is all I say. Then I end the call and read Paul's message three times in quick succession.

Rick—

I really can't talk about this. But maybe if you have access to a university library, you should know that Court Martial summaries are sort of public. They're printed in a legal journal called Military Justice Review. When shit goes really bad at a military academy, sometimes personnel are CMed. You can read bare bones summaries of these motions in the logs.

But look—if you find this thing—there's two guys mentioned, right? You might wonder which one you are. Please know that I was the target. It was me. And you got hurt trying to stop it.

By the way: we were friends. Absolutely. It makes me sad to hear you're not sure about that. I was lucky to call you my friend.

That's all I have for you. Maybe someday I'll be able to call you and say all the words out loud. Maybe I will be fearless, and say what needs saying.

But today is not that day. Not yet.

—P

I get up from the coffee shop and hightail it toward the library.

THIRTY-NINE

DAPHNE

Rickie is acting strangely, and it's stressing me out.

Yesterday he'd said he wanted to make dinner. But then he didn't. I waited for him for two hours before texting to ask, *Where are you?*

Sorry! Library. I'll be home late.

So I'd made myself a bean quesadilla, with a side of disappointment. Then I fell asleep in his bed at midnight. He came in so late I didn't even hear him.

I mean, sure, he tried to make it up to me in the morning. I woke up to his urgent mouth on my nipple. Things escalated quickly from there, and I ended up on all fours, gripping the headboard, with Rick's hand clasped over my mouth so I wouldn't wake up the entire house with my moaning.

It had been a very effective distraction technique. Reduced to a whimpering heap of sexual satisfaction, I'd failed to inquire about his distant behavior the day before.

Now he's right beside me in the old Volvo, driving me to Connecticut. Sitting here in the passenger seat as we cruise down 91 should feel like a big déjà vu for me.

But it doesn't, because Rickie is so quiet. "There's something wrong, isn't there? You haven't said a word for twenty miles."

"No, baby," he says, his voice scratchy from disuse. "I'm fine."

Feeling unsettled, I close my eyes and try to fight off a horrible sense of foreboding. I don't take naturally to performing spy maneuvers at my former place of work. Just the thought of breaking into an office to peek inside a file folder has my good girl complex pinging like crazy.

Maybe *I'm* the only one who's acting strangely.

But then I glance at Rickie, and see a worry wrinkle across his forehead that isn't usually there. He's keeping something to himself. I'm sure of it. "I swear, Rickie, I had a better sense of what was in your head that first time we rode together. When we were strangers."

This comes out of my mouth sounding very bitchy. And I expect him to call me on it.

But he doesn't. "Strangers are just friends you haven't met yet," he murmurs. "They taught me that at Sunday school once. Then I lost my memory. And I learned that strangers could also be people you have met before."

The hair stands up on the back of my neck. "Did something happen this week? Another déjà vu?"

He hesitates for a beat longer than feels right. "Not a thing."

"Are you okay?" I press.

In answer, he reaches out and gives my hand a squeeze.

And then says nothing for ten more miles.

"Can I put some music on?" I ask as the silence threatens to choke me again.

"Sure, baby girl. You go ahead."

I turn on the radio. But he doesn't sing along this time.

Even though it's a splurge, I booked us a room at the Harkness Inn, the nicest hotel I could afford. Now I glance around the luxe bathroom with its plush robes and bamboo fixtures, and I wonder what the hell I was thinking. This isn't some kind of vacation, although God knows we need one.

There is no way I'm going to be able to relax until after this is all over—until I've brought some anonymous attention to Reardon's cheating. Until I get justice.

It has to work.

Rickie is sitting on the bed, texting furiously. He doesn't even glance at me as I parade past him in lace panties, opening my suitcase to pull out my blouse.

"Is there something wrong?" I ask as he taps out another message with his thumbs. "You seem preoccupied."

"It's nothing. Lenore always worries when I blow off an appointment."

"Your therapist?" I clarify. "You're missing an appointment? We could have left later."

"Don't worry about it, Shipley." He still doesn't look up. "It's fine."

But nothing is fine. There's an icy chill rising off him that I don't understand. "Would you *please* tell me what's wrong? I'm already freaking out here."

Finally he lifts his gaze to mine. "Please don't panic. I don't want you to be afraid. Not ever. We can get back in the car and drive home if you want to."

"God, it's tempting. But I can't do that. If I give up, he wins."

"Daphne…" Rickie's beautiful face is grave. "I don't like you hanging yourself out there to fix a problem you didn't create."

"I did, though."

He shakes his head. "That's not true. Some people are just bad seeds. And it goes against everything I believe to let you walk in there and try to beat him at his own game. What if you can't? What if he's willing to do whatever it takes to win?"

Words fail me for a moment, because he looks so deathly serious. But then I find my voice. "If it feels like too big a risk, I won't go through with it."

He swallows. "Tell me your plan, then. We're running out of time."

"It's very simple. I swear."

I button the blouse, and then I tell him my plan.

Forty minutes later we're parking the car on the north campus. It's the golden hour, so slanted sunlight infuses all the red brick buildings with a rosy glow. I used to love walking around Harkness. I was so starstruck by this place, founded three hundred years ago. This vaunted institution where presidents, icons, and Supreme Court justices were educated.

Being starstruck was my Achilles' heel. I let myself be dazzled by a senator's son with a spray tan and a perfect smile. And then I paid the price.

Rickie slips his hand into mine as we approach the doors to the new wing. Normally you'd need key card access here. But there's a young woman at the door with a clipboard. I hand her my invitation and she waves us right through.

We proceed into the atrium, where the party is held. The ceiling is three stories up and made of glass. Offices ring the space above us, the hallways open to the atrium below.

"Do you see him?" Rickie murmurs.

"Not yet," I say, feeling shaky at the idea of coming face to face with Reardon. "But there's his father."

Rickie turns his head casually to take in the senator. He's surrounded by well-wishers. The Halseys have money and influence. And when his son decided to get a degree in public health, he began shining both attention and cash on the place.

This is why I have to be careful. If you accuse the son of a powerful man, you can't do a half-assed job of it.

"Let's head right for the dean," I whisper. "She's over by that sculpture. And I need to say hello."

His hand gives mine a squeeze, and I feel calmer. Rickie is a charmer. This part will go fine. He's my rock.

"Daphne!" the dean says, turning to greet me as I approach. "How lovely to see you!"

"I'm so glad I could make it," I say in an almost normal voice. "Dean Reynolds, this is my friend Rickie Ralls." I introduce Rickie, who gives her a winning smile. And we make small talk about Vermont for a couple of minutes, until someone more important than I am wants her attention.

With that over, I make our excuses and I steer Rickie toward the wine and cheese, where I allow myself to be waylaid by a couple of research assistants who used to share an office space with me in our old building.

Rickie stands at my side, holding a glass of wine, and playing the part of the perfect date.

Until I feel him tense up and turn his body by ninety degrees, as if shielding me from something. When I glance past him, I find Reardon Halsey a few yards away, staring at me.

And if looks could kill, I'd be dead already.

FORTY

RICKIE

The fight-or-flight response is well described in the literature. It's recognized as the first stage of Hans Selye's general adaptation syndrome. As a response to acute stress, the body suddenly releases hormones which activate the sympathetic nervous system and stimulate the adrenal glands. Respiration, the heart rate, and blood pressure also accelerate. Pupils may dilate. Muscles may shake or tremble.

I experience all of this in the span of about five seconds, until I take a deep breath, expanding my lungs, collecting oxygen, and ordering my body to calm the fuck down.

It's about two percent effective. Because when I glimpsed Reardon Halsey a moment ago, I knew. He's the one. He's the reason I lock the doors. He's the one who stole months of my life. He almost killed me.

And I can't let him anywhere near Daphne.

Inside, I'm all turmoil. But adrenaline is a powerful drug. I slip a hand onto Daphne's wrist. "You were going to give me that tour," I say silkily.

"Right," she says tightly. She's spotted him, too.

Her friends smile and say something gracious that I miss, because I'm calculating all the ways to get out of this room. There's the door we came in, but Halsey is blocking it. There are glass elevators at either side, probably leading up to the offices that surround this atrium.

I don't like any of those choices, so I lead Daphne to the side of the room, under the overhang, where we'll be less noticeable. "Talk to me," I whisper. "We can leave now, right?"

"No, I need to go upstairs," she says.

"That's a bad idea," I insist, guiding her to stand beside a large, potted topiary.

Daphne blinks up at me, trouble in her brown eyes. "Why are you freaking out right now?" she whispers. "What aren't you telling me?"

"Nothing," I lie.

Her eyes narrow. "Do *not* lie to me. That's what *he* did."

Shit. There's a knot of pressure in the center of my chest. "I recognize him."

"You mean..." She blinks. "From the Academy?"

I lean my body outward for a quick glance toward Halsey. And it's a huge mistake. He's not looking at us right now because he's talking to a woman. His girlfriend, from the looks of it. But it doesn't matter that he's smiling. I know that face when it's angry. I know he's responsible for other people's pain.

"*Rickie*," Daphne orders, squeezing my hand. "Tell me what you know."

"There's no time. It's a long story. Let's go."

"*No*," she insists. "And screw you and your long story. We just spent four hours in a car, with you acting all jumpy and weird. Seems like you had plenty of time to say whatever you had to say then."

"I'm sorry," I grunt. "Let's go somewhere else and discuss this."

"Don't even try it," she hisses. "This ends now."

Then? She jerks her hand out of mine and walks away from me. She marches half the length of the atrium and smacks the button on the elevator. It opens immediately, and she steps inside.

Shit! I take a few steps in her direction, but the doors close immediately.

And now I am on fire with panic. I turn in the opposite direction, heading for that set of open stairs I'd spotted. I leap up them two at a time, my eyes following the glass elevator, which stops on the third level.

I stop on the third floor, too. And then I position myself against the wall, where I can see most of the O-shaped third level, but I'm largely hidden from the atrium floor.

My heart is trying to climb out of my mouth as Daphne walks slowly around the third-floor loop. She's trying to look casual, stopping to look at the construction work that's still in progress. There are paint chips taped to the walls, and the odd ladder here and there. But then she stops in front of an office and tries the door.

I don't breathe again until it fails to open. *Thank fuck*. Maybe now I can get her to leave.

With my head down and my hands jammed casually in my pockets, I start toward her. But as I watch, she pulls something from her pocket. A card. She slips this between the doorjamb and the door, which is never going to work.

The door opens, and a light flickers on inside the office.

Fuck fuck fuck. As a reflex, I look down toward the atrium. My gaze finds Reardon Halsey immediately. He's staring upward at the third-floor office with the light on.

Then he turns, his girlfriend's hand in his, and leads her over to the other glass elevator on the opposite side of the atrium.

My heart nearly detonates.

Hugging the wall, I hoof it toward Daphne. I'm able to move quickly for a few seconds. But then the glass elevator opposite me glides into view. So I slow my pace and turn my face away. I also grab a ladder that's leaning against the wall and carry it the last ten paces to the office door where Daphne disappeared.

"He saw you," I grunt toward the door that's ajar. "He's coming."

"Shit!" she squeaks. I don't see her. She's hidden from view, possibly kneeling behind the desk.

I open up the ladder while my brain whirls.

"Can I walk out right now?" she asks in a trembling voice.

The elevator doors are already open across the atrium, and Halsey and his girl have begun to walk the loop. "No. Stay put." If she exits now, he'll easily see her.

And if he's going to tangle with one of us, it's going to be me.

I drag the open ladder right in front of the office door. Then I grab a toolbox that's sitting on the floor, and I climb the damn ladder toward the dropped ceiling. I put the tools on the fold-out shelf. Then I lift my hands, displacing a fiberglass ceiling tile, setting it aside, creating a hole in the ceiling.

Climbing one more step, my head disappears into the blackness above. Looking down, I open the toolbox with hands that somehow aren't shaking. I choose a heavy pair of wire snips, with sharp, fierce-looking tips.

And I wait.

I don't know how long it takes for Halsey and his girlfriend to approach. It's probably only about sixty seconds, but it feels like a year.

It's long enough for me to conjure up his face from my nightmares. That smirk he made in the dark when I realized I was roped to my own bunk. The shout that caught in my throat because I'd been gagged, too.

He and his pals had pulled off an act of cunning and violence. They'd upended lives. And—with a little help from Paul—I'd picked a hell of a day to remember it.

I'm sweating through my shirt when two pairs of shiny shoes appear at the foot of the ladder. "That's my office you're blocking."

That *voice*. I feel it like a splash of ice water. Dread curls into my gut. That voice whispered sick things to me in the dark. I'd turned my head away from it. But I couldn't move. I'd been immobilized.

Oh, God. I grab a joist near my face and hold onto it with a white-knuckled grip. There's not enough air up here.

"I need you to move," he says, the sneer only partially concealed behind a thin layer of good breeding.

More memories are drowning me. His sneer. His casual violence toward the plebes.

And now he's waiting for me to say something. "Give me five to ten," I grunt. My hands feel ice cold. It's another stress response—the body reserving blood for the brain and the essential organs.

Breathe, Rickie. Just breathe.

"Could you just step aside *now*?" he barks. "And did you *open* my office door?"

"Needed the light," I growl. "You need the internet to work, right? Your kind always does. But it's after hours, buddy. I need five to ten."

By which I mean—I need him to go to prison for five to ten years.

His silence seems to last a week. God knows I'm doing a shit job of looking like an actual maintenance worker. Thank Christ his girl-friend is at his side. He's less likely to make a scene.

"Two minutes," he grunts. "And close my damn door." His foot-steps retreat.

I count to thirty, then lower the snips to the toolbox with a shaky hand. "Thirty seconds," I hiss.

"Right here," comes a meek reply from behind the door.

Dipping out of my hiding place, I see Halsey and his girlfriend disappear into the elevator on our side of the ring. I force myself to take one more breath to let the doors slide closed.

"Okay, count to ten and then open that door."

Quickly, I replace the ceiling panel, jump down the ladder, and grab the tool box. Then I fold the ladder and park it against the wall as Daphne slips out, her purse over her shoulder, her face bright red. "I'm sorry."

"Shh." I take her hand and walk her quickly, heading for the stair-well again. "I can't tell if he went up or down. But there has to be another door out of this place."

"There is. At the bottom of the stairs."

"Let's move." Tightening my grip on her hand, we gun it across to the stairs, and then trot down them as quickly as I dare.

I can't see Halsey anywhere. But I won't let go of Daphne. Not until we're far away from here. The stairs continue down another half flight past the atrium. And then I see a blessed sight—a set of double doors with a red EXIT sign glowing above them.

We're pushing through them a minute later. "The car should be that way." I point to the right.

"Yes." Daphne is flushed, her eyes pinched. "I really fucked that up. I can't believe you got rid of him."

"Shh," I say, forcing us to walk at a mostly normal pace around the building. It's going to take some time, seeing as the place is huge. The grass is perfectly mown, and chrysanthemums bloom in a care-fully landscaped row.

Meanwhile, my heart is still ready to explode. I'm remembering the ropes cutting into my skin as I tried to escape. Halsey trussed me to my bed, and somehow broke several of my bones. I still don't remember how I got injured. But I remember Paul's gagging sobs on the bunk above me.

They raped him. I'm ninety-nine percent sure. It took me twelve hours of digging, but I'd found the court martial summary early this afternoon. I'd printed it out and folded it up in my wallet. Then I'd gotten into the car to drive here. I'd put two hands on the wheel, at two o'clock and ten o'clock.

And that summary is still burning a hole in my pocket, and my brain:

Decision: Sergeant A.P. Horst was relieved of his command at the United States Tactical Services Academy, and demoted to O-4. Crime: dereliction of duty, and endangerment of students in his care. Incident: two students assaulted on campus by upperclassmen. Both victims admitted to the infirmary and later hospitalized, one with multiple fractures, one with contusions, internal injuries and anal bleeding. Further action: three students expelled, one infirmary tech reassigned.

That's it. That's the whole writeup. But the moment I'd read it, I'd known. And I'd begun to remember.

Our hands still in a sweaty hold, Daphne and I finally reach the corner of this monolith, and we turn. At last the Volvo comes into view. I let go of Daphne's hand, and pat my pocket for the keys. "I don't want to stay here overnight."

"Okay," she says immediately. "But I need my stuff from the inn."

"Right. I walk toward the car, stopping on the passenger side so I can open the door for Daphne. The Volvo was made before remote key entry was a thing. I slide the key into the lock and turn it.

Someone steps out from behind an SUV and appears in my field of vision.

Daphne gasps behind me.

It's Halsey. He's alone.

I let go of the keys and square off toward him, my instincts jumping. I will not be caught off guard by this man again.

"*You*," he says. "I thought I was losing it. But it is you, Ralls." He takes a step closer. "Miss me?"

"Get the fuck away from us," I snarl. "I promise it'll be harder to take me out when I'm awake. You won't enjoy it."

His mouth goes hard. "I don't care about you, dumbass. Whatever Daphne took from my office, she's going to give it back now."

"She didn't take anything," I growl. "Get out of my face. You're lucky I don't drive right to the nearest police station and turn you in for assault and rape."

Daphne makes a shocked noise.

"That'll work well," Halsey says. "Seeing as you can't remember a thing. Your therapist calling around looking for answers isn't going to win hearts and minds. Thanks for that, by the way. My cousin got a kick out of it when he answered the phone. He took careful notes. You're a stupid fuck, Ralls. And so is your whore of a girlfriend."

They call it *fight-or-flight* for a reason.

I lunge at him.

FORTY-ONE

DAPHNE

The next sixty seconds are the longest of my life. I've seen fights on TV. Men circling each other, building the drama before a punch is thrown.

This is not that. This is Rickie hurtling at Reardon, crashing him to the asphalt, fists flying. This is Reardon letting out a warlike shout and then going silent again when Rickie smashes a fist into his mouth.

His rage steals my breath. Thick, choking rage. Rickie is a blur. His fists land several times before Reardon can mount a defense, punching Rickie so hard that his head snaps back.

The fight only burns hotter. Rickie pushes Reardon to the pavement and punches once. Twice. The sound of his fist colliding with Reardon's face is terrifying. He hits him again and my fear is so sharp that I can feel bile climbing my throat. "Rickie!" I shriek.

Miraculously, he freezes.

I don't breathe at all for the next few seconds, as Rickie staggers to his feet.

Then I see Reardon move. And for one awful moment I think I've made a horrible mistake, placing Rickie at a disadvantage.

But Reardon only rolls to his hands and knees, his head dropped. "You will fucking pay," he spits. And there's blood dripping down his formerly perfect cheek.

On autopilot, I grab the keys to the Volvo out of the passenger door. "Get in," I snap at Rickie.

And Rickie does. There's blood on his lip, and a wild look in his eye. But I block out the image of that blood. And I don't even look at Reardon. Stiffly, I walk around and open the driver's door, sliding in behind the wheel.

With shaking hands I start the car. My breath is coming fast. I feel as though I'm watching a movie of someone else's life as I look carefully over my shoulder to check for obstacles before I back out.

When I look back at Reardon before pulling away, he's covering his face with two hands. But I can still see his eyes. And the rage in them is on a plane I've never seen before in my life.

I've never been so scared. But I'm angry, too. And that anger fuels me as I press down on the accelerator and get the hell out of that parking lot.

An hour later we're cruising up 91. I'm still too angry to breathe. But I'm no longer driving.

First, I'd made a stop at the inn.

"I can't go inside with you," Rickie had said when I pulled in. His delivery had been flat and cold, which terrified me almost as much as watching him try to kill Reardon. "Get your things. Don't speak to anyone if you can avoid it. Leave the key in the room but don't check out at the desk."

I'd cut the engine and turned to look at him. His lip was bloody and already swelling, along with one eyebrow.

But the worst evidence of the fight was the look he held in those beautiful gray eyes. It was nothingness. Like someone had drained all the Rickie right out of him.

I'd been in shock myself. I'd gone upstairs and retrieved my things exactly as he'd suggested, leaving the key on the unused bed.

When I'd returned to the Volvo he was sitting in the driver's seat dry-swallowing a couple of aspirin. His mouth was no longer bleeding.

"Are you really okay to drive?" I'd asked, tossing my bag in the back. He hadn't even answered. He'd just started the engine.

Now we're driving up the right lane at a startlingly cautious sixty-four miles per hour in absolute silence, Rickie's eyes never leaving the road.

And I'm practically climbing out of my skin. "What happened ?" I finally gasp. "Do you remember Reardon?"

"Yes," he grunts.

"If you remembered him, you should have *said* something. You should have stayed home."

At first I think he won't respond. But after a long beat, he does. "I was never letting you tangle with him alone."

My anger notches up another couple of levels, and my voice goes high with hysteria. "Oh, so this is better? Watching you try to kill him? Everything is fucked. He'll tell the dean I broke into his office, and that my boyfriend attacked him. He could have you arrested."

There's silence from the driver's seat for several miles. And when Rickie speaks again, his voice is pure ice water. "Take out your phone. I need to give you a number."

"Whose?" I gasp. There isn't enough oxygen, suddenly. *Take out your phone.* He'd said that to me before. On our first trip up 91.

Before I'd met Reardon. Before Rickie had been—

I'm afraid to finish that thought. The words Rickie had hurled at Reardon were terrifying. I put that thought in a drawer and close it. For now.

"Your phone," he repeats.

"Whose number?" I gasp again. The air is too thin. I can't think.

"My father's. Take this number. And try to breathe slow."

So I take out my damn phone, and I tap in the number he gives me. Then I plug my phone into Rickie's charger.

And, as we drive up the highway, I eventually breathe more slowly. I close my eyes and I absolutely do not think about everything that just happened. I can't. Not yet. I put my fear into that same imaginary drawer and close it.

Instead, I picture Rickie's house on Spruce Street. In a few hours we'll be there, the door closed and locked. Nothing bad ever happens on Spruce Street.

And in the morning it will all be less terrifying. Maybe then I'll be able to think what to do. Maybe I'll be less angry.

I'm *so* angry.

"You should have told me," I repeat. "When did you realize you recognized him?"

Silence.

"When, Rickie? Don't lie to me. You said you'd never lie to me."

"I didn't," he grunts.

"Really? Then tell me when you realized you knew Reardon."

He sighs, which is proof—just barely—that he hasn't been snatched by aliens and exchanged for a robot. "After your birthday," he croaks. "I Googled him. I knew his face, but I didn't know why. This week my Academy roommate finally wrote me back. And I learned some things about my accident."

"You learned some things," I repeat, while fury blooms in my chest, bright and dangerous. "You should have *said!*" I shriek. "You're probably in trouble now. And I'm in trouble. I'm in *worse* trouble than I would have been alone."

"I'm sorry," he croaks.

But it doesn't help, because I'm working myself into a real lather now. Anger is easier on my breaking heart than cold, cold fear. "You're *sorry*," I hiss. "That's nice. That's an uptick from the last man I trusted, who screwed me over *without* saying sorry. Yay, me! Screwed over again, but I get a *sorry* this time."

"Daphne, listen—"

"*Why?*" I shriek. "So you can be *sorry*?"

"*Listen!*" he shouts. He also puts the blinker on and decelerates, even though we're nowhere near an exit. "You say whatever you need to. You tell them whatever you want. Don't spare me, because I don't deserve it. But do *not* talk to them when you're angry, okay? And don't do it alone."

"Talk to who?" I gasp. And then I notice a flash of blue in the side view mirror out my window.

A cop car. Holy shit. Rickie is being pulled over.

"We're not speeding," I say, as if I could make more sense of this.

"He works fast. Senator's son." Rickie stops the car. "It's probably on every cop's radio for three states."

My head swivels like an owl's, and now there are *two* cop cars. One of them pulls to a stop in front of us. The other behind us.

And the cop up ahead gets out of the car with his hand on his gun.

Slowly, Rickie lifts his hands where they'll be visible above the steering wheel. "I'm sorry," he whispers, and I can barely hear him over the sound of blood pounding in my ears. "Call your family, okay? They'll help you. And call my father."

The next few minutes are surreal.

"Step out of the car, sir," the cops say. "You too, miss."

It's windy on the side of the road, and the cold goes all the way to my bones.

The cops are calm, in their commanding way. But I'm not. I watch them bend Rickie over the hood of the car. He doesn't look at me. My throat closes up as they cuff him, his hands behind his back.

They read him his rights. They lead him away to the back of a cruiser, and shove him inside.

He still doesn't look at me.

Again, it's like I'm watching a film of someone else's reality. Until the cops turn their attention to me. One of them, a woman with a tight ponytail, asks me for ID. I give it to her, and she makes a note of everything on my license.

"We'll have questions for you," she says. "You have to follow me to the station, back in Harkness County. Or else I'll take you in the back of my cruiser."

"I'll drive," I say, barely processing her words. I don't want to go anywhere in a cruiser.

"All right," she says. "You are right on my tail, then. If you're not, we're going to have a problem."

"Got it," I say, my good girl complex answering for me.

"I'll give you a minute to get situated," she says. "You flash the headlights when you're ready for me to pull out."

"Okay."

She heads to the cruiser, and I get into the driver's seat. My phone is right there on the charger. I pick it up, noticing that my hands are clammy and slick. I wipe my hands on the skirt I put on hours ago. A *lifetime* ago, really. And I unlock my phone.

Rickie wanted me to call his dad. But as my eyes fill with tears, I realize there's someone else I need more right now. I hit a different name on my contacts list. The family lawyer. And then I hold my breath, listening to it ring.

"Daphne?" my sister's voice says. "What's up?"

"May?" I gasp. "I need your help. So badly. I fucked up. The police have Rickie!"

"What? Slow down. Tell me where you are. *Exactly* where you are."

Instead, I burst into tears.

"Whoa, Daphne. Honey," she says, her voice steady. "Are you in Burlington?"

"C-C-Connecticut," I stammer between sobs. "On the s-side of the highway."

"Where is Rickie?"

"Arrested! He punched Reardon!"

"Who?"

"My ex."

May blows out a breath. "Okay, first I need you to move the car to a safer place, and then wait for me."

"I *can't!* The police expect me to follow them to the station."

"Wow. Okay. First up, don't drive until you're calm, and you can see clearly. Then you can follow the police to the station, but *do not talk to them*. Wait in the car. No interview room for you until I get there. You tell them you're waiting for your lawyer. You have *no* obligation to answer their questions. Got it?"

"*Yes*," I sob. "Thank you."

"Share your location from your phone, then wait for me."

She hangs up before I can say anything more.

I put my head on the steering wheel and cry.

FORTY-TWO

RICKIE

The holding tank smells like piss. It's hard to focus on deep breathing exercises when every new breath is sharp with the scent of urine.

It's also hard to breathe deeply when your nose is broken. Which mine is, thanks to the cop that brought me into this cell and punched me in the face when I asked to make a phone call.

"That's for fucking with the senator's son," he'd said.

Spoiler: I didn't get that phone call. And my nose is killing me.

Now I'm seated on the floor at one end of the cell. On the other end, there's a bunk with nobody on it. Even though I'm alone in here, and exhausted, I can't go near that thing.

At least now I know why. Halsey tied me to one—the bottom bunk. My roommate was up top, the poor guy, when some number of cadets climbed up there with him.

And then? I think it broke. I'm pretty sure the bed fell on me, and the weight of those guys is what broke my bones.

I've worked this out while sitting here all night, thinking over everything that happened to me. I don't remember the moment I suffered the injuries. But Paul's assault is coming back to me in bits and pieces.

I couldn't help him. And then I woke up in a hospital with injuries consistent with falling from a high wall.

But there never was a wall. I remember watching that bed sway like a hurricane. I remember hearing the splintering of wood as the frame gave way.

After that, nothing.

So it's been a long, difficult night. I've had a lot of time to sit on this cold floor remembering. There were some moments when the memories got darker. There were chills, and trouble breathing. But I'm feeling pretty calm now, especially for a guy who's probably going to be convicted of assault.

Since I demanded a lawyer immediately, I'm stuck here 'til business hours, waiting for a public defender, or for whomever else shows up to help me.

Before they abandoned me in here, I overheard a policewoman saying that Daphne was waiting in the parking lot for her sister to show up. "She came inside to use the ladies' room and to tell me that her sister—a lawyer—was on her way down from Vermont."

That's helped me relax. I already knew Daphne was sharp. She probably hates my guts right now, and I don't blame her. But at least she called her family instead of letting fear and anger get the best of her.

Not that I can say the same. Beating on Halsey was a stupid ass thing to do. So fucking stupid. I completely lost my shit. And, yeah, my reasons were solid. But they don't matter very much right now.

If I'm convicted of assault, I can kiss my career as a clinical psychologist goodbye. It's pretty much a given that no state would want to license a violent felon. And no graduate program will want to take me on, either.

So this is what it looks like to hit bottom. It looks like screwing your own future. It looks like letting the Reardon Halseys of the world win.

Daphne was right. I should have leveled with her about my brand-new realizations. And I never should have come to Connecticut. But I couldn't quite put it together without proof. I wanted to see his face in person. I wanted to take measure of my own reaction. I wanted to walk toward the flame even if it burned.

But it burned too hot. I snapped. And now I'll pay the price. I'll lose my career path. I'll probably lose Dylan. And I'll probably lose Daphne. That's the worst part of all.

Hell, I might be starting over in a new place. Again. And this time my memory won't fail. So I'll be able to recall every single foolish thing I did, and every opportunity I've squandered.

I close my eyes and finally nod off.

And for once, that big fucking lock on the door of this cell isn't making it easier to sleep.

When I wake up, a uniformed officer is unlocking the door. At least it's not the guy who punched me. It's a new guy. My neck is so stiff I can barely lift my head to look at him. "Your counsel is here," he says.

I get up slowly and follow him into an interview room, where a guy in a suit waits. "I'm your lawyer," he says without preamble. "And I'd like some time with my client."

"You got fifteen minutes," the officer says. Then he leaves, closing the door behind himself.

"Don't tell me anything," the lawyer whispers. He's wearing a very natty pinstripe suit.

"Okay?" I'm so confused right now. "Who are you?"

"Robert Grant, attorney at law. Your father hired me on the advice of May Shipley."

"Nice to meet you," I say automatically, and my voice sounds all wrong because of my swollen nose. "So if I'm not supposed to talk to *you*, then who…?"

"Sit down. Your nose looks broken."

"I noticed that. It wasn't broken until my arrest."

"*Shit.* Okay, here's what's going to happen. You're going to listen to my advice. I may ask you a question or two. But we can't assume this conversation is private."

"Oh." I can't help but glance around at the four solid walls surrounding us. There must be cameras in here?

I sit down, and my lawyer does the same. "Look, the charge against you is aggravated assault. But the state's attorney is offering to plead down to simple assault. He says we have an hour to decide."

"Really?" I feel dizzy with hope. Or maybe that's just hunger and exhaustion. "Is simple assault a misdemeanor?"

"Yes."

"Then—"

He holds up a hand. "You're not speaking. You're listening."

I sigh.

"Look, most cases I get called on are boring. There's a bar fight. Somebody gets arrested. They set bail at the arraignment, or maybe I can wheedle a plea deal out of the busy state's attorney because it's a first offense and they don't want to clog the docket with boring little cases. But your case is different."

"I bet it is," I grunt. Not everybody mauls a senator's son in a public place, on the campus of a vaunted university.

"Look, my phone is blowing up with messages from the state's attorney's office. They're *panting* for you to plead this down. That is not how this usually works." He grins.

But I don't see what's so amusing. "Is that good?"

"Yeah, I think it is. I can think of a couple reasons why they're so hot to trot. The first reason is that maybe you're not guilty. Maybe you were defending yourself against an attack from the senator's son. Maybe they arrested the wrong guy." He winks.

"That's an interesting theory," I mumble. But of course it's not true.

"It turns out there aren't any cameras in that parking lot. The building is too new. It would come down to eyewitnesses. Those are thin on the ground, too."

"Oh, hell." I see where he's headed, but this is a terrible idea. The only eyewitness was Daphne. And I'm *never* asking her to take the witness stand and lie on my behalf. "My girlfriend has been through a lot," I say softly.

"Fine. Maybe you'd rather hear my other theory," he says. "Let's say the senator's son is a top-level creep who had it coming. I notice he was real quick to call the police after you two fought. He memorized your license plate. He mobilized the entire police force in two counties to hunt you down. That's how an entitled schmuck behaves."

"Sure." He's got that right. "But I don't see how that helps me."

"Right. So he did his thing, and now they've booked you on an assault charge that will derail your life for the second time in three years. That's really bad news, so you'll have to fight it. And now it's morning time, and daddy's lawyers have begun explaining what a trial will entail. For example, any history between the defendant and the victim will be examined in court. One potential eyewitness is your girlfriend, who used to be *his* girlfriend. So that will come out, too..."

My stomach lurches. "I won't throw Daphne under this bus. I'm never doing that."

"Uh huh. That's admirable. But I need you to think this all the way through. The Halsey family has got you in lockup. They don't want you to hit their baby boy. But on the other hand, they don't want a trial. Maybe you're willing to delve deeply into your history with the Halsey kid. Maybe your girlfriend has a few things to say about him, too. So this morning they're hoping you get a lazy lawyer who urges you to take this plea. You're still convicted of a violent crime, which you may or may not have committed. It's a deal, but it's not the best deal you could get."

"What is the best deal?" I have to ask.

"I got a real sensitive nose, Richard. I can smell fear. And I smell a lot of it this morning. If you plead not guilty, the judge sets bail and gives you a trial date. Then I'm going to start digging into the Halsey boy to try to defend you. Now, court cases are very public. Everything is on the record. If you'd been, say, assaulted by the victim before, we could introduce that at trial. If the victim has been expelled from a prestigious educational institution, he may not want that made public. Maybe the pain of going to trial is greater for him than the pain of his own broken nose."

Now I get it. And, yeah, Halsey doesn't really want me telling a packed courtroom where I met him. He has plenty to hide. "Maybe he hurt people before. Like me. Maybe he also threatened his girlfriend, and he doesn't want people to hear about it when she testifies."

"Now you're getting it." His grin is smug.

"Suppose they don't want a trial at all. So how does that work?"

"You plead *not guilty*. And then bail is set and the state's attorney has to dig in and make his case. So the newspapers get hold of this story and start writing about every motion that's filed. That gets more and more uncomfortable for them until the senator asks for the charges to be dropped."

"There's a lot of maybes in your theory, here," I point out. If I turn down that plea deal, then I have to expose myself to scrutiny, too. I'll have to tell people what happened to me. And, by extension, to Paul.

Shit. He'll get called as a witness. He'll be asked to describe a horrible thing in great detail. The same horrible thing that landed him in a mental institution. I don't know if I can ask that of him, just to avoid a misdemeanor charge that, let's face it, isn't frivolous.

And then there's Daphne. She'd also have to sit up there and admit to her relationship.

"I don't know," I whisper. "Do I have to make this decision without speaking to anyone else?"

"Yes," he says. "And you've got an hour, tops."

———————————

That hour goes fast.

I'm given a rubber bagel and some brown water that's supposed to be coffee. I brush my teeth with my finger and change into a fresh shirt that my lawyer brought me. I wonder if he buys them in bulk, for every time he needs to make a loser look presentable.

There's no help for my broken face, though. My face is throbbing with pain, and my nose is so swollen that it's distracting in my field of vision.

I'm handcuffed again for the trip out of my cell. The cops lead me down a series of hallways and into a dingy room where my lawyer is waiting. An ancient sign reading COURTROOM ENTRANCE is affixed to another door.

"You clean up nice," my lawyer says with a chuckle.

"Oh, we're doing comedy now?" I growl.

"Laugh or cry, kid. Sometimes those are the only choices. Listen— we step inside that courtroom, you let me do all the talking. You get one spoken line in this drama. After I enter your plea, the judge will ask if that is correct, and you'll say: *Yes your honor*. That's it."

"Okay."

"So don't keep me waiting. What's it going to be?"

"I haven't decided."

"Oh, Richard. They told me you were a genius."

I snort. "Who did?"

"Your girl and her sister."

"They're not *here*, are they?" I don't know how I'm supposed to make this choice, knowing that other people will be affected.

He actually rolls his eyes. "Don't look to the girlfriend for advice. It's your ass on the line. No handcuffs on her."

"But she's affected by this. If there's a trial..."

"Let's go!" says a uniformed bailiff. He swings the door open.

"Chin up," my lawyer says, stepping into the courtroom ahead of me. And then I hear him add, "Holy smokes, that's a big crowd."

I follow him into a large room. We're up front, by the judge's dais. There are already several handcuffed defendants seated on benches near the front, most with a lawyer seated beside them.

But my lawyer's gaze is on a cluster of guys with sharp suits, silk ties and shining haircuts on the other side of the room.

They're all staring at me. Every one of them.

Suddenly my skin feels hot and tight. And I'm way too conscious of my unwashed hair and my damaged face. I look like something dragged in from the gutter. And those men are here to make me feel small and afraid.

It's working.

"Look over there," my lawyer whispers. "They want your attention."

I turn and spot May Shipley. But *only* May, not Daphne. And then I notice the man standing next to her.

My father. His expression is... I can barely stand it. The man looks devastated.

So this is what total humiliation feels like. I thought I was done leveling up in all the ways I'd disappointed him. But this is much worse than suing his alma mater. He's here to watch me become a goddamn criminal.

Fuck. My throat goes dry and my eyes are hot.

"Follow me," the lawyer says. He grabs my arm and steers me up the aisle toward an empty bench at the back of the loser section.

I sit down and face the judge. I take a deep yoga breath, and I feel grateful that Daphne isn't here. I'm desperate to know what she'd want me to do. But I don't actually want her to witness this.

On the one hand, she wouldn't want Halsey to win. I know this.

On the other hand, I don't want to cause her any more pain than I already have. I don't want to make her testify on account of my screwups. She'd hate that.

It's all sinking in now. Daphne and I won't survive this. I've already lost her. It started the moment I failed to mention that Halsey's face looked familiar. And it ended when I attacked him in front of her.

Swear to God, losing Daphne will hurt more than having a misdemeanor on my record. But how many times can I fail her? First I stood her up. Then I held back information, even though I know she has trust issues. I can't make her testify at a trial involving *two* men who failed her.

I'll take the plea deal and spare her the rest. It's the least I can do.

Someone clears her throat behind me. "*Rickie*." It's May Shipley's voice.

"Son," my father whispers.

I don't want to turn around.

My lawyer pokes me.

Fuck. I swivel my busted face over my shoulder and lock eyes with May. "Fight it," she hisses. "Don't let him win."

I give a slow blink, because this is definitely surprising. May of all people should know what a trial will entail.

"And I'll help," my father says. When I crank my neck around to find him, his face is red. "It's not too late for that, right? I'll help you."

Hell, now my eyes are stinging.

"Docket number 2305547!"

"Game time," my lawyer says. "Stand up. Now what's it going to be?"

FORTY-THREE

DAPHNE

May: They called his case.

When I see my sister's text, my heart leaps into my throat. I should be in that courtroom. But I'm sitting outside the dean's office, because when I called her first thing this morning to beg for a few minutes of her time, she'd said "If you can get here by ten thirty I'll fit you in."

It's ten thirty right now. I'm glued to my phone. May and I were up half the night discussing Rickie's legal situation in the hotel room I'd planned to share with Rickie. My sister briefed me on his choices, and my stomach is in knots over it.

I need him to plead not guilty. I need him to fight it. Reardon Halsey *cannot* win.

This is all my fault, too. I shouldn't have dragged Rickie into my mess. I've spent the last year with my head up my ass, fixated on my own fall from grace. I should have known better than to imagine I could secretly fix this clusterfuck I've created.

That's stupid, not brave. And now Rickie will pay the price.

The office door opens, and Dean Rebecca Reynolds waves me in.

I sneak another look at my phone. There's no further update from May. So I shove the phone into my bag because I cannot let it distract me right now. I walk into the dean's office and close the door behind me.

"It's good to see you," she says immediately. "I'm still in the dark about why you quit your job last year. And now I hear that you've left the university? Could that even be true?"

"Yes," I say, and my voice shakes a little. Because I'm here to tell the truth. "I made some mistakes last year. I need to tell you some things, and you won't be happy with me."

"All right," she says, her expression grave. "Why don't you start at the beginning."

So that's what I do. "First, I had a sexual relationship with Reardon Halsey, even though I knew it was wrong, since I was his supervisor."

Her eyes widen, and I tremble. But I just keep on going. I explain how he ended things without drama. And that I'd felt guilty writing his evaluation, but I'd done it carefully.

Then I explain how I'd accidentally caught him throwing away surveys.

She gasps, but she doesn't say anything.

So I ramble on about my suspicion of his motive. "But of course I couldn't prove it. My next mistake was confronting him, instead of sharing my suspicions with you. He threatened me so fast my head spun."

She sits back in her chair at that. But she doesn't interrupt me.

"And then I was stuck. If I shared my suspicions, he was going to accuse me of horrible things. I'd be thrown out of Harkness, or at least I'd be under investigation. So I panicked. I quit working here. I couldn't write another recommendation for him, obviously. And I didn't have any proof. It took me until this past summer to think of a way to prove what he'd done."

I pull out my tablet and set it on the desk. "I think you'll find a mismatch between the postal expenses and the survey entries. Last night, I snuck into the team office and snapped this photo of the login information."

"*Lord*, Daphne."

"I *know*. That was the absolute peak of my stupidity. I wanted to prove it myself, and then write you an anonymous letter about it. But then Reardon saw me, and he threatened me again, and my boyfriend attacked him."

"Good *Lord*."

"Yeah," I say with a sigh. "This is the hardest, most embarrassing conversation I've ever had. But that's all. That's the whole story. And whatever happens to me, I deserve it."

She sits back in her chair and stares at me for a long time. I'm nervous about what she's thinking. And I'm nervous about Rickie's case. And my future. But I just sit there and take it. Because I brought this upon myself.

"It's hard to know where to begin," she finally says.

"I'll bet."

Then she barks out a laugh, and covers her mouth with her hand. "It's always the quiet ones."

"I'm getting that a lot."

"I trusted you."

"I'm sorry," I say quickly.

"No, I mean I trusted *you*, and I didn't trust Mr. Halsey. But I didn't act on that feeling, because his father is a very powerful man."

"I'm sure you're not the first person to make that mistake," I point out. "I let him charm me into dating him, even though I knew I shouldn't. I liked the attention."

"You're not the first person to make that mistake, either," she says drily.

"Noted."

"You understand that I have to investigate everything you've told me."

"Of course."

"And that will take some time."

"I hope it takes a very long time," I point out. "Because I really need a college degree. And I'm only a few credits short. If I get arrested for trespassing here and then thrown out of Burlington U, that's it for me."

She puts her head in her hands. "Daphne, nobody is going to arrest you. And you'll finish your degree."

I sag with relief.

"You should have just *told* me that you were involved with him. You're both undergraduates. It didn't have to be a big deal. I would have rearranged things. Maybe you would have been taken off the project."

"In hindsight, that sounds perfectly acceptable. But I let my ambitions get in the way."

She shakes her head. "If it makes you feel any better, I'd already noted the strange turnout pattern in Hartford. It's gotten worse in the last couple of months."

I let out a little moan of anguish. "I'm sorry. I'm so sorry." A scientist is lost without her data. "I've ruined everything."

"Did you throw any surveys away, Daphne?"

"What?" I yelp. "No *way*."

"Right. You didn't create this problem. And the fact that it's continued after you left is part of the reason I believe your whole crazy story. But I still have to verify it."

"Of course you do. And if there's anything I can do to help—aside from staying far away from your brand-new office building—I will do it."

"How's Burlington U?"

"Good. Fine. I like it there. I have a job working for Dr. Drummond. If I'm lucky, I'll be applying to graduate school in a couple of months."

The dean taps her pen on the desktop. "Can anyone else verify that Mr. Halsey threatened you?"

"Well, no." My face reddens. "Only my boyfriend. But seeing as he punched Reardon yesterday after another string of those threats, nobody will believe him."

She flinches. "Mr. Halsey said he'd accuse you of sexual harassment."

Burning with shame, I nod.

"If that's the case, he's the harasser, Daphne. You're the one with a case against him."

"If I hadn't panicked, you'd be right," I admit in a small voice. "And he'll never confess. His type never does. The best I can hope for is that you verify the damage he did to your study. He can't try to blame me if it continued after I left. That's the only way I'll be out from under him—by slinking off to earn a degree somewhere else."

Her sigh is heavy. "All right, Daphne. Thank you for telling me the truth. I have a lot of work ahead of me."

"I'm sorry."

"I know you are," she says gently. "Hang in there. You'll hear from us eventually. I'll probably need you to sign a statement about all the things you just told me."

"Okay," I say, my throat closing up. I did it. I told the truth. And it didn't kill me. "Thank you."

With that finally done, I duck out of her office and speed walk back to the old Volvo. I'm nervous about running into Reardon, but luckily I don't see him anywhere.

It isn't until I'm locked safely into the car that I pull out my phone. There are two new texts from May. First she writes: *Plea is not guilty! Lawyers convened at the bench.*

Then, five minutes later: *CASE DISMISSED! OMG!*

There's also a photo of Rickie in a bear hug with an older man. It must be his dad. We'd called him last night, just like Rickie had asked me to do.

Now I call my sister, and she answers on the first ring. "You okay?" she asks.

Once again I'm humbled. May dropped everything to rush to Connecticut and be by my side. She found the litigator for Rickie. She met me in the parking lot of the police station and made me tell her the whole story. And then, after I told her about breaking into Reardon's office, she made me unavailable to talk to the police.

"I can just refuse?" I'd asked.

"You can, and you will," she'd said firmly.

Then she'd bought me a fast food sandwich and made me eat it.

She'd sat up late last night fielding calls from Rickie's dad and Rickie's new lawyer and explaining it all to me.

I guess she doesn't hate me after all.

"Daphne, are you okay?" she repeats. "What did the dean say?"

"She was floored. But she listened. Now she has to go and dig her way through that mess."

"Not your fault," my sister says firmly. "Where are you?"

"In the parking lot. Can I come to you and Rickie?"

"Honey, his dad took him home. He needs to get a doctor to look at his broken nose."

"Oh." My heart drops. "I have his car."

"I know, girly. You're going to have to drive it home. Are you okay to drive? Do you need some food, first?"

I open my mouth to refuse her help. And then I think better of it. "Let's get some food," I agree. "And coffee. My treat. And then I'll let you get back to your life."

"Sounds nice," she says.

"I love you," I choke out. "Thank you for this."

"I love you, too," May says. "Now pick a place. I'm starved. Drama makes me hungry."

So I pick a pizza joint that I used to love.

But not as much as I love May and Rickie.

FORTY-FOUR

RICKIE

"I just want you to know that I'm sorry," my father says, both his hands on the wheel.

"You said, Dad. It's okay." Actually, he's said so about a million times in the last forty-eight hours.

It's Saturday, and my dad is driving me back to Moo U. I'd gone home with him after my dramatic court appearance—after I'd rolled the dice on a not-guilty plea.

The fact that it had worked, and worked immediately, is still hard to get my head around. My lawyer had been right when he'd guessed that the Halsey family didn't want a trial. That Reardon had too much to lose.

But I still feel raw—like it was a horribly close call. It's as if I almost got into a serious car accident, and can't stop hearing the squeal of the brakes in my head, and can't stop seeing the terror in the other driver's eyes.

I'm not over it.

And now my father can't stop apologizing to me. And my mother can't stop fussing. When I'd told them what really happened to me—and Paul—they'd been horrified. "I'm *glad* you sued them! They should *pay* for letting an animal run wild in a venerable institution." That's his new tune. Like I'm some kind of hero.

I don't feel like one, though. I feel like a loser. He'd wanted to drive me straight to the nearest hospital to have my nose looked at. "And you should sue the cop, too!"

But I'd turned down both those suggestions. I'd asked Dad to take me home instead, to my parents' house, where I hadn't been since Christmas. I'd just wanted a shower and a bed.

My mother had cried over me. The broken nose didn't help. I'd felt terrible for making her worry. But after my shower and a great meal and a full night's sleep, I let her take me to a doctor.

He'd pronounced my nose broken, and said to ice it. *Quelle surprise.*

But I'd stayed two nights with my parents, who were overjoyed. It seems they love me more now that there's a new villain in my story. I hadn't fallen off a wall and wrecked myself. It was someone else's fault. They *adore* this change in the narrative.

But I'm still the same old wreck who's sneaking back into town when Daphne won't be home. I don't know how to process all the harm I brought her. I haven't spoken to her because she has my car, and therefore my phone charger. My phone died forty-eight hours ago.

And because I'm a damn coward.

But now I open the glove box of my dad's car, and I find an old charger of mine in there. So finally I plug that sucker in. After ten minutes of driving, my phone reboots. I watch the apple glow on the lock screen as my phone wakes up and remembers itself.

I'm honestly afraid to look at my messages. It's hard to say how widely the inglorious news of my arrest may have spread.

And sure enough, my texts are brimming over with messages— most of them from people named Shipley. I see a text from Daphne, of course. My stomach actually rolls with the sight of her name. But there are messages from Dylan, too, and May. And even Ruth, and Grandpa.

That's the one I open first, because the stakes are low.

August Shipley: *I heard you clocked Daphne's ex. I also heard he had it coming. That's a real bad boy at work. Just remember that bones heal, and chicks dig scars.*

Huh. So that's one Shipley who doesn't seem to hate me. But not the one that matters. I scroll again, finding frantic messages from

Lenore. Uh-oh. I seem to remember leaving off in the middle of a conversation with her.

And, yup, she's been blowing up my phone, sounding increasingly panicked. So I text back in a hurry. *I'm sorry! I just got my phone back online. And that's not the only thing. It's been a hell of a week. But the good news is that my memory is suddenly coming back.*

I swear it takes barely five seconds before she's typing a reply.

Lenore: What's the bad news? I'm afraid to ask.

Rickie: Oh boy. Don't be mad.

Lenore: I'm not here to judge you. I'm here to listen.

Rickie: The bad news is that I was arrested for punching the guy who broke all my ribs.

Lenore: WHAT? OMG, After I make sure you're okay I'M GOING TO KILL YOU!

Rickie: Didn't you just say…?

Lenore: I lied. Why did you put yourself in that situation? Answer your phone.

It rings in my hand.

"Dad, I kind of have to take this."

"Is it the girlfriend?" he asks.

"Actually, my therapist."

"Ah." I see his flinch, even though he tries to hide it. Because real men don't see therapists, or train to become one. Real men fly aircraft. "Go ahead, son," he says. Because he's trying, I guess.

"Hey," I say into the phone. "I knew you'd freak."

"Did you put yourself in a dangerous situation?" she asks.

"Yes. I thought I could handle it. Or at least I hoped I could. But I was wrong."

"You didn't own your trauma," she says softly.

"No," I admit. "And it almost cost me everything."

"Do you need to come and see me?" she asks. "I'll make time for you. Even on a Saturday."

"It can wait until Wednesday," I say.

"You sure?"

"Yeah—but I promise to call if I'm struggling."

"This will be you someday," she says. "Worrying about a patient when you're supposed to be enjoying your weekend."

"I'm sure you're right," I agree. "But don't worry about me, okay? Except for my broken nose, the bruises all over my face, and the split lip, I'm fine."

She lets out a shriek, and I have to hold the phone away from my ear to avoid going deaf.

My father laughs in the driver's seat.

"Rickie! Have you seen a doctor?"

"Yes ma'am. I'm fine. I promise. But I am not quite the looker I was last week. This is going to cost me some applause on karaoke night."

"I'm glad you can joke about it," she says, her voice low. "But I'm still worried."

"It's just a setback," I insist. "We'll talk soon."

She fusses over me for another minute, and then I hang up, exhausted. In truth, I feel wrecked. And it's not just my face. I feel hungover—if not from alcohol, then from life. At least it's Saturday, and Daphne will be at the farm. I don't have to face her. Not yet.

"Tell me where to turn," my father says, exiting the highway. "Let's get you home. I finally get to see this house."

You were always welcome here, I want to say. It was his choice to stay away from this place, because he didn't approve of how I came to own it.

But for once in my life, I keep my trap shut. A guy can only fight so many battles on one day.

A few minutes later he pulls up in front of my house, and I've never been so happy to be anywhere in my life. "Come on in," I say, climbing out of the passenger seat. "The house has good bones, and a new roof. The kitchen is stuck in a time warp, but I don't mind it."

"Cool roofline!" he enthuses. "If you ever want to sell, we could do a remodel of the kitchen."

"I think I'll just stay put." Leaving Vermont is obviously hazardous to my health. And since I've somehow avoided becoming a convicted felon, I'm still hoping to apply to the PsyD program at Moo U.

I take my dad inside, and I use the last of my energy to give him a tour of the first floor. I let him crow about the moldings and the original wood floors.

"This is a nice place, son." He rubs the oak bannister distractedly. "I hope you're very happy here. I'm sorry I let shit come between us. None of it was your fault."

"Uh, thanks," I grunt, too exhausted to be more gracious.

"I'm serious. Let's not be strangers," he says. "Even if you *do* actually fall off a damn wall, Rickie. I don't care anymore. I've missed you."

Oh, hell. I don't have the fortitude for more emotions today. "Thanks, Dad."

He claps me on the back. "You look beat. I'm going to go so that you can get some rest."

"Yeah, okay." I hear a creak from somewhere upstairs. Must be the wind. "Thanks for the ride back to town."

"Anytime."

I show him out. And the minute the door is closed, I sit down heavily on the staircase. I'm almost too tired to get up and head for my room, no matter how badly I want to see my bed.

Behind me, I hear another creak, and all the hair stands up on the back of my neck. "Keith?" I call out. But his car wasn't in the driveway with the Volvo.

When I hear a footfall above me, I turn around fast. I'm startled to see that it's Daphne who's descending the stairs.

"Oh, hi," I say stupidly, scrambling to my feet. I'm so not ready for this.

"Oh God, your *face*," she whispers. "What *happened?*"

"It ran into a cop's fist. But it looks worse than it is."

Her eyes get red as she descends the stairs. "They *beat* you?"

"It was one punch. That's what a dumbass gets for hitting the son of the most powerful man in Connecticut."

A tear rolls down her cheek. "You didn't reply to my texts."

Shit. I hold up my phone. "It was, uh, dead until exit 10. Charger was in the Volvo." But I realize I'm just being a dick right now. "Daphne, look. I know I could have tracked you down. But I honestly don't have any idea what to say to you."

Her beautiful eyes narrow. "Maybe you could have begun by letting me know you're still alive?"

Shit. I guess we're doing this right now. I take a step backward, because I cannot reach for her. It would probably break me. And I have to get this out. "I failed you from the very start, right? No calls or texts when I stood you up. That's kind of a pattern with me. I tell you that I'm the man for you, and then I let you down."

"Rickie," she gasps. "There were a few extenuating circumstances. I wanted to tell you how happy I was that you pled not guilty. And that it worked. I've been waiting all day to see you. Don't do this."

But that's the problem. I'm basically a toxin in her life. "Yeah, I rolled the dice in the courtroom, and it came up lucky. That was selfish. I would have dragged you into my mess."

She shakes her head. "I wanted you to beat him. We were pulling for you. May said she'd tell you to go for it. But she wouldn't let me come, too. She said you wouldn't want me there. And anyway, I had to go speak to the dean. You want to hear what she had to say?"

Yes, yes I do. But that isn't what I say. "I hope it's all good things, Daphne. You deserve that. But I hope you understand that you also deserve better than me."

After I get those difficult words out, I turn and walk away, finally reaching my room. Where I lock the door behind me.

FORTY-FIVE

DAPHNE

My mouth drops open as he walks away.

I've been waiting—waiting in this empty house for hours, just hoping he'd turn up. Now he's here. He's home. And I feel like I've been slapped.

Once again, a man I trusted has thrown me overboard. I stand here, feeling foolish, heaving in a breath so deep it hurts my lungs.

But then I let it out again, and I realize a few things in quick succession. Rickie came face to face with our common enemy. At which point he put himself between me and Reardon, to try to save me from my own stupidity.

Then he flew at Reardon right after the guy called me a whore. After which he was punched by a cop and spent a night in jail, before facing down a judge.

That's a lot.

In fact, I've buckled under far less pressure than that, and I've done worse damage. Just ask my sister.

I take another deep breath, and then I do what needs doing. I walk through the house to Rickie's door, and then I knock.

No answer.

I knock again, but he still doesn't open the door. So I take out a credit card. Dylan and I taught ourselves to open each other's bedroom doors at a young age. And I opened Reardon's office door with this same technique just a few days ago.

But, damn it, Rickie's lock is made of sterner stuff. My card trick fails, and I'm foiled again. I put the credit card away. Then I back up a couple of steps, turn my body to the side, and ram the door, shoulder first. I hit with a loud crash, but the door doesn't give. And I bounce awkwardly to the floor.

My shoulder hurts, now.

This isn't going well.

The door is suddenly yanked open. "What the hell are you doing?" Rickie booms, looking down at my crazy self in a heap on the hallway floor. "Don't *break* yourself. We've had enough trouble already this week. Jesus Christ."

"Fine." I scramble to my feet. "But I'm not letting you do this. You're not shutting me out. We're a team, okay? Those were *your* words, asshole."

He gives me a look that's pure exasperation. Then he turns around and walks back over to his bed, where he lies down on his side, facing away from me.

It's not exactly a hand-lettered invitation. But I take it anyway. I close the door and follow him to the bed, where I curl up against his back. And I tuck an arm around his waist.

He doesn't move, or acknowledge me. But he doesn't fight it, either.

Suddenly I feel weepy again, which is really inconvenient. But he's so warm and solid, and he makes my heart ache. "I don't care whether you're guilty or innocent. I'm just glad you're here."

"You might have cared," he says dully, "if you had to take the stand and tell a jury everything you did on Wednesday night, and then everything I did."

"You're wrong," I insist with a shaking voice. "I'd do it right now if you needed me to—if it meant I could spend another night right here with you." I tighten my arm around his waist and breathe in his scent.

"Daphne..." He sighs. And then finally, he lays a hand over mine. "I don't deserve you."

"That's crap," I whisper. "Lenore would agree."

His abs contract under my hand, as if he nearly laughed. "Dirty play, Shipley."

"Am I wrong?"

"Nope. But I probably wouldn't believe her, either, so…"

"You should." I press my face against his back. "Maybe today you just can't hear me. I have those days, too. But this will pass, Rickie. And I'll still be here when it does. Because we're a team. And…" I take another deep breath. "Because I love you."

Rickie goes very still. And my poor, bruised little heart braces itself.

Slowly, Rickie rolls over to face me. And when I see that black-and-blue face, it's hard work not crying. But then I make myself focus on his clear gray eyes, and I feel calm again.

"Baby," he whispers. "I love you so much it hurts."

My whole being relaxes. "That's just your broken nose," I whisper back. "Do you need some Advil?"

"Yes," he says, with a sheepish smile. And his eyes look suddenly wet. "But first I need to hug you." He reaches out and pulls me closer.

We fit ourselves together right there in the center of the bed—my face in his neck, his hands stroking my hair.

"Thank you for not giving up on me," he says softly.

"I could say the same," I point out. "You're the one who told me not to give up hope."

"Don't," he says, rocking me against him. "Let's never give up."

FORTY-SIX

RICKIE

With Daphne in my arms, I'm truly calm for the first time in days. My heartbeat slows, and my thoughts lengthen into slippery, shiny things. I fall asleep in spite of my pain. And when I wake up a couple of hours later, Daphne is curled up to me, her back to my front. She's breathing so peacefully that I don't move for a few minutes, afraid to wake her.

Eventually, I need those painkillers. So I ease away from her just long enough to venture out for some water and a couple of pills.

When I sneak back onto the bed, Daphne rolls over and cuddles up against me. "I should get up and go to the grocery store," she murmurs.

"Let me order in," I insist. "I'd rather not go out with this busted face. But I'll treat you to some takeout. I owe you big time."

"No you don't," she says, her eyes still closed. "But I'll take it anyway. Can we order wings from Biscuit in the Basket?"

"If that's what my girl wants."

She makes a sleepy, happy noise. And I stroke her hair and marvel at my own luck. I *don't* deserve her. But I am not dumb enough to say so again. So instead I pick up my phone and scroll through all the messages from the people who are also crazy enough to care about me.

Keith: Did you really spend the night in the slammer? I hope cavity searches are not really a thing. LMK.

Dylan: Did you really punch Daphne's ex? I thought I was going to do that.

Lenore: I know you said Wednesday. But I'm here if you need me!

I also read Daphne's texts, which alternate between worry and more worry. *Oof.* I guess all I can do is try to make sure I don't put her in that position again.

Then I open up my email, which is basically a habit at this point, since I spent several days waiting for Paul to write me. To my surprise, there's a new email waiting.

Rick—

I haven't heard back from you. I know I did the whole "I can't talk about it" thing to you. But then I sent you off to see that posting, and since you're the smartest guy I ever met, I'm thinking you must have found it.

Now your silence is making me nervous.

If you need to talk, I'm @Luigi2000 on AppSnap.

—Paul

A shiver runs through me. Because I've never played a *Mario Brothers* game, and yet I suddenly remember that Paul likes them, and that Luigi is a character. I just know it, but I don't remember the context.

Getting your memory back is weird. I guess it's not all going to materialize in front of me like my fairy godmother. It's going to come back in little awkward flashes and insights.

I'd better brace myself, then.

I open up AppSnap and make a login for myself—@McFly2000. Then I tap in his handle and send him a message.

Hi. It's your dotty ex-roommate. Thank you for this. I'd never try to screensave anything you say on here. Just thought I'd put that out there.

Paul comes back only a minute later. *Appreciate that. And I trust you. Did you find it?*

I sure did. And I learned a lot. Unfortunately I then came face to face with a certain ex-cadet and was arrested for attacking him. You won't find it in the news, though, because his powerful daddy decided not to let the state's attorney press charges.

There is the digital equivalent of a stunned silence on Paul's end. Maybe I shouldn't have gone there.

But then he sends me a photo. It only stays on-screen for ten seconds, but I drink it in. There's his face—his *familiar* face—registering an expression of comical horror. *Say what?*

I laugh out loud. God, it's great to see his face. He's thin and a little nerdy. And that ten-second glimpse reminds me how I felt about him. I knew him as a force for good in the world.

I can't send you a selfie today, I tell him. *I have a broken nose. But when it heals, I'll show you the long-haired version of this sexy beast.*

Don't ever change, he says. *Since we're doing this, what else do you need to know?*

That's a good question, isn't it? Lenore has been trying to tell me that I don't *need* to know anything. And maybe she's right.

It's strange, but now that we're actually talking, I find it doesn't matter so much anymore. You're here. I'm here. My girlfriend is napping beside me.

That's great, man. Someday I want to hear the story of your arrest. Over beers.

Yes! That MUST happen.

Congrats on the girlfriend. I expect to see a cute selfie of you two at some point.

Yessir. Wait, I DO have a question! Do you remember me talking about Daphne? I was supposed to pick her up on the Saturday night of Open Weekend. But I stood her up at 8pm. I realize that night ended horribly a few hours later. But it would be super cool if you knew why I blew off my date beforehand.

He comes back right away. *Hold on. There's no way you could have picked her up that night. You were probably being transferred to the hospital right about then. Because our troubles began on Friday night.*

I'm stunned. *Really? My hospital record says Saturday.*

Yeah. That's why they fired the infirmary guy. Somebody decided to keep us in the infirmary a whole 24 hours before admitting we

*needed the hospital. You had internal bleeding. I had to listen to them
argue about whether or not you could die.*

I must gasp or something because Daphne shakes herself, sits up,
and reads over my shoulder. "Oh wow. Is this your roommate?"

I'm too stunned to answer.

But then Paul taps out one more thing. *I gotta run. But tell your
girl it wasn't your fault. You were really looking forward to that
date, too. You had a necklace made for her which was super weird,
and a dreamy look on your face. I made fun of you for it, but I was
super jealous. Later!*

Daphne and I slowly turn to look at each other. We're wearing
identical shocked expressions, before she leans in and kisses me. "I
knew it," she whispers.

"You did not," I argue, throwing down my phone and rolling on
top of her. "You thought I stood you up."

"That was before I got to know you," she argues. "Now I'm
mostly a believer."

"Mostly?" I tease. Then I cup one of her breasts and gently stroke
it. "How can I seal the deal? Can you think of a way?"

"I can," she says, smiling. "Order two different kinds of wings,
and some french fries, too."

I bark out a laugh. "Okay, Shipley. Anything else?"

"A private karaoke performance. Naked."

I let out a hoot of laughter. "Sure, baby. Anything for you."

FORTY-SEVEN

DAPHNE

We don't wake up until Chastity raps on the door of my farmhouse bedroom. "Daphne? Rickie? Family meeting in half an hour."

"Okay," I mumble.

"There's bacon," she adds helpfully.

"Mmm. Thanks."

But I don't get up. Rickie is curled tightly around me. That may have something to do with the modest size of my bed in the farmhouse. Or maybe he's just in a very snuggly mood.

Either way, I like it. Except it's giving me ideas. And we can't get busy here in my childhood bedroom.

"Rickie," I whisper. "We have to get up. Family meeting."

"I'm not family," he slurs. "I'm not anybody's family before at least ten in the morning."

"Be that as it may, it's also breakfast time. I heard there's bacon."

"Mmf. You know what would really motivate me to wake up?"

"I'm sure it involves sex," I guess.

"*Ding ding.* Shower sex. Let's go. I have some very fond memories of you and me in that shower on a hundred-degree day after baking pies."

"Not today, McFly. Wake up and come downstairs if you can." Against all my deepest desires, I slide out of his comfortable embrace. I have to, because it's going to be a very busy April Friday, and I need that half hour to get ready.

So I head to the bathroom, bracing myself.

First, there's a family meeting. That wouldn't be a big deal, except that I'm going to open up my grad school financial aid packages and compare them. It's always terrifying to confront your future head-on.

Then again, I'm pretty grateful that I have a few options. Reardon Halsey didn't break me. In six short weeks I'll have a degree from Moo U, and then in the fall I'll head off to one of the three grad school programs that accepted me.

Two weeks ago I found out that I didn't get into Berkeley. Or Johns Hopkins. Although Berkeley wrote me a lovely letter encouraging me to get more work experience and reapply.

That had been a blow to my ego. But in hindsight it's not that surprising. I have a funny-looking resume, and I lack the real-life experience that many public health masters' candidates have.

Still, I have choices. I'll make the most of them.

Grad school decisions aren't even the biggest thing on my mind this weekend. May is getting married tomorrow. That's why we're all here in the farmhouse, to celebrate her wedding weekend. Today there will be a quick rehearsal at the church, and then the men are all headed out to play paintball in the woods somewhere. The women are getting a yoga class, followed by mani/pedis and mocktails.

Then, tomorrow, there's a church wedding, followed by May's reception at *Speakeasy*. The gastropub's private upstairs space will be decked out for dancing and a barbecue buffet.

It will all be great. Just as soon as I get through the scary financial aid parts.

Mom went all out for brunch today, so I nibble on some extra strawberries while I wait for the family meeting to begin. In front of me on the table are three large envelopes. Sealed.

"You haven't opened them?" Griffin asks, sipping his coffee.

"No," I admit. "I promised myself that I'd open them here, where you could remind me that prestige isn't everything. If North Carolina isn't a good deal for me, then I'll have to let it go."

"Prestige isn't everything," my big brother says.

"Thank you."

"Neither is money."

"Now you're just confusing me." He grins.

Mom hurries into the room and takes a seat at the head of the table. "Sorry. Are we all here?"

"Almost!" Dylan yells from the kitchen, before appearing in the doorway. "I'm here. Let the party start."

"First order of business," my mother says. "The battery in my new pickup truck is dead. So if one of you can't jump it, that's an expense I wasn't expecting."

"Again?" Griffin mutters. "Huh. Someone must be running the heated seats or the radio too long with the engine off."

Grandpa's voice comes from the TV room. "It's been a cold spring! Somebody probably had to keep his tushie warm."

"But not without the engine running," I point out. "Why stay in the truck if you're parked?"

Dylan snorts. "I can think of a couple of reasons."

"In April?" I argue, because arguing with your twin is a God-given right. "Brrr."

Dylan shrugs. "Maybe you really were snatched by aliens, because you clearly didn't grow up in Vermont."

There are a few chuckles around the table. And then Griffin calls out, "Hey, Gramps? Didn't you take Mabel on a date in the truck last night?"

"Don't pin this on me," he grumbles. "Something must be wrong with the truck."

There's a stunned silence among us.

"Okay!" my mother says too brightly. "Next subject—Daphne's grad school decision. Open up those envelopes, honey."

"This one can wait. Let's get the drama over with." I pick up the envelope from North Carolina and slit it open with my thumb. I pull the financial aid letter out and drop it on the table.

"Dear Miss Shipley," Griffin reads. Then he trails his finger down the column of numbers. "They gave you some aid," he says. "Next year would cost us twenty-two thousand dollars."

"Ouch," I say. "That's...a lot."

"Don't panic yet," my brother says. He hands me the envelope from the University of Massachusetts. "Let's have some more data points, first."

I open that one, and it's better news. They've funded me for everything except for thirteen thousand dollars. "Better!" I say cheerfully. Except I'm not as wild about that school, even though it has a good reputation.

Griff slides the third envelope toward me. Everyone watches while I open an offer from the Burlington U. I pull it out and slap it on the table. I read the letter.

Then I read it again.

"Full ride!" Griffin hoots. "Yes, baby, yes!"

There's a note written in ink at the bottom. *I really hope you'll join us, Daphne. We'd love to have you. —Dr. Drummond*

"Who's that?" Griffin asks.

"The Dean of the whole program," I say in a hushed voice.

"Nice," my brother says, slapping me on the back. "You think it all over. But sometimes it's pretty great to stick with the people who love you."

"True," I murmur, lifting my eyes from the page. And there stands Rickie in the doorway, a mug of tea in his hand. Our gazes lock, and he smiles at me.

Then he gives me a wink and turns to go back into the kitchen.

"Wait!" My mother says, pulling another envelope out of her folder. "You got one more yesterday." She hands it to me.

"Ooh, it's from Harkness," my brother says. "Didn't know you applied there."

"I didn't," I admit. "I have no idea what this could be." A girl can't apply to a program after admitting to breaking and entering. That's just bad form. So I have no idea what's in this envelope.

"Don't keep us in suspense," May chirps.

So I rip it open. It's a letter from the other powerful woman in my life—Dean Reynolds.

Dear Miss Shipley—
The matter of survey tampering has finally been resolved. An

employee *was removed from the study. And an undergraduate was removed from the college. Thank you for your cooperation.*

Per our investigation, it has come to light that harassment by a member of your program led to your transfer. We do not condone harassment in any form.

Meanwhile, since you completed more than 75% of your Harkness requirements—and then fulfilled the rest at an accredited institution—you are technically eligible to receive your Harkness BA in lieu of graduating from Burlington University.

If you wish to ask for reinstatement, please write a letter indicating your interest before May 8ᵗʰ to be considered for commencement in June.

Sincerely,

Dr. R. Reynolds

"Wow!" May says. "Check it out!"

"Who knew?" my mother asks.

"You *have* to do this," Griffin insists.

Somehow my whole family has crowded around in order to read over my shoulder.

"You're going to get your fancy degree after all," Dylan chuckles. "Of course you are. I knew it all along."

I didn't, though. The whole year has been harrowing. And I can't believe I've come out on the other side of it. The paper grows blurry as my eyes fill with grateful tears.

A firm hand lands on the back of my neck and squeezes lightly. It's Rickie. He doesn't say anything. He doesn't have to.

He's just there for me.

FORTY-EIGHT

RICKIE

"Alec, receive this ring as a sign of my love and fidelity. In the name of the Father, and of the Son, and of the Holy Spirit." May slips the ring onto her new husband's finger.

Father Peters, his job nearly done, smiles gaily at the two of them. "There is no mention in the Catholic liturgy of kissing. However…"

Alec promptly leans in and kisses May, while everyone cheers.

Seriously, the Shipley clan really knows how to throw a wedding. The bridal party is up there looking sharp in a style I'd call Vermont Formal. The three groomsmen are in pressed khakis, crisp blue shirts and matching tawny vests instead of jackets. While the women wear pink dresses that are totally cute but not fussy. Daphne's long legs are particularly eye-catching in a skirt that ends just above her knees. I heard that there's dancing later, and I can't wait to whirl her around in it.

For now, I'm sitting on a pew next to Grandpa, who gave May away at the start of the ceremony. He spent the last half hour mopping tears away with his handkerchief.

Father Peters says one more prayer, although the business of marrying Alec and May is done now. The bride and groom are smiling at each other, hand in hand. And the wedding party looks ready to get to the next part of these festivities. Dylan and Keith stand up from the first pew and pick up their instruments. When Father Peters nods, they begin to play an Irish reel as a recessional.

We all rise, and the bride and groom join hands to lead the way out of the church. It's slow going, as people keep thumping Alec on the back and blowing kisses at May.

The wedding party is next. Daphne takes the arm of Benito, one of Alec's three brothers. Then comes Lark, May's best friend, with Damien, another Rossi brother. Then Audrey Shipley links arms with a man I've never seen before. Griffin was supposed to stand up for Alec, too. But at the last minute Alec's oldest brother turned up in town after a long absence. J.M. is striking, with long, badass hair and a broody look in his eye.

"Well, son. Let's shake a leg," Grandpa says when it's our turn to leave. "I heard there's bacon-wrapped scallops for the cocktail hour. We could be first in line. Most of these suckers are going to walk down the hill to the bar. But you could drive me in that sweet old Volvo of yours."

"Yessir," I say. Because you do not argue with Grandpa Shipley. Not when there's bacon on the line.

A few hours later I'm sipping a Shipley cider as Daphne pounds a Coke. We're both full of barbecue and flushed from dancing.

"I heard there's karaoke next," I say, teasing my girl.

"You wish," she says, setting her empty glass down on a tray.

"You're right." Instead, the band segues into a slow song. I finish my drink as couples begin to sway to the music. "Is it true that this cider has magical properties?" I ask. They're serving the Audrey cider at the wedding, which has been rumored to be an aphrodisiac.

"How would we know?" Daphne whispers, sneaking a hand underneath my vintage velvet jacket.

"Good point, baby," I whisper back. The two nights we've spent in her childhood bedroom have been our longest dry spell in months. "Although others may be affected."

We scan the room full of slow-dancers. The bride and groom are dancing together and laughing about something. Griffin is dipping Audrey while she giggles. Dylan and Chastity are staring meaningfully into each other's eyes. Her grandpa is dancing with the woman who may or may not have kept him company on the truck's heated seats.

Even Ruth Shipley is out there, dancing with Gil, the same man who accompanied her the night we bumped into them at the noodle shop. They're a couple now. "But taking it slowly," Ruth had explained over the holidays. He's a nice man, too. Even Daphne thinks so.

"Baby, dance with me?" I ask, closing a hand around hers.

She puts her hands around my neck and tows me out to the dance floor. The song is a gorgeous fiddle ballad. I rest my cheek against hers and sigh. "I feel lucky tonight," I whisper.

"Mmm," she agrees.

"Although you seem a little distracted," I point out. "Are you having deep thoughts about grad school?"

"Some," she admits. "You haven't asked me about it at all."

"That's intentional," I say, kissing her jaw quickly. "I don't want to influence your decision. It's not my place." I'd never ask Daphne to pare back her dreams on my account.

She pulls back a titch and studies me. "I'm trying to figure out how much is at stake."

"Thousands of dollars," I point out. "Is that what you mean?"

"I guess." She tilts her head uncertainly. "Would you think it was odd if I stayed in Vermont?"

"Odd?" My feet forget to move, and we come to a stop, while couples sway around us. "Not odd, baby. I'd be a lucky man if you stayed in Vermont."

"Oh," she says, her voice breathy. "I didn't want to assume. I'd always said I was leaving."

"Whoa. Don't leave on my account. Although if you end up in Carolina, we'll deal. I'd have to stay behind in Burlington and finish my degree. But that won't take forever. Then, unless you throw me over, I'll probably end up applying to grad school near wherever you are."

She blinks. "You'd do that?"

"Of course I would. I'd sell my house and follow you anywhere, Shipley. If that's what you needed."

"Rickie," she says, placing a hand over my heart. "That's a lot for me to ask."

"When I find something good, I don't let it go. How long does a public health degree take, anyway? Two years, right?"

"Or four, if I have to go part-time. There are a lot of variables."

I tuck my arm around her waist, and guide her to dance with me again. "Make a spreadsheet, baby. Figure out your next move. Choosing a school is hard. Once upon a time I chose the wrong one. I went against my gut, and it almost blew up my life. What does your gut say?"

She takes a breath and blows it out. "My gut really likes the idea of getting a full ride and finishing in two years."

"*Really.*" I think that over for a moment. "I thought you wanted to pick the best program."

"I thought I did, too," she admits. "But I like the people I work with now. I trust them. That means more to me than it used to."

"Okay. How long do you have to decide?"

"Two weeks."

"That long, huh?"

She smiles up at me. "I spent my whole life trying to do better than Moo U. I thought I needed the top of the list. Someone's external seal of approval. But Moo U took me in when I had nowhere to go. My family bails me out when I need their help. It really annoys me to be wrong, but—"

"You? Really?"

She pinches me. "Behave. I'm trying to be humble, here. It doesn't come easily to me."

"Sorry. Go on."

"I like my life in Burlington. I *love* you…" She traces her fingertip across the nape of my neck. "And it sounds so lovely to just say yes to Moo U, and the people who already love me."

"I could get on board with this," I agree.

"I'd be around when my family needed help. I'd be close by for Dylan and Chastity's wedding."

"Mmm," I murmur in her ear. "You'd be close by when I needed you underneath me. Naked."

"That too," she says. "That too."

I can't take it anymore. So I kiss her slowly, right there in the middle of the dance floor.

That's when the song ends. And someone picks up the microphone and declares that it's time to cut the cake.

"Break it up, you two," Dylan says, elbowing me. "There's cake to be had. Hey, Daph? Did you decide about grad school?"

Daphne pulls back and smiles up at me. "I think I just did."

"No way!" her twin brother says. "What's the verdict?"

But she can't even tell him. Because I'm kissing her again.

The End

ALSO BY SARINA BOWEN

TRUE NORTH

Bittersweet (Griffin & Audrey)

Steadfast (Jude & Sophie)

Keepsake (Zach & Lark)

Bountiful (Zara & David)

Speakeasy (May & Alec)

Fireworks (Benito & Skye)

Heartland (Dylan & Chastity)

Waylaid (Daphne & Rickie)

And don't miss Boyfriend in the World of True North

THE BROOKLYN BRUISERS

Rookie Move

Hard Hitter

Pipe Dreams

Brooklynaire

Overnight Sensation

Superfan

Sure Shot

Bombshells

Shenanigans

THE COMPANY

Moonlighter (Eric Bayer's book)

Loverboy

THE IVY YEARS

The Year We Fell Down #1

The Year We Hid Away #2

The Understatement of the Year #3

The Shameless Hour #4

The Fifteenth Minute #5

Extra Credit #6

GRAVITY

Coming In From the Cold #1

Falling From the Sky #2

Shooting for the Stars #3

HELLO GOODBYE

Goodbye Paradise

Hello Forever